# THE LONELY ASSASSIN

## MILAN THRILLER SERIES BOOK IV

# JACK ERICKSON

REDBRICK PRESS

*To Grace, William, Preston, Lukas, Campbell, and Desiree'*
*And, of course, for Marilyn*

## Milan Thriller Series

*Thirteen Days in Milan*

*No One Sleeps*

*Vesuvius Nights*

*The Lonely Assassin*

## Novels

*Bloody Mary Confession*

*Rex Royale*

*A Streak Across the Sky*

*Mornings Without Zoe*

## Short Mysteries

*Perfect Crime*

*Missing Persons*

*Teammates*

*The Stalker*

*Weekend Guest*

## True Crime

*Blood and Money in the Hunt Country*

## Noir Series

*Bad News is Back in Town*

# TABLE OF CONTENTS

There is a long history in Russia and the former Soviet Union of political leaders or revolutionaries assassinating opponents. Here is a short list that traces the history from the 19th century to the present.

## 19TH CENTURY

On March 13, 1881, Czar Alexander II was assassinated by Russian revolutionaries who tossed bombs at his bullet-proof carriage along a canal in St. Petersburg. Alexander II was considered a reformer who freed the serfs in 1861 and sold Alaska to the United States in 1867. He had already survived several assassination attempts but would not on that fateful Sunday.

## 20TH CENTURY

On July 18, 1918, Bolshevik guards murdered Tsar Nicholas II, Tsarina Alexandra, and their five children in the basement of the home in Ekaterinburg where they had been detained. Tsar Nicholas II was the grandson of the assassinated Alexander II.

The Tsar and his family had been removed from Petrograd (formerly St. Petersburg) after the February 1917 Revolution that overthrew the 300-year-old Romanov dynasty. A weak Provisional Government assumed control but was overthrown by the Bolsheviks led by the leftist Vladimir Lenin in October 1917. The Bolsheviks created the Union of Soviet Socialist Republic (USSR) in 1922, which lasted until 1991.

In 1918, two attempts were made to assassinate Vladimir Lenin. Lenin was wounded but survived. He died in 1924, possibly as a result of oxidation of the bullets remaining in his body.

Leon Trotsky was one of three Bolshevik leaders (along with Lenin and Joseph Stalin) who led the October 1917 revolution. Trotsky became the Commissar for Foreign Affairs and signed a peace treaty with the German government, ending Russia's involvement in World War I. Trotsky was leader of the Red Army, which was victorious over the White Army during the Russian Civil War (1918–1921). Stalin maneuvered Trotsky from power, and he was exiled in 1929.

Trotsky ended up in Mexico, where he survived several attempts on his life by Soviet agents. He died from injuries suffered in May 1940 by a Soviet assassin who sliced open his head with an ice ax.

In 1934, Sergei Kirov, a popular Bolshevik leader and friend of Stalin's, was murdered in Leningrad (renamed from

St. Petersburg) under suspicious circumstances, reportedly on the order of Stalin.

On 7 September 1978, Bulgarian dissident Sergei Markov was poisoned by a pellet coated in toxic ricin injected into his leg while waiting to cross the street on his way to the BBC, where he worked. Markov turned around, seeing someone pick up an umbrella and disappear in the crowd. Markov died four days later from what was called the Umbrella Murder.

## 21ST CENTURY

After the collapse of the Soviet Union in 1991, Vladimir Putin was elected President of Russia in 2000. Putin consolidated his power, choosing a few close allies to join his inner circle. Some who were not included in his circle became opponents, speaking out against what they thought was corruption and opposition to reforms. Putin tightened his grip and punished those who criticized his leadership. Many of those who did died. Here are a few:

Russian investigative reporter for Novaya Gazeta, Anna Politkovskaya was murdered in the elevator of her Moscow apartment in October 2006. Politkovskaya had written extensively about corruption and received international awards for her books and articles, including her 2004 book, *Putin's Russia,* a critical description of Putin saying he was leading a police state. Since 2000, five other Novaya Gazeta journalists have been murdered or died under mysterious circumstances.

Alexander Litvinenko, a former FSB (Federal Security Service of the Russian Federation) agent defected to the UK and was given asylum. Litvinenko wrote books about Putin's criminal acts and said he was responsible for the murder of Anna Politkovskaya. On November 1, 2006, Litvinenko was poisoned with radioactive polonium slipped into his tea at a London café. He died November 23. British authorities charged a former FSB agent with his murder and sought his extradition from Russia. It was denied.

Boris Nemtsov was an ally of Boris Yeltsin's after the collapse of the Soviet Union. After Putin was elected in 2000, Nemtsov became a critic and led protests against him during local elections. Nemtsov promoted economic and political reforms and was considered a possible candidate for the president of Russia in 2008. Nemtsov was shot four times in the back in February 2015 near the Kremlin and died. Nemtsov had told associates that he feared Putin was going to have him murdered.

Boris Berezovsky became a wealthy oligarch after the Soviet Union collapsed in 1991. He helped Putin's rise to President of Russia in 2000 but quickly lost influence. He feared for his life and fled to the UK, where he was granted political asylum. Berezovsky was found hanged with a noose around his neck in a locked bathroom of his ex-wife's Berkshire home in March 2013. No one was arrested.

Alexei Navalny, who once announced he'd run for president in Russia in 2018, became an activist against the repression and corruption in Putin's United Russia party, calling it a place for "crooks and thieves." Navalny led demonstrations across Russia, was beaten by police, arrested, and jailed. Navalny may have been poisoned by a toxic agent when he was in jail in 2019.

In August 2020, Navalny was flying to Siberia to join protests in local elections against Putin's United Russia Party. He became ill on the flight and was hospitalized in Omsk. A German charity airlifted Navalny from Siberia to a Berlin hospital, where he was in a coma until doctors revived him. Forensics determined that he had been poisoned by Novichok, a deadly neurotoxin produced in laboratories around Moscow.

CHAPTER ONE

MOSCOW—APRIL 2017

"Gennady, come look at this," Komarov said.

Komarov and his colleague, Gennady Titov, were seated at separate consoles of computers on the twentieth floor of a Russian bank, looking across the Moscow River toward Red Square, the Kremlin, and Saint Basil's cathedral.

Unusual early April snow flurries had layered a thin white blanket over Moscow and its suburbs, like frosting on a wedding cake. Morning sun had melted most of the snow, revealing signs of spring, with bouquets of yellow flowers and green grass shoots sprouting in parks and undeveloped parcels of land.

"What is it?" Titov said, rolling his chair over to Komarov's console. A row of desktop computers and terminals were linked to international banks, stock markets, and Bloomberg analyses of trading in interest rates, foreign currencies, and commodities.

Titov studied his boss's profile with concern. Nicolai Andreivich Komarov was a sick man, recovering from a bladder-cancer diagnosis in January followed by three months of chemotherapy and radiation treatments. Komarov was a ghost, his bald head shiny as a cue ball, his complexion like wallpaper paste.

The two men had been in their bank office since 8:15 a.m. But the mood had been somber, lacking the familiar chatter and joking about the weather, families, and movies they'd watched on TV the previous night. Not this morning.

Komarov had said little all morning, engrossed in what his terminals and computers were telling him. Titov had heard him mumble curses under his breath, push back from his console, and struggle to stand. Komarov would stare at the screens, reach down to flick a mouse to reveal an account, stare at a screen some more, and then shuffle into the small kitchen to pour a cup of green tea. He was on his third of the morning. The tea had not stopped Komarov's coughing bouts, which ended in hacking. Which he was doing when he returned to his desk.

"You look tired, Kolya. How are you feeling?" Titov asked, saddened by the appearance of his sixty-two-year-old friend and colleague, a former athlete and fitness fanatic. In his physical prime, Komarov had played semipro soccer until his early thirties and had then become an avid weightlifter. He had worked out on a rowing machine and a stationary bicycle at his apartment on the prestigious Garden Ring Road, where he lived with his wife of thirty-two years and two large husky dogs.

Komarov had invited Titov and his wife to a birthday party the previous November, when he had appeared to be healthy and in good spirits. Komarov had proudly shown him and other guests the recent additions to their luxury apartment: a wall-sized Oriental rug purchased in Iran, a forty-gallon tank with tropical fish and coral, and a telescope on the balcony so he could see the International Space Station with its Russian astronaut aboard. Komarov had boasted that he knew the father of the astronaut, one of his many well-connected Moscow friends.

"How do I feel?" Komarov said. "Try hungry but can't keep food down. Tired all the time but can't sleep. Sick of taking pills. And bored recuperating at home."

He coughed, reached for a tissue, blew his nose, and tossed the tissue in a wastebasket under his desk. He reached for a fresh one and crumpled it in his hand. "Then I got this miserable cold. I cough all night and wake up exhausted. That damn cancer will kill me. And this cold is making me *want* to die," he said, with a hacking cough into the tissue in his fist.

Komarov frowned, looking at Titov, his eyes hollow and his cheeks and jaw wrinkled. Titov was saddened by his colleague's appearance: a rumpled shell of a dying man, his suit draped over his formerly broad frame and muscular arms, making him resemble an oncology mannequin.

"Don't you think you should go home? Your cough sounds serious. Shouldn't you see your doctor?" Titov said, moving back to avoid spittle landing on him.

"Hell with him." Komarov scowled. "He'd tell me to go home and rest. I've been doing that for months! I need to get back to work. Otherwise, I'll go crazy."

"But your health, Kolya. That's more important."

"I don't want to go back to my apartment. It's a prison! I had to get out and do something. I'm bored, watching TV, reading newspapers, and taking pills. I'm sick of it all."

"I know it's hard on you and Olga, but you shouldn't do too much until you're well."

"I'll never be well again. I'll likely die from this cancer!" Komarov said, slapping the table. He reached for another tissue to wipe his nose. "All my life I've been in good physical shape, a stud! Now look at me. Another month and I'll be a skeleton!" Another slap on the table.

Titov had missed his colleague when he had been out of the office receiving treatments. Before he'd been diagnosed, they would banter back and forth, their backs to each other, drinking coffee and tea, sharing gossip or family stories. It was just the two of them in a private office where other bank employees weren't allowed. Komarov and Titov didn't have clients like the bank's financial advisors did.

Their clients, if that were the term, were Russians spread across the world: political higher-ups comfortably secure across the Moscow River in Kremlin government offices; Russians managing megacorporations in all sectors of the economy; ultra-rich oligarchs living lavishly in Europe and Asia on money gained from corruption, government slush funds, political malfeasance, and criminal activities.

"You've been preoccupied all morning. I miss our bantering," Titov said.

"I know, I know. My fault, sorry. But I don't like what I'm finding in Dima's accounts," he said, squirming lower in his deep chair and rearranging the sleeves of his suit, which sagged across his chest and stomach like a blanket after his loss of forty pounds during treatment.

"What do you mean?"

"I'm not sure, but some transfers look suspicious," Komarov said, pointing to a screen on one of his computers with rows of accounts intersecting with banks. In the top row were Russian banks, the Russian Treasury, Heritage, the Privat Group, and decals of the Russian flag.

"Dima's accounts start in our bank, rubles converted into US dollars. Dollars flow from our bank to banks in former Soviet republics, ending at the Bern bank, where Dima works," Komarov said, pointing to the logo of their bank linking to banks in Latvia, Ukraine, Moldova, and Estonia, labeled with their national flag decals.

"When the money arrives at the Bern bank, Dima converts dollars into euros, British pounds, and Japanese yen." Komarov clicked his mouse, opening an account with the logo of a Bern bank. Below the logo were a number of accounts with names and numbers. "These are fictitious limited partnerships that Dima manages," he said, pointing to the blocks, pronouncing their titles: "PromWest... PromNorth... Invernewl... Oust 2... Prim... Provost... Glasberg... Viebo... Coburg... HauseAlt... ArcSix... GroupoNove... DomNas."

Under each partnership were account numbers starting with a row of X's and ending with the last four or five digits. Komarov clicked his mouse again. The screen showed lines connecting the limited partnerships with accounts in banks in Denmark, Sweden, the Netherlands, England, Spain, and France. He pointed at a limited partnership labeled Provost.

"The Provost account, like others, supports our political ventures, cyberattacks, and political campaigns in America, Europe, and Canada."

Titov nodded, fully aware of the Kremlin-sponsored campaign to influence elections and fund "friendly" politicians using computer hacking, malicious bots, and bogus social media sites.

"Other limited partnerships are private accounts for, shall we say, 'personal reasons,' so Putin's friends can purchase villas in Italy, Greece, and Portugal, along with yachts in Monaco, Nice, and Marseille."

"And luxury homes in Mayfair and Kensington," Titov added.

Komarov scoffed. "That's not all. Some money ends up in accounts of their mistresses, their ex-wives, and their spoiled children."

"Who don't have jobs and don't need to," Titov added.

"It's ridiculous, isn't it? And those spoiled family members send their kids to private schools so they can learn English, French, and Italian. Some haven't been to Russia in years."

"What has this world come to?" Titov said in exasperation.

"Putin's friends like expensive toys, yachts, villas, gambling in casinos. They waste hundreds of millions of rubles having fun and bragging to friends about how rich they are."

"They live like kings and queens," Titov said, shaking his head.

"And Romanov czars," Komarov snarled. "We know what happened to them."

Titov nodded. "Sure do. Money corrupts—I mean, too much money corrupts. I don't think we'll get that rich. I certainly don't need to."

Komarov smiled. "Me, neither. I have all I need: a nice apartment, a dacha with fruit trees and a garden, and grandchildren who spend the summer with us. I hope I see them this summer—if I'm not buried in the ground."

"What about your vacations in Paris?" Titov asked.

Komarov shook his head. "That's for my wife. She loves shopping for purses and shoes, walking along the Seine, and eating snails."

"Snails. Oooh, I'd never eat snails," Titov said with a grimace.

"Me, neither, but I like goose pâté and Burgundy wines."

"What about Dima? Does he have expensive toys?"

"None that I know about," Komarov said, shaking his head. "He doesn't have to. He and his Italian wife live in a nice apartment in Bern that the bank pays for. And his car is an expensive SUV. They visit their daughter in Milan, who has some kind of job in fashion Dima told me about."

Komarov shrugged, reached for his teacup, and pushed back in his chair. Neither one spoke for several moments, pondering the dilemma that Komarov was in, its meaning, and possible consequences.

Titov went into the kitchen, opened the refrigerator, and returned with a can of Coke. He opened it, sending fizz and bubbles over his hand and onto Komarov's desk. "Sorry," he said, reaching for a box of tissues on the desk and wiping up the Coke.

Titov knew that suspicious transfers in Dmitri Volkov's accounts were causing Komarov intense anxiety. Volkov was a longtime friend and someone Komarov admired. And now Komarov was hinting that Volkov was possibly betraying him, skimming money from accounts. If so, both Volkov and Komarov were in serious trouble.

Before Komarov's cancer diagnosis, he had told Titov that he was considering retiring in a few years. He wanted time to travel and spend more time at his dacha in the summer and someplace warm, like Greece, in the winter, where he and his wife had vacationed. But instead of a well-earned retirement, Komarov was facing imminent death from cancer. And acknowledging that a friend might be a thief—was this Komarov's reward for a career helping Russian friends manage their money and promoting the Kremlin's political causes?

The office was quiet for several minutes. Titov knew these serious issues were haunting Komarov, as it would be difficult for him to reveal what his computer screen and databases were telling him.

Komarov sipped his cold tea, staring at the computer screen with the chart of banks and fictitious partnerships. Finally, he sighed and said, "Dima knew I would be out of the office for treatment. And he knew I was the only one monitoring his accounts. I asked my supervisor if he'd like to take over, but he said he didn't have time. I told him you were busy with your accounts and that I trusted Dima. He agreed and said he'd check the accounts occasionally and not to worry. I'd only be out a couple of months. What could happen in a couple of months?"

Komarov scowled and shook his head, pointing at his screen. "This is what happens when Dima's accounts weren't monitored," he said, tracing his finger from fictitious partnerships in the Bern bank to transfers to other banks and partnerships. Then he pointed at another screen, where a database was open.

"When I returned to the office, there were no notes that my supervisor had made. I doubt he even looked at the transfers. So I started my review on Wednesday. I noticed a few transactions that didn't quite look right—less money at the end of a transfer or foreign exchange than at the beginning. Yesterday I dug deeper and found more suspicious transfers. Today, well, take a look. See why I'm worried."

Titov moved closer so he could read the screen and the amounts of transfers. He traced his finger over a few accounts and mumbled a few amounts in high numbers of euros, British pounds, and American dollars.

He sat back in his chair and looked at Komarov. "Kolya…I think Dima's in serious trouble."

# CHAPTER TWO

# BERN, SWITZERLAND

**"I** want to make a toast, *amore*," Valeria said, raising a flute of Franciacorta Brut Rosé to her husband at their favorite Italian restaurant in Bern. They were seated at a table on an enclosed outdoor patio lit by streetlamps, looking down on the Aare River and the Kornhausbrücke.

Sunday dinner at the restaurant was quiet, unlike Fridays and Saturdays, when foreign tourists reserved every table from 7:00 to 11:00 p.m.

Only two tables were occupied on the patio, both beside a stone fountain decorated with pots of flowers. The atmosphere inside the restaurant was subdued: Italian red and white-checked tablecloths, Renaissance art replicated on the walls—da Vinci, a

Giotto ceiling in Padua, a Raphael fresco. In the corner, a woman pianist played arias from Rossini, Bellini, Puccini, and Verdi.

"Another toast?" Dima said, smiling as his wife's dark eyes sparkled from the twin candles on their table. "We already toasted with champagne at our apartment."

"*Sì, amore,* but that toast was to our last night in Bern. I want to propose another."

"To my wife," he said with a grin, "always full of surprises. Let me guess. Could it be to our last dinner in Bern?"

"Not really," she said, raising her glass between the candles. "This one is from my heart."

"From your heart. I like that."

They clinked glasses, and Valeria said, "To my loving Dima, who has given me what I wanted in life: a happy marriage, a beautiful daughter, and a life in Europe." She touched her lips and flicked an air kiss. "And most of all, he has given us a new home in Italia!" They clinked again. Dima's face glowed from toasting earlier at home before walking to the restaurant.

"My turn," he said, clearing his throat. Following her example, he held his wineglass between the candles. "To my beautiful, loving, and patient wife."

Valeria laughed, a soft rumble from her throat. She furrowed her brow in a mock gesture of objection. "Patient—me? You have to be kidding! My dear Dima, I'm never patient when I know what I want. Like this beautiful necklace, a nice surprise on our last night in Switzerland."

She placed her palm over the jade necklace he had given her when they had toasted at home.

"Your persistence is admirable," Dima said.

"Many women shrink from being clear about what they want," Valeria continued. "Not me! You're the reason I'm persistent. I know what will make you happy, too, like our new home so we can live closer to Chiara."

"She'll be our first guest," Dima said. "It's rustic, not what she's used to, living in a nice apartment in Milan, near all the shopping and elegant restaurants."

"She is a bit spoiled, I agree," Valeria said, taking a sip. "But she wants to see us more and not have to take a flight or a train. We'll be only a couple of hours from her."

"We'll see her often, mostly on weekends, when she doesn't have a date with a gorgeous Italian man. She's eligible and very attractive. Almost as attractive as her mother was when I met her in Roma. My, thirty years ago."

Valeria shook her head. "Can you believe it?"

"And we'll be living in Italy again. Took almost three years, but it's perfect for us: remote, difficult to find, and safe. Our friends in Moscow will never find us."

"Let's not talk about that," Valeria snapped. "Don't spoil our evening."

Dima nodded and gestured to Silvio, who was watching them from inside. He stepped down onto the outdoor patio and greeted them warmly.

"*Buonasera, signora, signore. È sempre un piacere rivedervi nel nostro ristorante.*"

"*Buonasera, Silvio. È un piacere anche per noi,*" Valeria said. "For us, too."

"*Prego.* Please, please, *vi lascio il menù.* Here it is, and the chef suggests his excellent *pici cacio e pepe* tonight."

"*Sì, grazie. Lo prendo io.* I'll take the *pici cacio e pepe,*" said Dima.

"*Molto bene.* Very good, very good. *Per la signora?*"

Valeria pointed. "I'll have the veal scallopini and roasted vegetables."

"Very good," said Silvio. "May I ask if you've chosen the wine?"

"I'll go with the Franciacorta," said Valeria. "Maybe you'd like a red?"

"Yes, please. I'll pair the pasta with a Tuscan wine. A bottle of Nobile di Montepulciano will do."

Silvio excused himself and headed to the kitchen.

Dima sipped his wine and reached for a piece of bread in a basket. "I have to admit, I will miss Bern." Valeria nodded, also taking a piece of bread.

"What a beautiful city," Dima said. "The Aare River, all the bridges, the gardens and flowers starting to bloom, and the bears in the Bärengraben by the river."

"I won't miss the snow," Valeria said. "Switzerland and snow—they go together. Almost as much snow as Moscow." She shuddered. "In Calabria, we have to go north if we want to see snow. I don't like cold weather. I look like an Eskimo when I'm all bundled up."

"Or an Italian bear. I like the image," Dima said, sipping his wine and nibbling on his bread.

"I've had it with snow, *caro.* I need sunshine, hot weather, and no freezing rain."

"Snow is in my blood." Dima smiled. "Even Russians say winters go on too long. Then comes glorious spring. It's like life begins all over—at least until the first snow in October."

Valeria shivered, as if she'd felt a blast of freezing winter wind from Siberia. "It will be hot where we're going. I can't wait."

"Let's take a last look at the Aare. I'll miss that amazing river," Dima said. They stood, and he took her hand and led her to a waist-high stone wall looking over the river. Tall trees lined the riverbanks, and leaves fluttered in a cool breeze. Even from that height, they could hear the soothing sound of the Aare rapids flowing over stones and winding around a turn where the river formed a loop around the peninsula of the old city center.

"Beautiful, isn't it?" Dima put his arm around his wife.

"Yes, but chilly. Let's go back to our table. I need my sweater."

They returned to their table. Silvio came from the kitchen, carrying a tray, and set it on a stand by their table with two platters.

"Ooh, that looks delicious, Silvio. Grazie," Valeria said.

"The chef knows you're one of our best customers."

"And this is our favorite restaurant in Bern," said Valeria. "It's almost like home for me. As you know, I'm from Calabria."

They shared pleasantries with Silvio as he served their dinner and replaced the basket with one full of freshly cut bread. When he left, they both started eating, enjoying their food and feeling mellow from the effects of the wine and champagne they had drunk at home.

"I can't wait to move," Valeria said, slicing into her veal scallopini. After she took her first bite, she sliced the baked potato, which was the size of a tennis ball, and cut small slices of the roasted zucchini, onions, squash, and carrots. They ate in silence for a few moments. Then Valeria said, "This is such a pleasant way to enjoy our last meal in Bern. But I'm anxious to move into our new home."

Dima rolled his pasta and raised it to his mouth. "Yes, so am I. Three years of looking! It will be quiet in the mountains. No traffic or crowds."

"I can't wait to cook my first meal in my new kitchen—your choice, as long as it's pasta. We'll have to go shopping for food tomorrow. The refrigerator and cupboards are bare, like in a fairy tale, even though we've already moved a lot of our stuff there."

Dima smiled. "No worries, darling. We don't have to worry about anything, especially money. We have enough to live for a long time, years and years."

"You need to retire; you've worked hard for years. Now you can do what you've always wanted: gardening, planting flowers and vegetables, especially tomatoes, basil—"

"What about garlic?"

"No, we can buy garlic at the market."

"I'd like to grow fruit trees—lemons, limes, maybe apples and cherries."

"Will there be enough sun?"

"Yes, on the roof after the workmen finish resurfacing and clearing trees so we can get sunlight. Carlo, the gardener in Croce, has seeds for vegetables and small fruit trees. He's bringing fresh soil and compost this week. The security system is installed. I'll turn it on tomorrow when we arrive."

"You've thought of everything, dear. And you'd pass for an Italian. You're fluent, with a slight Calabrian accent. And all the weight you've lost, almost thirty pounds. Your beard makes you look like a scholar. You wear only Italian clothes—suits, shoes, and that funny beret...even though Italian men don't wear berets."

The meal was over, and their bottles of wine were empty, as well as two glasses of grappa. Not a crumb of tiramisu was left on either plate. Tomorrow they would leave Bern for the last time.

After paying with a credit card, Dima left two 100-euro bills in an envelope on the table for Silvio, who caught their eye as they walked toward the door. Valeria and Dima waved, and Silvio bowed and walked over to them. They all said parting words, hugged, and exchanged goodbyes. The waiter's last words were *"Buon viaggio."*

"I'm going to miss him," Valeria said as Dima opened the door for her. A gush of chilly April evening breeze ruffled her hair. "Glad you left a generous tip."

Dima tugged his coat collar close to his neck, shivering in the chilly night air. "He's a gentleman. I'll miss him, too."

They walked down the tile steps to the stone driveway, Dima's arm around her shoulder, she squeezing his hand. She said, "I wonder what Silvio will think when we don't show up next Sunday. Pity we couldn't tell him."

"No one has a hint that we're leaving, except the super at the apartment. I left a forwarding address in Moscow, but nothing about where we're really going."

"But Silvio—what about him?"

"I took care of that. In a note with the tip, I told him we'd be away for a few weeks so he won't think we're going to another restaurant."

"That was thoughtful. Thank you for doing that. I'll miss him. He was always nice to us."

They reached Kornhausstrasse arm in arm, the wind rustling the pine trees along the street. They followed streetlights, reminiscing about good times in Bern over the past six years. But that was over now.

When they got home, Dima pressed the code to open the gate.

"Our last night," Dima said. "I feel a bit nostalgic."

"Me, too, I guess," she said, her voice trailing off as they entered the building. "Tomorrow we sleep in Italia. I'm so happy!"

# CHAPTER THREE

The next morning, Dima retrieved their white Fiat 500X SUV from the underground parking garage and parked in front of their apartment, three blocks from the Kornhausbrücke over the Aare River, which formed a bend around Bern, a turbulent rope of chilly water that descended from the Swiss Alps.

Valeria was waiting on the curb next to their two pieces of luggage, a boxed crate of ceramic dishes, and three framed Russian icons. In her arms, she held a carrier with their four-year-old cat, Cookie, a ball of white and orange fur coiffed by a cat trimmer.

While Dima loaded suitcases into the trunk, Valeria arranged Cookie's carrier on pillows in the back seat so she could look out the window. Valeria slipped a seat belt over the carrier as Cookie meowed anxiously, her gray eyes peering through the slits of the carrier. She was not used to being outside their apartment.

"There, there, Cookie," said Valeria. "In a few minutes, you can wave bye-bye to Bern. It will be a beautiful drive, with lots of mountains, rivers, and lakes, all the way to Italy—your new home!"

Cookie meowed and Dima groaned, hearing Valeria pampering the cat like a favored child. Valeria reached into the carrier and stroked the cat's furry head. "In your new home, you won't have to be afraid of traffic, loud noises, and sirens. Papa is building you a large porch enclosed by wire so you can enjoy the fresh mountain air. You'll love the birds and tall trees...and all the squirrels."

"Get in, *cara*. It's time to go. She's a cat, not a baby. She'll be fine!" Dima said, slamming the trunk. "We need to be on the road before ten so we can get there before dark."

"She'll need fresh air. I don't want her to be afraid and get sick. Remember when we were gone that weekend? The cat sitter said she wouldn't eat, she missed us so much."

"Please, let's go," Dima pleaded. "It's four hours to the border and another two hours till we're in our new home."

Valeria stroked her fingers over Cookie's head, relaxing the cat until she purred. She climbed out of the back seat, shut the door, and got into the passenger's seat.

*"Andiamo!"* Dima said, releasing the brake and driving down the street for the last time.

Valeria turned around, watching Cookie crouch lower in the carrier, her eyes wide through the narrow slits, no longer purring, emitting a noise between a whine and a snarl. Dima turned on Kornhausstrasse and climbed to Viktoriastrasse. Morning commuters were headed in the opposite direction, into Bern's city center.

Valeria looked out the window at the modern apartment buildings, large homes, and trees lining Viktoriastrasse. "It feels strange to be leaving Bern for the last time. I'll miss the old clock tower, the Altstadt, the Rosengarten, and the bears in the park along the Aare."

Dima stopped at a red light. "It's like no other city I know. I especially enjoyed kayaking on the Aare, but the water was ice cold and choppy. So easy to fall in. I always got tired, paddling around rapids, over the falls, getting soaked."

They drove on, Valeria gazing out at the suburbs, Dima following signs for the Autostrada 2 toward the Thuner See.

"Bern is a remarkable city...even if it's freezing in the winter. Just like Moscow," said Valeria.

Dima ignored her comment. Valeria rarely passed up an opportunity to say something negative about Moscow, a city that she said had never welcomed her. They had argued frequently about Dima's hometown, but after moving to Bern, she rarely brought up how much she had disliked living in Moscow. A truce of sorts had come about as she grew more comfortable in Bern, making frequent trips to visit Chiara and enjoying the historic landmarks in Milan: the Pinacoteca di Brera, the Castello Sforzesco, Teatro alla Scala, the San Maurizio church with its beautiful frescoes, and the Duomo.

They drove in silence, broken occasionally by Cookie's meowing until she fell asleep. Dima tuned in to a Zurich classical radio station playing operas. "Yes, leave it there. I know this," Valeria said, humming along to the aria *"Si, mi chiamano Mimi"* from Puccini's *La Bohème*.

When the aria was over, Valeria turned down the radio and looked at Dima. "*Caro*, does it bother you that we didn't tell our neighbors we were leaving?"

He shook his head and tapped on the steering wheel. "Not really. They were just neighbors, not friends. The Swiss are cool to foreigners, especially to Russians. They won't miss us. Rudolf saw me carrying suitcases to the elevator this morning and said he'd be moving out the rental furniture for the tenants moving in soon. He asked where we were going. I told him back to Moscow. No more questions."

"I think the Swiss have a superiority complex," said Valeria. "They think everyone else is inferior."

"Well, I wouldn't go that far," Dima said. "In six years, only a few Swiss invited us to their home, even though we invited them. I felt they shunned us because we're Russian."

"*You* are, dear. I'm Italian, remember?" she said, reaching over to squeeze his shoulder.

"Being married to me makes you Russian," he retorted, glancing at her and smiling.

"But once people meet me, I make sure they know I'm Italian. I greet them in German, then Italian, and ask if they know Italian. Really, *tesoro*, you're one of the good Russians. People hear so much about bad Russians who cause trouble in the world. Almost every week you read about Putin's bullies killing reporters, police beating up demonstrators, and the terrible civil war in Syria backing that criminal Assad."

Dima drove, understanding what Valeria was saying and agreeing with her, but not wanting to have their drive to Italy become a discussion about politics. He much preferred that they talk about the good news, their new lives, which he had devoted himself to planning for three years.

"The Swiss aren't interested in Moscow or Russia," she scoffed. "Few have been to Russia, except if they take a Baltic cruise and spend a day or two in St. Petersburg. In any case, you're not like other Russians, Dima. You're kind, thoughtful…a real gentleman."

"Let's not get into politics, Vale. Let's enjoy our drive. It's a beautiful day. We're driving through the Alps, along Interlaken and Lago Lugano. The scenery in Switzerland is some of the best in Europe."

"You're right. I'm sorry, *tesoro*. I want this to be a special time, our day of liberation."

They exited Bern, following traffic headed to Interlaken. Every few minutes, Valeria turned around to check on Cookie, who was looking out from her carrier, and then gazed at the landscape of hilly green pastures and villages along rushing rivers against a background of snow-covered Alps.

Valeria checked her cell phone and said, "Do you think you'll ever go back to Bern?"

Dima shook his head. "No, I don't want to. No reason. We had six good years there. I'm ready for a change. We're starting a new—and very different—chapter in our lives, one that has perils, but also rewards. It was time for us to make our move and shut down everything in Bern. If we stayed, we'd get a knock on the door and have to answer questions from Moscow or the embassy. I don't have answers they'd want to hear. I was able to deflect them until last week. Kolya left voice mails that I didn't return. They'll send someone from the embassy to look for me, no doubt."

Valeria bit her lip, fearing what Dima was saying. A knock in the middle of the night. She had read Soviet history and knew about the millions killed during Stalin's long and bloody reign. KGB raids in the middle of the night, banging on doors. Innocent people snatched from their families, shoved into cars, driven to Moscow's Lefortovo Prison, tortured into false confessions, and sent to Siberian gulags to perish.

"I can't wait to see Chiara. I miss her," Valeria said, looking out the window, imagining their new lives in Italia. "Bern and Moscow never seemed like home to me. Russian was such a difficult language to learn. The Cyrillic alphabet was very confusing, and all those declensions—I was lost the first year."

"You did fine, Vale. You had an accent, of course, but everyone who learns Russian as a second language has an accent."

"But it didn't come naturally. You know, the way Italian comes naturally and easily."

Dima reached over and patted her leg. "*Amore*, if it was up to you, everyone would speak Italian."

Valeria laughed. "Of course, they would! Who would want to miss out on such a beautiful language…all the things you can say, the subtleties. I want to speak Italian all day, not German. It's stiff, pompous, and chilly as Swiss wine, pinot blanc."

"You know how much I like Italian wines and liqueurs."

"You're like papa. He had *liquore alla liquirizia* every night after dinner."

Dima smiled. "I have a bottle waiting for us at our new home."

They drove past the Thuner See and later into valleys between snowcapped mountains and many lakes, rivers, and modest waterfalls. High on the steep hillsides, cattle and horses grazed in fields of tall grass.

"Beautiful, isn't it, Vale?" Dima said, reaching over to take her hand in his.

"Like a dream," she said, squeezing his hand.

They continued driving. It was a perfect day for a long drive, with blue sky, puffy clouds, and bright sunlight. They passed through quaint villages with two- and three-story gingerbread houses painted in red, blue, green, and yellow. The houses seemed to compete to see who had the most blooming geraniums and pansies spilling over from flower boxes on their balconies.

"I'll miss these villages, Vale. They remind me of a fairy tale."

"But where we're going is also beautiful. Villas along Lago di Como, and mountains and forests."

"Yes, we're moving from one scenic country to a neighbor with similar attractions."

"I can't wait," she said. "Oh, and after we get to Italia, I need to shop for groceries. I can't wait to have real Italian products— Parmigiano-Reggiano, Calabrian *'nduja*, the pasta extruded through bronze, the fruit and vegetables grown under the sun!"

"We'll have dinner in Porlezza after we cross the border. There're restaurants and a *supermercato* along the highway."

They reached the western suburbs of Lugano, in a steep valley between mountains that plunged into the dark blue Lake Lugano. Four hours after leaving Bern, they were winding along a steep mountainside bordering the lake. They entered a tunnel cut through the mountain, exited into the bright sunlight, and then entered a second tunnel, half a mile long. Headlights came on as cars slowed to fifty kph.

When they exited the long tunnel, a sign indicated the Swiss-Italian border was near. Rounding a curve, they saw three Swiss police cars parked by a metal fence, with uniformed officers checking license plates as cars crept slowly forward. One officer waved them along. Dima accelerated, winding along a curve. A low metal fence prevented drivers from plunging into the lake a hundred meters below.

A quarter-mile later, they saw two blue Polizia di Stato vehicles and a van parked, with officers on both sides of the road and a billboard with the Italian flag and greeting, *Benvenuti*.

"We're almost there. I'm so excited. I love that sign!" Valeria said, pointing to the billboard as they crossed the border. "Such a beautiful day, isn't it? God wanted us to have a memorable homecoming. Thank you, God!"

In a festive mood, they drove along the lake, feeling the warm rays of a late afternoon sun. A few minutes after they crossed the border, Dima slowed when he saw a sign that indicated a viewpoint ahead.

He turned on his signal and eased into a parking area with marked spaces. A white Audi was the only other car at the viewpoint. A young couple was taking pictures of the shimmering Lake Lugano and the mountains across the lake.

Dima waited until the couple left. "Last assignment," he said, as he reached into a side compartment to take out two cell phones and put them into his pants pocket. "Yours?" Valeria handed over her phone, which he held in his hand as he opened his door. "We'll use only our Italian phones from now on." Dima got out and stepped over to the guardrail above a steep cliff looking over Lake Lugano.

He shielded his eyes as if he were admiring the view and then looked over his shoulder to watch cars and trucks passing in both directions. When no vehicles were visible, he swung his arm back and flung Valeria's phone, watching it fall, splash into the lake, and make ripples like a trout grabbing a fly off the surface.

He reached into his pocket and took his two phones, again glancing back for a lull in the traffic. When the highway was empty, he flung the larger phone high in the air. It tumbled end over end, dropping into the lake with the aerodynamics of a hammer. Then the second phone, splashing in the wake of the first.

He turned around and wiped his hands theatrically, like he was getting rid of an annoying pest.

"Say goodbye to our Russian phones," he said when he got in the car. "I don't know if our embassy can track SIM cards from cell towers, but I don't want to take any chances. We will use only our Italian phones from now on, with only Italian phone numbers. When someone calls our Russian phones—and they will—they'll ring at the bottom of Lake Lugano."

"And scare the fish!" Valeria said, laughing. "Swiss fish don't want to talk to Russian thugs."

"Especially because they wouldn't understand Russian."

Valeria laughed. "But are you sure we'll be safe? I don't want the FSB knocking on our door one day."

Dima reached across to pat her knee. "They won't. No way they can track us to our new home. We're safe, Vale. They'll never find us. I've taken care of it."

They drove the last few miles overlooking Lake Lugano, the bright sun reflecting off the blue waters. Twenty minutes later, they arrived in the small town of Porlezza, turned at a traffic light, and continued on Highway 340. As they were leaving town, Dima slowed and pulled into a parking place at a roadside trattoria called Bellavista. Above the building, a sign said *Typical cuisine—today risotto con pesce persico.*

"I'm hungry. Time for dinner," Dima announced.

"I'll be right in. I want to bring in Cookie's carrier and put it under our table. I'll ask the waiter if we can have a bowl of water and some boiled chicken for her."

Valeria opened the back door, unbuckled the seat belt, and lifted out the carrier as Cookie meowed, her eyes darting around.

"We're in Italia, Cookie! *Benvenuta!*"

# CHAPTER FOUR

At 8:30 the next morning, two men stood in front of Dima and Valeria's gated, four-story apartment near Kornhausstrasse. Security consisted of a locked gate and metal bars with trident spearpoints.

The taller man wore a dark suit, a white shirt, a blue necktie, and stylish Italian dress shoes. His companion was shorter and paunchy, and he wore a tan sport coat, a turtleneck sweater, and loafers, like he was on his way to lunch at a Swiss pub. Both carried umbrellas at the prospect of morning rain threatening from gray, low-hanging clouds.

The two men could have passed as bankers, accountants, or lawyers, of which there were many in Bern. Or they could have been representatives from a mortuary making a house call on a prospective or current customer. But they weren't bankers, accountants, lawyers, or undertakers. In their coat pockets they carried Russian passports and business cards from the Russian embassy in Bern, which did not indicate they were FSB intelligence agents assigned to contact Dima.

Oleg, the senior agent, wore wire-rimmed glasses. Vladimir, his pudgy companion, was a recent arrival in Bern from his last assignment at the Russian embassy in Cuba.

"How well did you know Dima?" Vlad asked, reaching into his coat pocket for a pack of Gauloises cigarettes. He lit one and tossed the match in the street.

"I guess you could call him a friend. He had me over for dinner once after he moved to Bern with his wife five or six years ago. His wife is Italian, nice looking. She's an excellent cook, but her Russian was atrocious. Her German was a bit better, but she mentioned that she preferred to speak in Italian. So she and I didn't have much to talk about. Dima, on the other hand, was quite friendly. We shared stories about Moscow. He said he missed his friends there, but I don't think he has any family anymore. His parents died some time ago."

Vlad puffed on his cigarette, looking up at the apartment, not the kind he would have seen in Cuba. "I'd like to get assigned to Italy," he said. "My assignments have been to Lagos, Saudi Arabia, and Cuba. I hope I can stay in Europe after Bern. No more Africa or the Middle East for me. The cigars and rum were good in Cuba, but the only alcohol you get in Saudi Arabia is at the embassy. Can you believe they don't drink—at least, officially?"

"You'd like Italy. Go there on vacation when you have time," Oleg said. He pressed the buzzer to apartment 26 outside the gate and stepped back. Vlad, unfamiliar with Bern, turned around to survey the quiet neighborhood of apartments and a wooded park across the street. People were taking their dogs for a morning stroll. Young mothers pushed prams. Several parents led children wearing uniforms to a nearby Lutheran church school.

No voice answered Oleg's buzzer call.

"Ring it again," Vlad said.

Oleg pressed it once more. Again, no answer. "Dima hasn't been to the embassy recently. I asked around, and he hasn't invited anyone for dinner in some time. Maybe he has other friends—Swiss, Italian. I don't know."

The apartment building's front door opened, and a middle-aged man exited, wearing a suit and a raincoat over his shoulders. He carried a briefcase in one hand and an umbrella in the other. When the man opened the locked gate, Oleg said in German, "Excuse me, sir, do you know Dmitri and Valeria Volkov?"

"The Russians on the second floor?" he said, wrinkling his brow.

"Yes, apartment 26."

He shook his head. "I don't know them personally, only to say hello. Sorry, late for work," he said and crossed the street toward the bus stop.

Oleg took a few steps along the gated fence and pointed to an apartment on the second floor. He saw an empty metal table on the balcony against a door with shutters. "That's their apartment, 26. A nice place, with a view of the park and the Rosengarten in the hills."

"Nicer than Moscow?" Vlad asked.

"Are you kidding?" Oleg said, stifling a laugh. "You'd pay a fortune to have an apartment like that back home."

"I hate where we're living now," Vlad said. "The embassy assigned us to a cramped basement apartment. Our windows face a brick wall, the parking lot, and a security fence with cameras. It's cold, damp, and dark, even during the day. To get to work, I have to walk past garbage cans and up the parking garage ramp. Disgusting. My wife bitches about it all the time."

"You're new. Everyone new to the embassy gets a starter apartment in the basement. You'll get a better one when someone gets transferred back to Moscow. In a few months, you'll get on the second or third floor. No view, except the same one you have now, behind the embassy."

Oleg pressed the buzzer again. "One more time. Then I'll try to find the supervisor."

"We're wasting time. They're not here. You said he didn't answer his phone over the weekend."

The building's front door opened again. An older woman wearing a wide-brimmed hat mostly covering dyed-blue hair stepped out. In one hand, she held a leash attached to a small white dog wearing a collar of fake jewels that made it look like a toy, not a live animal.

The dog was anxious, whimpering, its legs prancing like it had to find a tree before its bladder leaked. Its thin body had been sheared, leaving a crown of white fur on its head, around its neck, and on the middle of its stomach. Its curved tail ended in a white snowball of fur.

When the woman opened the gate, Oleg greeted her in German, "*Guten Morgen—*"

The dog lunged at the men, barking in high-pitched sounds that pierced the air: "Yip! Yip! Yip! Yip! Yip! Yip!" The dog jerked the leash so taut it almost spilled the woman to the sidewalk.

Oleg and Vlad jumped back, almost tripping into the street. Vlad inched behind Oleg as a shield.

The wiry dog was the size of a shoe but had the raw energy of an enraged pit bull. It snarled, its needle-sharp teeth glistening with spit. "Yip! Yip! Yip!" It lunged at them from its hind legs, front paws clawing the air, jaws snapping within inches of the men's knees.

"Yip! Yip! Yip!"

"God damn!" Vlad swore in Russian, tensing his leg to kick the dog if it got close enough to bite them.

The old woman yanked the leash, almost losing her hat. "Cleo! No! Stop!"

The dog snarled and landed on its front feet, its barking replaced by growls. "Grrrrrrrr!" It dashed behind its master, wrapping the leash around her legs, emerging on the other side. "Grrrrr!"

"Sorry," the woman apologized, reaching down to pat the fur-ball head. "Cleo gets soooo excited when she sees someone she doesn't know. She's a good dog. She only barks at strangers."

"Does she bite?" Oleg asked, stepping back, glancing suspiciously from the woman to the dog.

"Cleo? No. Well, maybe once in a while when she's scared."

"She scared me," Oleg said.

The growling lowered into a snarl as the dog crouched, as if it was about to take another leap at them. Oleg and Vlad took another step back.

"Are you waiting for someone?" The woman asked, as if her dog's behavior was as normal as yawning.

"Ah…do you know Dima and Valeria Volkov?" Oleg asked.

The woman tugged the leash so she wouldn't trip. "Of course. Such a nice couple. Russians. We moved here about the same time, just before my husband died, poor dear. I miss him. So does Cleo, don't you, dear?"

Snarling became growling again.

"Valeria is very sweet. She makes me cookies for my birthday."

"Have you seen them recently? They don't answer their phone."

The dog bared her teeth, snarling, eyes bulging. Her mistress ignored her. "No, I haven't…not for a week or so. Why?"

"We're friends…from Moscow."

"Oh, nice. You're Russian, too. I could tell by your accent. I've never been to Moscow. I'd like to go sometime and see your Orthodox churches. I saw a TV show about Russian churches; they looked so lovely. My father was a Lutheran pastor. I love old churches—so much history."

For an older woman, she seemed eager for a spontaneous conversation with strangers on the street. But she was a lonely widow, starved for a few kind words, even if her dog was as friendly as a coiled cobra.

Oleg ignored her comment about Russian churches and said, "Do you know how I can contact the apartment super?"

"Of course. I'll show you.…Buzz him here," she said, raising the hand that was holding the leash. She pointed at the lowest buzzer on the panel gate, labeled 00. "His name is Rudolf. A nice man. I call him Rudy. His wife is Charlene. She's Jewish and from Poland. Friendly people. You would like them."

"Do you think he's available?"

"I don't know. He's busy all the time with people bothering him—something wrong with the plumbing, a broken window from a bird that tried to fly in. I don't bother Rudy, except once, when I had a problem with my toilet. He fixed it right away. He has all the tools to fix things. I barely know how to use a hair dryer," she said, laughing and patting a wave of her blue-tinted hair.

"Thank you," Oleg said with a slight bow.

"Excuse me. Cleo needs her morning walk in the park. If I'm late, she lets me know. All her dog friends in the park are out this time of the morning. She can't wait to see them. Her favorite is a poodle just a bit bigger than she is. I think Cleo barked at you because she wanted to go see her poodle friend. They jump and roll on the grass. They're so funny to watch. I wish you could see them play. I call her "Cleo" because my husband took me to Egypt the year before he died of cancer. We went to museums and saw sculptures and things about Cleopatra—such a romantic name. That's why I gave her that name. I taped postcards from Egypt around her fluffy bed, where she sleeps next to me. I tell her about Egypt and show her the postcards." She giggled again. "She even does funny things. She'll climb up on the sculpture of the Sphinx like she's trying to mate with it." Another giggle. "Have you ever been to Egypt? It's so hot, dreadful even. I almost fainted when I was on a camel. I don't like hot weather. Swiss weather is the best, don't you think?"

"I agree," Oleg said, eager for the woman to leave so they could get back to their assignment and not have to endure the woman's rambling.

Both men smiled politely as the woman walked around them, tugging the leash of her dog, who didn't take her eyes off them. When the woman stepped off the curb to cross the street, the dog offered one last chorus of barks and yips, nearly choking on her rhinestone collar as her master tugged her along.

"Damn dog," Vlad hissed when the woman reached the park. "I hate dogs who bark all the time. I'd shoot them, every last one."

"Toss them in a lake and let them drown," Oleg said. "My wife wants a dog. I refuse and say, 'All we need is one cat. Nothing more.'"

Oleg pressed the 00 buzzer. Moments later, a female voice answered. "Yes? Can I help you?"

"We're friends of Dmitri and Valeria Volkov in apartment 26," Oleg said. "I called, but he doesn't answer. I'm afraid he might be sick and may have to go to a hospital. Can you let me into his apartment?"

"I don't have the keys. My husband is the maintenance man. He'll be back around eleven."

Oleg sighed and looked down at Vlad, shaking his head. "Thanks. We'll be back then," he said.

Oleg and Vlad stepped back from the gate. People came out, smiled, and greeted them in German, *"Morgen,"* and went on their way.

Vlad took out his cigarettes, lit one, and took a puff. "We're wasting our time. I'm sure they're gone for good. He's skipped."

"That's what we have to find out. If he did leave, we need to find out where he went."

"His daughter lives in Italy. They probably went there. We'll find them. No one escapes from the FSB."

Drops of rain began splattering the street, making damp spots on the pavement. The two men opened their umbrellas. "Let's come back at eleven. Want to go for a coffee?"

"How about a morning beer?"

"Sure. Why not."

When they returned at 11:15, Oleg pressed the 00 buzzer. A minute later, a man answered. Oleg, who had been in Bern for three years and is fluent in German, said, "We're trying to reach Dima Volkov. Can you help us?"

"Wait there. I'll come out," the man said. Five minutes later, a man in work clothes, boots, and a cap opened the apartment building door and walked to the gate, not unlocking it.

Oleg asked, "We're looking for Dima and his wife. We're friends from Moscow."

"You have identification?"

They reached into their coat pockets, pulled out red Russian passports, and held them up between the bars in the gate.

The man glanced at their passports, squinting at the Russian text, shaking his head. "I can't help you. They aren't here. They left over the weekend. I removed the rental furniture from their apartment yesterday for the new residents moving in tomorrow."

Oleg and Vlad exchanged glances. Oleg said, "Do you know where they went?"

The man shrugged, looking annoyed with someone taking up his time. "I don't know. Back to Russia, I think."

"When you got the notice to remove their furniture, did it say where they were going?"

He shook his head. "No, I'm just the maintenance supervisor."

"He must have left a forwarding address," Oleg persisted.

"Try the rental agency. They probably know, not me."

"Do you have the address of the rental office?"

The man reached into his wallet and took out a business card. "Write down the address. This is the only one I have with me." Oleg took out a pen, scribbled the address on a newspaper, and handed the card back.

When the supervisor returned to the building, they crossed the street to the park and climbed a knoll a few meters higher, level with the second floor of the apartment building. They could see through an open-shuttered door into the darkened apartment 26: a chandelier dangling from the ceiling, two partitions that led to other rooms, pots and pans hanging from a rack in the kitchen. On the balcony, a metal table stood empty, with no chairs.

Oleg took out his cell phone and called the embassy. When the phone was answered, he said, "No sign of Volkov. The maintenance supervisor said they moved out over the weekend. He doesn't know their forwarding address. He said the apartment rental agency probably has it."

"Go there and get his forwarding address. He must have left one. You can't just disappear, not in this day. Putin wants to know. He called the ambassador today and asked about Volkov. Don't waste time. We have to find him."

"We're going to the rental agency now. I'll call you when I find out."

"Don't stop there. Go back to the apartment building tomorrow. See if you can find someone who knew him. Maybe he told a neighbor where they were going. Keep searching."

That afternoon, Oleg and Vlad went to the rental agency and asked to talk to someone about the Volkovs' forwarding address. The receptionist asked them to wait while she called her supervisor. Half an hour later, the supervisor came out, a bureaucrat. Oleg showed him a letter from the secretary of the Russian embassy requesting the Volkovs' forwarding address.

"Let me take this to the manager. He would need to give permission. I don't have the authority."

They waited another hour. The bureaucrat came back and handed Oleg a photocopy of a form with names, phone numbers, and addresses. Printed in German, it included Dima's full name, Dmitri Leonovich Volkov, a phone number, and a forwarding address: a Moscow bank and phone number.

Oleg and Vlad parked across the street from Dima's apartment the next morning, watching a crew unloading boxes and crates from a moving van parked in front of the gate with a ramp onto the street.

The movers off-loaded dressers, sofas, chairs, beds, dining tables wrapped in tarps and sealed with masking tape. They loaded them onto carts and wheeled them through the open gate into the apartment building.

Oleg and Vlad walked along the fence, looking up at the open doors of apartment 26, facing the street. "Lights on. New tenants in already," Oleg said. "I wish we could get up there and see if Dima left a forwarding address, or maybe find some mail that came in over the weekend."

"I don't know," Vlad said. "I see a woman walking back and forth. I don't think we could get in."

They walked across the street into the park and sat on a bench that faced the apartment. While they waited, first one car and then another arrived and parked in front of the building. Three couples, all with young children, emerged from the cars and walked to the gate. The women carried bouquets of flowers and wrapped gifts. Two of the men had grocery shopping bags. One held an open carton containing wine and champagne bottles.

One of the men pressed a button on the gate panel and spoke German. The gate opened with a click, and they entered the building.

"Let's get over there. Maybe we can get in," Vlad said.

At the back of the moving van, two workers struggled to ease a large crate with four legs and wheels down the ramp. When the crate was secure, the movers took a smoke break, leaning against the ramp to rest. A few inches exposed under the tarp revealed the polished legs of a piano. When the smoke break was over, one of the crew walked up the ramp and came down with a wrapped piano bench. He carefully placed it onto the piano crate, and he and his fellow workers pushed the crate through the gate, which they propped open with a brick.

Vlad and Oleg watched, seeing an opportunity. "Let's go in and see if we can get information from the new tenants," Oleg said. "Maybe Dima left a note about their mail or a forwarding address."

"Let's hope the supervisor doesn't see us."

They followed the movers into the building. The movers wheeled the piano crate to a freight elevator at the end of the hall. Oleg and Vlad went through the lobby and took the stairs to the second floor.

When they reached the floor, the freight elevator door opened. The movers guided the piano crate and bench toward the open door of apartment 26. Oleg and Vlad waited in the hallway, hearing German and the sounds of tearing and ripping. When the movers left the apartment, they pushed a crate stacked with cardboard sheets and wrapping tarp to the freight elevator.

"Let's see what we can find out," Oleg said. They walked down the hall and stood in front of the open apartment. Inside they could see the living room with unopened boxes, chairs, tables, and a sofa. The guests who brought gifts were in the kitchen, putting trays in the refrigerator and opening bottles. A young woman holding a baby wrapped in a blanket was seated on the piano bench, running her fingers over the piano keys.

Oleg stepped up to the open door and rapped lightly. "Excuse me. Mind if we come in? We are friends of the former tenants, the Volkovs."

The woman looked over with a puzzled look on her face. "Who are you? I have guests here. I'm not alone," she said, clutching the baby wrapped in a blanket.

Oleg and Vlad took a step into the apartment, remaining in the foyer. "Did you know Dima and Valeria Volkov, who lived here before?"

"No," the mother said, glancing at her friends in the kitchen. "I saw their names on one of the forms we filled out to rent the apartment."

"Is there any chance they might have left something, some mail, a set of keys or anything? They asked us to stop by to see if you found something of theirs."

The woman shifted the baby to her other arm. Two of the male guests came into the living room, holding champagne glasses.

"I didn't find anything," the mother said. "Maintenance probably took anything they might have left."

"We asked him, but we just wanted to see if there was anything you might have found in a drawer or closet."

The mother looked nervously at her guests, who had stopped what they were doing in the kitchen and were following the conversation between her and the two uninvited men. She held her baby tightly and said with a strain in her voice, "There was no furniture here when we moved in. That's all I'm going to say. How did you get into the apartment? Did the supervisor let you in?"

They didn't acknowledge her question.

The huskiest man, who was holding a champagne bottle, stepped toward them. "Excuse me, but do you have permission to come into the apartment?"

"We told the maintenance man we wanted to stop by and see if the former tenants left anything."

"Did he give you permission?" he repeated, taking another step toward Oleg and Vlad.

Neither spoke.

The man pointed at the woman holding the baby. "Then you'd better do what the woman told you. Leave and shut the door behind you."

Quickly, the mother said, "They didn't leave anything. You shouldn't be here. Please leave now, or I'll call someone."

Oleg made a slight bow. "I'm sorry. I didn't mean to cause any problems. The former tenant asked me to stop by in case they left something."

The man started walking toward them. "Do you mind? You're making Lynn nervous. Leave now."

Oleg and Vlad stepped back into the hallway, hurried down the hall to the stairs, and heard the door slam behind them. Neither spoke until they were outside and going through the gate.

"Well, we tried," Oleg said. "We'd better leave. I don't want the maintenance guy to come out."

When they were outside, they walked toward their BMW, hearing a dog barking. They both flinched. The old woman with the dog was on the curb, ready to cross, her white dog barking at them.

"Damn, it's that stupid dog," Oleg muttered, scowling.

"The woman's the stupid one," Vlad said. "You have to be crazy to have such a pain-in-the-ass dog."

The woman waved at them. The dog barked, straining at her leash, raising her front legs, baring needle-sharp teeth. "Yip! Yip! Yip! Yip!"

"Cleo remembers you!" the old woman said as she reached the sidewalk. Oleg and Vlad walked around their car, not letting the dog get closer. The dog continued barking, straining at the leash. "See, she recognizes you." She reached down, patted the top of the dog's head, and walked through the open gate. "Next time, she probably won't even bark," the woman said cheerfully.

When she'd entered the building, Vlad said, "I wish I had a gun."

"You do."

"But not here. It's in the embassy."

"Too bad."

"I'll bring it next time."

"Let's get a beer."

"Yeah. And brats. I'm hungry."

They walked a block, entered a bierkeller, and ordered hefeweizen beer and a platter of bratwurst, sauerkraut, and red cabbage. They had chocolate cake for dessert. An hour later, they were back at the apartment building, with Vlad smoking and belching from the beer.

The moving van was gone. Lights illuminated apartment 26, and the shuttered door to the balcony was open. Inside they could hear children laughing and someone playing scales and chords on the piano. The pianist stopped playing, and they heard boisterous, throaty toasts as guests welcomed the new residents into their new apartment.

The metal table on the balcony terrace had been replaced by an antique wooden table with stout legs, on which a blue ceramic vase held a large bouquet of red roses.

As Oleg and Vlad walked away, they could still hear the laughter and someone playing a jazz tune on the piano as a male voice sang in German.

# CHAPTER FIVE

MOSCOW—TWO DAYS EARLIER

"How much? Do you have an idea?" Titov asked, with a tone that hinted he was afraid to hear the answer.

"I'm working on it. All I have is early estimates, not all tallied."

Titov made a face like he was about to hear bad news. "How much? A million euros?"

Komarov shook his head. "Higher," he said, stabbing his hand up in the air. The sudden move of his arm above his head initiated a cough. Then another, ending in a throaty wheeze. He pulled his hand down and grabbed for a tissue. He covered his mouth and hacked into the tissue, a prolonged rasping that sounded like it came from a plugged sink.

When Komarov raised his head, his face was flushed. He wiped his mouth and looked at Titov with bloodshot eyes. "Sorry...damn coughing spells. Drives me crazy." He reached for a bottle of pills beside a computer, put several in his palm, tossed them in his mouth, and washed them down with a sip of his cooled tea.

"Kolya, can I get you something? This is upsetting for you."

"No, thanks. Yes, definitely upsetting. Maybe my friend is up to funny business," he said with another hacking cough. When he was finished, he wiped his mouth again, blinked several times, and gripped the edge of his desk to keep from collapsing in his chair.

Titov reached over and put his hand on Komarov's arm, feeling the folds of his suit and his arm of soft flesh and bone. "Kolya, please, you're sick. Let me call a doctor. You should go home."

"Not yet. I have to brief you in case I can't come back to work Monday."

"But your health!" Titov protested. "That's more important. This can wait."

"It can't," Komarov said, shaking his head and keeping a tissue close to his mouth. "I need to explain so you can take over if necessary."

"I'm not as familiar with Dima's accounts as you are."

"You'll be fine. Where was I?"

"How much Dima had stolen."

"Take a wild guess," Komarov said, tossing the tissue in the basket below and reaching for another. "Let's do this: Pretend you're someone contemplating how much you could skim from accounts that total more than 300 million euros. How much would you take?"

Titov shook his head. "I can't even imagine, K-Kolya," he stammered. "I wouldn't."

Komarov chuckled, waved his hand. "Pretend you could, and pretend you've been thinking of doing this for a while. You come up with a way to do it, and you know your supervisor isn't going to be watching your accounts. Play along with me."

Titov sighed, his face pale at the thought of committing a crime. "I'd be afraid to steal more than a single cookie from a plate. My mother taught me, 'Never take something that belongs to another person. You'll go to hell.'"

"Or the gulag."

They chuckled. "Same thing…hell…the gulags."

"Give me a number, any number," Komarov insisted.

"I don't know. Let's say a million euros." Titov made a face, feeling uncomfortable at the thought that he would steal anything, even a single cookie.

Komarov smiled. "A round number, a little low. I haven't totaled it all up yet. I need to go through each transfer and currency exchange one more time. Here's what I have so far," he said, clicking on a tab at the top of a browser that took him to a Google Sheets database.

He clicked on a link that said *February*. At the top were columns with limited-partnership names and abbreviated account numbers in parentheses.

In the first box after the February 1 date were horizontal rows with amounts of euros, British pounds, Swiss francs, and US dollars transferred from fictitious accounts.

Komarov pointed to the rows of February dates: "The first month I was out," he scrolled to the bottom, "almost six hundred thousand euros."

Titov's eyebrows rose. He was stunned by the amount. "One month?"

"And it's a short month, only twenty-eight days." Komarov clicked on the file button and then to one labeled *March*. He scrolled down through the March dates. "Another eight hundred thousand."

Titov whistled and shook his head in astonishment. *"Bozhe moi,* I don't believe it."

Komarov closed that file and opened a third labeled *April*. "In the second week in April, another four hundred thousand."

"Almost two million?!" Titov said with a stifled gasp. "Where did the money go?"

"I. Don't. Know," Komarov said with emphasis. "Somehow, he skimmed the money into an account that's not on his list."

"Can you find it?"

"I'll have to, hopefully before I report this. The bosses will want to know where the money is and how to get it back."

"When will you do that?"

"Damned if I know. I can't report that something doesn't smell right until I've tried everything to track down the money."

"How long will that take?"

"Who knows? I called Dima on Wednesday, my first day back. I didn't accuse him of anything; I just told him I noticed transfers that didn't look right. He said he'd check the paperwork from the receiving banks with his figures. All the paperwork from the accounts are mailed to him, not me. He said he'd get back to me and that there was nothing to worry about. Thursday I called again. His voice-mail greeting said he would return his calls shortly, but he didn't call back. That's not the Dima I know."

"So if he did skim, and you called him about it, he knows he's in trouble."

"That's why he doesn't answer his phone."

They were both quiet. Titov finally said, "You want more tea? I'll get it for you."

Komarov shook his head. "Not now. I need to tell you the whole story." Komarov cleared his throat.

"When I was in the hospital and then at home recuperating, Dima called me at least once a week to see how I was doing. That wasn't unusual. We've known each other for years."

"You told me that when I came to see you."

"He said he was working with an algorithm that would give him a fraction more in foreign-exchange trades and transfers in the morning, selling at the end of the day. I would have asked him about it, but I was full of painkillers. I couldn't think straight, fighting pain and nausea and just wanting to sleep and pop pills. He asked about my family, sent me flowers and boxes of Swiss chocolates. Imagine that…I'd never received flowers or chocolates from a man—so unusual. Each time we talked, he asked when I was coming back to work. I thought he was just being considerate. Now I'm not so sure. He hinted that he knew no one was checking his accounts."

"So it was premeditated. He planned it knowing when you'd be out of the office."

"It looks that way. I hope it's not true. I'd hate to think of the consequences."

"You trust Dima, don't you?" Titov asked, in a tone of voice that betrayed a sense of disbelief.

"I did, but I'm not sure about now. We had dinner with our wives when he was here at Christmas before his wife had a stroke after they returned to Bern. He called me and said she was in the hospital in Bern. Her doctors said she needed bed rest and no travel. So Dima hasn't been back to Moscow since January."

"When was the last time you talked to him?"

"Wednesday afternoon, like I told you. But I have to try again to get some answers." He picked up his cell phone and punched Dima's number. After four rings, the call went to a voice-mail greeting: *"Hello, this is Dmitri. I'm away from my desk. Leave a message, and I'll call you right back."*

"Dima, this is Kolya. Important: Call me before the markets close. I don't understand transactions the last couple of months. It's 10:30 in Moscow."

Komarov was about to hang up but needed to express his frustration. He waited a couple seconds and signed off with, "I don't like what I'm seeing in your accounts, Dima. Since you're not taking my calls or calling me back, I'm going to have to call my supervisor in the Kremlin. He'll want an explanation."

He set his cell phone on his desk and shook his head in disbelief and anger. "Damn it, I know he's there. I know he is. He works from 8:00 a.m. until lunch, and then he's back in the office until about 4:00."

"He's avoiding you," Titov observed, shaking his head.

"I hate to admit it, but I think he is. I don't want to accuse him of something if it could just be that algorithm he told me about," Komarov said, the corners of his mouth turned down in a frown, like a mask from the opera *Pagliacci*.

"What will you do?"

"I don't know. I've known him since university. I met his wife when he returned from the Rome embassy with her and their baby daughter. Our wives became friends, and also our children when they were young. His wife didn't like living in Moscow, so she took her daughter back to Italy every year. Dima was upset because they'd spend several months with her family. Then his wife gave him an ultimatum: She wanted to live in Europe, not Russia. She left, and Dima arranged to follow her by getting a job working at the Bern bank laundering money for the oligarchs. Now this," he finished, pointing at his computer screen.

"What will you do, Kolya? This is serious."

"Very serious," Kolya agreed, frowning. He picked up his phone. "I'll just have to call my contact in Putin's office, tell them what I have, and send over a file. Maybe they know something I don't. But if my figures are right and Dima isn't answering his phone, they can send someone from our Bern embassy to find out what's going on."

Titov nodded. "That won't be a friendly meeting."

"Not at all. Putin's friends will want quick answers. They'll demand to know where the money is and get it back. It could get bad for Dima."

"You mean like Litvinenko, poisoned in London with radioactive polonium?" Titov shuddered.

Komarov nodded, frowning. "You know as well as I do that Litvinenko isn't the only one who paid the ultimate price for betrayal."

"It's a long list."
"Very long."

# CHAPTER SIX

## QUESTURA, MILANO

During the Monday briefing for the DIGOS anti-terrorism police *(General Investigations and Special Operations Division),* Giorgio Lucchini stood with arms folded in the back of the briefing room, letting his deputy Antonella Amoruso run the meeting. She called on agents to update the status of investigations, interrogations, possible arrests on antiterrorism cases, and reports from the weekend football matches at San Siro, including the arrest of ten Inter supporters who set a few cars on fire outside the stadium at the end of the match.

Amoruso closed the meeting with her usual precaution: "Be safe out there. Protect yourself and your colleagues. Your commitment to protecting our nation is vital." She paused, raised her hand, and added: "And remember, my door is always open. See you next week." She stepped away from the platform as the agents filed out of the room, pairing up on their way back to their offices down the hall.

Lucchini raised his hand and motioned to Amoruso. "Good briefing. Should be a good week for us. We'll close some cases. New ones always come up. Sorry I was late."

"Not a problem. I saw you on the phone when I passed by."

"Yes, a call from Rome. Can you stop by? I have to brief you about it."

"I'll follow you. I'm free now."

"Good."

From the intense look in Lucchini's eyes, Amoruso knew it was important, possibly critical. Lucchini rarely revealed emotions, and his calm manner was a model that he expected DIGOS agents to follow. Act professionally at all times. Don't express anger or frustration when interviewing people or possible suspects. The seriousness of their work required total attention. Emotions could get in the way of making objective decisions.

Amoruso picked up her pace as she followed Lucchini to his office on the third floor of the Milano Questura, the joint headquarters of Polizia di Stato offices, including administration, immigration, Polizia Stradale, DIGOS, and DIA (the antimafia investigation department).

As Lucchini and Amoruso walked past other offices, agents dressed in street clothes stood outside, nodding to Lucchini out of respect. Lucchini was always professional, wearing designer suits, white shirts, and muted ties to work. At any moment, he could be called upstairs to the *questore*'s office for a meeting with judges, prosecutors, or commanders of other police branches. More than once, Lucchini had been called at the last moment to fly to Rome for a high-level meeting at the Ministry of Interior on national security issues regarding top-secret cases of international terrorism, given his experience with such investigations. For those occasions, Lucchini kept a small suitcase with a change of clothes, toiletries, and personal items in his office.

On such occasions, a police car would meet Lucchini at the Questura's arched entrance on Via Fatebenefratelli and whisk him to Linate Airport, with red lights flashing but no siren. When Lucchini arrived at Rome's Fiumicino Airport, another police car would speed him downtown to the headquarters of the Ministry of Interior.

When Lucchini reached his office, he stepped aside to let Amoruso enter. She enjoyed these spontaneous meetings with her boss. They usually meant something important had come up based on recently received information.

Lucchini lingered in the hallway for a moment while an agent asked him about a case he was working on.

Amoruso relaxed in a chair in front of Lucchini's desk and looked around his office, which resembled an academic's study as well as a police commander's nerve center. On opposite walls were shelves lined with histories and biographies in Italian, English, and German. Alongside the shelves were historic drawings of eighteenth-century Milano, the San Cristoforo church in the Navigli area, a horse-drawn carriage passing the La Scala Opera House, and Roman columns in front of the San Lorenzo church.

Modern technology and commemorations dominated Lucchini's working spaces: secure telephones and computers on his desk; a computerized map of Milano programmed to zoom in on any location in the city and suburbs with real-time satellite imagery; photos of Lucchini with Sergio Mattarella, the president of the republic, as well as with police commanders from

Italy, the US, and NATO nations; and diplomas and plaques honoring him and his agents.

When Lucchini ended the conversation with the agent and walked in, leaving his door open, Amoruso said, "You looked preoccupied in the briefing."

"I was. That's what I need to tell you about. The Ministry called me at home last night and again this morning. They're assigning us to a case with a Russian connection."

"Russia? What's that about?" said Amoruso with a puzzled look on her face.

"We don't have all the details, but we're going to be looking for a Russian."

"A Russian. What about?"

"I'd tell you, but we don't even know his name."

"Why us?"

"It's in our backyard…or maybe on our doorstep, according to what we know."

"That's unusual. There are a lot of Russians in Milano—immigrants, some businessmen, and finance people. But we haven't had any trouble with them."

Lucchini picked up a file and was about to hand it over. "By the way…you studied Russian, didn't you?"

Amoruso laughed, ending in a smile. "Well, better to say I *tried* to study Russian but gave up after one semester."

"That's all, one semester?"

"I learned to say '*da*' for yes, '*nyet*' for no, and '*dasvidaniya*' for goodbye. And I can't begin to pronounce hello—something like '*zdravstvuyte*.'" She laughed as she slurred over the difficult consecutive consonants. "Whew, that was always a tough one. I always murdered it."

Lucchini smiled. "And you took a course in Russian literature, didn't you?"

Amoruso's eyes widened in surprise. "How did you remember? That was a long time ago. I struggled through Tolstoy, Dostoyevsky, Lermontov. That was the end of my interest in Russia. I found Russian novels tedious—such a different culture and history. I got about three hundred pages into *War and Peace,* about aristocratic families and Napoleon's invasion, but then I gave up. I did like Tolstoy's *Anna Karenina,* about a wife who betrays her husband with a lover and then kills herself by jumping in front of a train. So sad. I liked her character."

"I did read Solzhenitsyn," Lucchini said, "who won the Nobel Prize in Literature. He wrote *One Day in the Life of Ivan Denisovich.* He spent years in a Soviet gulag. Grim. Depressing."

"Oh, I forgot," Amoruso said. "I also read Pasternak's *Doctor Zhivago.* Did you know it was published first in Italy? A copy was smuggled out, and someone published it, and it was made into a movie. But, Giorgio, why are we talking about Russian literature?"

He smiled. "Because, as I said, the Ministry is assigning us a case with a Russian connection, and I remembered you had studied Russian."

"So, what did the Ministry tell you?"

Lucchini picked up a file from his desk. "This is all we have. American CIA picked up an intercept from their Moscow embassy, an encrypted message that FSB, Russia's secret police, is looking for a Russian traitor suspected of living near Milan."

"Really? Maybe I'll have to brush up on my Russian."

"The FSB claims he embezzled money in a money laundering operation in Switzerland."

"Money laundering? Switzerland? I've read about that in the papers. They launder money to interfere with politics in the West and bribe corrupt politicians."

"It seems this Russian embezzled from accounts in Switzerland, skimming off the top."

"Isn't that a matter for Guardia di Finanza and Polizia Stradale?"

"One message hinted that the Russians might send someone after him, probably in Milano. Apparently, the FSB sent someone from their Bern embassy to talk to him, but he wasn't there. He left his apartment with no forwarding address."

"A Russian stole from other Russians?" Antonella laughed. "Russian rulers—going back to the Romanov czars, Soviet communists, and Putin's thugs—have always cheated fellow citizens. The oligarchs are crooks, thieves."

"As a common prejudice, you don't think of Russians as the most honorable people, especially at the top, Putin and his crowd. That's how they got their political power: stealing from the masses after the Soviet Union collapsed. Oligarchs became billionaires. Bought yachts in Nice and luxury homes in London."

"Putin's dangerous. He has no tolerance for dissidents, protesters, or the media. He's shut down independent news media and murdered reporters."

"And former officials," said Lucchini. "Litvinenko was given radioactive poison in London by a Russian agent. What a terrible way to die, with your body rotting until death comes."

"You think the oligarchs will send an assassin to find and kill this man?" Amoruso asked.

"Litvinenko's murder was tied to Russia's Federal Security Service, the FSB, which Putin headed before he became president. They also have a military intelligence branch, the GRU."

"And Putin would have approved Litvinenko's assassination?"

"Of course. Apparently, poison is a common way Russian assassins work. They also did it in Sofia, Bulgaria. Smeared it on the car handle of an arms manufacturer. He and his son became very ill and almost died. They recovered, but they attempted to assassinate him again at a resort on the Black Sea."

"Why did they try to kill him?" Amoruso asked.

"Russians go after anyone they suspect as traitors or defectors. In 2012, a Russian scientist, Alexander Perepilichny, died of a heart attack after he was poisoned by a toxin while he was running near his rented home in London. He was only forty-three years old, a bit young for a heart attack."

"I understand they have a secret laboratory where they make these toxins," Amoruso said.

"The Russians also try to interfere with elections, like they did in Moldova a few years ago," Lucchini said. "They also attempted a coup in Montenegro by trying to assassinate the prime minister. Fortunately, that failed."

"Ruthless," Amoruso said with a shudder. "It's like they're at war with Western democracies. And now Italy?"

Lucchini nodded. "That's why the Ministry isn't taking any chances. They suspect the Russian who embezzled is living in or near Milano. His daughter lives here. She does something in fashion."

"A Russian model?"

"We don't know. We don't have a name. In messages, they only call him a traitor who must be stopped."

"Hmm. The fashion industry. *Ispettore* De Monti has a connection with a guy who works in fashion and knows almost everybody in Milan. You remember that he gave us important information during the terrorists case at La Scala a few years ago. Maybe we could ask her to talk to him," suggested Amoruso.

"Have her and Volpara come by. We'll see if she still has that connection. Could be a good place to start if we can track down the daughter and get her name."

"I'll get them before they leave the office," Amoruso said. She stood, brushed her suit pants, and headed to the door.

\* \* \* \* \*

Ten minutes later, Simona De Monti and Dario Volpara joined Amoruso in Lucchini's office. He briefed them on the intercepted intelligence and the Russian daughter working in fashion.

"*Ispettore* De Monti," Lucchini said, "I remember a key link you came up with in our search for the Islamic terrorists. You met some guy who had something to do with the fashion industry."

De Monti smiled. "You're right. His name is Gianluigi Marinoni, nicknamed Giangi. He's one of those people who's in the 'right place at the right time.' The place was Deus, a nightclub and trattoria in Isola near my apartment. Giangi hangs out there, drinks too much, brays like a donkey, and makes a scene sometimes. He writes a fashion-gossip blog and articles for major women's fashion magazines. That's how he makes his living. He gives hints and suggestions for clothes and makeup based on the new collections. I understand his blog is read by top clients and employees in the fashion industry. He knows everybody and writes good copy. He's a sort of professional in his field. His errant behavior is a part of his personality and his being a VIP in that world."

Lucchini said, "I'm trying to remember. What was his connection to the Islamic terrorists, again?"

"I learned that Giangi was friends with the American funding the terrorists. He bought them a van and gave them cash. His brother, an army officer, was killed in Iraq. Giangi was bitter about American politics and wanted to do something, I guess as a protest."

"Ah, yes, now I remember. You found photos on his Facebook page."

"Yes. It turns out Giangi knew the American and was a link to meet him."

"And he led us to the terrorists."

"That's right."

"That was the break we needed. All because of this Giangi character?"

"Yes."

"Have you seen him at Deus recently?"

"My boyfriend and I go to other restaurants in Isola; there are so many good ones. But a couple of weeks ago, we were walking out of Deus. Giangi was with a boyfriend, arguing with the concierge to let him in. He said he was 'dying of thirst.' It was hilarious; everyone in line was laughing. The concierge threatened to call the manager, but Giangi's boyfriend got him to settle down. I didn't want him to see us, so we walked out behind another couple who was leaving. Therefore, he didn't see us, thank God."

They all chuckled, picturing the scene.

"Do you trust him?" Lucchini asked.

"No! He's a heavy drinker, shoots off his mouth, and brags about the people he knows and all the parties he goes to."

Lucchini said, "Maybe he knows this Russian daughter who works in fashion. A long shot, I know, but we don't have anything else at this time."

"I could try. What do you recommend?"

Lucchini looked at her. "Well, if you and Volpara happened to be at Deus and he came in..."

"Oh, he'd make a fuss. He'd holler, 'Siiimmooo, where have you been?' And he'd come running over. He does it whenever he sees me there, mooing like a hungry cow. His voice is high and squeaky. When he sees me, he makes a big fuss. He even asked for my phone number once."

"Did you give it to him?" Amoruso asked.

"Yes, he has it. But he hasn't used it lately. I'm not a fashion VIP, after all, and I'm probably pretty dull company for his social events. But I could text him, ask how he is, and see if we could meet for a drink."

"Good," Lucchini said. "Do you think you could find out, without raising suspicion, if he knows any young Russian woman who works in fashion? We don't even know exactly what her job is, or her age, so it's like searching for a needle in a haystack. You could use a little manipulation. You'd know how to do that."

"I'll give it a shot. He doesn't know I'm with DIGOS. He thinks I work for a law firm, transcribing boring legal reports. I'll have Dario with me and introduce him as one of my colleagues."

"Good idea," Lucchini said. "You'd want him there to give you a little security."

"Dario and I could buy him a drink and casually ask about his blog and whether he meets models from different countries, not mentioning the Russian. We could just let him babble on. He loves to brag and says he knows everyone. If he knows her, maybe we could get a name."

Lucchini nodded and looked at Amoruso. "Is it worth the risk?"

She nodded. "It could work. And we don't have any other leads." Turning to Simona, she said, "Come up with a way to get him talking about his Russian connections in fashion. Last time, we were lucky with him. Maybe something good will come from him this time, too."

Dario raised his hand. "How about this: I could tell him my brother's wife is Russian, and their daughter wants to be a model."

"That will get him talking," Simona said. "He loves to brag about how much he knows about the fashion industry."

Antonella raised her thumb. "That's it! Get him babbling about how many people he knows. He'll fall for it."

# CHAPTER SEVEN

On Saturday morning, Chiara Volkov left her apartment
dressed for a casual weekend, wearing gray slacks, a
yellow and orange scarf, a pale blue blouse, and low heels. On
her head rested designer sunglasses. In one hand, she carried a
Ferragamo purse, and in the other, a Dolce & Gabbana shopping bag.

Chiara boarded the metro at the Porta Romana station and
exited at Stazione Centrale, one of the busiest train stations in
Europe. She ascended the escalator to the first floor, weaving
among throngs of travelers wheeling luggage, pushing prams,
and carrying shopping bags through the station. She reached
the ground level of the station and proceeded to a Trenitalia
ticket kiosk.

She purchased two tickets, a one-way to Monza, a Milano
suburb, and another from Monza to Como. With the tickets,
she ascended two levels on another escalator into Centrale's

spacious lobby, which resembled a cathedral with its high vaulted ceiling and walls decorated with fascist-style bas-reliefs of gladiator helmets, shields, crossed swords, and tapestries of medieval Italian legends.

Centrale's lobby was a menagerie of commercial advertising, principally for designer clothes, shoes, perfumes, and sunglasses. Banners, neon signs, and revolving posters featured young Italian women and men, including sexy women in skimpy bikinis in poses just shy of pornography.

Chiara surveyed the travelers exiting the main station into the lobby like salmon swimming upstream in multiple currents. Standing alone, she watched a platoon approaching, unshaven men and women with clumps of uncombed hair, fresh from a camping or hiking adventure. They wore grungy pants, wrinkled T-shirts, and hiking boots while lugging backpacks bulging with blankets, pillows, bottles of water, hiking sticks, skateboards, and helmets. Stitched on their backpacks were cloth flags and decals of their adventures in Croatia, Greece, Turkey, Italy, Spain, France, and Portugal.

Chiara stepped aside as the backpackers fanned out, speaking German, Polish, and a language that sounded Eastern European. They forged aggressively through the lobby, carving a path as other travelers maneuvered to escape their invasion. The backpackers split as they approached Chiara, brushing against her arms and shoulders. She clutched her purse, standing firm so they wouldn't knock her down. As they passed, she whiffed odors of sweat, tobacco, and smoke. And a trace of marijuana.

After the backpackers regrouped and headed for the stairs to exit Centrale, Chiara walked toward the women's restroom. She pushed open the door into the crowded restroom of women and girls of various ages washing their hands and checking their hair and makeup in mirrors. Chiara went to the end of the restroom and pushed open an empty stall. She locked the door, hung the Dolce & Gabbana shopping bag on a hook behind the door, and set her Ferragamo purse on the floor. She retrieved from it a smaller black Armani purse.

From the Dolce & Gabbana bag, she also pulled out a Prada shopping bag. She slipped out of her blouse and slacks and changed into beige linen slacks, a gray sweater, and a shawl. She exchanged her low-heeled shoes for flats and arranged a blond wig around her head. Off came the designer sunglasses, replaced by a modest black pair. Into the Prada shopping bag went her Dolce & Gabbana bag. Into the black Armani purse she folded her Ferragamo purse.

After she changed her appearance, Chiara opened the stall door and headed to the sinks. She soaped her hands and rinsed them, glancing sideways in the mirror at the other women doing the same, waiting for them to leave the bathroom. She lingered, soaping and washing her hands again and putting them under the dryer. When she saw a mother with an adolescent daughter and an older woman head for the exit, she picked up her shopping bag and purse and followed them, staying close to the older woman, whom she greeted with a casual *"Buongiorno."* As the three women entered the lobby and merged into the crowds, Chiara walked alongside the older woman and then separated with a polite *"Buongiornata."*

She looked up at the electronic bulletin board on an arched entrance into the station. It showed a list of departing and arriving trains from various *binarios*. The electric tiles clicked and moved up the board as trains departed. Chiara put down her shopping bag, took out her phone as if she were talking on it, and swiveled slowly around to see if anyone was watching her. No one, it appeared, had noticed her. Hopefully, her disguise had worked: a different purse and shopping bag, a wig, and a different outfit from when she had entered Centrale.

The Monza regional train 2588 was leaving in twelve minutes from *binario* 23. The nasal drone of an androgenous voice announced over loudspeakers departures to Venezia, Roma, and Firenze on *binarios* 6 and 7. Chiara joined a line of travelers going through security, showing tickets to bored guards who waved them into the main station. Once inside, she turned right toward the regional train, *binarios* 23 and 24.

When she reached *binario* 23, she validated her ticket at the yellow terminal box and walked along the platform between *binarios* 23 and 24. The green and white regional trains were old and tired, soiled with grease, grime, and lurid graffiti, popular targets for marginally talented street artists. She passed the engine, which was wheezing like a sick dog, and stepped up into the second car, pushing open the glass door and walking through to the third car, which was less than half full with older passengers and families with young children. She chose a window seat where she could observe passengers boarding the train. No familiar faces since the security check.

Two minutes later, the train jolted and departed slowly, emerging from under the station's steel canopy into morning sunlight. The train jostled along the rails, slowly picking up speed as sleek, bullet-nosed Frecciarossa, SBB Swiss, and Deutsche Bahn trains eased into Centrale.

Chiara looked out the window at Centrale's rail yard, a broad wasteland of abandoned railcars, twenty-four pairs of rails stretching like oversized steel pencils, floodlight towers, and crisscrossing overhead wires. The yard was littered with debris, dried leaves, twigs, plastic bags, discarded water bottles, rusting tools, and broken concrete ties. A no-man's-land.

The train accelerated and approached a junction where tracks angled north, east, and west. It swerved onto the northern junction, picking up speed as passenger cars were jostled as if they were passing over potholed roads. The train whizzed by apartments with balconies of drying laundry, planter boxes with flowers and small trees, and children waving at the train.

The train reached maximum speed, passing through the suburban stations Greco Pirelli and Sesto San Giovanni for the eleven-minute journey to Monza. Chiara relaxed, feeling secure that she hadn't been followed. She felt soothed by the clickety-clack of the iron wheels running over the rails, sounding like a metallic whisper, lulling passengers to shut their eyes for a brief doze.

Chiara opened her purse and reread a postcard that had arrived on Wednesday. It displayed Bern's iconic giant clock in the historic city center. On the back was a scribbled greeting in Italian: *Come stai? Baci*, followed by a sweeping letter M for Mamma. Familiar handwriting and no information other than the simple greeting, a coded message inviting her for the weekend at her parents' new home near Lago di Como.

When the train arrived at the Monza station, Chiara lingered to let other passengers go ahead. Then she followed them into the lobby. The station was small and ordinary compared to Centrale's massive size and commercial excesses. Inside the lobby, two rows of wooden benches faced the electronic bulletin board, a small café, self-serve ticket kiosks, a *tabaccheria*, and a *gelateria.* A lone pair of blue-uniformed police, looking bored, ignored the few passengers entering and leaving the station.

No one had turned around to look at Chiara. She felt safe and went to the café and ordered coffee. She stood at the bar and casually turned around to observe arriving passengers greeting friends and families. After hugs and handshakes, they left the station, climbing stone stairs to the Via Enrico Arosio bus stop.

The electronic bulletin board clicked and displayed the train to Como San Giovanni, which would depart in twelve minutes on track 4. Chiara finished her coffee, returned to the station, walked down the steps into the underground passage to track 4, and climbed up to the platform between tracks 3 and 4.

She walked past the first bench and sat on the next, setting her Prada bag on the concrete and holding her purse on her lap. She held her phone and mumbled as if she was having a conversation while watching passengers coming up the stairs to the platform. She studied their faces and clothes for anyone familiar. Apparently, no one had followed her.

Chiara boarded the train when it arrived and chose a window seat so she could watch late-arriving passengers. The train departed for the forty-three-minute journey to Como San Giovanni. The time allowed her to check her phone. She texted her father and received an immediate response. She put the phone back in her purse and looked out the window, enjoying scenes of villages as the train whizzed past pastures with horses, cattle, and sheep; small farms; creeks; and groves of tall pine trees.

When the train arrived in Como, Chiara departed, walked through the station, and exited where taxis and buses waited for passengers. She walked down the concrete steps and entered a wooded park for the ten-minute walk to the Como ferry terminal, in front of the Como cathedral. At a kiosk, she bought a one-way ticket to Menaggio and then proceeded to the benches in the outdoor departure lounge.

The morning was warm, sunny, and unpolluted, a refreshing change from Milan's hazy smog. Chiara took a deep breath of the fresh, moist air of Lake Como and slowly exhaled. She gazed up at the mountains bordering the long, narrow lake that had been carved from Alpine glaciers eons before.

A loudspeaker announced the arrival of the ferry and asked passengers to form lines to board. Chiara watched two ferries, one departing and one arriving, as they belched smoke from blue stacks. The arriving ferry tooted its whistle, pivoted, and eased alongside the terminal docks. Uniformed crew tossed rope loops onto wooden posts, securing the boat to the terminal. Onboard passengers lined up and crossed a gangplank to enter the terminal.

When the announcement came for passengers to board, Chiara got in line, crossed the gangplank, and took the stairs to the top deck. She stood at the railing, her eyes sweeping the stunning view of Lago di Como, snowcapped Swiss Alps to the north, and sailboats and ferries cruising across the still blue waters.

With a jolt, a gassy blast from the smokestacks, and a whistle toot, the ferry departed with a rolling bump, pivoting until its bow was pointed north and chugging into the open lake.

The moment reminded Chiara of her happiest experiences, coming here as a child with her parents, weekending with lovers, attending weddings and birthday parties in lakeside villas, and enjoying occasional solitary holidays when she wanted to be alone to relax, read, listen to music, and hike on the trails around the lake. A cool wind came off the lake, swirling her long hair and caressing her face, ears, and neck. She closed her eyes, took a deep breath, and said a prayer. She felt blessed. Her life was full of joy, love, and beautiful memories. How had she gotten so lucky?

For two hours, the ferry cruised north, docking briefly at Argegno, Colonno, Tremezzina, Isola Comacina, Tremezzo, and Griante, crossing to Bellagio and Varenna and back to Menaggio on the western shore.

Chiara disembarked at Menaggio. She mingled with crowds of tourists and weekenders strolling along the embarcadero, which was lined with luxury hotels, outdoor restaurants, souvenir stands, and upscale clothing stores. She wanted to escape from the tourists, so she walked along the beachside embarcadero to the *lido*. She watched swimmers splashing in the chilly water and sunbathers relaxing on towels and in beach chairs on Menaggio's smooth, stony beaches.

Chiara was thirsty. She headed to one of her favorite locations on the beach, a brewpub with outdoor tables under the shade of a cypress tree. She ordered an artisanal ale and a plate of chips. When her order arrived, she walked back into the bright sunlight and sat at an empty table. After taking a few sips of cold beer and munching her chips, she reached into her Armani purse, pulled out her cell phone, and punched a number.

When a familiar voice answered, she said, "*Ciao,* Papa. I'm here."

"Same place?"

"Same place."

"Pick you up in half an hour."

"How's Mamma?"

"She can't wait to see you. We've missed you."

After finishing her beer and chips, Chiara walked along Menaggio's narrow streets, which were lined with restaurants, souvenir shops, wine bars, small hotels, and clothing stores.

She knew Menaggio well, and, again preferring to escape the tourist crowds, she followed a street that passed a cemetery and a monument to fallen Italian soldiers from the Great War and World War II.

She passed the regional bus terminal, a Carrefour Market, and the local church. She crossed the street and continued up a stone staircase to the walls of a former castle. When she reached Via Monte Grappa, she stopped at a café, ordered a coffee, and waited.

*Papa will be here soon.*

# CHAPTER EIGHT

The next night, Simona and Dario went to Deus, a popular restaurant in the trendy Isola neighborhood that was well known for funky music, a full bar of exotic liquors and wines, and decent regional foods. It had become one of the more popular meeting places for Milano's young professionals looking to connect with others in finance, engineering, technology, fashion, and media.

They stood behind a cord across the entrance, waiting for the concierge to allow customers to enter, which he did every two or three minutes to keep a steady flow in and out of Deus. The restaurant featured an outside dining area, private rooms, a long bar, and a room displaying sports equipment, Vespas, mountain bikes, skis, and walking sticks.

When Simona and Dario reached the front of the line, a concierge asked, "Aperitivo or dinner?"

"Aperitivo, please," Simona said, pointing to the bar. The concierge raised the cord, and they headed between outside tables to the four-step entrance to the bar. Most of the barstools were taken up by well-dressed Milanese as bartenders served drink orders. Multiple TV screens behind the bar showed a soccer game, a quiz show, and Formula 1 car racing at Monza. All of the TVs were muted, since bar customers were engaged in lively conversations with friends and bar companions.

Simona and Dario found two adjacent stools, and, within seconds, a cheerful bartender wearing a colorful green shirt with birds, flowers, and butterflies set napkins in front of them and greeted them. "What will you folks have?"

"A fruit cocktail. Nonalcoholic, please," Simona ordered.

"Negroni for me," Dario added.

"Your drinks are coming. In the meantime, help yourself to the *aperitivos*," the bartender said, pointing to buffet platters at the end of the bar.

"That's quite a shirt he's wearing," Dario said after the bartender had set clean glasses on the bar and filled their order.

Simona said, "You could go blind looking at his shirt—exotic flowers, tropical birds, and what looks like bees and butterflies."

"I bet that cost a few hundred euros."

"Bartenders don't make much money. Maybe his girlfriend bought it for him for his birthday or something."

Dario nodded. "Yeah. Wonder what the rest of his wardrobe looks like."

Simona and Dario stood and went to the buffet. They picked up plates and eyed the varieties of meat slices, couscous, cold pasta salads, fried chicken, mixed vegetables, cheeses, pizza slices, and fresh fruits.

"I'm hungry. I only had a panino at lunch," Dario said, filling his plate with meat and cheese slices, olives, pasta, and two slices of pizza.

Simona forked strawberries, grapes, melon, and pears onto her plate.

"That's it?" Dario said as they came to the end of the buffet platters.

"I'm trying to eat a little healthier. I'm shying away from bread, meats, and pizza. My stomach has been a little queasy recently, so I'm even avoiding alcohol. "

"Not me. I love all that rich food."

When they returned to their stools, their drinks were on colorful Deus-logo placemats alongside a menu card with the evening's specials: risotto with courgette flowers, shrimp, and farro salad with baby tomatoes, Parmigiano petals, and pesto.

Simona looked around to see how long the line was to enter. "Giangi texted he'd be here by eight. Hope he's not too late," Simona said, sipping her fruit cocktail and nibbling on melon slices.

"I'll bet he was surprised to hear from you. It's been a while."

"It has been. He was typing so fast he made a few mistakes, but he said he would be thrilled to see me again, and he has a new boyfriend he wants to show off."

Dario laughed. "That will be exciting, meeting two gays in love."

"Stop it. You sound homophobic. You have gay friends."

"I do, but they don't dress like that."

"From what I gathered," Simona said, "Giangi goes through lovers like people change clothes. One a month, maybe more."

"He burns through them. Probably has quite a reputation among the gay crowd."

They sipped their drinks, nibbled on their food, and chatted casually about vacations they were planning to take over Ferragosto. Dario would be traveling with his boys to his hometown, and Simona would be spending her summer break between Salzburg and Kitzbühel, as Armando, her lover, was due to conduct Mozart's *Così fan tutte* at the Salzburg Festival.

Half an hour later, their plates nearly empty and only drops left in their glasses, Simona glanced back at the line. "He's here!" she whispered. "The short one with goofy pants. And there's his boyfriend…and Giangi has a dog in a bag! *Mio Dio*, inside a Birkin bag! I can't believe it!"

Dario pivoted on his barstool and saw two short, trim men waiting for the concierge to raise the cord. Giangi was wearing red-and-white-striped pants with stars, a linen scarf around his neck, a blue silk shirt, and leather Prada sandals. His boyfriend was dressed in a more subdued manner: gray pants, a beige shirt, and circular-rimmed eyeglasses…with a bun of dyed-red hair on top of his head.

Giangi was carrying a miniature black poodle inside an expensive Hermès Birkin bag. The dog's head looked like a black tennis ball peering over the bag. The tiny creature seemed at ease in the crowded place. It was probably used to bars and social events.

"Giangi's pants look like an American flag," Simona joked.

"Think anyone will salute?" Dario said with a snicker.

Simona guffawed, almost choking on her last slice of watermelon.

"Good one! I've never seen the guy with the bun. He looks like a skinny rooster."

Dario snorted. "What a pair. They look like characters in a SpongeBob SquarePants video."

"Got that right."

As Giangi and Red Bun weaved through the outside tables toward the bar, Giangi was laughing, blowing kisses, and waving at people who glanced up and then looked away, avoiding contact.

Giangi bounced up the steps into the bar, his poodle bobbing in the Birkin bag. He stretched out his arms when he saw Simona. *"Siiimmmooo! Daahlinggg!"*

He tried to embrace Simona, who braced his arms so he wouldn't smother her. His scarf fell on the floor, and his poodle whimpered, yipping like it needed to pee.

"So wonderful to see you again, *tesoro*," he gushed. "I'm so glad you texted me. It's been, like, *forever* since I've seen your beautiful face! You look *faaabulousss* with that smart Ralph Lauren polo shirt, even though I suggest you go shopping more often. This was an item of the 2015 collection!"

"*Buonasera*, Giangi. It has been a long time. How have you been?"

"Maaavelous, dahling! Guess what? I'm in love again! I love being in love," he said, draping an arm over Red Bun's shoulder. "Meet the love of my life, Giuliano!" he squealed. "He's the creative director for Amerigo Lunari. We met on the set of a photo shoot two weeks ago."

Red Bun waved with his fingers. "*Ciao*, Simona. I'm Giuliano," he said, his voice high-pitched and squeaky. "Actually, I was promoted to creative director only a month ago. I've been the chief stylist for Amerigo for ages. And then he discovered my true talents! Do you know the last spring/summer campaign we shot at the abandoned factory outside Los Angeles? I'm sure you've seen it. It was all over Milano and in all the fashion magazines and on social media. Well, the factory was my idea, and Amerigo was sooooo impressed."

"Isn't he just the cutest thing you've ever seen?" Giangi slurred.

Giuliano put his hand over Giangi's. "Slow down, *tesoro*," he said. "Don't make a scene like last night, pullleez. You embarrass me sometimes."

Simona said, "Let me introduce you to my colleague, Dario. We work in the same law firm. His girlfriend's out of town, so I invited him to come tonight."

"Helllooooo, Dario," Giangi giggled. "Any friend of Simo is a friend of mine, although you should take more care about your appearance. Is your hairdresser the same as your grandma's? You need a new haircut, but you're cute. Does your girlfriend know you're with Simo?" He made a face like he was shocked and then winked. "I won't tell her," he whispered.

"*Ciao,* Giangi…Giuliano.…Do you come here often?"

"Oh, it's been ages since I was in Deus," Giangi said.

"Giangi, we were here last week," Red Bun corrected. "Don't you remember?"

"Like I said, it seems like ages. I've been *soooo* busy, you wouldn't believe it!" Giangi's eyes looked glazed, as if he had just woken up or was feeling the effect of multiple glasses of wine consumed before he arrived at Deus.

"How are things in the fashion world, Giangi?" Simona asked.

"Hellish, as usual. Fashion is such a terrible world, but someone has to do this job, right? And I'm willing to sacrifice my life for it!" he said, waving at the bartender. "Two Proseccos. Please, Andrea or whateveryournameis. Come here. We're dying of thirst!"

The bartender rolled his eyes, reached down for the open bottle of Prosecco, poured two glasses, and set them on the bar. No Deus placemats.

"Simona told me about you, Giangi. How long have you been in fashion?" Dario asked.

"Oh, forever, almost since I was a little boy," he giggled. "It seems like forever. Isn't that true, *amore*?"

"You probably know everyone in fashion," Dario said.

"Oh, I do, I do. So many friends. They're all so beautiful and fun."

"My brother's wife is from Russia. Their daughter would like to be a model."

"Wonderful! Tell me, does she have long curly hair, or maybe long, long legs? And she has to be skinny as a pole. No chubby ones, forget it!"

"She does have long wavy hair, blue eyes, and a cute nose, at least I think so. She's only sixteen but is very attractive. Just like her mother."

"Sixteen's a good age, before girls start putting on weight or have any wrinkles. But everyone wants to be a model. Isn't that right, *amore*?"

"Why, of course," Red Bun agreed. "I'm partial to Asian models. Their faces are just stunning. Don't you agree?"

"Oh, I do, and I like the African models who are coming to Milano by the absolute boatload!"

"My niece is quite thin and has long blond hair and pretty eyes," said Dario. "Do you know any models from Russia?

"Of course! And from Spain, Morocco, Brazil, all over the world."

"Interesting," Dario continued. "A friend of mine went to a party and said he met a Russian lady in fashion. But he didn't get her name. Do you know anyone like that?"

"Oh, it's probably Chiara Greco-Volkov! What a faah-habuulous name, don't you think? She's a lovely, lovely girl. So sweet and very sexy," he smirked. "Long, beautiful curls, like a corkscrew," he gestured, making swirling motions with his fingers. "I danced with her at the last New Year's party. Her boyfriend went to get drinks, and she and I went on the dance floor. We danced to an old Bee Gees disco song, 'Saturday Night Fever,' I think it was. We were *soooo* good on the dance floor. When her boyfriend came back, he was insanely jealous. A nice boy, but so rude! What he said to me was truly awful! I won't even tell you what he called me."

"Is Chiara a former model?"

"Yes. She was a model when she was a teenager and absolutely gorgeous, but fashion doesn't like models who don't age well. They want them to look like starving teenagers, not healthy girls in their twenties who eat pasta and pizza and drink wine. Models absolutely can't eat. They'll get fired if they put on a pound. They even weigh them...dreadful! They put each one on a scale like she's a pig going to slaughter for pancetta."

Dario smiled, not knowing how to answer. "Have you seen this Chiara recently?"

"No, I haven't. By the way, why are you interested? Is your girlfriend not enough for you, you rascal? *Simooooo*, is he a Don Giovanni? I hope not. Anyway, Chiara is Ruggero Rossini's right hand. She works in Rossini's agency. You know him, of course, the most famous fashion-show director and producer in Italy. And, incredibly, Ruggero listens to her. She's becoming quite powerful in the fashion world. I hope Ruggero will not get bored with her too soon."

"I hope so, too," Red Bun said. "Amerigo has worked with Ruggero since the nineties, but a producer such as Chiara is very difficult to find. Patient, competent, strict with models. And she's the only one who can make Ruggero see reason when he's too full of—well you know what I mean," he giggled.

"Simo, have I told you the latest?" Giangi asked.

"No, tell me."

"Oh, this is *sooo* exciting! I have a friend who works at Cinecittà. I told him Chiara is beautiful, half Russian, half Italian, and could play a sexy spy or something. He asked me to send photos. I called Chiara. She sent me some pictures, and when I sent them to my friend, I included a few of my own. I hinted that I'd *love* to be in a movie, too. I could play a gay James Bond. Maybe my code name could be Jimmy Boy, something cool. Don't you think it's time they start making movies about gay spies? Isn't it a *faahhabuulous* idea?"

Giangi giggled, hiccupped, and released a slight belch. "Whoops! Sorry about that. This Prosecco is bubbly. I like it."

Neither Simona nor Dario spoke, befuddled by Giangi's rambling, drunken monologue, interrupted only by him slurping his Prosecco. His eyes were out of focus.

Giangi held up his empty glass and waved at the bartender. "Yoo-hoo, lovely man. Can you bring another drink?"

The bartender looked over and shook his head. "Coming up. My name is Angelo."

Giangi didn't hear him. He was reaching into the bag to pet his dog, who licked his hand and nuzzled his palm. "Oh, *caro,* you are so sweet. Isn't she, Simo? I love when she licks my hand." He held the Birkin bag toward Simona.

"Simo, meet my darling Miss Twiggy. Isn't she the *cutest* thing you've *ever* seen? I absolutely love her. She's so spoiled! Exactly like me! And you know what? I wanted to call her "Choupette," like Karl Lagerfeld's cat, but I couldn't open a social media account with that name. You know that Miss Twiggy has more than 30,000 followers on Instagram?" He kissed the dog's nose.

The bartender delivered another glass of Prosecco. Giangi grabbed it and raised it to his lips. "I won't burp this time. Promise." He giggled.

He drained the glass and set it on the bar. And hiccupped. "Oops!"

# CHAPTER NINE

On Saturday morning, Simona and Dario arrived at Chiara's apartment near Porta Romana. When they entered the building, Dario commented, "Nice place—arched doorways, classic windows, and modest chandeliers."

"I think it's a historic building, put up after World War II by a famous architect," Simona said. As they walked across the polished tile floor, their soft-soled shoes made little squeaks.

Chiara had buzzed them in from the street-level intercom and waited while they took the elevator to the fourth floor and walked down a hallway to her apartment.

"She's living well. Must have a good salary," Simona commented.

"Fashion pays well, doesn't it?"

"If your boss is a famous director, of course. Remember what Giangi said? She has a lot of influence, which means she's probably paid very well."

Dario knocked on the door.

Chiara opened it and greeted them. *"Benvenuti,"* she said, looking first at Simona and then at Dario. "Do you have identification, please?"

They took out their DIGOS identification and showed her. She looked at Simona's first, using a finger to scan her name, her rank, the DIGOS logo, and the address of the *Questura*. She glanced at Dario's identification for only a couple of seconds. "Thank you," she said, stepping back.

*"Grazie. Buongiorno,* signora Greco-Volkov," Simona replied. She and Dario entered a foyer with a brick wall and a shelf with an array of fashion magazines. Under the shelf, a bicycle and helmet rested on a stand.

"It's just Volkov now. Greco-Volkov was the name I used in modeling, and many people still call me that, even though I go by just "Volkov" now. It helped, when I entered modeling, to have an unusual last name. Greco was my mother's maiden name."

Simona stopped to look at a poster of an Asian woman wearing a long coat and carrying an expensive purse and displaying bracelets on both wrists. She pointed at the poster. "I remember this cover. Was it from *Vogue* or *Marie Claire*? The model was very famous a few years ago, wasn't she?"

Chiara smiled. "Yes. The model is Liu Dupont. She was discovered by the Elite agency here in Milan, and my boss immediately cast her for five fashion shows in three days back in 2011. Poor thing, she was going back and forth like crazy without having time for either lunch or dinner. But she made a lot of money that season. Then she married a British banker and quit. She lives in Notting Hill now. She's from China. She has European blood; her father was French."

"Beautiful eyes," said Simona. "Almost like…"

"A bird," Chiara interrupted.

"So true. What do you think, Dario?"

He shrugged. "The model is pretty, but I don't like girls who look like storks. For me, she's too thin."

"So you'd never date a model, even a gorgeous one?" Simona asked, poking him in the arm as they made their way into a living room with stylish furniture: an arched Castiglioni lamp, a plush sofa with room for three people, and a blond wood table with fashion magazines. Morning sunlight beamed into the living room.

Chiara directed them to the sofa. "Tea? Coffee? Water?"

"Water, please," Simona said.

"Same for me," Dario said.

"Two waters, coming up." Chiara headed into a small kitchen. While she was away, they surveyed the living room. Across from the sofa was a Russian icon of a sad-looking Madonna with baby Jesus on her lap, holding up two fingers. There was a golden halo over his bald head. The flat, two-dimensional Byzantine style with primary colors looked out of place in Chiara's modern living room. Below the icon, a vase on a desk looked Daliesque, with twisting branches in bold colors and a lip that dripped down the sides.

On both sides of the vase were family photos, one apparently of her parents' wedding in front of a Baroque church. Her mother wore a long, white, flowing wedding dress; her father was dressed in a blue morning suit. They looked so young, especially her mother. Another photo showed the family on a beach, possibly with Capri in the background. Chiara looked about eight years old. In a third photo, the family was holding skis, with the Dolomites in the background. The family was dressed for winter, wearing ski boots, heavy coats, scarves, and gloves. Chiara looked like a teenager, standing between her parents and flashing a bright smile.

Chiara came back into the living room and handed them bottles of water and napkins. Chiara had high cheekbones, a button nose, and a small chin, possibly inherited from her father. Her narrow, dark eyes and coal-black hair were likely inherited from her Italian mother.

Chiara's hair was in braids. She was wearing shorts, a short-sleeved V-neck T-shirt, and running shoes, as if she were going to a gym for a Saturday morning workout.

"Needless to say, I was a little surprised to get a call from you, inspector De Monti. I don't think I've talked to a police officer before. Sometimes when I see police officers on the street or in cars, I wonder what their lives are like—catching criminals, shooting people. I don't even like to watch cop shows on TV."

Simona smiled. "I don't, either. They're awful—as if they can discover a crime in the first scene, investigate suspects, and interrogate one who confesses, all in an hour. That's ridiculous. So far from the truth."

"What is the truth?"

"Well, a case comes to us. We investigate, collect evidence, and talk to a lot of people, each of whom might reveal a small detail that's important. Investigation can take months, or even years. It's rarely easy."

"Do you and inspector Volpara work together?" she asked, nodding toward Dario.

"Yes. All police, including DIGOS, work in teams. Dario and I are a team. We do the tedious legwork: talking to people, visiting crime scenes, meeting victims, looking for suspected criminals."

"So, tell me, why do you want to talk to me?"

Simona looked at Dario, who nodded in a gesture that meant *Go ahead. She likes talking to you.*

"As I told you on the phone, *signora* Greco, it's about your father in Bern," Simona said.

Chiara shook her head, causing her braids to move back and forth. "Not anymore. My parents left Switzerland. Did you know that?"

"We learned that they possibly had."

"Can you tell us where they moved to?" Dario asked.

Chiara turned to look at Dario. Their eyes locked for a few seconds until Chiara said, "Why? Are you going to arrest him?" Her voice was brittle, like she was being asked to betray a family member. Dario's tone had been gentle, not threatening, as if he was merely seeking information, not probing in a way that could get someone in legal trouble.

Dario shook his head. "Not at all. We just want to talk to him." Dario's voice remained casual. A simple request.

"Why?" Chiara insisted. The brittleness was even sharper, very defensive, hinting that she wasn't going to cooperate.

"We think he might be in trouble," Simona said calmly, attempting to soothe Chiara's emotions. They had been in her apartment less than ten minutes. What had started as an official introduction had turned tense, the last thing Simona and Dario wanted. "We just want to talk to him. We've come across information that he should know about." Like Dario, Simona kept her tone mild, merely asking for Chiara's cooperation.

"Tell me. I can pass it along," Chiara said, ratcheting down the brittleness to just a cool response.

Simona answered, "I can share with you that your father has come to the attention of officials in the Russian government who are looking for him. They believe he's not in Switzerland anymore."

Chiara looked from one to the other, possibly pondering who she should engage with. They were clearly a team, trained for encounters like this, asking for information, not demanding it. When she answered, she lowered the stakes, wanting to share information but not yet ready to reveal where her parents were.

"For your information," she said, her voice calm, "my father worked in government after he completed university. He knew Gorbachev and Yeltsin and has met Putin." She shook her head, expressing displeasure. "Putin calls him Dimka, a familiar name, not the formal Dmitri."

Simona and Dario listened, not wanting to interrupt Chiara, hoping she would continue with biographical as well as political information that they hoped would help them in their investigation. So far, all they knew was merely that the Russian government was searching for someone they thought was a traitor and possibly should be pursued and killed. In Italy.

After a pause that might have meant that Chiara was believing that Simona and Dario were there to help her father and mother, she continued. "And my father's father, who died before I could meet him, was a high official in the Communist party before the Soviet Union collapsed in 1991."

Another pause for emphasis as Chiara was becoming more comfortable revealing important information. "Going back further, my father's grandfather knew Lenin. And Stalin." It occurred to Simona that this sweep of Russian and Soviet history might explain why Chiara had been defensive when the questioning had begun.

Simona and Dario were gratified that they were getting significant background information while listening to Chiara's explanation of the historical connection between her father and the Russian government that wanted to locate him.

"I'm proud of my *father*...and his *heritage*," she said, emphasizing *father* and *heritage* in a manner that couldn't be misinterpreted. "You need to know that I will do anything to protect them now that they are in Italy, my mother's homeland. I have Russian blood, but my heart and soul are Italian."

There was silence for several moments. Simona and Dario felt relieved that their mission had already uncovered important information. They now knew that this was more than a sensitive political situation. It was also about a family seeking security and safety.

Nodding in appreciation of Chiara's revelation, Dario said slowly, "*Signora* Volkov, thank you for sharing this with us. We understand your father has attracted interest from high-level Russian officials. From what we've learned already from our sources, his situation seems potentially threatening."

"Threatening how?"

"Moscow is trying to locate him. They think he might be in Milano."

"He's not." A tone of brittleness again.

"Can you tell us where he is?"

Chiara's hands closed in her lap, making tiny fists. "He's with my mother, but I can't—won't—tell you where. I talk to them often and see them occasionally. They're safe. They don't want to be found. Papa has security at their home. He speaks fluent Italian, which my mother taught him. He has an Italian passport and a *carta d'identita* because he married my mother."

"Is he aware that the FSB is after him?"

"He knew they would come one day. He and my mother planned on leaving Bern and finding a remote place where they would be safe. He thinks they're safe where they are."

"How do you know you're not being followed?"

"I'm half Russian," she boasted. "I know about the KGB and the FSB. My father was KGB at one time. Did you know that?"

"No, we didn't," Simona said. Another important fact for the investigation.

Dario had an idea: Ask questions to keep Chiara talking, to learn more about her parents. "Could you tell us where they met? I haven't heard of many Russian and Italian couples."

She nodded and made a gesture that seemed to convey nonchalance. "In Roma, when my father was assigned to the Soviet embassy."

"And when was that?" Simona asked.

"In 1988, before the Soviet Union collapsed. My mother was only nineteen. She was working part-time in a clothing store while she was a student at the University of Roma. Papa, sent by the embassy, was studying Italian. My mother is from Calabria. I was born in 1991 in Roma, so I have Italian and Russian passports."

Another important fact that they could verify at the office. In less than half an hour, they had learned vital data that would help their investigation.

"Was your father's last name on your Italian passport?"

"Yes, Volkov, although I relate more to my mother's Italian heritage than my father's Russian heritage. I was going to change to her last name, Greco, but it was a legal hassle and not really that important in my career. An unusual name helped when I started in my fashion career, so I used it."

Dario was tempted to take out a notebook and write down details, but he was sensitive to the fact that he wanted this to appear to be an information-gathering task, not official police business. Both he and Simona had good memories and could record the details after they left Chiara's apartment.

Chiara asked, "Do you think my mother might be in danger also?"

They nodded. "We expect she is," Dario said. "You said you know about the FSB. They have eliminated political opponents in the past—poison umbrellas, radioactive doses in tea, murder on the Moscow Bridge. A good example is Anna Politkovskaya, a journalist who wrote a book critical of Putin and the Kremlin crooks."

"There's a memorial to Politkovskaya in Milano," Chiara said.

"At Porta Garibaldi," Dario said. "I was at the opening. We knew Russian intelligence agents would be there."

"I was there also," Chiara responded. "I took pictures for my father. He warned me against it, but I wore a disguise."

"Russian FSB agents filmed it all," Dario said. "So did we."

"I'm sure they wanted to identify any Russian who might be sympathetic to Anna's senseless and brutal murder."

"I'm sure you know about Alexander Litvinenko, who was poisoned with polonium and died in London."

Chiara frowned. "Of course, I know about that," she said with a shudder. "It was a horrible crime, what they did to him.

Murdered him in a foreign country. And they got away with it, the bast—" she stopped and didn't finish the word.

"That's why we are here talking to you, *signora* Volkov," Simona said.

"Call me Chiara."

"All right, Chiara. Then we're Simona and Dario from now on."

No one spoke for several seconds until Chiara finally said. "Thank you. I understand a little better now. I called my father after you called me. He encouraged me to talk to you."

Wanting to learn more about Chiara's background, Dario asked, "Did you grow up in Moscow?"

Chiara nodded, seeming more relaxed now about talking to them. "Until I was fourteen. I learned Russian from my father and in school, and I had a tutor teaching me piano. One of the things I enjoyed most about living in Russia—almost the only thing—was having a dacha where we went in the summer."

"What's a dacha?" Simona asked, appreciating Chiara's openness about her upbringing. Nothing sensitive, just memories.

"A summer cabin in the woods where you can grow a garden, bike on country roads, and swim in a lake away from crowds. I didn't like Moscow—all the dirty streets, too much traffic, cheap cars, and terrible food, mostly potatoes, beets, and carrots. And bread that tasted like sawdust," she said with a shudder. "Mamma felt the same, so she cooked Italian whenever she could get pasta and make sauces. Fortunately, my father's position got us entry into special stores, where she could buy imported food that other Russians couldn't."

"When did you move to Milano?"

"Permanently, in 2005, when Mamma threatened to leave Moscow without Papa. I had been to Italy many times. My mother would bring me to see her family in Calabria, where we spent summers and some Christmases. Moscow is brutally cold in the winter; it's like living in a freezer. I hated it, and so did Mamma. In 2005, she told my father she wasn't coming back. He moved to Switzerland in 2008, where he worked in a bank, and she joined him there."

"You lived there, too?"

"Yes, I went to Swiss schools. Learned German but didn't like it. I was bored. Mamma had a friend in Milano who worked in fashion. I was a model for a while when I was a teenager, but my legs were short, and I was a little plump." She smiled and pressed her hands on her thighs, which were indeed a little stout for a woman in her mid-twenties. "In fashion and modeling, they want girls with legs like storks who look like they haven't eaten in weeks." She laughed. "Some of them showed up for photo shoots and hadn't eaten anything in days except for crackers, tea, and seltzer water. Never sodas, bread, or pasta."

"They look so skinny. I don't know how they do it," Simona said.

"They want models with unusual hair styles, sometimes long hair down to their waist, and sad eyes, like their dog died. They teach them to pout, look depressed...and hungry. They look like they'd kill for a pizza."

Simona and Dario laughed. "I'd never make it as a model," Simona said.

"Actually, I didn't, either, but it got me a start in the fashion industry. I liked Milano. I knew a few people, and they hired me to work behind the camera, setting up shoots, arranging wardrobes, working with those pathetic-looking waifs. The models show up every day, some teenagers, not well educated sometimes. They're looking for an exciting life where they can make a lot of money and become famous. The more exotic looking, the better—some with pale complexions like ghosts, others with dark skin as black as the night sky. Also, unusual features—long flowing hair like a lion's mane, sharp chins or noses like you could cut bread with, or large lips. Unusual eyes, narrow or quite large. Not like the people you see in the streets—more like people you stop and look at in the streets."

"Yes," Simona agreed, "you recognize models on the street. Just like you say, most have some unusual features, but they're all very attractive. However, in my opinion, they don't look happy."

"It's because they're hungry!" Chiara exclaimed. "But I have a much better job now. I work for a famous director, Ruggero Rossini. You might have heard of him. He's considered one of the most famous fashion-show directors and producers in Italy."

"Yes, I have," Simona said. "I've seen his photo and stories about him in the newspapers when there's a big fashion show."

"Especially in September and February, for women's fashions, and January and June, for men's."

Dario interrupted this line of conversation, wanting to focus on their purpose for meeting Chiara. "Will you see your father soon, Chiara?"

She shrugged. "Maybe. Why?"

They pulled out their wallets and gave her their business cards. "When you see your parents, please have your father call us," Dario said. "We'd like to talk to him."

"He's careful about using mobiles. He thinks he can be traced."

Simona raised a hand. "How about we write your father a short letter and include our business cards? Do you have paper so I could write a note?" Simona looked around the apartment.

"Give me a minute," Chiara said, walking over to the desk with the family photos. She opened a drawer, took out a box of stationery, and handed a sheet to Simona.

Simona turned to Dario. "Let's write a couple of sentences. Tell him we'd like to meet him."

"And the sooner, the better."

# CHAPTER TEN

Summer had arrived in Milan, with occasional drizzles in the morning and hot, steamy afternoons with temperatures in the mid-nineties.

Simona and Dario stood outside Amoruso's office while she was on the phone. It was the middle of the week after they had had their meeting with Chiara at her apartment the previous Saturday. On Monday, they had briefed her and Lucchini about what they had learned about Chiara's father.

When Amoruso put down her phone, she greeted them. "Come in. What's going on? Anything about our Russian friends?"

"As a matter of fact, yes. This was just delivered," Simona said, handing her an open envelope containing a one-page note.

"What's this?" Amoruso asked, putting on her reading glasses.

"The latest in communications—a handwritten letter," Dario said with a smirk.

"I recognize this stationery. It's from Pettinaroli. They have a nice store in Brera," Amoruso said, pointing to a small gold logo on the back of the envelope.

She read aloud:

> *Simona and Dario,*
>
> *I have communicated with the person you want to meet. Pick me up at my apartment on Saturday at 9:00 a.m. I will wait on the curb.*
>
> *Bring hiking poles, insect spray, bottled water, hiking boots, long-sleeved shirts, and pants.*
>
> *We will return to Milano around 6:00 p.m. Do not call.*
>
> *Chiara*

Amoruso smiled and set the letter and envelope on her desk after examining the empty back page. "I guess his daughter is serious about protecting their location. Where do you think they are?"

"Not a clue," Simona said. "According to the timing, it looks like we'll drive for about three hours, maybe spend two or three hours with the father, and then return. So the location could be in the Apennines near Bologna, Piacenza, La Spezia, or Torino. Alto Adige is too far. Same with Tuscany."

"To the north, it could be Bergamo or one of the lakes: Como, Maggiore, Varese. Maybe even Garda," Amoruso said, looking again at the envelope addressed to Simona at DIGOS headquarters. "Intriguing. It will be an adventure for you."

"Have you ever had someone send you a letter like this?" Simona asked.

"Not since I joined the police. Now everyone uses cell phones to text or send emails. This is the first handwritten, personal note I've seen in a long time. Interesting. From the way you described Chiara, she's a bit touchy and wants her way. I'd advise you to follow her instructions and bring what she says. If you don't, she's likely to refuse to take you."

"You're right about her behavior. We'll do exactly as she says. I'll have to buy hiking poles and get bug spray," Simona said. "I've never used hiking sticks before. I'm curious what that means."

"Don't bother. I've got an extra pair of hiking poles," Dario said. "But get some bug spray for me, will you, please?"

"I'll pick some up at the pharmacy on the way home."

Amoruso stood up and picked up the note and envelope. "Let's show this to Lucchini. I'll bet he'll be surprised, too. First time for everything."

As they walked down the hallway to Lucchini's office, Amoruso told them. "If Chiara doesn't mind, check in with me when you're on the way and when you leave to come back home. I'm curious where she's taking you. It's certainly not in a city or suburb. You're going out into nature. Make sure you have plenty of bug spray."

"We will," Simona assured her.

"I'll be happy to be at home Saturday," Amoruso said. "I won't need bug spray there."

## GENERAL INVESTIGATIONS AND SPECIAL OPERATIONS DIVISION

On Saturday morning, Simona and Dario drove an unmarked police car out of the downstairs garage at the *Questura* to pick up Chiara at her apartment. As she had indicated in her note, she was standing at the curb. She was wearing a long-sleeved blouse and jeans and was carrying a cap. In one hand, she carried a cloth bag, with the handles of hiking sticks exposed.

When she got in the back seat, she said, "Thanks for being on time. Did you bring hiking sticks, boots, bug spray, and water?"

"In the trunk," Dario said. "Are we going mountain climbing or meeting your father?"

Chiara smiled and settled into the back seat, laying her cloth bag with the hiking sticks on the floor. "Both. I thought you liked exercise. You said you played soccer."

"I'm in pretty good shape," said Dario. "I work out at a gym, mostly with weights and a walking machine."

"Good. You'll need to be in shape to meet Papa." She laughed.

"I've been in police for twenty years," Dario said, pulling away from the curb. "But I never used hiking sticks on duty or had to use bug spray."

"First time for everything," Simona said, turning around to smile at Chiara.

When they drove down Viale Pasubio, Dario said, "Where are we going, Chiara? I need directions."

"Como."

"Como?" Dario said in surprise. "You said your parents are in a remote location where they wouldn't be discovered. Como's not remote. Tourists flock there like ants, crawling over every beach, café, and ferry. It's like a Disney nature park."

"Not *in* Como, just the direction to drive. I'll tell you where to go from there. It's in the mountains a few miles from the lake."

They continued on Viale Pasubio, passing the Cimitero Monumentale, and then drove on Via Cenisio until they reached

Viale Certosa, at which point they took Highway A8 for several miles, and then A9 to Como.

Once they were on the Autostrada and Dario was driving faster, Chiara reached into her purse and took out a pack of cigarettes.

"Mind if I smoke?"

"No problem. Just roll down the window."

Chiara rolled down the window and lit a cigarette with a plastic lighter. "I'm curious, Simona: How did you become a police officer? Not the type of career most women would consider. It's dangerous. Most police are men."

"That doesn't bother me. I started in Bergamo, my hometown. A few years ago, our boss at the Milano *Questura* brought a team of DIGOS agents to Bergamo to hunt down a terrorist who had kidnapped an American mother and was hiding near there."

"I remember. There was a shooting at Centrale, and the terrorists had some connection to Brigate Rosse."

"That's right. Good memory. We tracked down the terrorist and rescued the American mother. Our boss shot and killed the terrorist. Last I heard, the American mother is living with her daughter in Menaggio. She moved from New York after her parents died. Her father's parents were Italian, and he vacationed near Como and bought a villa in Menaggio. Her father was a Wall Street banker. Pretty rich, I understand."

"How did you meet Volpara?"

"That came later. I was recruited to DIGOS by my boss, whom I met in Bergamo during that case. After training, she assigned Dario and me to a team. We've been partners for a couple of years."

Simona reached over and patted Dario's shoulder. "He's a good guy, but we bicker like a married couple. We have different personalities and interests. I like to read, study art, and listen to music. My boyfriend is a conductor who's performed at La Scala. Now he's the conductor at the Seattle Symphony in the US. Dario, on the other hand, is a sports freak. All he thinks about is soccer, boxing, and skiing. But he's a good father. He has a couple of kids."

"Do you have children?"

"No, not yet," Simona said. "Maybe in a couple of years."

"Don't wait too long. It's better to have children when you're young."

Simona didn't respond, resistant to talk about personal details with someone she'd only recently met and who was an important connection in their investigation. She didn't need to ask Chiara if she had children. There had been no sign of toys, photos, or anything related to kids in her apartment. She wanted to try to limit questions to what was relevant to their investigation.

"Is your father near Como?" Simona asked, changing the subject.

"No, closer to Menaggio."

"Menaggio?" Dario interjected. "That's tourist central. Mobs of Germans, French, Americans, and Italians go there every summer. How can anyone be in hiding in Menaggio? Hikers, bikers, and campers could stumble across them."

Chiara smiled. "Well, not exactly in Menaggio. You'll see."

Dario shrugged. "I would have thought your father would have found a place more remote, like in the Abruzzo, a rural area in the Po Valley, or in the Apennines. There are lots of almost-deserted villages in the mountains."

"My father is smart. He and my mother looked all around northern Italia before they decided to move where they are. I'll let him tell you why he chose their place. You'll see."

Simona sensed that Chiara was irritated by Dario's skepticism. She didn't want their relationship to be about confrontation. Cooperation was important in sensitive affairs such as this.

"Do you visit your parents often?" she asked Chiara.

"A few times. They've only been there a number of weeks," she said, not being specific.

"How do you go there? What if you're followed?"

"I take a train from Centrale to Monza. I change clothes, into kind of a disguise, and watch to see if anyone is following me. Then I take a train to Como and take a ferry or a regional bus from there. I'm cautious, always looking around to see if someone is following me."

Dario said, "How do you know the FSB hasn't sent a couple of agents to follow you? Surveillance isn't just one person. Three or four could be on your tail—women agents, older men—with radios or phones to take turns following you."

"I have a good memory. I think that if there was a team, I'd notice. I watch everyone. My disguises include wearing different clothes, sometimes a wig, sunglasses, and switching shopping bags. It's a good system, I think."

When they approached Como, Dario took an exit in the direction of Menaggio and drove along the west side of the lake, passing through Cernobbio, Argegno, and Tremezzina, frequently on one-lane roads squeezed between apartments on both sides.

"Always heavy traffic on weekends," Dario said, patiently following a stream of tourist buses, taxis, limousines, and motorcycles creeping along. He shifted gears and touched the accelerator and then the brakes to keep moving at the pace of a brisk walker. "I was stuck here once when a bus bumped into the car in front of it, which hit another car ahead of that car, and then another car collided with the bus. What a mess. We spent an hour waiting for the police to show up and get traffic moving again."

As they drove through Colonno, the traffic snaked around a bend and stopped. Ahead, cars, a tour bus, and three motorcycles were stopped in the middle of the road, where a narrow stretch allowed one lane of traffic to drive south until a police officer motioned for the northbound traffic to inch through the narrow passage. When they reached the police officer, he held up his hand, motioning them to stop. Dario slammed his hand on the steering wheel and cursed.

"*Cazzo!* Didn't he recognize a police car? I should get out and—"

"Patience, please, Dario," Simona said, reaching over and putting a hand on his shoulder. "We'll make it."

Ten minutes later, they passed through Tremezzina, following the green highway sign toward Menaggio. Simona looked out the window and saw a small fleet of ferries and sailboats leisurely slicing across the deep blue waters of Lake Como.

Chiara leaned forward, pointing to a road sign after they departed Tremezzina. "Pay attention here. Don't go to Menaggio. Take Highway 340 toward Lugano."

"Lugano?" Dario said, frustration in his voice, looking in the rearview mirror so he could maneuver from the right lane to the left, where a green sign with an arrow pointed to Lugano. He sped up after he veered from the Menaggio-bound traffic and went under a bridge. The road started to climb. "This right, Chiara?"

"Yes, keep driving. I'll tell you where to exit. It's about six kilometers ahead."

"Your father lives between Menaggio and Lugano, two tourists traps?

"Cool it, Dario. Let Chiara show us the way," Simona said.

Dario checked traffic behind him and ahead, slowing as they emerged from a tunnel. The highway climbed a steep mountain covered in forest and granite cliffs, following a winding ridge above a narrow valley, with villas along the way. The road twisted in a series of hairpin curves on which cars slowed when it changed from two lanes to one in both directions.

"This is a bit tricky," Dario said, accelerating on the short straight road and then decelerating on the curves. "I was on this road a long time ago. It's a bit treacherous and slow with these tight turns. Miss a turn, and you could roll down the hill until you hit the trees. Lots of accidents on this highway."

"But it's beautiful scenery," Simona said. "Lago Piano ahead, then Porlezza and Lake Lugano. A nice drive as long as traffic keeps moving."

It was quiet in the car as Dario concentrated on the winding road climbing the mountainside, rarely able to drive more than forty kilometers an hour. Chiara sat forward and pointed to a sign indicating destinations ahead. "Croce is the next town… and then another mile or so beyond."

Dario slowed, passing through the village of Croce. They passed a few homes resting on hillsides, as well as a small church with a steeple. He stopped at a red light where two small roads intersected with 340. A man was walking a dog across at the intersection, and two boys were riding bicycles on the sidewalk. When the light changed, Dario drove on, passing two small hotels, a *gelateria*, and a coffee shop where customers were reading newspapers and drinking coffee under an awning.

In less than a minute, they were out of Croce. The highway flattened and straightened out. They passed small farms, modest homes with gardens and fruit trees, and cattle grazing in green pastures.

Chiara leaned forward again and pointed to a small wooden sign that read *Grandola ed Uniti* with the names of *agriturismi*. "We're going to turn off soon. Slow down. You're going to make a right turn."

Dario decelerated. Immediately, three motorcycles behind him whizzed around the car and accelerated, engines roaring as the riders shifted gears and sped ahead.

"Turn here, a sharp turn," Chiara said, pointing to a narrow road between a house and a rural pizzeria.

Dario touched the brake, executed a hard right turn, and navigated along a narrow asphalt road. There were no pedestrians, cars, or bikes visible. He continued to proceed slowly. Within seconds, they had left a busy highway and entered a quiet village with no signs of life. Dario rolled down the window, and a draft of summer air warmed the interior of the car.

"The fresh mountain air smells good," Simona said after rolling down her window, too.

"A sleepy village—not what I expected so soon," Dario said. "This place looks almost deserted."

The only sound was a slight squishing noise as the car's tires rode over old asphalt heated by the sun. No trees. No people. They arrived at a deserted piazza, boxed in with a boarded-up church, three-story apartments, and a vacant former restaurant. Perched on the church cross, a bird chirped, flapped its wings, and flew off, disappearing behind an old apartment building.

"Anybody here?" Dario said, stopping in the piazza, looking around, and not seeing anyone. The only sign of life was a black dog lying in the shade of the church, watching them but not barking.

"Keep going," Chiara said, pointing to a weathered sign with the name of an *agriturismo* on the stucco wall of the deserted restaurant. "Head toward the *agriturismo*."

Dario drove slowly, glancing up at the sign with the name of the *agriturismo* barely legible. They left the piazza and drove down a narrow, shadowed street until they reached a roundabout. He drove through, climbed a small hill, turned sharply at another sign pointing toward the *agriturismo*, and passed a small hotel with a closed door, a couple of stone houses, and a gravel area with parked cars and vans. No one in sight yet.

The asphalt road turned into a one-lane road with smooth stones. Dario slowed as the tires bumped along. He took another sharp turn through a growth of pine trees.

"No traffic here...or people," Dario said quietly. "Where are we going? I almost feel lost, and we only left the highway two minutes ago."

Chiara smiled. "Just wait. You'll think you left civilization when we get there!"

Dario said, "I feel that way now."

The stony road narrowed, more a pedestrian path than a road for vehicles. Another sign nailed to a tree pointed to a sharp left turn and down. Dario braked and eased left. The road dipped, and tree branches brushed against their car, causing Dario and

Simona to roll up their windows so as not to be swiped by the branches.

"Is this where we leave civilization?" he joked.

"Almost there…careful…this road is a bit tricky—"

"It sure is. The tree shade makes it dark, and it's almost noon."

Chiara pointed over Dario's shoulder. "You'll see a wooden bridge ahead. I think it was built by Romans."

The car inched down, trees continuing to brush alongside. Dario touched and released the brake, his hands gripping the steering wheel, eyes narrowed as he navigated cautiously along the single-lane stone road. Another set of arrows pointed to the next sharp turn, and they plunged even lower. When they reached a small clearing, rays of bright sun illuminated a narrow valley below with a shallow creek flowing over smooth stones. Flocks of chirping birds flew across the valley and disappeared into the forest.

The road's smooth stones looked polished by centuries of traffic—soldiers, farmers, wooden carts, metal wheels of premotor vehicles, early autos, motorcycles, and adventurous hikers.

Simona gripped the armrest as their car inched across a stone bridge. "Amazing. Beautiful. Peaceful. Remote. I like this."

Dario touched the brake pedal, letting gravity ease them across the one-lane bridge. The sides of the bridge were wrapped in tree branches bound with wire and tattered ropes—the only means of rickety support.

"Turn right after the bridge, and follow the stone path," Chiara said, pointing to a gravel area in bright sunlight. Dario released the brake slowly after the path ended.

"Park there," Chiara said, pointing to a shaded spot between two boulders along the shallow creek. Dario tapped the accelerator and crept into the open place between the boulders.

Dario stopped the car, shifted into park, and turned off the engine. He leaned back in his seat and said with a chuckle, "Where the HELL are we?"

"We made it. Congratulations," said Chiara. "You're a good driver."

"Wait till I tell everyone back at the office," he smirked. "They won't believe me."

"Time for our hike," Chiara announced. "I hope you brought what I told you. It's hot, and we have a long hike ahead."

Dario got out of the car and shaded his eyes. He gazed around the narrow valley flanked by thick pine forests between steep mountains and a stony creek.

"A few tile roofs there," he said, pointing up the valley, "and telephone lines. That's it." He pointed to barely visible wires crossing over the valley and utility towers almost covered by the trees.

"Listen!" Simona said, cocking her head and pointing to a flock of sparrows, chirping as they flew in the sunlight and then disappeared into the forest. "Hear the birds? I love birds, especially in the wild. Free to soar. No traffic, pollution, or buildings. Amazing. I like this place."

"Just hawks and wildcats to look out for," Dario said. "Plenty of predators out here."

"You and your jungle perspective," Simona teased.

"Hey, that's nature. Either hunt and catch things or get eaten by them. Your choice."

Chiara said with a smile, "You two *are* like an old married couple, always bickering."

"And guess who usually wins—me!" Simona boasted. "Right, Dario?"

They all laughed, and then Chiara said, "Get your hiking poles, bug spray, and water. You'll need them."

Dario opened the trunk and handed poles and water bottles to Simona.

"Where to now, Chiara?" Dario asked, stretching out his hiking poles.

"Follow me. Ready for a little mountain climbing?"

"Show us the way!"

# CHAPTER ELEVEN

Dario put two water bottles in his backpack, reached down to tie his boots, grabbed his hiking sticks, and put on his backpack. "Hard to believe," he said, shading his eyes from the bright sunlight that penetrated the forest around them. "Ten minutes ago, we were on a highway between Menaggio and Lugano. Now we are in a remote valley with only a few signs of civilization: an *agriturismo,* the roofs of a couple of remote homes, and power lines. No traffic, shopping centers, or people. I like it here."

"So do I," agreed Simona, tying on a waist belt with a water bottle and a tube of bug spray. When she finished, she tugged her shirt to cover her holstered weapon. "Show us the way, Chiara."

"Follow me," Chiara said. She led them to a stone pathway. They walked single file, Chiara in the lead, passing a two-story building with a sign that read *La Vecchia Chioderia.* Two older men were watching them, seated at wooden tables in the shade of umbrellas and drinking glasses of beer. Chiara waved at the men as the three of them passed by.

The stone path continued along a mountainside covered in tall trees, climbing vines, and granite boulders. "That's the *agriturismo* I told you about. It's also a trout farm."

"A trout farm, out here?" Dario exclaimed.

"You'll see it ahead," Chiara said, continuing along the stone path as it rose along the mountainside.

When they passed behind the *agriturismo*, Chiara pointed to a row of long, rectangular metal tanks below ground level with walls a meter above ground. In the tanks' greenish gray water, trout of various sizes swam randomly, causing ripples across the surface. In one tank, thousands of inch-long fingerlings swam in swarms below the surface. In other tanks swam slightly larger trout, some four to six inches and others six to eight inches long. In two of the tanks, mature, foot-long trout, plump with flesh, swam lazily in groups of three or four until they meandered away. Occasionally, one mature trout broke the surface to snatch a bug and then splashed below with its prey.

The trout tanks were in a grassy field along a barely visible creek below the overhanging pine trees. Rakes, shovels, hoses, nets, and other tools lay strewn on the ground or were propped against metal sheds. Mud- and dirt-speckled tractors, a road grader, and a crane were parked haphazardly, looking discarded.

Two men wearing rubber boots and gloves were draining one tank, shoveling debris and oozing mud into wheelbarrows, while a third man aimed a stream of water from a large hose along the tank's concrete floor, guiding the muddy water toward a drain.

Another booted and gloved worker siphoned medium-sized fish from one tank to another. Four- to six-inch-long trout were sucked up a hose and then cascaded from the other end of the hose into a neighboring tank. The siphoning briefly exposed the fish to sunlight, creating flashes of iridescent blue, red, and green scales before the trout plunged into the receiving tank.

Dario said excitedly, "Look at the beautiful trout! Hundreds, thousands, all sizes. Amazing. I've never seen a trout farm!"

"Whew, a bit smelly," Simona said, laughing. "I don't like to *smell* fish, but I like to eat them."

Chiara pointed through the fence at the closest tank. "That tank has mature trout ready for harvesting. They ship them on trucks like the one over there," she said pointing to a hazy green truck that looked like a small oil tanker. "They deliver fresh trout to a fish market in Como, where they gut, clean, and refrigerate them. Restaurants in Milano, Bergamo, Verona, and as far away as Firenze and Bologna buy them and serve them within a day or two. They're never frozen. As fresh as you can get."

"I love trout. Such a delicate taste," Simona said.

"What a fascinating place. I want to bring my girlfriend here. She loves fish, too," Dario said.

Chiara let them watch the men working. Simona and Dario walked slowly along the wire fence, gazing into the tanks. "Okay," Chiara said at last. "We're not tourists. Time to start hiking. We have a ways to go."

"Another story to tell at work. Let me get a couple of photos," Dario said, taking out his cell phone and snapping pictures.

Chiara led them down the smooth stone trail for a hundred yards and then stopped and pointed to a metal pole covered in vines and tall weeds. Barely visible was a sign.

"*Pietra pendular, Barna, 2 kilometres,*" Simona read. "Are we hiking to Barna? I've never heard of it."

"Not all the way. We'll get close. Start up this stone path. Careful of your footing. These rocks can be slippery. But first, bug spray time," Chiara said, taking out a vial from her pants pocket and dousing her arms, neck, face, and ankles, then lathering it around her skin. Simona and Dario did the same, laying their hiking poles in the weeds and lathering spray on exposed skin, which would hopefully protect them from pestering insects.

"Let's go," Chiara said when they were finished with their bug spray. She stepped up into the vines and weeds, using her hiking poles to climb the stone steps. Dario and Simona followed, pushing aside vines and weeds to proceed. They were on a handmade stairway that was no more than layers of small stones with a larger perpendicular stone leading to the next step.

Chiara made the first turn to her left, ascending a few steps and then turning right as the trail zigged and zagged up the steep, pine-forested mountainside. After another zig-and-zag turn that climbed higher, she slowed, turning around to watch Simona and Dario following as they used their hiking poles to progress up the stone stairway.

The air in the forest was damp, still, and warm, not blazing like in full sunlight. As they progressed, the only sounds were their boots on the stones and a chorus of songbirds flying from tree to tree high overhead.

They hiked in silence, except for sounds of heavy breathing as they ascended, turned, and slowly made their way up the stone stairway, partially obscured by thick vines and shoulder-high weeds. Bugs swarmed over their arms, heads, and legs, some landing and being swatted away.

"Man, bugs are everywhere," Dario said, slapping bugs on his lathered arms.

"It gets a little better," Chiara said. "For some reason, they're mostly in the lower elevations. When we get to thicker forest, there aren't as many."

"Thank God!" Dario said, ducking from a swarm of bugs crossing in front of his face.

They continued upward. At a flat stretch, Simona stopped to catch her breath. "Whew, I'm glad you had us bring hiking poles," she said. "This is steep climbing."

"We've just started," Chiara said over her shoulder. "Our destination is about half an hour from here. Lots of turns along the way. You'll get used to it."

Their pace slowed as they followed Chiara, who seemed to be in excellent physical shape and was frequently a turn or curve ahead of them. The longer they were on the trail, Simona and Dario began to get accustomed to their journey, using their hiking poles for stability and brushing aside weeds, vines, and low-hanging tree branches from their shirtsleeves and pant legs.

They hiked without talking, a squad of adventurers striding over the stone path, turning to reach the next higher level, and repeating as they moved up through the dense forest.

Chiara stopped, turned around, and pointed below with her hiking pole. "You get a better view of the valley from here—the trout farm and the creek that flows down the valley."

They turned to look back. Below, through a gap in the pine trees and vines, the trout tanks looked smaller. They were a hundred meters above the farm. The distance and their vantage point allowed them to see more clearly the narrow valley below, the rear of their parked car, the roofs of the *agriturismo*, the trout tanks, the creek, and the steep mountains across from them. The colors seemed almost like a plein-air painting, with brushstrokes of green pine branches, brown tree bark and a dirt trail, a hazy blue sky, and a wisp of white clouds.

"Beautiful," Simona said, nodding her head. "What a view."

"I need a photo," Dario said, taking out his phone. "A few hours ago, we were in Milano. Now we're hiking in a pine forest. Quite a day so far." He slapped his wrist. "Except for these damn bugs!"

Simona laughed. "They live here too, Dario. It's their forest."

"That's why they're attacking us. They want it to themselves," he said, flicking a dead bug off his wrist.

"Let's go," Chiara said. "Long hike ahead." They continued climbing, the trail becoming steeper and offering only piles of stones, not stone steps like in the beginning. As they climbed, Simona and Dario wiped sweat from their brows. The warm temperature and the exertion of the strenuous hike were more than they were used to as office workers.

After several steep turns, Chiara stopped and held up her hand. "Tree down across the path. It wasn't here the last time I was here."

Ahead, at the angle of the next upward turn, a tree had fallen, leaving thick branches strewn across the trail. The exposed tree trunk had ripped up the ground, revealing jagged slashes of blond wood stabbing from the mountainside.

Chiara looked up the trail along the steep mountainside, which was covered in high weeds and snarling vines. "We'll have to crawl under. No other choice," she said. "I'll go first. Careful, those branches can gash your skin."

She bent to her knees, covered her head, and pushed through the thick branches and twigs. The branches and leaves were so thick that Simona and Dario could see only Chiara's poles and boots as she inched her way through, stooping low as branches brushed across her body and then snapped back.

"Made it!" Chiara said, panting after she had crawled through. All Simona and Dario could see was her boots and the top of her head.

Simona took a deep breath and turned to Dario. "I'll go next. Stay back a bit. Those branches snap back. They could poke out your eye." She bent over and started crawling under the largest branch. Smaller branches brushed against her body, snagging her hair.

"Damn, I'm stuck!" she yelled, kneeling and unsnarling branches from her hair.

Ahead, Chiara was ducking under another branch from the same fallen tree, higher on the trail and not as thick.

Dario surveyed the obstacle. He was taller and wider at the shoulders than the two women, and he was unable to duck under the branches. Instead, he got on his knees, lowered his head, and crawled, grunting, wheezing, and cursing as his knees landed on stones. He pushed branches aside and kept crawling, panting at the struggle. After almost a minute of crawling, he stood, slowly brushing away pine needles and leaves from his shirt and pants.

"You made it," Simona said.

"Yeah," he said, breathing heavily. "Another ahead. Looks a little easier."

He waited while Simona crouched and crawled through the branches until she was through and standing next to Chiara, her poles in the ground to keep her from sliding down the trail.

"You're next, Dario. Take your time," Chiara said.

He grunted. "If two women can make it, so can I," he muttered. He inspected the branches of the fallen tree, saw an opening, and dropped to his knees. Within a few seconds he emerged, sweat pouring down his face.

"I had rigorous training in the army," he panted, "but I never had to crawl on my knees over stones and through branches. Can we take a minute? I want to sit down and catch my breath."

"We could all use a break," Chiara said. She turned to examine the fallen tree. "A storm caused this," she said, pointing with a pole at the broken trunk. It was a meter wide and splintered with jagged pieces of fresh wood as sharp as razors.

"The trunk grew from a pile of rocks," she continued. "Maybe the roots didn't go deep enough. A storm could push it over, snapping the trunk like it was a twig. A storm passed through here a week or so ago. That's probably when this happened."

Dario wiped his brow, flinging sweat away, and turned to Chiara. "Your father lives near here? Does he hike this way, too? He must be in great physical shape."

Chiara smiled. "I'll let him tell you. He's older, but very smart. That's why he chose this place."

"It's very remote and hard to reach. How did he find this place? And how does he get here?" asked Dario.

Chiara smiled. "That's what you'll learn when you meet him."

"I want to know the whole story. What's ahead?"

"We're about halfway."

"Halfway?" Dario said, his eyes widening. "More downed trees?"

"I don't think so. Some areas are flatter, but we still have a ways to climb. And one area that's dangerous."

"'Dangerous'? What do you mean?"

"You'll see. Let's get going. They're waiting for us."

Dario brushed debris from his pants and shirt. "I'm ready. Show us the way."

The stone path continued, twisting and turning up the rock-covered mountainside. Some areas of the path had steps, but mostly it was just dirt and gravel on the trail. They hiked another ten minutes. Sweat popped out on their foreheads and arms from the heat of the day and the exertion.

Dario finished one bottle of water, opened another, and took a long drink. He and Simona struggled to keep up with Chiara, who stopped and waited for them along the way. When she reached a flat stretch, she said, "Stone bench ahead. Let's take another break."

After two more turns, they reached a stone wall about three meters long covered in green and brown moss. Chiara sat down, resting her hiking poles on the wall, and took out a water bottle. When Simona and Dario reached the wall, they plopped down on the stony surface and reached for their water bottles, too.

"Hotter than hell, even though we're in the shade," Dario noted. "I thought we were driving to your father's home, not rock climbing. How does he get back and forth? Does he take this same trail?"

Chiara smiled. "Again, ask him. We'll be there in about fifteen minutes."

"More climbing?" Dario asked.

"A few more turns, but not as steep," Chiara said, pointing at the stone path, which disappeared around a bend and reappeared meters higher.

Simona looked up, watching birds flying between trees, chirping and whistling, perching on branches for a few seconds, and then flying off to another tree.

"Birds like it here," Simona said wearily. "But they don't have to hike, just fly from one tree to the next, carefree and happy."

"Hunting for bugs, that's what they're doing," Dario muttered. "Birds won't starve up here. There's a feast of bugs." He slapped his arm where a fly had landed. "Got him!"

Chiara smiled. "Ready to move on?"

"Let's go," Simona answered, standing and looking up at the forest.

They continued on a flat stretch of path along the side of the mountain. As the path narrowed, a steep ravine appeared on their left.

"Careful. Stay on the trail. Don't get close to the edge," Chiara said, pointing down into the ravine, which plunged a hundred meters with no sight of the bottom. Only the tops of trees and bushes were visible.

Chiara inched along the narrow, treacherous path with the ravine on their left and a granite hillside on their right. "Don't fall here. They'd never find you."

"Oh, my God, that looks so dangerous!" Simona said, inching closer to the granite wall.

She and Dario peered into the ravine, a wedge that started in the mountain ahead of them and widened to ten meters across. More ominous, a boulder the size of a car, shaped like a jagged spear, had lodged between the walls of the ravine, pointing down. Weeds, small bushes, and a tree sprouted from cracks in the boulder.

"That is scary," Simona said, her voice quavering. "That boulder must have rolled down the mountain and then fallen into the ravine."

"Which caught it," Dario said, "like a goalie catching a soccer ball before it went into the net. Amazing. I've never seen anything like that. Shows the power of nature. I've got to get a photo," he said, reaching for his mobile phone.

"It's almost like a sculpture," Simona observed, stepping back from the ravine. One of her boots dislodged a stone, which rolled into the ravine and plunged below, disappearing into the canopy of trees.

"Let's keep moving. I don't like this," she shuddered.

The narrow path continued along the ravine and then veered back into the forest. Although it was midday, the temperature had cooled a few degrees, making it more pleasant to continue their journey. They kept climbing. The click-click-click of their hiking poles over the stones was the only sound in the forest. For five minutes, no one spoke, their labored breathing making it difficult to talk.

Chiara stopped when the path straightened for a few meters. Simona and Dario paused, looking into the forest, where a concrete structure was ensnared in twisting vines. They reached the structure, about three meters high with a wire barrier hammered into the stone.

Inside was a small statue of Mary in a robe, holding baby Jesus over an altar the size of a Bible, covered with a film of dust and dirt. In front of the altar were rusted bronze candleholders with no candles, broken vases with faded plastic flowers, and torn pages from a prayer book—all decayed and long forgotten.

"Look at this: a shrine, abandoned in the forest," Simona said. "Children from villages probably came here many years ago to light candles and leave plastic flowers. They're probably all dead now. I wonder who even remembers that this shrine is here."

"I've seen shrines like this before in forests and parks," Dario said. "Churches are closed, boarded up. A sign of our times."

"I asked someone in Barna about this," Chiara said. "They said children would build such shrines in the forest; this is just one of them. But clearly, it's abandoned."

Simona nodded, crossed herself, and kissed her thumbs. "I'll remember," she whispered.

"We're getting close," Chiara said, turning and walking along the path, climbing and making another turn.

Dario and Simona followed in silence as the trail became easier to hike. Dario's breathing had returned to normal. He looked around at the forest and the birds flying through the trees. He stopped, squinting and looking up a tree as they approached. "Simona, look," he said, pointing up with his hiking pole. "A video camera under that branch. See it?"

Simona looked where he was pointing, narrowing her eyes until she gasped, recognizing metal cones with camera lenses. "You're right. Like a CCTV. Why here? We're deep in the forest."

"It's aimed at anyone on the path. Someone's watching us," said Dario.

As they continued on the trail, he searched for more cameras. "Another one," he said, pointing at a tree. "And a third."

Ten meters later, searching in the trees, he stopped. "Simona, look. What's that? A house…a shed? And a fence back in the trees. New fence and wires."

"I see them," Simona answered. "What's that for, here in the forest?"

Chiara was ahead of them, looking into the forest where the fence was visible. When they reached an open area, they saw a two-story stucco farmhouse against the side of a hill.

A man was waving at Chiara, dressed in casual clothes: a short-sleeved shirt, slim pants, and linen walking shoes.

*"Buongiorno,* Papa!" Chiara said, turning around to Simona and Dario. "I've brought the agents from DIGOS I told you about. We just had a nice hike."

*"Benvenuti a casa nostra,"* the man said.

"Simona, Dario, meet Papa! This is where he and Mamma live."

# CHAPTER TWELVE

D ima embraced his daughter. They exchanged cheek kisses, and when they parted, he held her hand. "Papa, meet Simona De Monti and Dario Volpara, the police I told you about."

The resemblance of father and daughter was apparent: narrow eyes, high cheekbones, and pug noses. Dima was slightly taller than his daughter. He put his left arm around Chiara's waist as he greeted Simona and Dario.

*"Buongiorno, signor* Volkov," they echoed as they shook his hand.

"Welcome to our home. I've been watching you make your way up the trail," Dima said, speaking fluent Italian with a slight Calabrian accent. He looked like a middle-aged Italian, with his modest beard, neat haircut with no sideburns, open-collar shirt with the two top buttons unbuttoned, tight pants, and casual walking shoes.

"Papa has sensors and cameras along the trail. Part of his security."

"I saw surveillance cameras about a hundred yards back," Dario said, "but no sound sensors."

"You wouldn't see them unless you stepped off the trail. They're close to the ground, partially covered in leaves," Dima said. "I check them every couple of days. Sometimes when I hear something, I'll check the cameras and see animals moving around nearby."

Simona and Dario smiled, partly at the image of animals setting off sensors, but also at Dima's seemingly casual, friendly manner. He didn't look like a man who felt at risk, with his friendly voice and his arm around his daughter.

Dima said, "The sensors picked you up by the ravine where the trail is narrow and treacherous. That's where I put the first sensors, since hikers likely wouldn't notice, being more concerned about falling into the ravine."

"The hike here was challenging," Simona said. "Dario and I spend most of our time in an office or a car, not hiking. Do many people come up here?"

Dima shook his head. "Not really. Mostly experienced hikers who climb the trail like they're getting ready for a competition. They're not interested in scenery, like weekend hikers who are looking for views of mountains and Lake Como. At the back of the trout farm, most hikers choose an easier trail along the creek that has a few benches to stop and rest on. If hikers stop at the *agriturismo* and ask about trails, the men recommend the creek trail and tell them that the trail up here is strenuous, not for beginners or families with young children."

"I saw a sign where the trail begins that said Barna was two kilometers away," Simona said.

"That's right, over the hill there," Dima said, pointing up a slope. In the distance was the top of a church steeple.

"Is that how you get here? Not the trail, I hope," Dario said.

Dima smiled, dropping his arm from Chiara. "I'll tell you all about it. I'm sure you're hungry," he said. "Let's go into the house. Mamma's waiting. I'll bet you're ready for a glass of wine or cold water."

"Please!" Dario said. "I'm exhausted and thirsty."

"Follow me," Dima said, taking Chiara's hand and leading them through a grove of trees that partially revealed their home. The pine trees were native and mature, with small shoots coming out where rays of sun filtered from treetops, allowing photosynthesis. As the four of them approached the house, the native trees gave way to landscaping, flowering bushes, and newly planted olive and lemon trees.

When they reached the porch, Dima sat on a bench and took off his boots, setting them on a mat with other pairs of boots and an umbrella stand containing hiking poles and folded umbrellas.

"If you don't mind, please take off your boots," he said. "I have slippers inside. My wife doesn't like it when I track dirt and leaves into the house. You can leave your hiking poles in the umbrella stand." He pointed at the circular metal bin.

The tired hikers sat on benches, took off their dusty hiking boots, and dropped their poles into the stand. When they entered the home, they stepped into cotton slippers on a mat near the door.

From the exterior, the home looked like a village farmhouse. But when you stepped inside, the interior resembled an urban apartment, with a wall-mounted TV, new sofas and chairs, and posters of modern art from Triennale in Milano. Simona and Dario followed Chiara and Dima into the dining room, where a small chandelier hung above a linen-covered dining table set with ceramic plates, napkins, silverware, a bread basket, wine-glasses and water glasses.

"Chiara's here with her friends!" Dima shouted toward an open door to the kitchen, from which they could smell aromas of baking bread and pasta sauce.

*"Benvenuti!"* a cheery voice greeted them. Chiara's mother came into the dining area wearing an apron over a flowered summer dress.

"Mamma!" Chiara squealed as they exchanged kisses and hugs. Simona and Dario noticed that Chiara's mother was an attractive, middle-aged woman with long black hair streaked with strands of gray. Mother and daughter resembled sisters—same height, similar hairstyles. Valeria radiated mature beauty and grace. She was slightly plump, with wide hips, fleshy arms, and faint wrinkle lines around her eyes and chin.

Chiara turned to Simona and Dario, her arm around her mother's waist. "Meet Mamma Valeria, the best person in the world," she gushed. "Mamma, this is Simona and Dario from DIGOS, from the Milano *Questura*. They came to my apartment and told me why they wanted to meet you."

*"Ciao, ciao,"* Simona and Dario said, reaching to take Valeria's outstretched hand.

"I'm so happy you could come," Valeria said, her voice warm and welcoming. "Chiara wanted you to visit our modest home and see how happy we are to be back in Italia. Lago di Como is not Calabria, my home, but it's close enough to see Chiara and enjoy all the delights of northern Italia."

Simona imagined that Chiara would look like her mother in twenty years, an attractive woman, fashionably dressed and happy with her life. Subtle differences between them were Chiara's higher cheekbones, narrower eyes, and daintier nose, inherited from her Russian father.

"Oh, Mamma, I'm so glad to be back," Chiara said, again putting her arm around her mother's waist. "I've got so much to tell you! I'm working at a prestigious fashion show next week. And guess what! I met a very nice man at a wedding. He asked me to dinner next week."

"Really, another boyfriend? What's his name?" Valeria asked.

"Carlo. He's Spanish and very handsome, like an actor. But he works for a bank. He makes a good salary and travels a lot for work to Roma, London, Amsterdam, and New York."

Dima cleared his throat. "Ladies, we have guests for lunch. Can you wait until after dinner for gossip?" He smiled and pulled out a chair at the end of the table.

"It's not gossip, *amore*," Valeria protested. "She's our daughter. If she has a new boyfriend, I want to know about him. So should you!" She said with a twinkle in her eye. "We both want grandchildren before we get too old and feeble to play with them."

Dima laughed. "Yes, we do, but let's feed our hungry guests before they collapse."

Simona and Dario were enjoying the warmth and hospitality from Dima and Valeria. The couple seemed content and carefree, despite the serious situation they were in and the possible dangers they faced.

"Please sit down," Valeria said. "Chiara, let's bring in the wine and *aperitivo*."

"And water, please. We're a bit dehydrated," Simona said.

"Of course," Valeria said. "I have chilled bottles of Pellegrino in the refrigerator. Could you get those, dear?" she said, looking at Chiara.

Simona and Dario sat down across from each other, with Dima at the head of the table. There was a chair for Valeria at the other end of the table and an empty chair for Chiara to sit next to Simona.

Looking around the dining room, Simona saw framed photos of the family in Roma, Moscow, and Milano on the wall above a blond table holding silverware, plates, cups, and glasses.

Valeria and Chiara went into the kitchen. Chiara returned with two opened bottles of Pellegrino. She set them in front of Simona and Dario, who poured full glasses for themselves, drained them, and then refilled them.

"Oh, that water's nice and cold. We really needed that," said Simona.

"It certainly is hot today," Dima said, "much hotter than it would be in Bern. And after a long climb, you do need plenty of cold water."

Chiara came back with opened bottles of Chianti and Pinot Grigio and set them in front of her father. Behind her, Valeria carried in a colorful ceramic platter of cheeses, prosciutto, olives, tomatoes, and bruschetta slices.

"Red or white?" Dima asked his guests.

Dario paused and looked at Simona and then at Dima. "Well, we're on duty. We're not supposed to drink."

"But you've had a long hike, and you're thirsty. How about just one glass?" Dima said, smiling at them, his hand on the Chianti bottle. "And no one will know. It's just us. You won't be back in Milano until this evening."

"I think it's okay, Dario," Simona said. "Just one glass. But I want mostly water."

"Me, too," Dario answered and looked at Dima. "One glass of Chianti for each of us."

Dima poured their wine and reached over to pour Pinot Grigio for Chiara and Valeria.

When all were seated, he raised his glass. "A welcome toast to our guests, Simona and Dario. We've had guests from Barna at our home, but you are the first police officers. I hope you will help keep us safe!" he said with a smile and a wink.

Everyone clinked glasses across the table, "*Cincin...Cincin,*" and Chiara passed around the platter. They forked slices of cheese, prosciutto, olives, and bruschetta slices onto salad plates and started to sample.

"I'm famished," Dario said, gobbling one bruschetta in two bites and reaching for another.

"Enjoy, enjoy," Valeria said. "I have more in the kitchen, but don't spoil your appetite. Lunch is coming soon."

Dima munched on a cheese slice, sipped Chianti, and said, "So, tell me, Dario, how was your hike?"

"Exhausting! I'm in pretty good shape, but it was a challenge to hike up a steep mountain over stones with twists and turns. The hardest part was crawling under a fallen tree that covered the trail. There's no exercise I do at the gym that trains me for mountain climbing."

"Ah, yes. You have to be physically fit to live in these mountains," Dima agreed. "No sidewalks, stairs, or flat runways."

"I'm curious," Dario said, wiping the crumbs from his third bruschetta from his lips. "Do you hike the same trail when you leave and return?"

Dima smiled. "I'm not as fit as when I was in my twenties. I'd never leave if I had to hike over that trail. Too many possibilities to fall and break an arm or leg. But I wanted Chiara to show you how strenuous the trail is to our remote home. No one is going to stumble onto our house by accident."

Simona asked, "But how do you get into town to shop for food and other necessities? I don't even know what town it would be."

Dima smiled and raised a hand to Valeria. "Later I'll explain. But let's have lunch first, okay? Valeria prepared one of her special meals."

From the kitchen, Valeria brought out a platter of steaming pasta with Bolognese sauce and passed it around the table. Everyone forked pasta with ragù sauce onto their plates.

"This smells heavenly, Valeria," Simona said. "A perfect meal for starving hikers."

They all forked rolls of pasta coated in the ragù sauce and eagerly began to eat, making pleasant sounds as they began to satisfy their hunger. After a couple of forkfuls, Dario said, "This pasta is delicious, Valeria. My favorite meal. A nice reward for us."

"You're welcome. You like to hike, and I like to work in the kitchen," Valeria said to gentle laughs. "I learned cooking in Calabria from my mamma and *nonna*. But it wasn't easy to get fresh pasta in Russia, unfortunately. So I traveled back and forth from Calabria with suitcases full of pastas, sauces, and meats."

The casual lunch conversation flowed smoothly. They talked about the warm weather, Simona's and Dario's families, and the joys and frustrations of living in Milano—but not about the *Questura*.

As the pasta platter emptied, the conversation changed from casual to business. Dima leaned back and said, "I'd like to hear about your investigation. I suspect the GRU is trying to find me."

Simona and Dario wanted to hear more from Dima before they volunteered their information about the intercepted communications out of Moscow. Dima rolled his empty wineglass in his fingers. The tone of his voice was direct. "I knew they would try to track me down. But Valeria and I planned for three years to leave Switzerland and relocate to a remote place. Isn't that right, *cara?*"

Valeria nodded, a serious look on her face. "It is. We wanted to be close to Chiara, but not in Milano or a suburb where people would know we were newcomers. You know, Italians like to gossip. People would want to know more about us, which was not what we wanted, in order to keep safe. Choosing the right place to live was critical for our safety."

"We started staying at *agriturismi* within a couple of hours of Milano, away from towns, especially where tourists go," said Dima. "If we liked an area, we drove around, looking for homes for sale. We toured a few when they had open houses. I wanted a remote location where cars and motorcycles don't come around. We liked the lakes, Maggiore, Orta, Varese, and Como, but most are within a few kilometers of a town or village. About two years ago, when we stayed at the trout farm *agriturismo* in the valley, we asked about buying a home near there. 'Quiet and remote' were the words we used."

Valeria smiled and nodded.

"There were homes for sale in the village you drove through to get to the trout farm," Dima continued, "but they were only minutes from the Menaggio-to-Lugano highway. Not remote or safe. After more searching, we met a lawyer in Barna who knew about this place."

"Barna. Where is that?" Simona asked.

Dima smiled and pointed over her head toward the ceiling. "Not far from here, but difficult to find unless you know where you're going."

"I hadn't heard of Barna until today," Simona added.

"No reason you would unless you're searching for it."

Simona nodded, wanting Dima to continue. Both she and Dario were learning important background information. Investigators learn more by listening than by talking.

"About a year ago, the lawyer called me and said he knew the owner of a remote farmhouse who had abandoned it several years ago. He couldn't find a buyer and eventually gave up. Our lawyer was persistent, talking to many people until he heard about that owner with an abandoned farmhouse. He called us, and we drove over from Bern and met the lawyer and the owner. When we asked to look at the home, the owner acted like it was Christmas. He couldn't wait to sell and get a payment."

Dima winked at Valeria. "We were in a good negotiating position. If we didn't buy his place, he'd have to wait another five years until someone else showed up."

Dima poured the remains of the Chianti bottle into his glass. "We struck a good deal, didn't we?" He laughed, a rolling laugh, enjoying his tale, eyes bright, pleased with his good fortune.

Valeria said, "I thought the owner was going to have a heart attack, he was so excited. He named a price, Dima lowered it, and the owner reached across and hugged me with tears in his eyes. He was so happy to take our offer—"

"Which was insanely low, I'm almost embarrassed to say," said Dima. "But he got what he wanted, and so did we. And now we have our new home!"

Valeria pumped her fist. "Yes! And we love it here."

Dario said, "Very clever, *signore*. You knew what you were doing. This would be a very difficult place to find."

"You think I'm safe, then?"

"Yes, but you still need to be cautious," Simona said. "Why is Moscow sending someone to find you?"

"It's a long story. I don't want to get into all the details. Just know that I took money from wealthy Russians—oligarchs—who have various financial interests in Europe, some legal and others with political objectives. I'm sure you know about them."

"We do," Dario said, arms crossed over his chest. After a long drive to a remote *agriturismo*, a strenuous hike up a steep mountain, meeting Dima, and enjoying a pleasant lunch with wine, they had reached the time for a serious exchange of information. "How did you do that—and why are Russian agents looking for you?"

Dima waved a hand. "Too long to go into detail. Just understand that, every day, I transferred millions of euros into American dollars, Swiss francs, British pounds, Danish kroner, and a few other currencies. I would transfer assets from various accounts and skim off a small percentage to transfer to accounts no one knew about. After a few weeks, a supervisor noticed, and I knew the clock was ticking. We had to leave Bern. Officials in the Kremlin were notified—including Putin, since his friends are oligarchs. They don't get rich...or stay rich...if they don't kiss Putin's ring."

Dima smiled and nodded slightly before adding, "Or some other place I won't mention." Everyone around the table smiled.

Dario said, "And you know the FSB and GRU have ways to track people using technology."

"I do."

"Not just cell phones, but taking photos of people's gait, height, style of walking. They can even follow people who are disguised."

"I'm aware of it. I have guards you didn't even notice once you left the *agriturismo* and started the hike. I have surveillance cameras in trees, sensors on the path, and night-vision goggles Russian troops used in Syria."

"Do you think you're safe?" Simona asked.

"Why?" Dima asked with a slight look of concern. "Is DIGOS interested? You don't get involved in spy cases, only terrorism."

"This is international, sir," Simona corrected. "We consider what GRU agents have been doing to eliminate Russians they claim are traitors."

"Of course. Litvinenko in London and others, as I'm sure you know."

"We do," Dario confirmed.

"Is your Italian Ministry of Interior involved?"

"The Ministry provides us with intelligence from various sources," said Simona.

"Your embassy in Moscow?"

"That's one of the locations, yes. There are others."

"Of course. Are Americans involved, the CIA?"

Simona looked at Dario. They both understood that they could neither confirm nor deny the source of their information, one of the cardinal rules of intelligence. Sources and methods had to be protected. It was not necessary for Dima to know that information. As the senior agent on their team, Simona answered, "I'm sorry, *signore*. We can't confirm anything other than what we've just said."

Dima nodded. He understood, even though he had asked more out of curiosity than as an attempt to interfere with their investigation.

To change the mood and direction of the conversation, Valeria said, "*Amore*, maybe they should learn how we met in Roma. It's a wonderful story, our love story."

Simona said, "Why, yes, we would like to hear that. I love learning how people meet and fall in love."

Dario smiled at her, gratified that Simona was trying to encourage a more personal conversation.

Valeria also smiled, looking at Chiara and her husband, who met her gaze and nodded.

"My wife, always the romantic," said Dima.

"Now, now, Dima, this is a nice story. I was a young university student, and Dima was enrolled to learn Italian as a new foreign service officer at the Soviet embassy."

Dima picked up the story. "The Soviet embassy wanted all the officers to learn at least some Italian. One of my responsibilities was processing visas and attending receptions with Italian officials. Some—not me—were collecting intelligence and meeting Italian Communists. You can't expect to learn anything if you don't know the native language."

"Of course, we understand," Dario said. "Our embassies do the same, but many foreign service officers already speak other languages, especially English, German, and French."

"I want to tell them how we met, *amore*," Valeria said with a smile. "It's a nice love story. We met in a coffee shop on the campus. I'd see him walk in, order, and sit by himself. One morning during a break, he sat at a nearby table and started talking to me. His Italian was basic, with a heavy accent. I could barely understand him. I helped him with a couple of phrases that he mispronounced. He thanked me, and the next day, we sat at the same table and continued talking. He was at the university for only a month, but by that time, his accent was already better. I told him to watch TV, listen to local radio stations, and go to markets and cafés and listen to other Italians. You can pick up a lot by listening."

"Your Italian is very good, sir," Simona said. You speak almost like a native."

"Yes, but not from Roma," Valeria said. "I started teaching him my dialect from Calabria."

"I noticed," Simona confirmed.

"Thank you, *dottoressa*," said Valeria. "Dima asked me to have coffee with him one Saturday when we didn't have class. We started seeing each other often. His Italian was improving"—she looked at Dima and smiled—"and soon I was falling in love with him. He was so handsome and kind, and he brought me flowers. We'd walk along the Tiber. I remember the first time he kissed me. There was a full moon, and it was springtime. And I wanted him to kiss me."

"Mamma! You're embarrassing me," Chiara said in mock protest.

"You already know this. I've told you before."

"But these are police officers. They're not interviewing you to go on some silly TV show."

Dima smiled. "You know your mother, Chiara. She likes to talk about people falling in love. And your new boyfriend. She is a romantic. You know how she loves to read romance novels and listen to opera, even though most are about romances that don't end well."

"Please, Dima, let's stop talking about me," Valeria said. "Now they know how we met, but they're here to learn more about you and how we got this home and your security."

Simona and Dario nodded.

Valeria continued, "They should also know how much you've changed since you left Russia. He lost weight; that was important for his health. Russian men get fat as they age. They eat bad foods, don't exercise, drink too much vodka, and smoke like chimneys. Dima didn't want to end up that way, so he started exercising, and he lost weight."

"I quit smoking when Chiara was born," Dima added.

"But you still drink vodka, Papa," Chiara said with a smile.

"Yes, and I prefer grappa occasionally. But the drinks I liked best are Italian wines, the best in the world. My favorites are Valpolicella and Chianti from Tuscany."

"Good choices," Dario said approvingly. "Valpolicella is one of my favorites, too."

Dima nodded. "I like to sample wines. I have a small wine cellar in the basement." He paused. "We take little vacations often. I like to go to the Lake District. We were in Garda last week, and we'll go to Lago Maggiore next, and then Bergamo."

"My hometown," Simona said with a smile. "It's a charming city, and the upper part is quite historic."

"I've heard nice things about Bergamo," said Dima. "I'll take that as a recommendation, thank you. It's boring when we're here

all the time, a remote farmhouse next to a small village. I want
to see more of northern Italy, especially in the warm weather."

The conversation was meandering, making Simona anxious.
They needed to discuss the reasons for their coming. "I hope you
don't mind, sir, but could we talk about your safety, please?" she
asked, hoping he wouldn't be offended.

"Of course, *dottoressa*. Come to my office. I'll show you
where I monitor the cameras and sensors."

He rose from the table and gestured for them to follow
him as he led them back through the living room and down a
hallway into his office. They followed him in, and he stepped
back to let them see the TV screens and computer monitors
on the walls, the type you might see in a police station, not
in a secluded home in the forest. Simona and Dario stepped
closer to examine two monitors with multiple screens showing
outdoor scenes from the CCTV cameras hidden in the trees.
They recognized the fence and trail they had come up. On the
other screen, the cameras pointed away from the house. In the
distance, they could see a modest hill and the tops of buildings,
including the spire of a church.

"As you can see," Dima said, pointing to the screens, "I have
cameras that monitor all directions from which people could
approach, from up the trail and over the hill from Barna. Not
quite 360-degree coverage, but on the other side of the house,
it would be hard for anyone to approach. It's a dense forest with
ravines, not the way hikers would come."

He pointed to a computer screen on his desk and a small
device that looked like it projected sound. "On this computer,
sensors from both directions record sounds at certain decibel
levels so I won't be alerted every time squirrels or small animals

are moving through the forest, but I would pick up the sound of a person walking on twigs and leaves. I tested it a few times. I had Valeria walk toward the house and noted the decibel level."

He pointed at a device similar to a computer mouse with a dark bulb. "And if a sound is triggered, this red light goes on and sends an alert to an app on my phone."

Dima took out his phone, scrolled down the screen to an app, and opened it, showing a pulsing track like a heartbeat monitor. Near the middle of the screen was a red line with a decibel number in the low hundreds. "If a tree falls, the monitor would pick it up. This would spike, and I'd hear a beep and come into my office and check the monitor for what made the noise."

Dima stood back, letting Simona and Dario examine his surveillance equipment. They were familiar with the technology he had installed to keep him and his wife safe. Dario and Simona moved around the room, looking at the walls: a map of Russia, a small old Soviet flag, plaques written in Cyrillic, and a photo of Gorbachev posing with men in military uniforms and what appeared to be high-ranking Soviet politicians in an elegant setting with large chandeliers, gold-leaf designs on the walls, floral wreaths, and propaganda banners. Dima pointed at a man standing close to Gorbachev. "That's my father. He knew Gorbachev for many years. They were friends."

Simona and Dario stepped closer to the photo, looking at Dima's father: similar size and facial features, with a modest smile, like his son.

"Very impressive, *signore*," Simona said. "What you've set up here is remarkable."

Dima made a slight bow. "I learned about surveillance working in intelligence in Moscow. You can buy even more technologically sophisticated equipment in Italy, equipment that's even more advanced. I wanted only the best. I'm satisfied."

Simona and Dario nodded, taking one last look around the office.

"When you're ready, let's go up to my deck. I want you to see what I have up there," Dima said, walking out into the hallway and over to a stairway. "Valeria will bring biscotti and strawberries for dessert. Let's enjoy this splendid weather and the sunshine."

"Sunshine?" Dario asked. "It was shady on our hike. We didn't see much sun."

"Ah, yes, but I like the sun, and I took measures to get sunshine in the afternoon. Come, follow me."

Simona and Dario followed, reaching a rooftop terrace that resembled a patio at a hotel, with a terrazzo floor, a table, and deck chairs. Around the deck were planter boxes with flowers, *rucola,* tomato and basil plants, potted lemon trees, and an olive tree with tiny green olives sprouting on branches.

"Welcome to my Italian rooftop garden," Dima said, gesturing around the patio. "We hoisted up composted soil and fertilizer in March from a farmer. This fall, I'll plant cabbage, carrots, and onions."

They heard the sound of steps on the staircase. Valeria and Chiara arrived with trays containing biscotti, grapes, strawberries, melon slices, and bottled water.

"Please sit down. We'll have dessert before you head back to Milano," Dima said, motioning to the deck chairs and the table where Valeria and Chiara had placed the trays.

Valeria said, "Isn't it beautiful up here? When we lived in Russia, Dima took me to the dacha where his father and grandfather planted vegetables so they would have something to eat during the winter."

"Sometimes, that was the only food families had during the bleak Soviet era," Dima said. "Those were hard years. My father and mother told me about them."

Dima paused. "Nazi tanks came within a kilometer of our dacha in 1942 when they reached the suburbs of Moscow," he said. "Trees around our dacha had bullet holes, and there were pits in the ground where artillery had exploded. My father told me stories that his father had told him. Nazi soldiers broke into the dacha, ransacked it for food, and stole a watch and a clock. Crazy! Why steal a watch and clock? But they didn't burn it down, just raided it for food.

"When I was ten, I was digging in the garden and found a Nazi grenade. I thought my father was going to have a heart attack. He pulled me back inside and called the police. The next day, an army truck pulled up, and a sergeant scooped up the grenade with a shovel and set it into a metal box with sandbags. Later, they said it was still live; they exploded it at an army base."

Dima stepped over to the edge of the terrace and pointed down the trail. "Here is where I watch anyone approaching when the sensors alert me." He put his hand on binoculars mounted on a stand and aimed at the path. "And with these, I can see who's on the path. Not many people venture here, except serious hikers."

Dario went over and looked into the binoculars. "Good range. Looks like it covers about twenty meters on both sides of the path."

"Yes. Occasionally on a weekend, I'll come up here and use the binoculars to spot hikers when I get tipped off by a fellow who works at the trout farm. I pay him to warn me when anyone starts up the path. After he tips me off, I come up on the roof and watch them."

"How long have you been living here?" Dario asked, stepping back from the binoculars, his eyes sweeping around the woods, the paths, weeds, vines, and sprouting trees.

"Living, or restoring? We bought it a year ago. I hired workmen to repair the roof and bring planter boxes up here for my small garden. They painted inside and out, installed new floors, put in new appliances in the kitchen, and brought in our furniture. They finished in March, and we moved in last month."

"How many people have come on the trail that you've observed?" Simona asked.

"Oh, maybe ten or a dozen each week. Occasionally, you'll have a group of hikers, three or four. They walk by, and some don't even notice the house. They're tired and want to climb the hill into Barna."

"And how do you leave? Down the trail?"

Dima shook his head. "No. Come here. I'll show you."

They walked to the back of the roof. Dima pointed at a garage behind the house. They could see tire tracks from the garage over leaves and dirt that climbed a hill, not near the hiking trail.

"Our car is in the garage. When we go shopping or pick up Chiara in Menaggio, we drive up that path through the trees to a fence that has an electronic gate. I paid the city and got permission from the *Carabinieri* to install the fence and gate. They can open it with an electronic key and drive down to our place."

"So you don't have to hike up the path we came on?" Simona asked.

Dima laughed. "When we moved in, I hiked down to the trout farm to buy fresh fish. But now I hire one of the men to bring me some."

Dario laughed. "We're twenty years younger than you, *signore*, and I wouldn't want to hike that trail more than once a year. We've done it this year; that's enough."

Dima smiled, appreciating Dario's comments about the strenuous hike to their home. "Tell me, Dario. You're an experienced police officer. What do you think of my security?"

"Well, to be honest, we didn't know what to expect. Chiara said you had a remote place with security. We weren't sure what that meant, but we see that you're not likely to be discovered by a casual hiker. This is more than we expected."

"Do you think I'm safe?" he asked, a confident look on his face.

Simona and Dario looked at each other, and then Dario spoke. "We're not experts on surveillance technology. We have experts at DIGOS who handle electronic surveillance. I could have them take a look at your system. Maybe they would have ideas on improving it."

"By all means. Let me know when they're coming."

Dario thought for a moment. "As thorough as your security system seems to be, sir, I'm curious: What would you do if you did see someone suspicious, possibly from the FSB or the GRU, approaching your house?"

Dima said with confidence, "I was in the KGB. I have the means to protect us if we were discovered. I have some arms in my wine cellar. Would you like to see them?"

"Maybe another time," said Dario.

Dima looked at his watch. "It's getting late. You have to get back to Milano. I'll drive you to your car at the trout farm. It takes about twenty minutes. Then two hours to Milano. You should be back by 7:00 p.m."

# CHAPTER THIRTEEN

"**G**ood morning. Let's start immediately with our debriefing about Saturday's assignment," Lucchini said, smiling at Simona, Dario, and Antonella in his *Questura* office the day after the visit to the Volkovs' home. "I've never heard of DIGOS officers hiking on duty. First time for everything, I guess."

They all chuckled, pleased that Lucchini was starting the meeting with a bit of humor.

"We did, and word will get around that DIGOS agents exercise while they're on the job," Dario said with a smile. "I'll be the first to admit that it was strenuous. We hiked almost an hour over a steep trail overgrown with vines and weeds. We had to crawl under the branches of a big tree that had fallen on the trail. That was hard, getting snagged in branches that snapped back and scratched our arms and legs. It reminded me of an obstacle course I went through during training when I was an army recruit. I was younger and stronger then. Now I'm middle-aged and several kilos heavier."

Lucchini smiled. "Did you take photos?"

"Yes," Simona said. "I'll put them in the file along with our report. Want to see some?"

Lucchini held up his hand. "Later. Tell me what you found at the end of the hike. You met Volkov and his wife?"

"That was the best part of the day," said Dario. "We had a nice lunch prepared by Volkov's wife. After lunch, Volkov took us into his office to see his security systems. He has CCTV cameras in the trees along the hiking path, as well as audio sensors to detect movement. He was in the KGB at one time and learned about surveillance technology."

Lucchini nodded. "He wouldn't have left Bern unless he knew how to set up security so it would be difficult for the Russians to find him and likely assassinate him. Tell me about their home."

Simona answered, "They live on a mountainside in an old farmhouse they've remodeled. It's quite comfortable. And his Italian wife, Valeria, treated us to an excellent lunch after our ordeal. She's a good cook."

"Where in Italy is she from?"

"Calabria," Simona said. "A very nice woman. The whole family was friendly toward us. After lunch, the father, Dima, took us into his office where we could see TV screens linked to the CCTV cameras and a speaker that allows him to hear forest sounds, including people hiking. Next, he took us up on the roof, where he has a garden and binoculars. Then he drove us back to get our car at the *agriturismo* where we started the hike."

"Are they safe there?"

Simona nodded. "I think so, for now. A few hikers pass by, and Dima's sensors and cameras follow them. But it's not just the remote trail that makes their home difficult to access. There are no roads, just a hiking trail. No one is going to stumble on them, that's for sure."

Dario added, "He planned this well. They have a car in a garage behind the house that they take when they go shopping for food or to see their daughter. Dima has cleared a path through the forest to the village of Barna, where there's a gate with electronic security. It's almost directly behind the Barna police station. Dima said a buzzer goes off in the chief of police's office anytime someone opens the gate."

"That's clever," Lucchini said. "It appears that Dima knows security. But that won't stop the Russians from trying to find him."

Antonella raised a hand. "We might want to send someone to check his cameras and sensors, as well as the gate."

"Good idea. Let's do that, Antonella."

"I'll arrange it. We'll let him know when they're coming. Do you have his phone number?" Antonella asked Simona and Dario.

Simona said, "Yes. He uses his phone sparingly, mostly texts to his daughter. He said they threw their Russian phones in Lake Lugano when they left Switzerland so they couldn't be tracked. They have Italian phones now. And he has an Italian passport because he got one when he married Valeria."

"Well, that's good. We consider him an Italian citizen. But the Russians are determined to track him down and most likely assassinate him. The Ministry of Interior sent us details of the political assassinations the military intelligence GRU has done in England, Ukraine, and Georgia. They send GRU agents with phony passports to get into the country and use radioactive poisons. They're ruthless, using assassinations for political revenge."

"Have you learned any more about them sending someone to find Dima?" Dario asked.

"Yes, more intercepts from Moscow to Roma and here. We don't know when they are sending an assassin or who he is. If we do intercept the name and when he is coming, we'll check when he registers at a hotel or B&B. Then we can follow him and see where he goes. He'll probably follow the daughter, thinking she will lead him to them. What's the latest with the daughter?"

"On the drive back from Como, she thanked us for going to meet her father," said Simona. "She'll let us know if she communicates with him or goes to see him again. We mentioned we could send a surveillance team to check out his situation."

"Soon. Antonella, would you like to meet them?"

She nodded. "Yes, I would. I'll call and introduce myself." *Ispettore* De Monti can arrange a time for us to talk. Will you take care of that?" she said to Simona.

"Of course, right after our meeting."

"Before you go, let me brief you on the intelligence we have on the GRU assassinations," Lucchini said. "According to intercepted messages, they're determined to find Volkov. We certainly don't want an assassination in Italy. That would be a crisis politically. The Ministry is briefing high-level members of the Chamber of Deputies. They insist we do everything to arrest the assassin and protect Dima."

"Of course," Antonella agreed. "It would be a crisis: a Russian murdered because we couldn't protect him. A scandal. The media would crucify us."

"Did Volkov explain why they want to assassinate him?" Lucchini asked.

"In a few words," Dario said. "He embezzled money from oligarchs he was laundering money for. These are mostly Russians close to Putin. Some are billionaires who buy yachts and villas in England and France. Some of the accounts are for political cyber hacking in the U.S., Germany, and France."

"Africa, too, according to the Ministry of Interior," said Lucchini. "No end to the disruption they're trying to cause in capitalist countries. They certainly created havoc in the U.S. in the election last year. Look what America ended up with: a pompous demagogue in the White House."

Amoruso said, "Volkov's embezzlement is Russia's problem, not ours. Our responsibility is to prevent someone from tracking him down and murdering him on our soil."

After the meeting, Dario stopped in Simona's office. "Still on for dinner tonight?"

She smiled. "Of course. Wouldn't miss it! I want to meet your new sweetheart…see if you're good enough for her."

He laughed. "Never give me a break, do you? Sure, I'm good enough for her. She told me I'm the best man she's ever been involved with."

"Really? I'll ask her and see if she agrees, or if she's just blowing smoke."

"Naw, I think she means it."

"I hope so, for your sake."

"You'll like her. And I'm looking forward to seeing Armando again. It's been a long time since I've seen the Maestro. How's he doing?"

"Fine," she said. "He's off to Berlin on Sunday—two weeks of rehearsals for the symphony. It's a big deal, the first performance of the season. He's conducting Beethoven's Ninth symphony. I'm sure you know it; you're such a cultural elite."

"Why, of course. I can even hum a few bars." Dario cleared his throat dramatically, hummed a long note, gestured with his hands like he was conducting, and then started humming a tune, bobbing his head to the melody.

After a moment, Simona cried out, "No! That's not Beethoven...it's Queen! 'Somebody to Love.' Get out of here!" she said, tossing a pen, which missed as he ducked into the hallway.

"See you tonight!" he said from the hallway.

# CHAPTER FOURTEEN

When Dario and Cecilia returned to her apartment that night after dinner, Dario turned on the TV to watch a repeat of a soccer game. He went to her liquor cabinet, poured a glass of Amaro Montenegro, and returned to the sofa.

Cecilia retreated to her bedroom, undressed, slipped on a robe and slippers, and returned to the living room. Dario lit a cigarette and watched the game, moaning when his favorite team, Inter, almost kicked in a goal. Cecilia stood behind him, running a hand through his hair. "So, how long have you known Simona?"

Without turning around, he said, "Oh, I guess about three years. We became partners on the Islamic terrorist case right after she joined DIGOS. We clashed in the early days. It was really funny."

Cecilia reached over, pushed back his hair, and kissed his forehead. "You told me about a couple of your bitching sessions. They did sound funny. Wish I'd been there."

"But, looking back, the bickering brought us closer. Right from the beginning, we respected each other as professionals. Our work is serious, sometimes dangerous, so bickering was a relief from the tension."

"Did it start right away or after you'd been a team?"

Dario reached up and put his hand over hers, which was on his head. "Right from the beginning. On our first case, we had to drive to Desio, and she complained about my smoking. She hated it and said it would kill me one day. And you know what? I cut back on smoking, down to probably half of what I did before we met."

"Good for her. You know I don't like it, either."

Dario nodded and said, "How many cigarettes have I smoked tonight?"

"Hmm…well you're smoking now…"

"But it's only my second since 6:00 p.m. And only eight or so all day."

Cecilia patted him on the shoulder. "Good. Maybe one day it will be *no* cigarettes."

Dario didn't comment. He took one more puff and then stamped his cigarette out in the ashtray.

"Thanks," Cecilia said. "So, she didn't like your smoking. What else did you argue about?"

"Our personalities aren't the same. You know me. I like to talk, joke, and tease people."

"I know that. You even tease me sometimes, mostly about my expensive clothes and shoes."

"It's just in fun; you know that. I also tell you how good looking you are and how I appreciate it that you always dress like you're going to dinner or a party."

"I like clothes, even shopping for them. Same with my girlfriends."

"And you have nice friends. I like that, too. I even get along with their boyfriends or husbands."

"You'd better," she said, squeezing his shoulders. "So, what's Simona like personally? I couldn't tell much tonight from dinner. She seemed quiet to me."

Dario nodded. "Yes, she didn't say much. Sometimes I think she's thinking about something else even when we're talking. She's more serious than I am. She reads a lot—serious books, histories, and literary stuff. You know I don't read much, mostly *La Gazzetta dello Sport*. I just skim the headlines; that's about it. Simona also likes to talk about politics. I think it's boring."

"I'm with her, *caro*."

He nodded and reached up to squeeze her hand. "But our partnership works, maybe because we're so different and don't try to change each other."

"That's good. A sign of maturity and professionalism."

"Right. She says I'm a dude who just likes sports and partying with my buddies. She and Armando get invited to fancy dinners where they meet celebrities and rich people. Not my style; I think you know that."

"I could tell," she said. "Can you turn down the TV? It's a bit loud."

"Sure," he said, grabbing the remote and muting the sound.

Cecilia walked into her kitchen, opened the refrigerator, pulled out a bottle of water, and returned, sitting in a chair with her back to the TV. "Is everything okay with them? I mean, are they serious?"

Dario looked at her, puzzled by her question. "Sure they are. They're a good match. They both like music, art, the theater. Armando travels a lot. He's a guest conductor in Europe and the U.S., where he has a position with a symphony in Seattle."

Cecilia studied his face, watching his eyes follow the action on the pitch. She glanced at the TV. When a period was over and a commercial came on, she said, "Please don't take this wrong, Dario, but something didn't seem quite right tonight."

He looked at her and blinked. "Really? What do you mean?"

"A couple of things. Simona didn't say much about herself but asked me a lot of questions. It was almost like I was at a job interview."

"She wants to get to know you. What's wrong with that?"

"She didn't drink wine, even though it was poured for her. She took one sip."

"So what?"

"She seemed anxious, distracted, looking around at people in the restaurant and not listening when Armando was talking. And she has these nervous tics—blinking a lot, tapping her finger on the fork."

"Yeah, it fell on the floor. The waiter got her another one."

"She kept on tapping. I wanted to ask her to stop, but I didn't want to be rude. She barely touched her food. She only nibbled some bread and the grilled vegetables."

"Yeah, I noticed. Maybe she had something to eat before they met us."

"Maybe. But other than eating the bread, she took one bite of her *branzino in salsa* and then pushed it to the side of the plate and didn't eat any more. But the fish was excellent. I loved mine."

"Yeah, your fish did look good. I snuck one bite."

"One? I think it was a couple."

Dario smiled. "Maybe I did. I liked all the lemon sauce. But you know me. I'm a meat guy. I loved my *osso buco con risotto.* The best I've had in a long time."

The commercial break was over. Dario watched the beginning of the next period. The referee tossed the ball into the circle, and the scrambling began. Cecilia said, "*Tesoro...*how well do you know Armando?"

Dario frowned, thinking for a moment before answering. "Not well, just what Simona says about him. I've only met him a few times. We talk a bit, but we don't have much in common, except Simona."

"All secondhand, then?"

"Yeah, you could say that. Why are you asking?" Dario finished his Amaro Montenegro, set the glass on the table, and looked across at Cecilia. "Something's on your mind. What is it?"

"Just observing, that's all. You've talked about Simona a lot, and I had the impression she was this very intelligent woman with a dangerous job. I found her to be a little...cold. Distant."

Dario looked away from the TV and listened to Cecilia's observations, knowing that she was perceptive about people. She was a therapist who listened every day to patients pouring out their souls to her, seeking counseling on how they could achieve more happiness and contentment in their somewhat tortured lives.

Cecilia's friends were similar: professional women, spirited conversationalists, opinionated, and smart.

When Dario had first met Cecilia at a holiday party the year before, he had been impressed by her intelligence and personality. Back then, he didn't know she was a therapist but was pleased that she asked him intelligent questions about his life and hopes. When they met a second time for dinner, she continued to explore what he was thinking and believing. He almost felt like he was being interrogated by a professional. While they were drinking a liqueur after dinner, she confessed regarding her profession, which made everything clear. "You know, Dario, I haven't told you, but I'm a therapist. I meet with clients every day. I want to know intimate details of their lives so I can help them with their problems."

He remembered that he'd reached over and squeezed her hands. "And you do it gently. I keep wanting to tell you important things in my life. I hope you don't stop. I want to tell you everything."

In his memory, she grinned, squeezed his hand in return, and said, "It's up to you. I'm a good listener."

Then he'd turned the tables, asking her probing questions. By the end of the evening, they both knew that they wanted to spend more time together.

Two months later, Dario had moved some clothes into her apartment, and they had started living together, mostly on weekends. Her apartment was an hour from the *Questura,* so most nights it was more convenient for him to stay at the apartment he shared with his male roommates, who were "DIGOS bachelors"—men whose job didn't allow for much contact with their wives and families.

Dario was in love with Cecilia. He was obsessed for the first time with a woman who was so different from his ex-wife and the other women he'd dated since his divorce.

Cecilia stood up, walked behind Dario, and put her hands on his shoulders. "Armando also seemed a bit distracted and anxious. He talked about his family, and a little about his career. He doesn't seem to like traveling as much as he has to."

"Right, I got that."

"But something was on his mind. He listened to me when I was answering Simona's questions, but his eyes were kind of blank, staring without seeing, like he heard my words but they didn't register with him. He seemed…distant…in a way."

"Really?"

Cecilia nodded. "I know how important Simona is to you, but I don't think we'll be good friends. I can't imagine them having us over to her apartment for dinner."

"It's a one-bedroom in Isola. I don't think they entertain much at home."

"Would you ever want to invite them for dinner here?"

Dario thought about it, watching the game but contemplating what she was asking. "Well, maybe…but with another couple. One of your friends."

"I'm thinking the same thing. Better if we have other people here."

Cecilia turned to watch the match: players running back and forth on the field, no shots on goal. Bored, she got up, went into her bedroom, lay down on the bed, and picked up a book on her nightstand. She flipped through the pages but discovered that she wasn't in the mood to read. Dario had said he couldn't be at her apartment the next night. She would be able to read in bed alone, a delicious thought. Reading helped her fall asleep.

She set the book back on her bedside table and returned to the living room. Dario had turned off the TV and was putting his empty glass in the kitchen sink.

As he walked toward her, he noticed she had a serious look on her face. "You okay?"

"Yes, I am. Know what I think?"

"What's that?"

"I think Simona is pregnant."

# CHAPTER FIFTEEN

Vladimir Putin slumped deep in his chair—almost a throne—resting on a carpeted platform in an ornately designed ceremonial conference room at his home in the Novo-Ogaryovo estate, ten kilometers from downtown Moscow. It was the former residence of Soviet Georgy Malenkov, the successor to Stalin after his death in 1953. Around the spacious room, paintings from the Pushkin Museum in St. Petersburg adorned the walls. A candelabra from the Hermitage in St. Petersburg rested nearby. A gold chandelier the size of a beach umbrella hung over a polished mahogany table. Thirty empty chairs surrounded a table. Behind Putin's throne was a row of red, white, and blue Russian ceremonial flags, the size seen in parades.

It was a Tuesday morning in late April and time for Putin's weekly briefing from GRU, the foreign intelligence directorate for the Russian armed forces and the first directorate's unit 29155, which was tasked with assassinations, sabotage, and political disruptions in Europe. Putin's briefer, Lieutenant Colonel Anton Lebedev, had placed a file of the briefing on the table in front of Putin's throne. While Lebedev read through the report, Putin followed along on his copy, reading glasses perched on the tip of his bony nose. As he read, he traced his finger down the pages, verifying that he was getting every detail and that there were no mistakes or deletions.

Occasionally, Putin looked up, his icy blue eyes staring at Lebedev's posture and bearing. Lebedev had briefed Putin for three years but still felt like he was being judged for the content of the report—every word, every topic, every nuance. If the president of Russia did not like what he was hearing, Lebedev feared a cell in Lefortovo Prison was waiting for him.

Ten minutes into the briefing, Lebedev cleared his throat, knowing the next topic was disturbing. Lebedev imagined Putin enraged, tearing up the pages, throwing them at him, and storming out of the conference room, slamming the door and retreating to his private study. But Putin never erupted; he smoldered like lava seeping from deep inside a volcano.

Lebedev's forehead and armpits were damp with sweat. His throat was dry and constricted, not from a lack of water, but from tension and fear. He trembled, reading without daring to look at Putin, his words sounding like rain falling on a tin roof. "I'm sorry, Mr. President, but the next topic is a disturbing one."

Putin flipped to the next page, skimming the first paragraphs, his finger sliding down the page. He adjusted his reading glasses and lowered his head until his eyes were inches from the open file.

Lebedev cleared his throat and started to read, a tremor in his voice. "It's possible…one of our colleagues, Dmitri Volkov, who manages accounts in Bern for our colleagues, has possibly stolen from them." He paused, not wanting to rush into the summary of the accountant's analysis. Putin kept reading, not looking up.

"How much?" Putin asked, his words sharp as knives.

Lebedev cleared his throat again, feeling Putin's anger. "Maybe three million euros," he said, expecting a lightning reaction from Putin. But it didn't come. The molten lava was below the surface but dangerous for anyone nearby.

Putin was reading each paragraph. At the end, he started over at the top of the page. A blush of crimson colored Putin's pale cheeks, which were normally the color of paper, a sign Lebedev knew signaled Putin's anger. Putin continued reading, flipping pages until he came to the end of the report on Volkov. Then he turned back to the beginning and read the first page again.

"Where is Volkov?" Putin snarled, taking off his reading glasses, leaning back in his chair, and staring with cold eyes at Lebedev, who knew the icy stare meant one thing: rage.

"Sir, we sus-suspect," he stammered, "that he has left Bern and is in an unknown location."

"Why don't we know where he is?" Putin snapped, his voice like a whip. "How did he get away without us knowing?" His words were harsh, loaded with venom.

"Sir, we're trying to locate him."

"*Trying?!* I don't want *trying*. I want you to find him!" Putin's words were bullets.

"Yes, sir, we are trying, but—"

"Arrest him! Bring him to Moscow. He's a criminal, if what you're saying is true."

"We suspect he is. Accountants are preparing a detailed analysis of his transfers, which I will bring over immediately, maybe later today. What you see in this report is their conclusion."

"I know Volkov. Why would he do this?" Putin growled, his fists balled up like grenades. He started to stand but then slumped back onto his throne.

"He's been a loyal supporter of yours. His father was an advisor to Yeltsin and Gorbachev—"

"Who destroyed the USSR! Traitors, both of them!" Putin snarled.

"Yes, sir, but from our records, Volkov has never been disloyal to you or United Russia."

"How did he steal money? Why didn't someone catch him?"

"We don't know. His supervisor, Nicolai Komarov, was on medical leave, being treated for bladder cancer. He had two months of chemotherapy and radiation. He lost more than eighteen kilos and most of his hair. He's still weak and only able to work a few hours. After he returned to the bank last week for the first time after chemotherapy and radiation treatments, he noticed discrepancies in Volkov's accounts. When he tried to call Volkov, Volkov didn't answer his phone."

"Of course not! He's a thief!"

"Yes, sir," Lebedev said nodding.

"He's a fool. Who would do something as dangerous as stealing our money?! He knows he'll be caught. What have you done to find him?"

Lebedev cleared his throat again, mildly relieved that they were having a conversation, with Putin asking for information and not exploding in rage like he had moments before.

"Last week, FSB officers from our Bern embassy visited Volkov's apartment. They learned that he and his wife had departed the day before and left a forwarding address of the bank where Komarov works. We've tried to reach him by phone and text, but there's been no response. We've tried many times. He's ignoring our pleas."

Putin put his reading glasses back on and flipped back to reread the Volkov report, his blade-thin lips pressed tightly, his ice-blue eyes narrowed into slits. While he flipped through the pages, he tapped an index finger on his temple. He came to the end of the report, closed it, and pushed it aside, one hand resting on it. "Appalling, stealing from friends. He's a traitor, a thief. He should be shot."

"Yes, sir. What are you going to do?"

"I need to know where he is!" Putin's voice rose again in anger.

"We think he's near Milano. His daughter works there. She lived in Moscow until she was about fourteen years old, when she moved back to Italy with her mother. When Volkov was assigned to Bern, his wife eventually joined him, but their daughter stayed in Milano."

"I remember some of this, secondhand," Putin responded, his anger subsiding. He blinked fast, as if something was in his eye.

"We have photos of you and him at your year-end press conference in December."

"I remember. But now he's a traitor and a thief. We know how to deal with thieves and traitors."

"Yes, sir. We have selected an experienced agent to find him."

"And kill him. He's a coward, running away, leaving no forwarding address, not answering his phone. He knows he's in trouble, and we'll find him. We always do. It's a waste of time to think we could bring him back to Moscow and face a court here. We don't want a trial. But we have to find him. Soon."

"Our agent will do that. He's tracked down traitors before."

"Who is the agent?

"Vasily Egorov, a veteran Spetsnaz intelligence agent, experienced in sensitive operations in Ukraine, Chechnya, and Syria. He's one of our best agents. I know him well. He assisted in the assassination of the Chechen rebel Yandarbiyev in Qatar in 2004. Egorov was arrested for espionage in Georgia in 2006 and then returned by the Georgian government. He recently operated our secret listening post in Syria."

"Egorov, yes. I met him at an awards ceremony a couple of years ago. A good choice. A very experienced agent."

"When he's not on a mission, he teaches new agents at the GRU training academy. His specializations are surveillance, explosives, and assassinations."

"Send him. Train him for this mission. It's not to Ukraine or Chechnya; it's Italy."

Lebedev relaxed momentarily, relieved that Putin had made the decision that only he could make.

"Sir, one reason we chose Egorov was that he was stationed at our consulate in Milan when he was in the army twenty years ago. He knew a little Italian. We'll train him so he can speak better Italian. Languages come easily for him; he learned Ukrainian and Moldovan when he was assigned to those places."

"Important: He has to speak Italian. Italy's police are experienced and well trained in terrorist investigations. Their state-of-the-art technology is maybe even better than ours."

Putin pushed back from his throne and stood. The briefing was over, even though there were more GRU cases to report. He stepped off the platform. Giving Lebedev an icy stare, he said, "Keep me informed. I want to know when Egorov has been successful. We'll give him a medal for heroism after he assassinates Volkov. Tell him his mission is to protect our national security. That's the truth."

"Yes, sir, it is."

Putin turned to leave the conference room and then turned back to Lebedev after a few steps. "Give him what we gave that traitor Litvinenko. Let it be a lesson to other fools who might be considering betraying us."

"Yes, sir."

"I expect to receive phone calls about this…this Volkov thief. No doubt I'm not the only one who's angry. Three friends have been robbed, maybe even more when I get your final report. They will want their money back. And justice. We'll get both eventually."

The next day, Vasily Egorov was in GRU headquarters, sitting at a table across from Lebedev and two senior officers for his annual review, usually a boring recitation of his assignments and his classes for new recruits. But the meeting wasn't his review, which usually would be contained in a thin file. Instead, in front of Lebedev sat a large file in which Egorov could see plastic folders that usually contained photos.

Lebedev lit a cigarette, signaling that he was about to begin. The two other colleagues also lit up. Egorov followed, reaching across the table for a metal ashtray containing cigarette butts.

"Good morning, Vasily. You might say this is a lucky day for you."

"It's not my review?"

"No, this is about your next assignment." Vasily was puzzled by Lebedev's smile and tone of voice.

"Oh, God, not Syria again," Vasily said. "I hate deserts, with their sand and blistering weather. It's brutal. I can't breathe with all the dust. I had to throw away my clothes when I returned— even my boots, as the sand had penetrated the leather. I'm still coughing. Dust stays in your lungs until you cough it all up."

Lebedev held up his hand. "No, Vasily, you won't need desert boots for this assignment. You're going to a much better climate for an assignment you'll find more interesting. We think you'll enjoy it."

"Where?"

"How would you like to spend summer in Italy?"

"Italy! I'd love to go back to Italy." Vasily grinned, pleasantly surprised. "You're not teasing me, are you?"

"No, I'm not."

"Why? What's in Italy?"

Lebedev patted the file. "It's all in here. Take this back to your office and read it. There are reports from our Bern embassy and from Putin's office, including photos and background information about who we want you to find."

"I'll read the report, but tell me more so I can ask questions. And where in Italy? Rome?"

"No, Milan."

"Milan?" Vasily repeated. A slight grin grew into a smile, revealing his teeth. He chuckled. "Milan. You know, I was assigned there as a security guard at our consulate. That was more than twenty years ago."

"That's one of the reasons you're going. Plus you learn languages fast—Ukrainian, even a bit of Moldovan. You're the only one in our department who knows Italian. You haven't spoken it in years, so we'll give you intensive language training."

"Where, a university?" Vasily frowned.

"No, personal lessons from one of our agents who just returned from Rome after a three-year tour. He speaks fluent Italian now. We've asked him, and he's agreed. He said the best way to learn the language fast is to live with him for a month. He's divorced and spending time at his dacha. He says you'll speak Italian all day, eat meals, go for walks, do exercises. He'll teach you what to say when you meet someone, how to ask for directions, how to carry on a conversation about football, the weather, even politics. He's very smart and eager to teach you."

"I'd like that. I'll be a student, not an instructor. I like studying languages. This will be easy. I'll learn fast."

"You'll have to. It will be important for you to speak Italian as soon as you land—and with the right accent. Your tutor told us that, when Russians try to speak Italian, they get some words right, but their accent is often crude and offensive to Italians. He said most Russians sound like their tongue is a hammer, hitting consonants hard, and they also miss the right accents on vowels. They slaughter the Italian language, according to him."

Egorov smiled. "Italian and Russian, such different languages. I learned some Italian when I was there, but it was elementary. I still have some old grammar books, but it's better to have a person teach you. Learning accents is very important."

"I'm pleased you're enthused. I think you'll learn fast. You don't go until your tutor says you're ready. You'll read Italian magazines and newspapers, watch Italian TV, and listen to Italian radio. We want you to melt into crowds and be able to discuss the weather, current events, and even football, their national obsession."

"I know about football. That will be easy."

"We don't want you to stand out as a Russian. You have another small advantage: Your ancestors were Tatar, so your skin color is a bit darker than that of most Russians."

"Of course. But what is the mission? What's in Milan?"

Lebedev patted the file again. "It's all in here. A banker stole money he was laundering for our friends. He was living in Bern but disappeared. We need to find him and get rid of him. Putin gave the order, and he knows you've been given the assignment."

"Putin, really?" Egorov said, pleasantly surprised. "It's a very high priority, then."

"From the top," Lebedev confirmed. "I briefed him about your experience, and he's confident that you'll be successful. And when you return, you'll receive a medal and a cash bonus. Enough to spend a couple of months on beaches in Sochi."

"Milan and then Sochi?" Egorov said, smiling as if he'd been given a surprise gift, which this was. "It's going to be a good summer. And thank God I won't have to endure another Middle Eastern blistering desert."

"What you'll learn in this file is that the man you're going to find left Bern with no forwarding address. His wife is Italian, and they have a daughter in Milan. She's a link to locate him— the only link we have at this time. When you arrive in Milan, your job is to follow her, learn her daily routines and where she goes. We expect she sees her father and mother, but we don't know how or where."

"Surveillance. I like that."

"And you're good at it. But you have to be able to look and talk like an Italian so you don't raise suspicions that could lead to the police questioning you."

Lebedev handed across the file. Egorov flipped through pages of text and then photos of a young woman: attractive, in her twenties, well dressed. The photos included scenes of daily urban routines: shopping at a market, entering and leaving an apartment, sitting with a young man at cafés and a trattoria, drinking coffee in the mornings, and eating pasta and drinking wine in the evenings. Walking with a young man in a park, hand in hand. Hugs and cheek kisses when they met or departed.

"She's quite attractive. Russian and Italian?"

"That's right." Lebedev pointed to a piece of paper. "This is her address in Milan and the office where she works. We had agents from our consulate follow her to get these photos, but we don't want to risk the agents being spotted by police and kicked out of the country. Italian police know we have intelligence agents at our consulate. That's another reason we want to send you. You're not known by the Italian police."

Egorov closed the file. "When do I leave?"

"First, you'll go through special training. You know how to do this: approach him in a park, at a café, in his car, or even walking a dog. You'll quickly swab him with poison before he sees you. Surprise is important. So is privacy. You don't want anyone else to see you."

"I understand. I've been in situations like this."

"Your experience is good. You'll follow Volkov a couple of times to learn his routines so you can intercept him and sprinkle the powder on his skin or put it into food or drink and walk away undetected."

"Won't he have guards?"

Lebedev shook his head. "We don't know. If he does, report back to us. We'll come up with a solution. We've arranged a room for you in an apartment run by a Russian woman we trust. When we have a sensitive mission to Italy, our agents stay in her apartment. Hotels and apartments require guests to turn over passports, which are registered with the local police so they can track you. Not necessary in her apartment. You'll have a Polish passport and driver's license in your name, and you'll carry cash. We'll give you 20,000 euros and supply you with more from the consulate if necessary. You'll have a credit card, but use it only if some place doesn't accept cash. Ask before you pay for something. Is that clear?"

"Yes, of course."

Lebedev reached into a drawer and took out four sealed envelopes. "After you finish your training and your tutor says you're ready to travel, we'll have another meeting, and I'll give you cash: 5,000 euros in each envelope. Keep a record when you spend more than 200 euros at a time. Don't squander or gamble. Also, no prostitutes. They'll steal from you and give you a nasty disease."

"Of course not. I'd never hire a prostitute."

"Anything else? We expect you'll be ready in four or five weeks."

Egorov held up his hand. "Before I leave, I need to go to St. Petersburg, maybe for a long weekend. My mother is very ill, and my son lives there. I'll tell them I'll be traveling but not tell them where."

"You'll have your Russian phone, which we'll use to reach you in Milan. But tell your friends and family not to call you unless it's important. We don't want Italian police to track you on that phone."

Egorov nodded. "My mother and son do sometimes need to reach me."

"When you arrive, buy a cheap Italian phone if you have to call people you meet. We want them calling an Italian phone number, not one in Russia. After you've been there a few days, go to our consulate to pick up a weapon. Don't carry it when you're doing surveillance—only when you are ready to assassinate Volkov. Just a precaution, as he might have a pistol as well."

"How long will I be in Italy?"

"You'll have a tourist visa for ninety days, plenty of time to find Volkov and carry out your assignment."

"Ninety days? I can find him in thirty."

"Just a precaution in case it takes longer. If you can't locate him in thirty days, we don't want to have to apply for another visa. It could cause questions. We want you to be a phantom visitor with no way for the Italian police to know you're in the country. Or why."

He nodded. "Of course. Ninety days will be sufficient."

\* \* \* \* \*

Egorov spent two hours reading through the Volkov file and looking at photos of Chiara Volkov, her father, and her mother, going back several years. Volkov's wife was attractive, like Italian women he had seen on the streets when he had had limited freedom to spend a few hours walking through Milan. He was excited about this assignment; he wouldn't have restrictions on time or where he could go, like he'd had when he was a lowly guard at the consulate.

When Egorov left his GRU office in eastern Moscow that evening, he walked to a bus stop for the thirty-minute trip to his apartment. When he boarded the bus, he was so exhilarated that he wanted to shout out to the other riders, who looked exhausted and weary, "I'm going to Italy!"

But he resisted, stifling a smile for so long he thought his cheeks would crack.

When he arrived at his apartment that dreary, rainy evening, he unlocked and pushed open his door. His exhilaration about his forthcoming assignment evaporated. Instead, an agonizing wave of depression swept over him. He flicked on the overhead light, which did nothing to ease his anxiety.

Katya, his girlfriend for nearly two years, had moved out of his apartment a month earlier, another sad experience in a year that had had many depressing events, including his mother's illness and growing dementia, as well as his son's animosity toward him. And Egorov had been living with a lingering fear that he would be assigned to another Syrian mission, one that he might not come back from.

His eyes went immediately to the coatrack by the door, where Katya used to hang her winter fur coat. In the month she had been gone, looking at the coatrack had been a reflex. But it had been empty since March, a depressing acknowledgment of her leaving him. He held on to the fantasy that one day he would see her coat hanging there again. It was futile to obsess about Katya, but he couldn't help himself. She was on his mind every day, but not every hour, as it had been in the first couple of weeks after she had abandoned him.

When she'd moved out in March, she had made sure he wouldn't be around. She had packed up when he was in St. Petersburg one weekend to visit his ailing mother, who was dying of emphysema, and his twelve-year-old son, Pyotr. Egorov had called Katya every day, describing his mother's hacking coughing spells from too many years of smoking unfiltered cigarettes. He had also shared with Katya what it was like to see Pyotr outside the home of his ex-wife, who wouldn't let him come into her apartment. Pyotr was becoming more hostile, on the cusp of being a rebellious teenager, just like Egorov had been with his own parents. In the hour he had spent with Pyotr walking around a park, his son had been sarcastic, spitting on the ground, cursing at his father for not caring about him, and telling him he was a bad father who came to see him only when it was convenient and who never brought him to Moscow.

That visit to St. Petersburg had been another bitter experience, one of many in the past two years. It had been painful to witness his mother's declining health and Pyotr's animosity. He had been eager to return to Moscow and Katya, whom he'd hoped one day to marry.

When he had returned from St. Petersburg, he opened the door, and Katya's fur coat was not on the coatrack. Her key was on the table next to the rack. She was gone. And he'd felt shocked that when he was with his mother and son, Katya had cleaned all of her possessions out of the apartment.

Around the apartment were so many memories of Katya, including a faded spot on the wall where an icon from her family had hung. The bookshelf of the romance novels she loved to read was empty. In the bedroom, empty hangers hung on her side of the closet, except one with a torn white blouse with lace around the collar and wrists, a reminder of the rough sex they had had the first night they slept together. It was a memory they used to laugh about when she would pull it out and show it to him, a leer on her face.

"Remember?" she'd say with a smirk that meant only one thing: *I want sex...now...here.* And they would tumble onto the bed, ripping off each other's clothes in a race to see who could get the other one naked first. She usually won.

From the desk in the bedroom she had removed a framed photo of them on the deck of a ship on a Baltic cruise. Her toiletries were gone from the bathroom, as was the blue robe she wore every night with her fluffy slippers. She had left her favorite blanket. He had been so distraught the first few nights that he had pulled the blanket off the bed and slept on the couch in the living room. He'd kept only one pillow, stuffing hers on the top shelf in the closet so he wouldn't see it unless he stepped on a stool.

It had been too painful to sleep in the bed where they had made love for almost two years, knowing she would never return.

They had talked and texted a few times. Katya had explained that she couldn't live with him anymore because of his moodiness, bad temper, swearing, and drinking vodka until he passed out in front of the TV.

"I just can't take it anymore, Vasily," she had cried in their last conversation. "I'm thirty-six. I want to get married and have a baby before I'm too old. But you don't want another child, as you've told me many times. Your son is all you talk about. He's a wonderful boy, so handsome. But he lives in St. Petersburg, and you see him twice a month. What did I do when you were gone? I waited, dreading when you would come in the door, because I'd have to hear your stories about what you did in St. Petersburg, and I'd always feel left out. All you talked about was Pyotr, and you never asked how I was or what I did, being alone all weekend."

"I'm sorry, Katya. I won't behave like that anymore. I promise," he had pleaded.

"No, you will. Pyotr's your son. I'm just the girl you screw when you want to. I want more than that. You live a life of danger, going off to Chechnya or Ukraine, not coming home for months. I would sit. And wait. All I could think about was when I was going to leave you. I had to. I needed a new life—but not with you."

# CHAPTER SIXTEEN

Vasily Egorov flew from Moscow's Sheremetyevo airport to Frankfurt, arriving in the late morning and taking an early afternoon flight to Linate. His briefcase contained maps and guidebooks of Milano, an Italian dictionary, and a copy of *Corriere della Sera* he had bought at a Frankfurt airport bookstore. He'd left two Moscow newspapers in Frankfurt that he'd bought at Sheremetyevo, where he also had exchanged rubles for euros.

Vasily traveled light. The suitcase he'd checked at Sheremetyevo contained a spare pair of pants and a shirt he would throw away once he had replaced them with new Italian clothes. The same with toiletries—nothing from Russia. Sewn into a side panel of his suitcase was a metal tube a little smaller than a cigar, secured with a double lock that required him to press buttons on opposite corners of his suitcase to open it.

When Vasily arrived at Linate Airport, he took Bus 73 through the eastern suburbs to the Duomo metro, where he took the yellow metro line to Stazione Centrale, Milan's main train station, a congested hub of passengers arriving and departing to major cities in Europe and Italy.

Vasily rode the escalator to Centrale's entrance and walked out into the humid, early evening air, which contained only a light haze of pollution, unlike Moscow's foul, oily smog. He wheeled his suitcase into the Piazza Duca d'Aosta, turning around to admire the massive white marble Centrale with its larger-than-life sculptures of horses, gladiators, and chariots on the roof.

Vasily savored his first look at the city where he had lived for two years as a guard at the Russian consulate at Via Sant'Aquilino 3. He looked down the wide Via Vittor Pisani, which flowed into Piazza della Repubblica, a congested street with trams, taxis, and cars navigating in Milano's commercial center. He gazed up at the Pirelli Tower, which he remembered, and the UniCredit Tower, the highest building in the city, with its impressive feature of overlapping sleeves of silver metal, like the petals on a flower.

Vasily felt a rush of anticipation, returning to explore a bustling city that had been daunting when he was a naive twenty-three-year-old guard. He was thrilled to be back. It had been twenty-two years since he had lived there, a city that reminded him of his St. Petersburg hometown, so much more beautiful and historic than dreary Moscow.

In the days and weeks ahead, he would seek out historic landmarks that he'd read and reread about in the travel guides—the Duomo, Galleria Vittorio Emanuele, La Scala, Biblioteca Ambrosiana, the Castello Sforzesco, and the Navigli, reportedly the hip area, with cafés, art galleries, and quaint bridges over the canals. Vasily had devoured the travel literature, underlining key details in the text, folding back corners of pages, memorizing dates and names.

As an experienced GRU agent, he had learned the importance of studying maps to become familiar with the territory he would be working in. He had developed a passion for studying the maps of Milano in the travel books, tracing routes from the apartment where he would stay to key metro stations, Chiara's apartment, and sites he wanted to visit when he had time. The Russian diplomat who had taught him conversational Italian had given him travel books in Russian and Italian. Vasily referred only to the Italian book and had left the Russian book back in Moscow.

He sat on a bench to absorb the city around him. A flock of pigeons careened around Centrale. He gazed at the pine trees in the piazza. African refugees hawked souvenirs, goofy toys that spun on wheels, small drones with wires, funny hats, and toys that beeped and whistled, appealing to four-year-olds.

After admiring Milano's skyline, he was hungry and tired from his flights. He wheeled his suitcase across the piazza, focusing on his reason for being in Milano: to track Chiara, who he thought would lead him to her father. He hoped it wouldn't be soon; he wanted to enjoy Milano for a few weeks. His assignment was open but was to be accomplished in no more than three months. Vasily was determined to make the most of his days there, to seek new adventures and enjoy Italian food and wine before he returned to Moscow.

He walked off the piazza and, following the map, reached Via Filzi and continued to the apartment where he would be staying. When he found the address, he pressed the button for the manager. A minute later, an old woman answered, speaking in Russian. He told her his name. A click, and the door opened. The old woman grunted a greeting in Russian and led him into the darkened hallway, walking with a pronounced limp. They passed a staircase with a tattered rug on the steps. Pointing up the stairs, the old woman mumbled in Russian. "Number six, on your left. The key is in the door. Come and pay me first."

Vasily followed her into a darkened lobby, sparsely furnished with a worn couch, a lamp, and an old desk piled high with paperwork, pens and pencils, papers that looked like bills, a package of cigarettes, and an ashtray. The one set of windows was shuttered, with curtains drawn.

The woman was blunt, mumbling so low that Vasily could barely understand her. "Four hundred euros a week. Forty additional euros a week for laundering sheets and towels. Twenty five euros a week for coffee and brioche in the morning," she said, gesturing at a darkened kitchen under the staircase.

Vasily took out his wallet, counted out five hundred-euro notes, and handed them to her. She stuffed them into her apron pocket, not counting the bills. She scratched her scalp, which was nearly bald on top. Her strands of gray and white hair looked like they hadn't been brushed in days.

"How long you stay?" she asked, looking up at him for the first time. She had bloodshot, pale blue eyes with wrinkles at the corners. Vasily estimated she was about seventy, but maybe younger and showing the effects of no exercise, heavy smoking, and little sunlight.

"I'm not sure. At least a month. Maybe more."

"Tell me before you leave. There may be other charges." He detected a possibly Ukrainian accent. She was not a Muscovite.

As Vasily wheeled his suitcase to the staircase, she snarled, "No whores in your room. Go someplace else, or I kick you out. Understand?"

"Of course," he answered. He watched her limp past him into the kitchen, where she opened an old refrigerator. She returned with a bottle of water and handed it to him. "You look thirsty. Return bottle when empty. I fill and leave in here," she said, gesturing to a table next to the refrigerator with another full bottle and salt and pepper shakers.

Their business was over.

He carried his suitcase up the stairs, unlocked the door to number six, and entered. Faded yellow curtains hung on the only window, which filtered streams of sunlight onto the metal-framed bed. It was covered with a green woolen blanket and two pillows, thin as a book. A metal table next to the bed held a bedside lamp that resembled a cigarette carton, with a cone-shaped shade the size of a plastic throwaway cup.

Vasily looked around the dingy room. An old TV rested on the *armadio* next to the bathroom door. Almost Soviet. On the ceiling, he noticed a stain of concentric rings of water marks the size of a brown cake projecting from a corner.

He went into a darkened bathroom and snapped on a light switch. The room was narrow, with a tiny sink, a toilet, a bidet, and a shower that hadn't been scrubbed. Above the sink hung a mirror with a crack running down the middle. He winced at the stench of an animal, a dog or a cat, likely the pet of a recent guest. He noticed a stain on the floor under the sink, possibly where a litter box had been.

Vasily closed the bathroom door and sat on the bed. The springs squeaked as he sagged toward the middle. He took out his Russian cell phone and texted Lebedev that he had arrived and would take a stroll in the neighborhood—code for locating Chiara's apartment.

He opened his suitcase and began unpacking. After his clothes were arranged in the *armadio,* he ran a hand down the side panel of his suitcase, feeling the slight bulge of a cylindrical metal container the size of a small cigar. He laid the suitcase on the floor and eased it under the bed with his foot.

Vasily undressed, took a shower, put on fresh underwear, and lay on the bed for a nap. An hour later he stirred, groggy, hearing trams and cars passing below. He got up, dressed in slacks and a long-sleeved Italian shirt, and sat on the bed, studying the map of the center of Milano.

At 7:00 p.m., he was on the street, a tourist map in his back pocket. He took the metro from Centrale to Porta Romana. When he arrived, he rode the escalator up to Via Crema and walked two blocks, peering into retail windows, coffee shops, a trattoria, and a small bookstore. He entered a restaurant and asked for an outdoor table. He sat down and looked across the street at an eight-story apartment building with small trees and bushes on the roof.

He ordered a salad, pasta with ragù, and a bottle of Chianti. When the waiter brought the wine and poured a glass, Vasily took a long drink, finished the glass, and refilled it. Sipping his second glass, he surveyed the neighborhood. Middle-aged and younger couples strolled on their evening *passeggiata.* They appeared to be carefree, chatting and laughing, texting and talking on phones—not what you'd see on a Moscow street. They looked like people he'd like to know: well-dressed men wearing long-sleeved shirts, trim pants, and expensive shoes.

Several women, a few alone but more in pairs, carried Prada and Gucci purses. Earbuds in place, the women were oblivious to Vasily studying them.

He took out his phone and scrolled to a photo of Chiara's apartment. One photo revealed her walking on the arm of a young man, another of them returning in the evening. He scrolled through a series of photos of her leaving her apartment in the morning, walking to Porta Romana metro, exiting at the Duomo station, walking to Via Borgonuovo, and entering an office building.

More photos showed Chiara going about her daily routine, and two pictures showed her leaving on a Saturday morning, taking the metro to Centrale, and entering a restroom. But there were no shots of her leaving. Why not? No more pictures that day.

After eating his dinner and finishing the wine, Vasily left the restaurant and returned to his apartment, tired but excited. Over the next few days, his surveillance of Chiara would begin, early in the morning and late in the afternoon when she returned from her office. In between those hours, he could explore Milano, one area of the city after another. He would shop for clothes and an Italian phone, and he'd visit museums, art galleries, and historical landmarks.

His daily surveillance would note variations in Chiara's routine. On the weekend, he would pay close attention to where she ventured, hopefully leading him to her father.

He hoped it wouldn't be soon.

# CHAPTER SEVENTEEN

Vasily followed the same routine every day, leaving his apartment at 7:00 a.m., taking the metro to Porta Romana, and walking to a café on Via Crema a few doors from Chiara's apartment. She lived on a tree-lined street with cafés, retail shops, a news agent, a tobacco shop, a pharmacy, and a Vodafone outlet. It was a quiet neighborhood. Morning traffic was light, not like other streets into the city center.

On the first day of surveillance, Vasily sipped coffee at the café and waited for Chiara to leave her apartment for work. When he spotted her on the street, he let her walk ahead as he followed her to Porta Romana. Once she went down the steps to the metro, he kept his distance, entering the car behind her and watching when she exited at the Montenapoleone metro. He let several people get ahead of him. Then he exited and watched Chiara walk to an office building on Via Borgonuovo.

Each day, after she reached her office, Vasily had free time to explore center city. He walked along Via Manzoni toward Piazza Cavour or in the other direction to Piazza La Scala. He'd have a leisurely lunch and a half-bottle of wine, go window shopping, and stop in a Feltrinelli bookstore or a Davide Cenci store to buy Italian shirts and pants.

When he was not on surveillance, Vasily watched political news and soccer games on TV in a café or a trattoria.

He'd return at 5:30 each day to Via Borgonuovo and wait for Chiara to exit her office, usually after 6:00 p.m. Then he'd follow her to the Montenapoleone metro and back to her apartment.

The first week, he wanted to understand her evening activities. On the third night of his surveillance, he saw her leave her apartment at 8:00 p.m. with a man. He looked about five years older than Chiara. He was handsome, tall and thin, and wore tan slacks, leather shoes, and a light brown turtleneck. They strolled along Via Crema and entered a nearby trattoria. Vasily waited across the street, sitting on a bench at a bus stop. After having dinner, the couple returned to Chiara's apartment around 10:00 p.m. The gentleman remained.

During the first week of his surveillance, Vasily noted the details of Chiara's daily routine on a spreadsheet that he emailed to Lebedev. Vasily commented that Chiara's daily routine was the same. She had a lover, but Vasily didn't know if they lived together. She dressed well and occasionally met friends on the metro or approaching her office. But there was no sign of her mother or father. He surmised that they didn't live in Milano and that they possibly met on weekends.

On the first Saturday of his surveillance, Vasily returned to the café near the intersection of Viale Sabotino and Via Crema.

Around noon, Chiara exited with the handsome man he'd seen before. They spent the day shopping in bookstores and going to an art gallery, and then they took a tram to the Navigli for dinner with friends. They returned to her apartment about midnight.

On Sunday afternoon, Chiara went out for a few hours without her lover. She had lunch with a woman friend, attended a movie at Cinema Orfeo, and shopped for food at a local market.

In the evenings, Vasily watched TV, flipping through channels offering schmaltzy romantic movies, talk shows, and quiz shows with voluptuous, scantily clad young women with long, flowing hair, short dresses, and high heels. His favorite channel was Rai 1, which showed Salvo Montalbano mysteries. Vasily was intrigued by the handsome actor who played the *commissario*, investigated murders, and met sexy Sicilian women. Vasily chuckled at episodes where Montalbano's lover, a beautiful blonde from Genoa, flew to Sicily for romantic weekends during which they indulged in a steamy love affair.

He wanted to learn more Italian, so he started reading *Corriere della Sera, La Repubblica,* and *Il Sole 24 Ore.* He also consulted an Italian dictionary and phrase book to improve his vocabulary. He would spend an hour reading one article, learning the vocabulary used by journalists, which was challenging since his tutor had taught him mostly basic conversation.

He would flip through the newspapers, scanning headlines about news from around Italia, Europe, and occasionally the U.S. and reading movie and TV schedules. The last pages of most newspapers reported on sports, mainly football, which he enjoyed. While reading, he'd underline words or phrases he didn't understand and then use his dictionary to improve his moderate level of reading comprehension.

Italian politics intrigued him, especially squabbles among Beppe Grillo's Five Star movement, Matteo Salvini's nationalist Lega Party, and the Democratic Party's Paolo Gentiloni. He learned that Grillo had been a comedian and attracted attention with attacks on government incompetence and widespread corruption among all politicians. Salvini ranted about African refugees arriving in Sicily seeking sanctuary; he claimed they were polluting the country's culture.

Italian editorials expressed criticism of politicians, so different from Russia, where the media toed the Kremlin's line on TV and radio as well as in newspapers, lavishing praise on Putin. Vasily had become so bored with Russian media that he only scanned headlines, knowing the conclusion of articles and editorials. Always the same: Support Putin. Don't agitate or demonstrate. Those who did ended up in jail.

But in Italy, politics was a free-for-all, with everyone throwing mud balls and debating political issues as if speeches and essays could change opinions. Vasily knew you could rarely change anyone's opinion. He had friends who despised everything Putin and the oligarchs did, but Vasily didn't engage them, valuing the relationships too much to ruin them with arguments.

By the end of the first week, Vasily was enamored with all he had observed and experienced in Milano. He looked forward to what was to come.

In his second week, he changed coffee shops for better logistics to be closer to the Porta Romana metro. From the coffee bar, he could watch Chiara walking from her apartment. He'd leave the café, walk ahead to Porta Romana, and descend to the train. When the train arrived in the station, Chiara always entered a middle car. Vasily waited at either end, getting in the first or last car and exiting as soon as the metro reached Chiara's station at Montenapoleone. He'd hurry up the stairs, mingling with crowds without looking back, knowing she was following behind.

He knew that if she had noticed him following behind, she might become wary. But if he was ahead of her, not following, she was unlikely to become suspicious. In the future, he would try new tactics, such as waiting for her to arrive at Porta Romana metro and then following her. If her routine continued to vary little, he might even position himself near her work and see what time she arrived. Varying surveillance was something he had taught GRU recruits, but only if the person's routine varied little.

By the end of the second week, Vasily was enjoying the new café. He would find an open space at the bar and watch to see when Chiara was on the street. He sipped a cappuccino or an espresso, eyeing caffeine-craving customers who entered for their morning fix, tossed back an espresso, and then went on their way. Vasily sipped until there was only a film of brown foam at the bottom of his cup, and he was always ready to exit and begin his daily surveillance.

He studied the café's customers, many of whom came in at the same time every morning. One morning, a woman entered the café alone. She stood out in the crowd of men who looked anxious on their way to work, thinking about the hassles they would face. The woman didn't look hassled; she looked relaxed, with a smile on her attractive face. Vasily guessed that she was probably in her mid- to late thirties.

She was shapely and stylish, not like a model or a movie star, but someone with poise and confidence. She dressed like she was about to go to a gym or a yoga class, wearing tan linen slacks over her long legs and attractive rear. Her yellow and blue cotton pullover revealed a long, sleek neck and modest cleavage. Her open-toed sandals looked expensive, as did her Prada purse. She liked jewelry: a necklace with strands of silver shaped like coins, bracelets on one wrist, an Apple watch on the other, and rings on two long fingers. Her hands looked like they were sculpted in white marble.

A customer next to Vasily left the bar, leaving a space where the woman eased in without looking at him. She raised a ringed finger to the barista, who greeted her: "*Ciao,* Betta. Cappuccino coming up."

In the mirror above the bar, Vasily glanced at the woman, whose back was to him. She carried herself in a self-assured manner, her marble white hand on her purse on the bar.

Vasily sipped his cappuccino, wanting time to slow so he could study the woman, whom several men in the café had noticed. After the barista set the saucer, tiny cup, spoon, and napkin in front of her, she sipped, set the cup on the saucer, and reached into her purse for her phone. Her purse tipped, knocking over her cup, spilling coffee onto his wrist, and staining his cuff.

"*Scusi! Mi dispiace!*" she cried out. She grabbed her napkin and dabbed at his stained shirt cuff. "Sorry. Sorry. Excuse me." Her pale cheeks blushed pink.

Vasily said in Italian, "Don't worry, it's only coffee. Wine will stain, but coffee washes out." He got the barista's attention and pointed to the woman's spilled cup. "Another for the lady," he said.

The woman grumbled a muted curse, "*Accidenti!*" as she dabbed his stained cuff and wiped up the spilled coffee. "Damn, what a stupid thing. Clumsy as an ox!"

Vasily's heart skipped a beat as he felt her long fingers rubbing his wrist, her other hand firmly around his forearm. "It's okay. Don't worry," he said. His eyes were inches from her forehead, and he could smell the shampoo she had used that morning, or perhaps a subtle perfume. Flowery, not citrus or heavy.

Other men in the café snickered, watching the mini-drama at the end of the bar, envious that Vasily was getting the woman's attention. In a low voice, one of them said, "Wish that was me, not that new guy."

When the barista brought her a fresh cappuccino, Vasily pushed a ten-euro note toward him while the woman fumbled in her purse for her wallet. "No, no, let me buy," he said as she grabbed another napkin, continuing to wipe up the spill on the bar.

"But I soiled your shirt!" she protested. "I should buy for you."

"Don't worry. It will wash out." Their eyes locked for an instant, hers dark, intense. They both looked away. Vasily's heart was pounding; something about her beauty and sultry voice aroused him. Her long fingers had touched him. The first Italian woman who had. He didn't know how to respond. He looked in the mirror above the bar and saw that she was looking at him.

He smiled. She smiled back. "I haven't seen you here before…" she said, her voice trailing off.

"No, that's true. I haven't been in Milano very long," he said.

"Yes, I thought you were new here," she said, picking up her fresh cup, taking a sip, and setting the cup back on the saucer. "I don't come here every morning, but I recognize most of the men. I've talked to a few of them before. They mostly work in finance, engineering, and media."

"Interesting. How about you?" he said, and then realized the question was too direct. He hoped he hadn't offended her.

"I work a few blocks away, but I stop here if I have time."

He smiled and nodded. He wasn't going to ask where or what her profession was. They both sipped their beverages, not looking at each other. She picked up her purse and said, "See you later. Late for work. I'll buy tomorrow." Her voice was almost a purr.

"I'll be here," Vasily replied, excited that they might talk more the next morning.

She walked out the open door, turned, waved at him with her long fingers, and disappeared. Only a few minutes had passed with her at the bar next to him, but it seemed longer. Intense. He felt exhilarated and full of energy, but not from the caffeine. Her brief appearance, her fingers rubbing his shirt, and her intense eyes had aroused him. He reached for his cup, his fingers shaking.

One man at the end of the bar smiled at Vasily in the way men do when a woman is involved.

The next morning, Vasily was standing in the same place when she walked into the café. He raised a hand and motioned to her. She walked over, setting her purse on the floor this time, not the bar.

"*Buongiorno*. You again, from yesterday," she said. "Let me buy you a cappuccino."

"No need, I'm finished," he said, pointing to his drained cup.

"Then get another," she said, raising two fingers at the barista. "One more for this gentleman. I'm buying."

She took out a ten-euro note and pushed it forward on the bar. "Like I said yesterday, you're new here."

"I just got into town recently."

"From where? You're not Italian. Is that a German accent? I'm not good at guessing where people are from."

He shrugged. "It doesn't make any difference, does it?"

The barista arrived with their cappuccinos. She picked hers up and sipped, not looking at Vasily. "I guess not, as long as you speak Italian. Why visit Italy if you can't speak a word of Italian?"

"Yes, such people miss so much. Italian is a beautiful language."

She finished in two gulps and picked up her purse. "Sorry, no time to talk. Have to go. Late for work. Let's talk more tomorrow."

He bowed slightly. "I'll be here. Have a pleasant day."

She didn't reappear the next day. Vasily hoped that their brief exchanges had not made her wary of him. Women were cautious of men who seemed aggressive. He didn't think he had come across that way.

The following morning, she walked in, looked down the crowded bar, and walked toward him, motioning to the barista.

"Sorry I didn't make it yesterday. Got up late. Had coffee at work."

He nodded and looked at her. A pale blue and white scarf covered the lower part of her long neck and cleavage. "Nice to see you," Vasily said, not wanting to be too direct or ask a question.

She turned to look at him. Those intense eyes again. He held his breath. "Where are you from?" she asked in a low voice. "Your Italian is good, but with an accent. From where?"

"Russia."

"Really?" She said with surprise. "I don't know any Russians. Are you here for business?"

He shook his head. "Just a tourist."

"What is life like in Russia? I don't know much about your country."

"You should go sometime. We have beautiful Orthodox churches, museums, the Kremlin, lots of shopping centers, and all types of ethnic restaurants."

"Italian restaurants?"

"Oh, yes, and they're very popular."

"Everyone loves Italian food." She paused. "So you're just here on a vacation?"

"Yes. I came to Milano many years ago and wanted to return. I was too young then to experience all the history and culture. I have been reading some travel books and exploring the sights...and enjoying the excellent food."

"Where have you been so far?"

"The Duomo, of course, the Castello, and the Brera museum."

"Don't miss La Scala's museum. They have costumes from famous operas—*Tosca, Aida, La Bohème* —and portraits of famous ballet dancers."

"Nureyev danced at La Scala."

She blinked as if surprised by his comment. "Why, yes. How did you know?"

"I'm from St. Petersburg. My mother worked backstage at the Kirov Ballet. I saw movies of his performances growing up. But, of course, no one talked about Nureyev after he defected to Paris and didn't return to Russia."

"So I've heard. He died some time ago, didn't he? He was gay and died of AIDS or something. Is that right?"

"He died in Paris, only fifty-four years old. My mother enrolled me in ballet classes when I was a boy. She said I could be the next Nureyev."

The woman laughed. "Really? Did you like it?"

Vasily smiled, enjoying the casual exchange with the first Italian who had shown any interest in him. "I liked football better. Ballet was hard work! Professional ballet dancers make it look easy as they float in the air and land perfectly with every leap. What audiences don't appreciate is how athletic you have to be to dance professionally. You could match a soccer player against a professional ballet dancer, and guess who would be the better athlete?"

"The ballet dancer?"

"I'm almost sure of it. They need to be slim and must have physical stamina, muscular development over all the body, and quick reactions. Some ballets are three hours long, and the stars are onstage in most of the scenes. You can't do that unless you're in extremely good physical condition."

She looked at Vasily with a bemused expression and then at her watch. "I should go. I have an appointment. Sorry. If you're here tomorrow, maybe we can talk more. You're interesting, not the kind of Russian you bump into on the streets here. They usually look rough, talk loudly, and don't speak Italian. And they walk on the street like they own it."

"Elisabetta's your name? A royal name, Queen of England."

She laughed. "No royal blood in our family, although my mother admired Queen Elizabeth. She bought a poster of her coronation when she was in London on vacation. She told friends she wanted to name her first daughter after her."

She reached out and offered her hand. "My friends call me Betta. What's your name?"

He shook her hand. "Vasily. My parents named me after an uncle killed in World War II. He died on the Eastern Front fighting the Nazis."

Betta frowned, the wrinkles on her forehead making her look angry. "War. I hate war," she said, her voice becoming almost shrill. "It's so barbaric. And it's always men, old men who send young men—mostly boys—to settle ridiculous political grievances. Why can't they do what women do: sit down, talk about the issues, argue, debate, and come up with a compromise, rather than grab guns and send boys they've never met to die for nothing? It makes me furious!"

Betta's opinion was startling. He'd never heard a woman speak so passionately against war. And politicians. She was right. It was always men who caused wars.

"You're right. World history is about men starting and fighting in wars."

"Especially in Europe," she said, holding up her hand. "You've got Kaiser Wilhelm starting World War I. Then Hitler, Stalin, and Hirohito in World War II, Lyndon Johnson in Vietnam, George Bush and Tony Blair in Iraq and Afghanistan, and your President Putin in Crimea, Chechnya, and now Syria."

Vasily was stunned. Her fury was impressive. He didn't know what to say. He couldn't argue, and he didn't want to. And he had been sent to Italy by orders from Putin.

Betta continued, "And who's left behind to heal the sick and wounded when they return from war? Women! I see it almost every day. It makes me sick."

Vasily was uncertain how to respond. "Really?" he mumbled. "Tell me more."

Betta's eyes were ablaze. "I work for a pharmaceutical firm, but I volunteer at a nonprofit clinic that provides free medical care to refugees and homeless."

He nodded. "I see them on the streets, holding cups for people to drop coins in. Very sad."

She made a fist. "So true. We're treating a poor boy who lost a leg when he was run over by a truck. He'll never walk again. Even his other foot and ankle were terribly mangled, like ground-up sausage. I'd like to find the man who drove the truck and didn't take him to a hospital. This poor boy will need medical care for years. His family are refugees from Libya who landed in Sicily. The father can't get a work permit and doesn't speak Italian. They need help desperately. That's what we do: help those in greatest need."

Her passion was persuasive. Most women he knew just shrugged and shook their heads if the topic of refugees came up. But not Elisabetta. "It's good you're doing something you believe in." Regrettably, he couldn't say the same thing about his reason for being in Italy.

"Come to our clinic sometime, Vasily. I'll show you around."

He raised his eyebrows, surprised at her invitation. He stammered, "Yes, I'd—I'd like to come."

"What are you doing tomorrow?"

Betta was determined and passionate about a cause, an experience that was new to him. "Ahhh, what do you mean?"

"Our staff is getting together for *aperitivo* tomorrow after work to plan a fundraising event. Come. Meet my colleagues. Have a drink."

"Are you sure? You barely know me," he fumbled, feeling suddenly awkward. In Russia, men invited women, not the other way around. Italy was so different from Russia. He liked it.

"Do you know Porta Ticinese, with the old Roman columns? It's near the Navigli."

"No, but I can find it. I have maps."

She opened her purse and poured onto the bar a bunch of crumpled papers and a pen. She scribbled on the back of a receipt. "Here's the address of the bar and my phone number. Seven tomorrow night. I'll tell my colleagues about you. They'd like to meet a Russian who speaks Italian. They're good people, politically progressive, committed to nonviolence and helping the needy. And they like to have fun. Why don't you give me your phone number?" She handed him her pen and a piece of paper.

Again, her forwardness. Such a pleasant and easy manner. He wrote the number of his Italian phone and pushed it toward her. She stuffed it into her purse without looking at it.

"Gotta run. See you tomorrow for *aperitivo*."

Then, with another wave of her long fingers, she was out the door and gone. Vasily was stunned, holding the crumpled receipt with the name of a bar and her phone number. He took out his phone, added her first name and number, the first in his Italian phone. He'd look up the address of the bar and go. He'd meet her friends and learn more about her and the clinic where she volunteered.

He'd been in Milano for two weeks. An Italian woman, beautiful, smart, and confident, had invited him to a social event. Nothing like this had happened to him in Russia.

He put the receipt with the address and her phone number into his shirt pocket and looked outside. He had been so distracted that he nearly missed Chiara walking past the coffee shop. He hurried out, letting her walk ahead to the metro stop. He'd follow her, not be ahead of her this time.

As Vasily scrambled to catch up, he replayed in his mind the previous five minutes. Betta's personality and manner had impressed him. He wanted to know more about her. What kind of woman was she? One thing he knew for sure: He wanted to see her again.

# CHAPTER EIGHTEEN

W hen Simona got home from work, she opened her apartment door gently, expecting that Armando Bongiovanni was working. Armando was a well-known symphony conductor, and he was preparing for a concert in Seattle in a few weeks.

She walked quietly down the hallway and looked into the kitchen, where he was seated with his back to her. His arms were raised, making modest conducting gestures with a baton. Over his shoulder, she could see the score to Bartók's Symphony in E-flat major on a small stand on the kitchen table.

She stood there in silence, not wanting to disturb him, smiling as he hummed. His hands and arms motioned to his left, then his right, as he pointed his baton at imaginary sections of violins, basses, and cellos onstage.

Armando's mind was always on his music. He often hummed when they took walks, making small gestures with his fingers and hands by his side. Often she would slow down and let him go ahead a few steps, enjoying how absorbed he was in his music world.

The first time this had happened, she'd asked him, "*Amore*, you're walking with me…it's a beautiful day. We were talking, and when we stopped, you walked ahead of me and started doing this," she'd said, mimicking his hand gestures.

He laughed and wrapped his arms around her. "You're right, Simo. I'm daydreaming, working on a passage that I enjoy conducting."

"I like it. But can we continue walking and maybe talk to each other? Join me back on Earth."

They continued walking, now hand in hand, talking about a vacation they were going to take to Lago Maggiore that weekend. When they left the park, they walked across the street, entering a café to order coffee. When their cups and saucers were placed on a tray, Armando took it outside to a table in the shade of an awning.

Simona was curious, still intrigued by his gestures as they walked. "I've seen you do those little gestures before. It's like you're in another world, on a journey far away."

He grinned, reached across, and squeezed her hand. "You know my little secret."

"Do you say that to make the ladies swoon?" she teased.

He laughed. "Oh, now, only you, whom I trust."

She wrinkled her brow, narrowing her eyes. "Really? I guess I should be flattered."

"I didn't say it to flatter you, only to let you know what goes on in my mind when I'm at the podium. Most conductors won't say what they're thinking when they're conducting. They only talk about music, chords, and melodies. For me, instruments are like chariots lifting the audience—"

"—to another galaxy?" she had said, sipping her coffee.

Their eyes locked, and his eyes widened. "Why did you say that…'galaxy'?"

"Tell me more. I like this conversation. I'm learning more about you."

He nodded. "Very well. I like this conversation, too. But I don't want it to be only about me. I want to know more about you."

"For now, I'm imagining how your mind works when you're conducting. Has it always been this way, when you first knew your life was going to be about music?"

"Since about the time I was ten."

"How did you know?"

"This is going to sound silly, but when I was that age, my father, who played a violin with the Rome Symphony, took my brother and me to see the first *Star Wars* movie."

"This is about *Star Wars*?"

"Yes, it is. You know the movie?"

"Of course. I loved it. Han and Leia, zooming around galaxies in the starship."

"The *Millennium Falcon*. Exactly. And you remember the score, written by John Williams, who composed many film scores?"

"It was fantastic. Lots of soaring themes. It was memorable, like Richard Strauss's 'Zarathustra' at the beginning of *2001, A Space Odyssey*."

"There you have it. I was in the theater with my father and older brother. The movie opens, the orchestra plays the overture, and the prologue crawls up the screen: "*In a galaxy far, far away...*" From that moment, I wanted to do something that had such a powerful impact on me. Music was my choice. And when I hear stirring music like symphonies, it takes me—like *Star Wars*—to distant galaxies."

Simona leaned back in her chair, transfixed by what Armando had shared with her about his youthful experience and his art. The men in her past had never touched her with moments like this. Rather, they droned on about sports, politics, business, and physical exercise, all of which she found boring. How could a woman live with a man who droned on about such trivial topics every morning or while having a drink or dinner? Her brain would freeze.

"That's a lot to think about," she said. For the first time in Simona's life, a man had touched a place in her heart that craved a deep connection. She admitted to herself that she was falling madly in love with Armando, a man who could express intimate thoughts that had nothing to do with sex. That would come later.

She knew Armando was in one of those galaxies as she watched him at her kitchen table, his head, arms, and shoulders moving as if he were actually conducting. She would never disturb him when he was on one of those journeys. She backed out of the doorway and went into her bedroom. Dropping her purse on the bed, she sat down to take off her shoes. She rubbed her feet, eventually falling back on the bed, closing her eyes and listening to Armando humming in the kitchen. She dozed off but awakened when the humming ceased.

She got up, brushed back her hair, and walked into the kitchen as he put down his baton. When he saw her, his eyes lit up. "Simo! Wonderful to see you. I'm glad you're home. How was your day?"

She leaned over and kissed him on the cheek. "I was watching you when I came in. You were so absorbed in rehearsal."

Armando blushed. "Sorry, I didn't see you come in. When did you get here?"

"Just a few minutes ago. I was tired and rested a bit."

"How was work today?"

She grimaced and went to the refrigerator to take out a bottle of sparkling water. "I've mentioned before that we have a challenging assignment at DIGOS."

"Can you tell me about it?"

She pouted. "Sorry, I can't. It's about that time we went to Como—" she stopped, not wanting to mention a possible assassination threat from Russia. She sipped her water. "I'm thirsty. It's been a long day. Let's find something else to talk about. When do you leave for Seattle?"

"Three weeks from tomorrow. I have a meeting with the production director at La Scala on Friday about next season's *La Cenerentola,* and after that an appointment with a student conductor I'm mentoring."

Simona sat down at the kitchen table and reached out for Armando's hand. "I have an appointment next week with my doctor." She paused, anticipating how he would respond to what she was about to say.

"Is it a routine appointment?" he asked, a hint of worry in his voice.

"Armando…I think I'm pregnant. I bought a pregnancy test today. I'll take it tonight."

He gasped. *"Mio Dio*! That's wonderful!" He stood up and wrapped her in a warm embrace.

Simona was surprised but happy with his rapid response. "Are you sure?"

"Of course! I'm happy that we're going to be parents."

"That's *if* the pregnancy test is positive...which I'm pretty sure it will be. I've missed two cycles."

"I hope it is. I really do," he said with a warm smile. He kissed her. A lingering kiss.

When she pulled back, she looked into his eyes. "So, are we going to get married?"

"Yes, of course we're going to get married! We're going to be parents. Aren't you thrilled?"

She reached for his hands and squeezed them, feeling as if she was about to cry. "I am," she said softly, "but I feel a bit anxious, too. All the changes a baby would bring in my professional life, my family...and us."

"Don't worry about us. We're in love. We'll have a child. Your parents will be thrilled! When will you tell them?"

"To be honest, that upsets me some."

"Why?" he said in disbelief.

"We're not married, and that's an issue for them. They're old-fashioned, devout Catholics, and they believe a couple should get married before they have a child. And they have to have a home to bring the child to."

"We have your apartment," he said, gesturing around the kitchen.

"Here? This is a shoebox. Where is the baby's room?"

"Wherever we want it, *amore*."

"There's no room," she insisted. "My apartment is for a single person, like when I rented it before I met you. We need something bigger—at least two bedrooms, a study, and a place for the baby to play. Look at you, rehearsing at the kitchen table next to the stove and refrigerator. You're not a student; you're a principal conductor at the Seattle Symphony. You need your own room to work, rehearse, have musicians over. But your books, music, and computer are in our tiny bedroom, your clothes stuffed in suitcases. Mine are jammed in my *armadio* or back in Bergamo. Since you moved in, it's like we're living in a closet."

"I know, but we're usually out all day, with you at work and me rehearsing or meeting musicians."

"But when we come home, all we have is a long hallway that leads to this small kitchen, the bathroom, a tiny closet, and our bedroom. We have suitcases and boxes in the hallway. I almost trip over them when I get home."

"Of course, we'll get a new apartment. That's easy," he said. "He—or she—will need their own room with toys, books, and pillows, and a play room when their little friends come over."

"Would you want a boy?"

"I'd love it. And we could start him—or her—to learn to play the piano. The younger children start, the more likely they'll have an ongoing interest in music."

Simona laughed and rustled her hand through his hair. "Listen to you. We don't even know if I'm pregnant, and you're already turning him—or her—into a musician. That's sweet."

"We'll start looking for a new apartment, next week, even."

"But you'll be traveling this summer—Seattle, Berlin, Copenhagen. I can't remember how many other places you have to go this fall."

"I'm reviewing offers to perform through next May. Summer isn't so busy, but I will be on the road a lot."

"But if you're going to be a father, how will you manage living away from her? Or him?" she said with a laugh.

His blue eyes sparkled, his grin showing perfect white teeth. "I'll manage. I'll bet you want a girl, a baby daughter. You'll be such a good mamma." He paused. "Boy, girl. Him, her. It doesn't matter."

"That's cute," Simona said with a smile. "I like that: him, her. Say that fast."

"Himher. Sounds like a German name." They both laughed. "What about names? Have you thought of any?" he asked.

"Way too early. First things first. I need to know if I am pregnant. I'll do the pregnancy test tonight, and if it's positive, my gynecologist can confirm it."

"And when we can expect to see our Himher? I'll bet it will be in January."

"You think so? Why?"

He paused, counting back in his head. "No, January. I'll bet it's January."

"Yes? Why?"

He grinned. "Where were we in April?"

She rolled her eyes, smiling as she recalled a memory. "April, our week in Majorca. You were very…affectionate," she said, patting his cheek.

He spread his arms, smiling. "Do you blame me? We were on the beach, you in your bikini, sipping Campari, asking me to put sunscreen on your back and legs. I was very aroused. That bikini was like a handkerchief."

"I bought it just for you," she said, running her fingers through his hair again.

"And how many times did I compliment you? Ten? Twenty?"

"Well, it was more than that little bikini, remember?"

"Yes, sleeping late every morning, and then…" he grinned.

"Not wearing clothes in our hotel room."

"Naked as birds."

"Birds and bees. Isn't that what it's all about?"

They embraced, kissed, and held each other tightly. He squeezed her and said, "*Amore*, will you marry me?"

She pulled back, a startled look on her face. "You're proposing? In our kitchen? After I tell you I think I'm pregnant?"

"Yes, yes, and yes," he said with a smile and a nod.

"Well," she teased, "let me think about it. How about you come up with a more romantic place for your proposal."

"Where would you like?"

She smiled, moving closer to him. "That's your choice. Men are supposed to think of the place before popping the question. Surprise me."

"Hmm, let me think about it."

"The clock's not running. We have some time before we have to tell everyone I'm pregnant. And then there's the wedding. My girlfriends will all want to know how and when you proposed. I don't want to disappoint them. Think of something we'll remember the rest of our lives."

Armando smiled. "I have my assignment. It'll be fun to think up a memorable place to propose.

"Enough of this mush. I'm hungry. What are we going to have for dinner?"

"Let's go out and celebrate. Our lives are going to change soon. I'm so excited!"

"Yeah, let's go out. There's no food in the refrigerator that I want to eat."

"When will you tell them at work? If the test is positive, that is."

"Something else I need to think about."

"Why?"

"I've told you before, the *Questura* is mostly men. Only about 15 percent are women, except for secretaries and admin types."

"You'll have to tell them, and soon, if it's true. You're thin and you'll start to show in a few weeks," he said, patting her stomach.

She put her hands over his. "I'll start showing in a month or two, if it's true."

"You'll look beautiful. A woman about to have a baby, her first child."

She wrinkled her brow and frowned. "I'm nervous about how I'll look with a big belly, like I'm carrying a watermelon."

They both laughed, enjoying their special moment. "My soon-to-be watermelon wife," he said, patting her stomach again.

"Oh, please, I never thought of myself as a fruit."

"A flower, maybe," he teased.

"You. You always have funny suggestions. Frankly, I've never thought about being either a fruit or a flower."

"Just a beautiful, intelligent woman."

"That will do."

"I'm thinking. When will we tell everyone?"

"Let's wait. First, the pregnancy test. Then my appointment with my gynecologist. Too much to think about. It makes me nervous when I think about how I'm going to tell Antonella. We're pretty close. She's a great boss."

CHAPTER NINETEEN

V asily took a tram to the Navigli and then walked down
the Quartiere Ticinese, a new area for him. As he waited
for a traffic light to turn, he looked ahead through a stone arch-
way with a portico at what looked like a blockhouse, possibly
an entry gate to Milano from earlier times. A narrow one-way
street passed under the arch and turned slightly, leading to a
row of marble columns in front of a piazza.

He had read in the Milano guidebook that these were fifth-
century Roman columns. How could they have survived centuries of commercial development and rebuilding after American
bombers had devastated much of Milano in 1943?

Vasily's emotions were torn between excitement and anxiety
about seeing Elisabetta again and meeting her friends in a social
setting. She had said his Italian was good, but so often he would
overhear people on the street or in restaurants talking so fast
he could barely understand more than a few words. However,

conversations with Betta were easier, more natural, just two people talking, asking questions and answering, not long monologues. Except when she had talked about hating war. He agreed with her; wars led to miseries that lasted lifetimes.

He walked past the Roman columns, admiring them, and across the piazza. He stopped to read a sign that identified the San Lorenzo church. In front, on a pedestal, he gazed at a religious statue that appeared as ancient as the columns. In most areas of Milano where he had walked, the city seemed bustling with modern architecture, high-rise apartments, and arcades with expensive retail outlets. But here was a landmark of Italian history from the fourth century, preserved in a modern city.

At the end of the piazza, Vasily stepped down into a narrow, busy street of trattorias, cafés, tobacco shops, a TIM phone store, a bakery, and a bookstore. In the early evening, the street was bustling with music and the laughter of crowds enjoying themselves, seated outside trattorias and cafés, drinking wine or coffee and chatting with friends.

As he slowly walked down the street, marveling at the evening socializing, he noticed a woman at an outdoor trattoria stand up and wave. Elisabetta. He waved back and picked up his pace toward the trattoria, his stomach churning with anticipation of what was ahead. He'd be meeting associates of a woman he barely knew. Another surprise that delighted him.

Betta approached him in the cobblestone street, smiled, and leaned up to give him quick pecks on his cheeks. "Thanks for coming, Vasily. My friends are looking forward to meeting you."

She took his hand and led him to a table where her friends were gathered. She motioned to an empty chair next to hers.

Before he sat down, Vasily was greeted with a hearty chorus of *"Ciao…Benvenuto…Piacere di conoscerti."*

He nodded and smiled nervously. *"Ciao, a tutti.* Thanks for inviting me."

Betta placed a hand on his arm and introduced him. "This is my new Russian friend, Vasily, whom I told you about. Vasily, meet my friends and colleagues," she said as she gestured around the table. "This is Mario…Beppe…Giovanni…Marco…Maria…Ludovica…Stefano."

They all smiled, greeting him warmly and raising their hands as she called out their names. They looked relaxed after enjoying wine from the three bottles on the table, as well as cheeses, olives, prosciutto, focaccia bread, open sandwiches, and crudités.

Betta's friends resembled the well-dressed Milanese he had seen when he'd followed Chiara and later strolled about the city. Some were as young as their twenties, others slightly older, and one couple looked to be in their fifties. All had wineglasses in front of them and cell phones on the table.

"Here, next to me," Elisabetta said, touching his arm as he sat down. On his left, a young man who looked like a teenager but was probably in his early twenties said, "Ciao, Vasily. My name is Stefano," and reached to shake his hand. "Welcome to Milano. How long will you be visiting?"

"A month, may—maybe a little longer," he stammered, pleased that he was comfortable enough to speak Italian to strangers.

"Where are you from, Vasily?" asked an attractive woman about thirty sitting across the table. Was she Maria, or Ludovica? Betta's introductions had happened so fast that he couldn't place names with faces.

"St. Petersburg," he answered.

"St. Petersburg! I've been there. Such a beautiful city," she said. "I loved the Hermitage. We spent a whole day there. Saw the czar's apartment, the coronation room, and enormous halls where they held balls. There was so much gold and so many chandeliers and long spiral stairs. Those Romanovs lived well."

The man who looked to be in his fifties quipped, "Until they were assassinated by the Bolsheviks. The whole family, even the children."

Stefano said with a grimace, "That's right. All murdered and tossed in a well or something."

"Hey," the woman who had brought up the Hermitage said. "Don't say things like that. Be respectful of our Russian friend." She turned to Vasily. "I'm sure you've been to the Hermitage often."

"Oh, yes," he responded. "It's an amazing place. So much history happened there. It was actually called the Winter Palace before it became the Hermitage, a museum."

The others peppered him with questions.

"Are you working, or on vacation?"

"What do you like about Milano?"

"Where did you learn to speak Italian?"

"What are your favorite Italian foods?"

One by one, he answered their questions, not using their names, which he couldn't remember from Betta's quick introductions. He felt that her friends were genuinely pleased that he had come. After he responded to everyone's questions, the others resumed their conversations with each other and discussed why they had gathered. As Betta had told him, this was a planning meeting for a fundraiser for the clinic. Each person told Betta how many people he or she had invited and how much they hoped to receive in contributions.

While they talked, Vasily took some bread and forked a few slices of cheese onto a small plate.

"Wait a minute. Vasily needs some wine," Betta said, touching his arm. "Gavi, Prosecco, or Gutturnio?" she asked, pointing at the bottles.

"Prosecco, please."

Betta reached for the bottle, poured a full glass for him, and continued talking to her associates about the fundraiser. She took notes on a piece of paper she had taken out of her purse and tallied how many guests would be coming. She urged everyone to invite more people so they could meet their goal of raising 10,000 euros.

When business was concluded, the group settled back, socializing with each other. Vasily watched, impressed with how friendly they all seemed. No arguing, no drama, no sarcasm. Just people enjoying the company of friends.

A waiter brought two more wine bottles and *aperitivo* platters as the group's conversation became more animated, with much laughing and teasing. Vasily sipped his wine and nibbled on cheeses and meats as a cool breeze and evening shadows darkened the piazza and the cobblestone street. After an hour, people started excusing themselves, waving goodbye and saying, *"Buonanotte…a domani…grazie,"* along with streams of *"Ciao, ciao, ciao."*

Betta touched Vasily's arm. "I've got to run soon, Vasily. I have to get home to take my dog for a walk. How are you getting back to your apartment?"

"I took a tram to the Navigli and walked here."

"I'm headed the other way—sorry. Will we have coffee in the morning?"

"I hope so."

"Good. We can chat more then. Can you come to the fundraiser on Saturday night at the Galleria d'Arte Orizzonti? The people who support our cause are left-wing progressives and environmentalists who are sympathetic to the plight of refugees and migrants."

Vasily balked, as Saturdays and Sundays were for tailing Chiara, who he suspected met her parents sometimes on weekends. "Aah, sorry. I—I don't think so," he stammered. "I have plans."

Betta winked. "A date with a pretty Italian woman?"

He was stunned by such a direct, brazen question. Was she hinting she would like to see him socially? It didn't seem like she was being blunt, just friendly.

"No, a friend is in town. I'm taking him on a tour."

"You could bring him to our fundraiser."

His heart skipped a beat. "Well, I don't know. Could I call you?"

"Sure. Don't worry, Vasily. You don't have to contribute money. I thought you might like to meet some more of my friends. We expect maybe fifty people—a few artists, professors, teachers, and politically active types who support the clinic."

"I'm impressed that you have so many people helping your cause."

Betta gestured with her hands as if she were being modest. "Those are the only people I consider friends: socially conscious people motivated to help those in need. There is so much trouble in the world and so much suffering among refugees, homeless, poor, uneducated. It's terrible. So much misery. We just want to do what we can to ease their hardships."

Vasily wanted to reach over and touch her arm, a gesture that seemed so natural for her. But he resisted. He didn't want to do anything that might push her away. He liked Betta very much and didn't want to risk even the slightest comment or move that she might misinterpret. Instead, he just smiled in a way that he hoped she recognized as sincere. "I admire you, Betta. You're such a good person. The world needs more people like you and your friends to help the impoverished."

She leaned over, stretching to peck him on the cheek. "Thanks, Vasily. You're very kind." He waited for her to make the next move. "But I've gotta run. My poor dog is probably peeing on the floor while I'm sitting here drinking wine with friends." She laughed. "He's used to it, though. Do you have a pet back in St. Petersburg?"

*No,* he thought. *Just a bitter ex-wife, an ailing mother, a son going through teenage turbulence, and a former girlfriend who had abandoned him and was probably with another man now.* And, of course, he didn't live in St. Petersburg, but in Moscow, which he hadn't told her. There was so much he had to keep from her, especially his reason for being in Italy: a mission to kill someone.

"Aah, no, I don't. I travel and I work late. I don't want to have to ask friends to take care of a cat or a dog. Maybe in the future."

"Pets are good for people. They make us happy and fulfilled. They love us unconditionally. They just want to be fed, taken for walks, and given a warm place to sleep." She laughed. "Like humans."

She got up and walked into the street, turning to face him as he stood by the table. She rolled her fingers in her departing wave and then strolled down the street, which was congested with people out for the evening. As Vasily made his way into the narrow street, he watched Betta as she caught up with two of her women friends. They walked together, talking and laughing, so comfortable and close. He was envious. He felt alone—a familiar experience.

It was dusk, and streetlights were on. Many people were on a *passeggiata*, out for dinner or meeting friends. As Vasily walked back along Corso di Porta Ticinese toward the Navigli, his mood soured. He felt depressed by the double life he was leading. An attractive, confident Italian woman was showing him a life of dedication to help the poor and ill.

How long could he keep this up, pretending to be on vacation but actually on a deadly mission? Should he change coffee shops so he wouldn't see Betta again? No, he needed to see her and talk to her. She made him feel almost normal, accepting him without knowing his true reason for being in Milano. How long could he continue to face her and answer her direct and probing questions? On previous GRU assignments, he had traveled with documents that hadn't revealed his true identity.

As he walked, watching people enjoying the company of friends or lovers, he felt so envious of their carefree happiness. He went down the list of people in his life. How few people really knew him, what he thought, his dreams, fears, and joys. His ex-wife despised him, his son avoided him, and Katya had left him. His profession required him to conceal many of his activities. After years of dangerous assignments, he wondered who he really was. He was traveling with a Polish passport, not a Russian one. Another lie to cover up the truth: He was a forty-five-year-old man who killed enemies of the Kremlin.

He knew who he was: a lonely assassin.

CHAPTER TWENTY

When Chiara exited her apartment at 8:00 a.m. on
Saturday, Vasily noticed a difference in her appearance. She was wearing jeans and carrying a large purse and a
shopping bag that looked full. Normally, she carried a smaller
purse and no shopping bag.

He left the coffee shop ahead of her and walked to the metro
station, arriving before she did. He watched as she followed her
routine of entering a middle car. He took the last car so he could
see when she exited. She didn't get out at the station near her
office but continued to the Centrale metro station. He followed
her out as she weaved among crowds, took the escalator to the
first floor, entered the train station, and continued to the ticket
office. Chiara stopped and turned around slowly, holding her
phone like she was making a call. She then put her phone back
in her purse and stopped at a ticket kiosk. As Vasily watched,

standing between a man and woman, she made two transactions using a credit card.

Vasily stepped to another kiosk and bought a round-trip ticket to Bergamo, not knowing Chiara's destination.

After purchasing tickets, Chiara returned to the escalator, taking it to Centrale's grand lobby, with its high-vaulted, cathedral-like ceiling and walls adorned with bas-reliefs of gladiators, swords, and shields from the fascist design of the 1930s.

Vasily kept his distance as Chiara weaved through the crowds. She turned abruptly and entered a woman's restroom. He bought a newspaper and circled the lobby until he spotted an empty seat on a bench alongside passengers waiting for trains, their bulky backpacks and oversized luggage on the floor beside them.

Vasily opened his paper and held it so he could see Chiara leave the restroom. After several minutes, he noticed a woman with Chiara's features exit, but she was wearing a different blouse and pants and was now carrying a brown purse and a different shopping bag. He recognized the short, quick steps of her gait from previous surveillance. She carried the shopping bag on one arm and her purse on the other. No doubt she had changed clothes in the restroom, an attempt to disguise herself in case she was being followed.

He left the bench, folded the newspaper, and tucked it under his arm. He let other travelers get between him and Chiara and followed her into the station, where travelers flashed their tickets to security staff. He watched her inside the busy, noisy main station and let her walk ahead of him. She turned right and made her way to the regional train tracks at the end of the station. She validated her ticket at an electronic monitor and walked down the passageway between two green regional trains. He followed, validating his own ticket.

He stayed behind to see which train she would enter, track 23 or 24. When she reached the engine at track 23, she turned around to see if she was being followed. Vasily dropped back behind two men carrying suitcases. He waited a few seconds and then stepped aside in time to see her board the second car behind the engine.

Vasily picked up his pace and looked up between the tracks at the electronic board with train numbers, destinations, and departure times. Chiara had boarded the 2570 regional train, departing at 9:25 a.m. with stops at Monza and Como. A uniformed train official blew a whistle and called out; the train was about to depart.

Vasily walked quickly to the last car of the five-car train and boarded. Seconds later, the train jolted and reversed out of the station. Vasily sat at a window and looked out as the train emerged into bright sunlight, accelerating slowly, its steel wheels clicking across the tracks. When the train approached maximum speed, Vasily stood and walked down the aisle, stopping at the sliding door between cars. He moved through the train until he got to the car behind the one where Chiara was sitting. He looked through the glass door and saw her, on his left, sitting at a window in the middle of the car, her back to him. He stayed in the third car and sat in an empty window seat so he could see when Chiara got off.

Eleven minutes later, after speeding through several suburbs, the train arrived in Monza. Vasily stayed seated, looking out the window and watching Chiara leave the train and walk toward the station. She stopped and casually looked to see who was behind her before she entered the station. Vasily remained in the open door of his car until he saw Chiara disappear into the station.

He stepped down onto the platform and walked slowly toward the station entrance, watching Chiara in the lobby. Once again, she casually turned to look behind her. Vasily moved slightly to his right and left to keep Chiara in view in the distance. Was she going to leave the lobby or possibly return to the station? He was in a position to keep her in sight without her noticing. He watched her walk into a small coffee shop and order something.

The coffee shop was in full view from the station. Vasily walked toward an enclosed newspaper and magazine store near the open double doors into the lobby. He browsed at racks of newspapers, bought a copy of *La Repubblica,* and sat on a weathered wooden bench inside the station. He opened the paper as if to read, holding it so he could watch Chiara. After she drank her coffee, she left the café, returned to the lobby, and sat on a long bench in front of the electronic board that flashed the times of departing and arriving trains.

Vasily raised his newspaper to shield his face, checking on Chiara every few seconds. After five minutes, she stood, left the lobby, and returned into the station. The train they had arrived on had departed, replaced by another regional train.

Chiara walked twenty yards in front of Vasily, who raised his newspaper so she couldn't see his face. When she came into view to his left, he watched her walk down the platform toward the regional train on the same track they had arrived on. She boarded the second car of the train and disappeared. Vasily stood, walked briskly down the platform, and boarded the last car.

The train departed, backing out of the station. Fifty-five minutes later, it arrived at San Giovanni station in Como. Seated at a window, Vasily saw Chiara leave the train and enter the station. He followed, keeping other travelers between them. He saw her descend a stone stairway into a park.

He let her walk ahead of him, always keeping distance between them. He crossed a street and followed her as she walked several blocks. Vasily looked left and right and saw a sign with an arrow that said the Como Cathedral was at the next intersection. Chiara entered a piazza and walked past a large Gothic cathedral where tourists were taking selfies.

Vasily watched Chiara cross the piazza without looking up at the cathedral and continue to a crowd of people in a queue to buy tickets for a Como ferry. Ahead, he could see sailboats on the blue waters of a lake and steep mountains that stretched for miles.

This was Lake Como, a famous vacation spot that Vasily had read about in his guidebooks. Although he was doing surveillance, he could now enjoy a popular and well-known tourist center. The sun was hot, but a gentle breeze was coming off the lake. The day was going to be pleasant, away from the traffic and crowds in Milano.

Vasily watched Chiara buy a ticket and walk through a gate to sit on a bench with other travelers waiting to catch a ferry. He couldn't see any ferries coming to the landing, so he had time for a diversion. He stepped over to a souvenir stand that sold caps, T-shirts, banners, guidebooks, maps, and plastic toys. He bought a tan straw hat—the kind that was popular with tourists—a polo shirt with the logo of Lake Como, and a pair of sunglasses. He slipped into a restroom to change into the Como shirt with the logo, put the hat on his head, and don his sunglasses. In moments, he was just another traveler out to enjoy Lake Como, mingling with tourists.

While he waited in a queue to buy a ticket, he could see a white Como ferry approaching, its twin smokestacks belching black smoke as it glided toward the terminal. With a jolt, the ferry reversed its engines, twin screws churning the waters and sending foaming waves over the surface as the ferry slowly approached the dock.

With a round-trip ticket to Colico, the farthest distance on Lake Como, Vasily sat on a bench several yards from Chiara. She couldn't see him unless she stood and walked toward him.

As the ferry docked, boarding passengers rose from benches and made their way into the terminal, covered by an awning that served as an umbrella from the bright sunshine. They waited in two roped lanes leading to gangplanks at the front and rear. When the ferry docked, uniformed crew wearing white hats and blue shirts with the ferry company's logo tossed circular rope lines around wooden posts and motioned for departing passengers to cross a wooden plank into the terminal. When the last passenger had left the ferry, boarding passengers showed their tickets to crew and crossed the planks onto the ferry.

When Chiara boarded at the bow gangplank, Vasily mingled with passengers boarding at the stern gangplank. While he waited, he saw Chiara take a seat on a bench on the lower deck. Vasily boarded in the rear and took the stairs to the top deck. He sat near a railing lined with orange life vests and coiled ropes.

The ferry engines belched, and a boarding bell announced imminent departure. Black smoke billowed from the smokestacks.

The crew unleashed the ropes, wrapping them and laying them on the deck. The ferry jolted, reversed from the terminal, and made a slow half-circle, churning the blue water into soapy foam. Hungry seagulls hovered above, seeking to snack on fish churned up in the ferry's wake.

Vasily relaxed on the top deck in the warm sun. He and Chiara were on the same ferry; she couldn't escape for as long as it took to reach her destination.

The ferry picked up speed as it entered the channel along the western side of the lake. Over the next hour, the ferry docked at ports on the west side—Cernobbio, Argegno, Colonno, Tremezzina, and Griante—but Chiara stayed aboard. As the ferry crossed from Griante to Bellagio, Vasily walked to the back of the ferry, came down the stairs, and sat on a rear bench where he could see the top of Chiara's head in the next compartment. She seemed absorbed, looking out a window at Como's scenery of villas nestled on forested mountains and sailboats cruising on the flat blue lake. Vasily ignored the scenery, his eyes locked on Chiara.

An hour later, the ferry departed Varenna and crossed the lake toward Menaggio. Chiara stood, went into the restroom, and didn't exit until the ferry had docked and the plank was laid.

*This must be her destination,* Vasily thought. He was ready for the next segment of his surveillance, confident that she had no idea he was following her. He wondered where she was going next. To see a lover? Her parents? Or was she simply on a day-long vacation? Time would tell. He had all day and all night, if necessary, to learn her plan.

He watched Chiara join a crowd of tourists preparing to disembark. She turned around to see if anyone was watching her. Vasily lingered in the rear, hiding behind other tourists, peeking once a minute to see where she was.

After the ferry docked, a double line of passengers stepped onto wooden planks and onto Menaggio's dock. Ahead, a line of boarding passengers waited behind a rope. Vasily surveyed Menaggio's sidewalks and piazzas, crowded with tourists enjoying a relaxing summer day on the lake.

Vasily followed Chiara, mingling with tourists who were strolling along Via Mazzini and taking photos of Menaggio, the ferries on the lake, and each other. Chiara walked along the embarcadero until she found a seat on a bench. She reached into her purse and took out her phone, gazing at the shining blue lake. The phone conversation was brief. When she finished, she stuffed the phone into her purse, rose, and walked to Piazza Garibaldi. She entered a café, where she stood in line, ordered, and took a metal numbered flag to an outside table. Five minutes later, a waiter delivered a sandwich and a glass of white wine.

Vasily stood in front of a souvenir shop that sold tourist baubles, postcards, caps, shirts, aprons, flags, calendars, and tourist guides.

Chiara ate leisurely, sipping her wine and checking her watch. When she finished, she left the table and returned to the embarcadero, dodging tourists snapping photos.

When Chiara glanced behind her, Vasily slipped into a crowd of older tourists being led by a female guide carrying a pole with a small German flag above her head. The German tourists walked by Chiara, and after twenty yards, Vasily slipped away from the group. Chiara passed behind him and walked up a street with restaurants, shops, and hotels.

Vasily took his time, letting her get ahead of him, clearly visible, proceeding without the crowd of tourists. He stood in the shadows of a hotel and watched her pass a bakery, a bank ATM, and a shoe store until she reached Via Lusardi. A traffic jam of cars, taxis, motorbikes, and tour buses inched their way through Menaggio.

Chiara crossed at a traffic light and climbed a stone path, passing a church. Vasily stayed in the shadows of the hotel, following at a distance. Chiara was alone, climbing stone steps between older brick apartments, boutique hotels, and restaurants shaded from the sun. When she was out of sight, Vasily hurried up the stone steps. When he reached the top, he walked a few steps to look into a café and then casually looked back.

Chiara was gone! *Where?* He hurried in the direction in which she had disappeared. Momentary panic. Had she entered an apartment, one on either side of the narrow street? It had been only ten or twenty seconds since he had seen her. Somehow she had managed to disappear. He was experienced in surveillance and trained to detect when a suspect was on to him: faking going in one direction and then reversing and coming toward him, or turning a corner and ducking into a store or an alley. But Chiara hadn't acted suspicious, other than her attempt at a disguise.

Vasily reversed his steps until he was at the place he'd last seen her.

When he reached an intersection, he saw her in the distance, climbing a stone path shaded by trees. A wooden sign said *Via Monte Grappa*.

He waited below, letting her get almost out of sight, until she entered a small coffee shop. He stood in the shade of an old stone wall on Via Monte Grappa. When Chiara exited the café, she was carrying a tray with a cappuccino and a biscuit. She sat at an outdoor table, took her phone out of her purse, talked for a minute, and then put it back.

Vasily lingered along the stone wall, walking up one side of the street and down the other, dodging passing cars, motorcycles, and children. He kept out of Chiara's sight, emerging every minute or two to see her still sitting at the outdoor table.

She had finished her coffee and was reading a magazine, turning pages, glancing up Via Monte Grappa, and then resuming her reading.

A black SUV came around a corner and braked in front of the café. Chiara stood, waved, and walked toward the car. A woman got out of the passenger side, and a man from the driver's side. When the three of them met, they embraced and exchanged cheek kisses, smiling and laughing. The driver picked up Chiara's shopping bag and purse, and put them in the back seat.

The driver was Volkov. Vasily recognized him from photos given to him in Moscow. He pulled out his phone and snapped pictures of all of them. And the car.

After a few moments of greeting and embracing, the Volkovs entered the car. Dmitri Volkov backed up, made a tight circle around the intersection, and drove up the street.

Vasily dashed up the cobblestone street as the car climbed a hill. He grabbed his cell phone and snapped photos of the license plate. He noted two initials, *CO,* for the province. His tutor in Moscow had told him that car license plates in Italy had two initials representing where a car was registered.

Vasily figured that *CO* must mean Como, which meant Volkov and his wife lived in the province. This would include popular tourist areas where a million people lived. Vasily needed more information: not just the province, but the town where they lived. How would he do that?

# CHAPTER TWENTY-ONE

V asily returned to Milano on the Como ferry. He felt
ecstatic; his mind was racing regarding his breakthrough
on surveillance: seeing Volkov and his wife and getting photos
of them and their license plate. The next time Vasily saw a car
that looked like Volkov's, knowing the license plate would allow
him to be certain it was the right car.

He pulled up the photos of Volkov he had received in
Moscow. Volkov had lost weight since those photos were taken.
He had also grown a beard, like many Italian men. He even
dressed like an Italian, in narrow dark pants, a tailless shirt,
loafers, and sunglasses.

Vasily had taken two photos of Volkov that day, one straight
on and the other a profile when Volkov had put Chiara's purse
and shopping bag into the back seat. Vasily also had taken two
photos of the license plate as the car was going up a hill.

Vasily would forward the photos to Moscow as part of a detailed report. To do this, he planned to go to the Russian consulate in Milano to use a secure communication. He'd tell Moscow that he was planning to rent a car the following Saturday to drive to Menaggio and park near the café where Chiara had met her parents on Via Monte Grappa. If they met again the next weekend, he'd follow Volkov's car to see if he could find where they lived. Once he discovered the location of their home, he could devise an execution plan after surveilling Volkov and his routines.

The prospect was exciting. He'd been in Milano only three weeks and would need possibly another two or three weeks to fulfill his mission. But completing his mission also meant he would return to Moscow—and likely never return to Italy. That thought was not appealing to him. He enjoyed Milano, with its vibrant lifestyle, historic landmarks, and good restaurants. And especially seeing Betta. His heart fluttered when he anticipated seeing her on Monday morning. What was that all about? He wasn't falling in love, but he was attracted to her personality and admired her carefree attitude, close friendships, and commitment to the clinic for the underprivileged.

To him, Betta's laughter seemed genuine and free-spirited. She came across as happy and self-confident. Then there was her gesture of waving goodbye with a finger wave, as if she was running her fingers over piano keys. An act, maybe, but one he enjoyed. He always returned it with a simple wave of his hand. Maybe he should be a bit more theatrical with his wave. How should he do that? Practice in front of a mirror? Never. How could he even contemplate adopting a more original way to wave at her? It was silly.

What was happening to him? A woman he'd met a few times was making him think such foolish things. What was it about her that caused this?

Betta was attractive, sexy, and provocative. Probably in her mid to late thirties, but carefree like a younger woman, with a love of life and many friends.

Had Betta always been that way? He knew little about her life but was curious. Was she married? He didn't think so. Did she have a lover? Most likely she did. She seemed irresistible to men seeking a beautiful, self-confident, mature woman to make love to. Many probably already had.

When he saw her again, he wouldn't dare to ask if she was involved in a relationship. But from her past behavior, he expected she would reveal this part of her life, not in a manner of seeking the same from him, but with an attitude of *This is a part of me, who I am. I'm completely comfortable telling you about my lovers, but I don't care about your love life. Don't tell me. I'm not interested.*

After the regional train from Como pulled into Centrale, Vasily stepped down and walked into the station, realizing he had replayed in his thoughts the mornings with Betta at the coffee bar and the evening *aperitivo*. Why couldn't he get his mind off of her? He was becoming obsessed. What did it mean?

Vasily stopped at a trattoria near his apartment and ordered dinner, *spaghetti alle vongole* and a bottle of Falanghina wine. He took his time eating, nibbling on bread dipped in olive oil and vinegar. He then took swirls of the warm pasta and enjoyed every bite of the delicious meal. His wine was silky smooth, with a hint of citrus blossom aroma and tasting of fermented grapes. He read the label: *Grown in Campania*. He wished he could visit Campania and the Amalfi Coast and drink more Falanghina wine.

He savored a few bites of tiramisu. His wine bottle empty, he drank mineral water to slake his remaining thirst from the trip to Menaggio. He was tired but grateful to have seen Volkov and to have snapped photos. His reward was this delicious meal and bottle of wine.

He felt different, not the man who had arrived in Milano focused on a deadly mission. He was one of the *siloviki*, following high-level orders to commit a crime on foreign soil. If he was successful, he would return to Moscow soon. His supervisor and GRU elites would award him a medal, a bonus, and some time off. When that was over, he'd wait for another assignment and resume teaching at the GRU academy. But never able to return to Italia? He held his breath. He didn't want that restriction in his future. But what could he do? It was unlikely that the Russian government would ever let him return there after he committed the assassination. It would be too risky.

The prospect of returning to Moscow was grim. His apartment was empty of Katya's things and full of sad memories. Katya had deserted him, probably never to return. No one had replaced her. His few hurried encounters with women had been with prostitutes and sleazy women he had picked up in bars. Those memories were fleeting and depressing. He hated them but still needed the companionship of a woman, even if just for a few hours.

He looked ahead. When he returned to Russia, he would travel to St. Petersburg and endure more painful experiences: his adolescent son's aloofness, his ex-wife's contempt, and his mother's growing dementia. All dismal.

Whenever he visited his mother in the nursing home, she would look up at him, struggle to remember his name, ask who he was and what he wanted, and then nod off into a deep slumber. St. Petersburg, his hometown and favorite city in Russia, had become a destination full of pain.

Living in Moscow had few joys. The city was very crowded, with polluted air; noisy, rude people; traffic; and boring Soviet architecture. Not like Milano.

When Vasily returned to his apartment, it was 10:30. He was tired but wanted a diversion from the stress and emotions of the day. He turned on the TV and flipped through channels to Rai 1 to watch another Montalbano episode. This one was about an immigrant boy murdered by Mafia criminals who trafficked in desperate people fleeing Africa and the Middle East. It was a depressing story, but Vasily was intrigued by the romantic scenes of Sicily, Grecian monuments, rows of sunbaked villas on hillsides, and the beach near Montalbano's apartment, where he swam in the morning and at other times when he was trying to work out a problem with a murder case he was investigating.

Vasily opened a bottle of grappa from his cabinet, drank two glasses, and lay on his bed. As he became sleepy, his mind wandered from the day's events and what would happen over the next few days. It was all happening so fast. He wanted more time in Milano—time to relax, enjoy the city's vibrant lifestyle, and see Betta again. With her on his mind, he drifted off to sleep.

Vasily slept poorly, tossing and turning, abruptly waking from dreams, recalling the previous day, falling back to sleep, and plunging into even more bizarre dreams. By the time he was awake, it was 7:30, but he was still tired from interrupted sleep. He lay, looking up at the ceiling and counting the concentric brown rings of water stains from the leak in the apartment above. Nothing planned for the day. As he showered, he thought that Chiara would likely come home on Sunday from Menaggio. He had something to do after all: go to her apartment in the afternoon and see if she returned.

He took the metro to Porta Romana at 3:00 p.m. and walked down Via Crema. He wandered a bit, stopping at cafés and finally sitting on a bench at a bus stop while watching families out for a Sunday *passeggiata*. Every few minutes, he'd glance toward Chiara's apartment. At 7:30, he had an early dinner, Milanese risotto and a bottle of Sangiovese, while seated at an outdoor table under a canopy of flowering magnolia trees. The Sangiovese went down his throat like liquid silk, leaving a trace of grapes on his tongue. He'd do a bit of research on Italian wines, try as many as he could, and maybe take a few bottles back to Moscow.

Vasily's mind was roaming, as free as the wind, thinking of wines and Italian food. So many restaurants and so many recipes to try. For a moment, he felt carefree and relaxed, remembering Betta. She had shown him what *carefree* and *relaxed* meant. And how good it felt.

He paid for his meal, left a generous tip, and walked out of the trattoria, a bit woozy from the wine and pleasantly full from the risotto. As he strolled down the sidewalk across from Chiara's apartment, he mingled among a group of lively teenagers texting and laughing, pet owners walking their leashed dogs, and lovers enjoying a warm evening together. Just another Sunday evening for Milanese. Did they know how lucky they were?

At 8:30, a black SUV stopped in front of Chiara's apartment, where there were no empty parking spaces. Vasily watched Volkov get out, open the back door, and take Chiara's hand as she rose, carrying her purse and shopping bag. Her mother joined them on the sidewalk for a brief exchange of hugs and kisses. Vasily snapped photos with his phone before Chiara's parents got back into the car and Chiara entered her apartment.

His diligence had paid off. More photos and details of Volkov's routine. His supervisors would be impressed. Tomorrow he would reward himself by finding a bookstore and buying a book on Italian wines. He looked forward to that. It was another new experience he wouldn't have anticipated back in Moscow.

\* \* \* \* \*

Betta arrived at the café a few minutes after 8:30 the next morning. She walked over to the bar, where Vasily had saved a place for her.

"Would you like to take a table outside? It's a beautiful morning," he said, hoping she would have more than the couple of minutes she usually allotted for her morning caffeine routine.

"No, but thanks anyway. You know me, late for work again," she said with a laugh. "Sorry you couldn't make it Saturday. We had a successful fundraising event. We made almost 9,000 euros. That will keep us going for another couple of months. How was your weekend? Did your friend like your tour?"

She raised a hand at the barista, who nodded and, in less than a minute, delivered her cup, saucer, spoon, and napkin.

Vasily remembered the story he had told her about why he couldn't come Saturday night. "Oh—oh, yes," he stammered. "He really enjoyed it."

"Where did you take him?"

Elisabetta was persistent, with little time for formalities. He felt her dark eyes looking deep into his soul, mining for something that she wanted to know. What was she searching for? Was it intimacy, or something else? She'd be an excellent cop or attorney: *Forget pleasantries, probe, and get down to the good stuff: Who are you, and what are you about? No secrets allowed.* Vasily's impression was that if she found something she didn't like, she'd be on her way, and he'd be left in the dark.

"Well, the Duomo, to start."

"Oh, the Duomo," she said. "Always crowds on the weekend, tourists by the thousands. My favorite time to go to the Duomo is in the winter, before and especially after Christmas. Tourists are gone, and there's time to appreciate that magnificent cathedral." Her eyes sparkled.

Betta's emotions were ignited. Vasily liked her spontaneity and passion.

He wasn't sure how to respond. All he could say was, "But… but we didn't go inside the Duomo. The line was too long."

"Where else did you take him?" she asked, sipping her coffee and glancing at her watch.

"We took a tram to the Castello and walked around Parco Sempione."

"You should have taken him to the Casa degli Atellani and Leonardo's Vineyard, in front of Santa Maria delle Grazie, the church with da Vinci's *Last Supper*. It's a beautiful place and a marvelous example of the Milanese Renaissance. Oh, and the San Maurizio Church. Such a majestic house of worship, with incredible frescoes. It's our Sistine Chapel in Milano. I recommend you go there before you leave."

"I will. I've read about these places in the guidebook but haven't had time to go."

"Where is your friend from, St. Petersburg?"

"No, Moscow. He teaches architecture at a university. He took pictures of many buildings: apartments with trees on balconies at Porta Garibaldi, the skyscrapers, and CityLife."

"I have friends who live at CityLife. I enjoy visiting them, strolling along the winding paths, stopping at the fountains, and seeing acres of trees. And no parking lots. I don't like the traffic in Milano. I much prefer the parks, where you can lose yourself watching families with children playing. That's one of my favorite activities when I'm alone."

Betta drained the last drops of her coffee, set the cup on the saucer, and picked up her purse. "Gotta run, Vasily," she said, starting toward the door.

"See you tomorrow?"

She stopped and came back. "Oh, I forgot. There's a party next Saturday—some of the people you met, along with others. It's my best friend's birthday. You'll like her. She's sweet."

With her familiar finger-roll wave, Betta was out the door. As she disappeared around a corner, Vasily's eyes moved to Chiara's apartment. She hadn't appeared yet. She might be late for work, like Betta.

Vasily finished his coffee and looked down into his empty cup. How long had Betta been standing next to him? Two minutes? Three? It had happened so fast, and then she was gone. His emotions were on a roller coaster. *Another party Saturday night: How could I? I'm renting a car to drive to Menaggio to follow Volkov's car if he shows up to meet Chiara. How can I be in two places on the same day?*

He feared that Betta might never forgive him for turning down two social invitations. He felt intimidated by her directness, which also intrigued him. He'd never met anyone like her.

# CHAPTER TWENTY-TWO

Armando fidgeted in the gynecologist's waiting room at Mangiagalli Hospital. He looked around at the seated women, mostly in their thirties, some accompanied by husbands. He and Simona had waited for half an hour until a nurse came out and called her name. For a minute or so afterwards, Armando felt anxious, wanting to be with Simona during the examination. But she had wanted to go in alone and had said she would be a bit embarrassed if he joined her.

He picked up magazines and flipped through them but felt too nervous to read. He just looked at the pictures. After three or four magazines, he knew the magazines were a waste of time. He looked at his watch and then his cell phone. He skimmed through his messages but didn't answer any of them. When he put his phone away, he looked up at the clock. It was 10:41 a.m. They had been there together for thirty minutes, followed by ten minutes where he was sitting alone. As he watched the clock, it made him think of watching an iceberg thaw: drip, drip, drip. A small slab falls into the ocean. Then drip, drip, drip.

A man across the room stood and came over to Armando. "Excuse me. Aren't you Maestro Bongiovanni? Sorry to bother you, but I thought I recognized you from La Scala."

Armando felt a flush of embarrassment. "Well, yes, I—I am," he stammered, noticing that others in the waiting room had looked over at him. "I do perform at La Scala. Thank you for noticing."

"If it's not a problem, could I have your autograph?" The man reached into his coat pocket and took out a pen and a pocket calendar. He opened to an empty page and handed the calendar to Armando.

Armando scribbled his name and the date and handed the calendar back. The man took it, bowed in respect, returned to his seat, and picked up a magazine. But before he opened it, he glanced over, smiled, and nodded as if they were friends after this brief encounter.

Armando could feel his face warming from the full blush that he was sure colored his cheeks rosy pink. He wanted to hide, but it was impossible. Everyone was looking at him, smiling and nodding as if he had just stepped off the conductor's podium at La Scala. Where could he hide? Nowhere. He was in a gynecologist's waiting room. Everyone knew why he was there. He must be an expectant father accompanying his wife—or lover—to her appointment.

He lowered his head, flipped through another magazine, and pretended to read, which he couldn't. The room returned to its previous state of friends and relatives waiting for news about expectant mothers from the doctors' offices behind the door.

Time passed slowly. His normal patience had evaporated. When would Simona come out? What would she say? How were their lives going to change? Would she learn if she was going to have a girl or a boy? No, it was probably too early for that. It didn't make any difference; he just wanted a healthy child. He prayed it would be healthy.

He looked up at the clock again: 10:45.

At 10:56, the door where Simona had entered with the nurse opened, and Simona came out. Her face was pale, but she was smiling at him.

He stood and was beside her in an instant, peppering her with questions. "How are you? What did he say?"

"Wait. Let's go out into the hall," she said. They entered the hallway, walking until they passed a couple coming in their direction. When they were alone, Simona said, "He's a nice doctor, a gentleman. I see him once a year for a checkup. He remembered me, even where I work. He confirmed I'm pregnant, eight weeks. He ordered exams, including a blood test next week. He said my nausea was normal and nothing to worry about. I can continue working, just no physical stress. I'm sure glad the hike at Como is behind me. I told the doctor about it, and he said, 'No more strenuous hikes.'"

"When do you come back for your next appointment?"

"Next month, when I'm twelve weeks. They'll do an nuchal translucency so we can see our little baby."

Armando listened carefully and took Simona's shaking hand, grabbing her purse before she dropped it as they waited at the elevator.

"Are you okay?"

"Just hang on to my hand," she mumbled, her voice quivering.

"But you're shaking. We're going to be parents!"

"That's why I'm shaking," she said. "I'm scared."

"Scared? You said the doctor reassured you. And you looked radiant coming out of his office. I loved the happy expression on your face."

"I did feel happy, but when I was in the doctor's office, I was nervous, listening to every word he said. I asked him to repeat himself a couple of times so I could tell you. He was so nice, patient, and gentle. He told me not to be nervous and said that everything looked good and I was healthy and should have a good delivery." She paused. "I need some fresh air. Hospitals always smell sterile. I want to go outside."

"We'll be there soon. Put your hand on my arm." The elevator arrived, empty. Armando pushed open the metal gate, and they entered. They were on the ground floor in a few moments. Armando opened the gate and held it so Simona could exit into the hallway. Soon they were out the door into the crisp morning air.

Simona clutched his arm, took a deep breath, and let it out with a deep sigh. "Oh, fresh air. I needed it." She took another breath, held it, and exhaled. "I'm okay now. Let's walk. I need to move. I feel a bit dehydrated. I need some water."

"Whatever you want. We'll find a place," Armando said, walking slowly. Their pace picked up as they reached an area with full sun shining on them.

"That's better," Simona sighed. "The sun feels good. But not too fast, okay?"

"Of course. Just hang on to me. You'll be fine."

"*Amore*, how did you feel in the waiting room?"

"Well, I was nervous at first. I was waiting, wondering what was going on with you and the doctor. This was my first time in a gynecologist's waiting room." He chuckled. "First time for everything, I guess."

"Can you believe it? He confirmed that I'm actually pregnant!"

"*We're* pregnant," he corrected.

She stopped and looked up at him. "What? No, *I'm* pregnant. You're the reason."

"No, we're *both* pregnant. We did this together."

She laughed. "You can't be pregnant. I'm the woman. Did you forget?"

"But *we're* pregnant. We're going to have a baby. It's ours!"

She laughed again. "No, *I'm* pregnant. I want to be the pregnant one. Let me be pregnant!"

They laughed and fell into each other's arms, hugging.

An older couple near them slowed, having heard their conversation. Their faces registered confusion.

Simona noticed they had attracted attention from the older couple and a few others walking nearby. She looked at them, smiled, and apologized. "It's okay. We just found out we're going to be parents. But *I'm* the one who's pregnant, not him!"

The impromptu audience returned Simona's smile. The older couple bowed, and the man said, "Congratulations. We're happy for you."

"Thank you. Thank you," Simona and Armando replied in unison. Then they resumed walking, stepping up their pace to escape the attention they had drawn.

"That was funny, *tesoro*," Simona said. "I've never attracted an audience on a sidewalk before."

"Neither have I," Armando responded. "Another first for me. Two today: the gynecologist's office and drawing a small crowd on the street." He smiled. "Let's get coffee for me and water for you. We need to sit and talk."

At the next intersection, they saw a coffee shop, crossed the street, and entered.

"There's an open table in the corner. We'll have privacy," Armando said, gesturing to a table next to a window.

"Get me a sparkling water and a green tea, please," Simona said. She took her purse from him and went to the table, sitting so she could look outside at the sunny street.

Armando ordered and joined her in a couple of minutes. He set down a plastic tray with cups, saucers, napkins, and spoons. Simona continued looking out the window.

"It is a pretty day, isn't it?" she said. She sipped her water and then reached for the cup of green tea.

"More than pretty. It's a memorable day. We'll never forget this."

She smiled and asked, "Are you going to tell your friends that you're going to be a papa?"

"Of course. I can't wait. We're going to have a baby!"

"I hope I'm ready to be a mother."

"What do you mean?"

"I just don't know if it's the right time for me to become a mother."

"Why not? A woman is blessed to give birth to a child that will change her life."

*"Our* lives."

"Yes, both of us."

"But I'm concerned about my job."

"Why?"

"I love my job. I don't know how I will handle staying home with a baby, nursing, getting up in the middle of the night, changing messy diapers, knowing what to do when the baby cries. Crying babies scare me. What if there's something wrong and I don't know what to do to stop the crying? And I'm worried about nursing. It hurts your breasts. They swell like balloons. You can tell new mothers when you see them on the street; their breasts are so big."

"Don't worry about that."

"But I am. Soon my stomach will bulge like I swallowed a watermelon."

"You'll look good. Pregnant women look happy, knowing what's coming."

"But I'm worried about the nursing. It hurts. And what if I can't?"

He grabbed both of her shaking hands. "You will. Don't worry. Most mothers love nursing. Just ask my sister. She says she likes having babies and watching them nurse."

"You never told me that before."

"Well, it wasn't important. Now it is. Call her and hear what she has to say. She'll help you."

Simona turned and looked out the window. Armando released her hands, and she picked up her cup and took a sip, looking at him.

"I'm also worried about my career."

"Why? You can have a career and also be a mother. Motherhood is a gift, the best you will ever have."

"I do want both, to be a mother and have a career."

"You will have both."

"I hope so. I don't want anything to interfere with my career."

"You'll have to tell people at work."

"Yes, I know, before my tummy becomes a small watermelon."

"Perhaps you should tell them soon and get it over with."

"Well, I should wait for the twelfth week, for our baby to be established and growing, as the doctor told me. But I'll at least tell Antonella and Dario tomorrow. I don't know what they'll say. I'm nervous."

"I know what they'll say. They'll congratulate you and tell you how happy they are for you. Guaranteed!"

"How much longer can I go into the office? When will I have to stop working?"

Armando shrugged. "Ask Antonella. She'll know about maternity leave."

"It's five months, isn't it?"

"You're a state employee, so yes, I believe you get five months of maternity leave and get to keep your job."

"I never asked, as I didn't think I'd be facing this. Few women working at DIGOS have babies. Some already have children and talk about them. They show you pictures and brag about how fast their kids are growing up and how much they like being moms."

"So will you."

She grinned. "Think so?"

"No doubt! You'll love it. I know you will."

Simona reached across and put her hands on Armando's. "*Tesoro*, I won't be able to sleep tonight, worrying about what they'll say when I tell them."

"Simo, you're making too much of this, and you're worrying instead of just enjoying today. This is good news—for you, for me, for her."

"A girl? You think so?"

"I hope so. Don't you? A baby girl. What will we call her?"

Her eyes lit up. "I would like a daughter."

Armando said, "A daughter first, and then maybe a little brother in a couple of years."

Simona stood. "Oh, please, one at a time. I can't think about having more than one baby."

Armando smiled. "Let's go home. We've had an exciting day already."

They left the coffee shop. When they got outside, the sun was casting shadows across the street. "I'm looking forward to going to bed tonight. I think I'll have pleasant dreams," Simona said.

"About her?"

"Yes!"

# CHAPTER TWENTY-THREE

Vasily pressed the buzzer on the gate at the Russian consulate, Via Sant'Aquilino 3, a narrow street near San Siro stadium. A camera on the inside gate peered down on him. He looked up and showed his Russian passport, not his Polish one.

He peered through the metal gate at the tiled road that led toward the consulate, which was partially hidden by tall bushes. He knew the area well. Hidden behind bushes and trees were a four-car garage for consulate cars, a storage unit, and a path leading to a backyard with a high wall and electronic sensors. The little-used backyard had a small kidney-shaped pool, lawn chairs, and a bird fountain empty of water.

Surveillance cameras on the roof focused around the gated complex, monitored twenty-four hours a day. The roof also contained a garden of antennas enclosed with hexagonal coverings to prevent cameras from identifying their function and bandwidth.

It had been more than twenty years since Vasily had been posted at the consulate as a guard. He wondered if the interior had changed. As he recalled, behind the metal double doors, a hallway led to three offices: one for the consul, another for his assistant, and a third for secretaries and admin personnel. Between the offices were two bathrooms, one for the consul and his deputy, and the other for everyone else.

Upstairs were modest offices for FSB and GRU staff and high-ranking officers in the Russian army, navy, air force, and coast guard. The last room was stacked with computers, electronic servers, and a booth for communicating with the Kremlin over secure telephone lines, with a two-way camera.

The basement contained a dormitory for bodyguards of the consul and his deputy, as well as twelve military guards who maintained twenty-four-hour security at the consulate. This level also contained two rooms for supervisors, one an army major and the other a GRU intelligence officer.

After Vasily waited five minutes, a uniformed guard marched down the tile driveway, his freshly pressed brown army uniform decorated with medals and rank. He was junior officer in his late twenties, trim, no smile. "Can I help you?" he said in an official tone.

"I have an appointment. Here's my passport," Vasily said, handing it through the barred gate.

When the guard took his passport, Vasily said, "I had your job twenty-two years ago, my first foreign assignment."

The guard said nothing.

"How do you like living in Italy?" Vasily asked, trying to be friendly and establish a bit of rapport, although he knew the guard likely had been advised to keep information about the consulate at a minimum, even to fellow Russians.

The guard blinked, a puzzled look on his face, momentarily caught off-guard at Vasily's question. "It's all right, but I wish I had more free time. My boss keeps me busy even when I'm not on duty, cleaning equipment, monitoring security. It's a bit boring, really."

"Nothing's changed. Sounds just like my tour here. I volunteered for extra duty, so my boss eventually let me have time off, a few hours every couple of weeks. I had a map and explored Milano, getting to be a tourist for a few hours."

"I've been here a year, and I've been out only four times," the guard said. "I wish I had more time. Maybe after I get back from Moscow next month to see my family." The guard saluted, handed back Vasily's passport, and unlocked the gate. "Follow me," he said, escorting Vasily to the consulate.

While being led down the hallway, Vasily noticed little had changed except for new carpet, fresh paint on the walls, color photos of Moscow landmarks, the consul's portrait, and official photos of Putin and Russian military brass.

After a brief courtesy call on the GRU ranking officer, Vasily was taken to a locked room at the end of the hallway. The officer punched in a code, the door clicked open, and they entered a room with no windows. The GRU officer flicked on a light, revealing a small room with a table, one chair, and a glass-enclosed cubicle.

"Here's the code to enter the secure cubicle," the GRU officer said. He waited until Vasily entered the code and entered the cubicle, and then the officer left the secure room. Vasily picked up a desk phone and punched in the numbers to reach Lebedev in Moscow.

After a couple of pleasantries, Vasily reviewed his progress since he'd arrived in Milano. "I follow the daughter from her apartment every day when she leaves for work, and I follow her when she returns home. Her routine varies little during the week. So I suspected she might see her father and mother on the weekends. She does.

"Last Saturday, she changed her routine and took a train and then a ferry on Lake Como to the town of Menaggio. I was careful, and I doubt she noticed me. In the afternoon in Menaggio, she met her father and mother outside a café. She got in their car and they drive off, but not before I snapped photos of Volkov, the car, and the license plate with a code that indicates they live in the province of Como. I suspect it's not far from Menaggio, which wouldn't be a good place to hide out. Menaggio is a major tourist town on the lake, so I doubt he lives in the town.

"Then on Sunday, I waited near the daughter's apartment and saw the parents bring her home. More photos. I didn't have a car to follow Volkov, but I will soon."

"Vasily, good work. Do you think anyone noticed you following?"

"I doubt it. The daughter made a very feeble attempt to disguise herself by changing clothes in a restroom and switching purses and shopping bags. But you can't change the way you walk. I teach recruits how to recognize someone by their gait. She's an amateur."

"You're a professional, Vasily. She's an amateur, and not a very good one. Following her will lead us to Volkov, where you can fulfill your mission. What's your plan to learn where Volkov's hiding out?"

"Already planned. On Saturday, I'll rent a car and drive to Menaggio. I'll park near the place where Volkov picked up his daughter. I'll follow them, and with luck, he'll drive to their apartment. I'll take photos of it so you can see the address and the surrounding area. I'll be cautious so people won't notice me and possibly alert him."

"Do you think he has guards? Maybe a private security company he's hired?"

"I don't know. I saw him for only a minute. He drove off, with no other cars behind him. No one else in his car except his wife. So he doesn't travel with guards."

"But he might have them at his apartment. I expect he would. Be careful."

"I will. They'll be easy to identify."

"Don't attract attention. You don't have to carry out your mission immediately, not until you know a little of his routine."

"I know. This isn't my first assignment to track down an enemy in a foreign country."

"When will you approach him with the 'treatment'?"

"Only after I learn a little of his patterns—where he goes to shop, to dine, and to walk, such as parks. Most people repeat their daily routines. I'll come up with a strategy where he's alone—at a park, walking down the street, or parking his car. Then I'll make my move. I'll come up behind him and wipe the serum on his skin."

"Good. You know how to do this. When will you have a chance?"

"I don't know. I'll learn more when I find his apartment and survey the area. I'll let you know."

"Your target is Volkov, not the wife or daughter. But if they happen to be with him, you have no choice. Call me after you find the apartment. Do you want someone to come with you?"

"No, I like working alone. I always have."

After the call, Vasily returned downstairs to the GRU officer's office. After Vasily updated him about the call and his assignment, the officer reached down into his desk and took out a slim metal container with a lock. He unlocked the container, lifted the top, and turned it around to show Vasily.

Secured in a fitted slot was an SR1PM pistol used by Russian Spetsnaz GRU forces. "For your protection, in case you need it."

Vasily lifted it out and stroked it with one hand and then the other. "My favorite weapon," he said without looking up.

"And these," the GRU officer said, reaching into the drawer again, bringing out a slender wooden box with Russian serial numbers, which contained twenty cartridges.

"Good luck. Maybe you won't even need to use this."

"I always want to be prepared."

# CHAPTER TWENTY-FOUR

On Saturday morning, Vasily rented a Fiat 500L sedan at Via Vittor Pisani, close to Centrale. Nervous to be driving for the first time in Italy, he eased into traffic toward Centrale, turning onto Via Tonale. His first task was to get on the autostrada and reach the suburbs on his way to Como.

His rental agreement included a GPS on the dashboard. He put in the destination of Via Monte Grappa in Menaggio and followed directions.

As he started to drive, the first drops of rain spattered the windshield. Within a minute, drenching rain fell, making visibility difficult. Vasily fumbled with a lever on the steering wheel for the wipers, but instead the headlights came on. He lifted the lever on the other side, which made one swipe of the windshield and then stopped. He raised the lever, and the wipers raced across the windshield fast, but at least he could see. He played around with the lever, finally getting the wipers to sweep rain away and not be distracting.

But the falling rain was hindering him from seeing out the back window. He again played with the wiper lever until he got it to sweep away the rain so he could see out the back.

While getting the wipers to work, he had not paid attention to the GPS instructions and had missed the intersection he was supposed to take. He drove another three hundred yards to the next intersection and made a left turn to go back. But he ended up on a one-way street and had to brake as two cars in both lanes were coming toward him, honking. He backed up until he could turn onto a side street and get out of the way of the approaching cars, which had continued to blare their horns at him.

Frustrated, Vasily tried to understand the directions from the female Italian voice on the GPS, who revised with new directions that only confused him. He backed up onto the street to continue going one way, but a car approached him rapidly and honked, as he was driving too slowly. The car jerked around him, the driver honking, flipping an obscene gesture, and yelling at him even though the car windows were closed.

Vasily drove through the intersection, now uncertain about how he could follow the GPS instructions and get back on the right road. The monotone female GPS voice told him to turn right at the intersection, take the roundabout, exit at the third street, drive another eight hundred meters, and take the on-ramp to the autostrada, which had not been marked on his map. Confusing.

He was lost, a trained assassin learning to drive in a foreign city with a rental car much different from his car in Moscow. He felt a bit helpless for the first time since arriving in Milano, where every day had seemed to be better and more interesting than the previous one. He had no one to turn to except the female GPS voice.

Vasily finally made it back to Viale Alcide de Gasperi. After a few blocks, he spotted a sign for the autostrada. Relieved, he listened as the GPS voice told him to drive another kilometer to get on the ramp to the autostrada. But at the next intersection, cars were at a complete standstill. He waited as other drivers honked. Peering ahead, he could see a car parked on tram tracks, blocking the road and halting traffic.

He had been driving for only a short time but had already missed a turn, gotten lost, ended up going the wrong way on a one-way street, and made several frustrating attempts to get back on the right road. His anxiety mounted. He was angry and frustrated at Milano traffic and felt desperate to get on his way.

When the traffic began moving again, the GPS voice told him to get in the right lane and prepare to take a ramp onto the autostrada. However, he saw another obstruction where he was supposed to turn. Construction crews had planted cones in the lane. Workers were drilling into the asphalt, tearing it up while other workers tossed the asphalt onto the back of a truck.

The car behind him honked. What could he do? A worker was holding up a stop sign and not letting him drive ahead. The honking persisted until the worker waved him around the construction crew toward the ramp. But the ramp was closed. No traffic allowed.

Where could he go? The GPS voice told him to take the ramp to the autostrada, but he had to drive under it as cars behind him continued to honk.

Ahead he saw a detour sign. He followed it. It took him through several streets until another detour sign pointed to the next ramp.

The rain continued hitting the windshield, making it difficult to see clearly. Vasily sensed his blood pressure rising as beads of perspiration dripped down his forehead. He felt hot and began fumbling with buttons on the console for the air-conditioning, punching one after another. A blast of hot air erupted from the vents so fiercely it ruffled his hair. He flicked it off and tried another. Moments later, a whir of cool air replaced the hot air.

It took him an hour to reach the suburbs amidst the streams of traffic heading north. As it was Saturday, many Milanese were leaving for a weekend of relaxation on Lake Como. Vasily was in the middle of the exodus. Traffic slowed to a crawl, with a line a kilometer ahead moving like snails.

My God, was it going to be like this all the way to Menaggio? He almost regretted the decision to see if he could find Volkov's car and follow him. The traffic crawled at ten kilometers an hour, bumper to bumper. High-performance Mercedes, Fiats, Porsches, and BMWs crept along. Vasily looked up at green destination signs, relieved when he finally saw the first sign for Como, with an arrow pointing to his right.

He pulled off at a petrol station, tired, angry, and desperate to find a restroom. He got out and jogged through the rain into the building, his hair and shirt damp. After the restroom break, he bought coffee and a brioche and got back into his car. He picked up the map and traced with his finger the route of the autostrada that continued north another thirty kilometers to Como. He didn't want to drive into the town and hoped there would be an exit to bypass Como and continue up the lake to Menaggio.

His anxiety irritated him. He was on a schedule to reach Via Monte Grappa by 3:00 p.m., hoping to see Volkov pick up Chiara so he could follow them to their home near Menaggio.

When he reached the suburbs of Como, it was 12:45. The rain had stopped. Bright summer sun was shining amidst clouds of white pillows, creating mists as the rain on the highway evaporated. Vasily followed the signs for SS 340, which snaked up the western shore of the lake. Fearing he might take the wrong exit, Vasily gripped the steering wheel and managed to make the correct turn that pointed to Lugano and Menaggio.

Within minutes, he was on SS 340. Traffic moved efficiently through lakeside towns until he reached Cernobbio, where the four lane highway became a two-way street with narrow sidewalks for pedestrians. Cernobbio's narrow main road ran between apartment buildings, coffee shops, and tourist hotels. Vasily glanced to his right and caught a glimpse of Lake Como and ferries churning through the flat blue waters, as well as sailboats lazily cruising with blissful unawareness of congested street traffic.

Progress was slow for the next hour, with a string of traffic lights and pedestrians crossing streets. Ahead and behind him, a continuous line of cars, taxis, noisy motorcycles, tourist buses, and trucks slowly made their way.

Vasily glanced at his watch. He needed something to eat. Two paper coffee cups were empty, discarded on the floor. Crumbs from his brioche littered the passenger seat. His rental car, sparkling clean when he had picked it up, already looked like vagabonds had camped out in it.

He followed SS 340 along the lake through Tremezzina and Griante. Green signs indicated that Menaggio was ahead. At 2:00 p.m., he arrived in Menaggio and turned into a petrol station on Via IV Novembre. He picked up his map and traced with his finger the road to Via Monte Grappa, a kilometer from the lake.

Vasily pulled out of the petrol station, his GPS companion telling him to turn on Via Como, a sharp turn that took him to Via Cadorna, passing villas and apartments with views of the blue lake glistening in the sunlight. His map showed an unmarked street that led to Via Monte Grappa. He took the turn, drove a few meters, and saw a wooden sign for Via Monte Grappa.

"You have reached your destination," his GPS companion confirmed. He switched off the GPS and drove slowly up the narrow road, looking to his left until he spotted the coffee shop where Chiara had waited for her father.

He drove past it, turned on Via Sonenga, and parked with a view of Via Monte Grappa. On a wall, a sign indicated "Via Cadorna," the road he presumed Volkov had driven to meet Chiara.

Vasily got out of the car and stretched, his shirt damp with sweat. He needed a cigarette, his first since picking up his rental car. The drive to Menaggio had been so challenging that he hadn't thought he should try to smoke. Even the momentary distraction of reaching for his cigarette packet, removing a cigarette, lighting it with a plastic lighter, and then flicking ashes into the ashtray could have been disastrous. He'd been craving a cigarette and finally felt safe to light one. He took several deep puffs and then walked around the corner to the coffee shop with the faded purple awning. He bought coffee, a panino, and a bottle of water and sat at the table where Chiara had sat. He looked down the street where she had walked the previous Saturday. No sign of her.

Vasily glanced at his watch: 2:15, close to the time Chiara had arrived. He ate his panino, sipped his coffee, and finished another cigarette as he watched pedestrians coming up the hilly street carrying bags of groceries, with children following behind.

He returned to his car, tired and anxious, hoping Volkov would arrive in his black SUV soon.

He did. At 2:45, Volkov's SUV slowly came down the road that led to Via Cadorna and turned onto Via Monte Grappa. Chiara's mother was sitting in the passenger seat, with Volkov driving. Vasily had been right! This was their weekend routine to meet Chiara. Now, if the Volkovs returned to their home, Vasily's persistence and intuition would be rewarded.

Volkov parked. He and his wife got out and walked toward the café. Vasily exited his car and took a few steps so he could see them in the distance. They entered the coffee shop to find Chiara waiting inside.

Moments later, Vasily saw the three of them walking up Via Monte Grappa, Volkov carrying the shopping bag where Chiara had stuffed her things in her amateur attempt to disguise herself.

Vasily hurried back to his car. He started it and backed up a few meters so he had a view of the road to Via Cadorna. Two minutes later, he saw Volkov's SUV driving up the hill and turning at the arrow to Via Cadorna.

He had them. All that remained was to follow them to their home.

For the next twenty minutes, Vasily followed Volkov, letting cars pass him, keeping one or two vehicles between him and the SUV.

Traffic was light, not like on the SS 340 highway. Vasily finally started to relax. His persistence had paid off, and now all he had to do was leisurely follow Volkov to his destination.

The hilly area became more rural as Vasily climbed through wooded mountains, passing homes and farms with wood or stone fences enclosing gardens, groves of lemon and apple trees, stables for horses and dairy cows, and a few chicken sheds.

The afternoon sun blazed down on the rural setting, making it look serene and inviting. Vasily continued to relax, enjoying for the first time that day a sense of calm and order. He glanced out the windows, noticing that almost every home and farm seemed to have pets: dogs running over open fields or cats drowsing on porches or in shade under trees. Flocks of chirping birds filled the air and soared into the pine forests or landed in local trees.

Clouds were building over the mountain peaks ahead, white turning to gray. On both sides of the road, tractors mowed hay, which would be allowed to dry before it was gathered to feed cattle. Fields of green cornstalks in straight rows stretched as far as the closest forest.

Vasily found himself enjoying the tranquil country setting. Although it was still hot, he turned off the air-conditioning and opened his window, allowing warm, humid air smelling like mowed hay to fill the car. He liked the Como countryside, with its towering pine forests, steep mountains, and peaks that looked to be 3,000 meters high. This was the most peaceful area he'd been in since he had arrived in Italy.

He wanted more of this serenity. It calmed him and made him long for a peaceful life. He envied the Italians who had the good fortune to live in this beautiful mountain setting with clean fresh air, no pollution, and quiet.

He wished he could disappear and change his life.

But he was on an important assignment, a responsibility he was in the process of fulfilling. He kept a distance from Volkov's SUV, watching as he made turns at intersections. Vasily would follow and enter an intersection in time to see Volkov make his next turn. He kept more than a hundred yards behind unless the road was short, in which case he would wait a few seconds before resuming so Volkov wouldn't see him in his rearview mirror. Traffic was light in both directions, consisting of cars, farm trucks, and a regional bus that stopped at benches for rural passengers.

It seemed to work. Volkov was driving at a constant speed, taking no diversions, apparently unaware that he was being followed. Minutes later, Volkov turned at an intersection with a wooden sign pointing toward the hills that said *Via per Barna*. Vasily let Volkov go on for a minute and then took the turn, seeing the SUV in the distance. Ahead, Vasily could see what appeared to be a small town or village on a hillside, where a church spire rose above homes and apartments.

Vasily slowed, letting Volkov continue, passing a sign that said *Barna*. Even at a distance, it appeared to Vasily that this was a sleepy rural town with no sign of industries, only homes and farms.

A regional bus left Barna and passed Vasily as he entered the village, driving slowly, looking down narrow streets lined with a few homes and small apartment buildings. He passed a schoolyard where children kicked a soccer ball in a grassy field. Farther along, he saw old men sitting on benches, smoking and idling until it was time to go home for a nap or an early dinner. Vasily passed a Carrefour Market, the busiest place in the village, with shoppers entering one door and exiting another. A mother pushed a stroller while a young girl, probably her daughter, walked alongside pushing a shopping cart full of grocery sacks.

Vasily stopped at a piazza in front of the spired church. He pulled into a parking spot near a circular stone fountain. Getting out, he stretched from the long drive that had started that morning, more than five hours ago.

He walked in front of the church and saw a faded stucco plaque that read *Chiesa di Santa Maria Maddalena*. A double wooden door was slightly open. He continued over the cobblestone piazza, where young children played with toys, and mothers sat on benches, talking with neighbors. He circled a tall fountain with a statue and small gargoyles spewing water back into the fountain as well as onto plants.

But no sign of Volkov. His SUV had taken a turn that Vasily hadn't noticed. He walked down narrow streets but didn't spot Volkov's vehicle. Volkov had likely parked in an underground garage.

Vasily couldn't risk continuing to walk around, looking conspicuous as a stranger in the village. Small towns were notorious for gossip. If someone new showed up, whispers began and quickly spread through such a town like a virus: *Who is the strange man? Why is he here?*

Vasily needed to be the invisible assassin, not a suspicious person roaming around Barna. He'd find Volkov. It was just a matter of time.

Vasily returned to his car and drove out of the piazza as dark storm clouds filled the sky in the distance. A jag of red lightning, and then another, crackled over Lake Como. A splatter of raindrops on the windshield quickly became a deluge. Vasily flicked on the wipers, heading down the hill from Barna as cats and dogs fled for homes and barns. Tractors remained in the fields, mowing hay. Long green leaves on cornstalks swayed in the wind that whipped through the countryside.

It was about 4:30 p.m., later than Vasily had imagined returning to Milano to attend Betta's party. Rain meant slow traffic, cars splashing in puddles, difficult visibility, and minor accidents. He was certainly going to be late, he realized. But it was the price he had to pay to learn what he had that day. He knew it was just a matter of time before he would find Volkov and carry out his mission to assassinate him.

# CHAPTER TWENTY-FIVE

V asily was glad he had a GPS on his rental car. Without
it, he likely never would have made it back to Milano in
time for Betta's party, even though he didn't arrive until 9:30. He
found a parking place a block away and dashed to the apartment
building. He found the hostess's name and apartment number
on the back of Betta's business card, pressed the buzzer, and
announced his name.

A woman answered with a slightly slurred voice, "Oh,
you're Betta's friend, the Russian. We've been waiting. Betta
said you'd better make it or she'd never invite you to another
party. Come on up!"

The door clicked, and he went inside. He took the elevator
to the fourth floor and walked down the hallway. He could hear
sounds of a party coming from the apartment.

He knocked and heard a burst of laughter, as if someone
had told a joke. A smartly dressed woman holding a glass of

wine opened the door. "Vasily, come in. I'm Federica. I'm glad you made it. I'm giving the party for Giulia."

Vasily entered the apartment and said, "Thank you."

Federica led him inside and pointed across the room. "There's a buffet table, and there's still plenty of food. Grab something to drink and come meet Giulia and the other guests."

Vasily surveyed the room, familiar with the raucous chatter of a party that had been underway for some time: boisterous conversations from small groups, an argument about politics from a circle of men who looked to be in their thirties or forties, lovers holding hands or standing with arms around each other, and women laughing in a corner. On facing couches, two older couples were deep in conversation, with one man making hand gestures as if he were telling a humorous story. When he finished, his audience emitted a burst of laughter.

The crowd appeared middle-aged, with more women than men, all fashionably dressed. No sloppy clothes, fat people, or drunks.

Federica turned to the crowd and announced his arrival. "Hey, everybody, guess who's here? Betta's Russian friend, Vasily!"

The partygoers nearest them turned their heads and welcomed him with a chorus of "*Ciao, Vasily...Ciao...Buonasera... Ciao.*"

Vasily waved, feeling somewhat overwhelmed by the boisterous partygoers. He was delighted to be there, even though he was sober and tired. He needed a drink or two to catch up with them.

Federica took his arm and said, "Come on, Vasily. I'll take you over to get some wine."

She led him through the small crowd to three tables under a wall-mounted TV screen. One table held food, another several open wine bottles and glasses. The third was decorated with wrapped presents, colored envelopes, humorous birthday cards standing on end, a half-eaten birthday cake, empty plates, small forks, and floral napkins.

"Help yourself, Vasily. Let me know if there's anything else I can get for you." He thanked her. The caterer behind the table smiled and said, "What would you like to drink, *signore?*"

Vasily surveyed a row of bottles: white and red wines, champagne, Prosecco, and liquor. "I'd like a cabernet sauvignon if you have it."

"Of course," the caterer said as he reached for a bottle. He poured half a glass and handed it to Vasily. "Try this. I think you'll like it."

Vasily sipped and then took a longer drink. It was very smooth. Slightly heavy, no acid. And it flowed so well into his stomach. He took another drink, finishing the glass.

"Let me refill your glass, *signore,*" the caterer said, still holding the bottle. This time he poured a full glass. "An excellent wine, *signore.* Cabernet sauvignon from Colli Euganei, in Veneto."

"Yes, it is excellent. Thank you." Vasily felt a touch on his shoulder and heard a familiar voice close to his ear. "Better late than never. I didn't think you'd make it."

He turned to face Betta, who was wearing a short blue skirt, a low-cut blouse, and a necklace between her cleavage: a silver chain, a second strand below it with what looked like a silver tear dangling from the center, and a third strand below in the same design, a thin chain with a silver tear. Concentric, stylish, certainly expensive. This was the most elegant he had ever seen Betta look.

She kissed him on both cheeks and said, "Follow me. Some people I want you to meet." She took his hand and led him toward a circle of women engrossed in conversation.

"Hey, everybody, this is my new friend, the Russian I told you about," Betta said. "We've been having morning coffee recently before work. He's from St. Petersburg. Vasily, meet Cecilia, Rosella, Sabrina, and Giulia. It's Giulia's birthday party. She's thirty-nine again."

They laughed at her comment and greeted him. "Thanks for coming, Vasily," Giulia said. She was a tall, sexy blonde with pale blue eyes that looked ceramic. "Betta calls you her mystery man, wandering around Milano. How do you like our city?"

"It's amazing. I love it. I'm enjoying my time here very much," he said, feeling welcome in the short time he'd been at the party. "Happy birthday, Giulia. It looks like you're all having a great time. Thanks for inviting me. It's nice to meet you all."

The woman he thought was Rosella said, "This is a party crowd, Vasily, as if you couldn't tell. Many of us have been friends since childhood. We grew up together, went to school, started work—and stayed friends. Some even married—"

Betta laughed, interrupting her friend: "—and some are still married, but not all of us, right, girls?" Her friends responded with a chorus of laughs. One answered, "Really, Betta. Some of us haven't found the right man yet."

"Well, are you in training to find the perfect husband?" she joked.

The woman he thought was Rosella answered quickly. "Some of us already have." She held up her left hand, displaying a wedding band and another ring with diamonds.

More laughter and smiles. The wine that had flowed for hours had served as a lubricant for their spirited conversation and humor, warm and not sarcastic. The women were clearly comfortable with each other from years of friendship and sharing intimate parts of their lives.

Vasily was puzzled. How should he respond? He just smiled and nodded, too embarrassed to comment.

"What brings you to Milano, Vasily?" Sabrina asked.

"Mostly, I'm a tourist. I start a new job soon and had time to take a vacation and visit Italia. I wanted to visit your museums, art galleries, and historic sites."

"Plenty here," Giulia said. "You'll be busy."

"I'm also collecting information for a friend who writes for a travel magazine. He couldn't make it, so I'm doing research for him."

"Really?" Betta said. "You didn't tell me that before. I've got friends who work in museums. They'll arrange a private tour if you're interested."

Again, Betta had offered a favor. "Maybe next week. Thank you for the offer."

"Not a problem. I'll make a few phone calls."

"What kind of work do you do in St. Petersburg, Vasily?" asked the woman he thought was Cecilia.

He paused. *What do I say?* "I'll start working for a bank soon. Just an admin job, mostly transferring accounts."

"Hmm. You didn't tell me that before, either," Betta said, with a look that seemed either puzzled or disappointed.

"Sorry. It just hadn't come up."

"Mmm, maybe you're right. Oh, well, now I know," she said, taking another drink of wine.

"I work in a bank, too," Giulia said, "but my first love was always art. I wanted to study art history, but my father told me, 'Go into business. You'll make more money so you can go to museums all over the world.' He was right! I'm off to Paris next month. The Louvre, of course, to start with. It will be my third or fourth time."

"Maybe you'll meet another handsome Frenchman, like the last time, right?" Betta joked.

They all laughed. Vasily felt a little uncomfortable around these smart and attractive women who were sharing fragments of their love lives. They seemed so relaxed talking about intimacy, something that he figured must be common among mature Italian women. Russian women rarely shared such details, and certainly not around men.

Betta touched his arm. "Excuse us, ladies. I want to take Vasily around to meet more friends." She looked at Vasily. "By the way, are you hungry? There's food at the caterer's table."

He nodded. "Yes. I just had a light lunch." In truth, he was half-starved and eager to fill his empty, groaning stomach.

"Come on. We'll get you a plate and fill it up. But first, let's refill your wineglass. It's empty."

She led him to a long table with food, next to where the caterer had poured his wine. But he wanted more wine first. The two glasses of cabernet sauvignon had pleasantly soothed his brain.

After the caterer refilled their glasses, Betta said, "Let's have a toast, shall we? To Giulia's birthday party!" They clinked glasses and said, *"Cincin."*

They both sipped and smiled. Betta took his arm again and led him over to the buffet table. Vasily felt a warmth inside that was from more than just good wine on an empty stomach.

"Lots of good food here, Vasily. Fill your plate."

Vasily was glad she had taken his arm. The wine was having an effect on him, and he didn't want to stumble and make a scene. He needed to be in control, not do something that would embarrass himself or Betta.

"Here, try this risotto. They just brought it from the kitchen," she said, reaching for a spatula and spooning a portion onto his plate.

"It's one of my favorites," she said. He picked up a fork, took a bite, and swooned at the first food he'd eaten in many hours.

"Mmm, so good," he said. "This is warm and delicious. Can I have a little more?"

"Sure." She spooned another serving onto his plate, then added pasta with *pachinko* tomatoes and basil, veal with tuna mousse, stuffed peppers, and zucchini pancakes.

"That should satisfy your appetite. Come back for more if you'd like some cheese, pizza, or salad."

"It all looks so good. Thank you."

"Why don't you find a chair and eat as much as you like. I'll come back."

She left, and Vasily was alone, eager to satisfy his hunger. With his full plate, he found an empty chair and sat down. He devoured the delicious foods, and when his plate was almost empty, he returned for some salad and a slice of pizza with cheese, basil, and tomatoes, which disappeared in three chomps.

When his plate was empty except for a little mousse and a zucchini pancake, he felt woozy. He had eaten too fast, and the wine was making him a bit sleepy. He relaxed, his hunger pangs soothed. Life returned to his tired body. The rich food was like fuel to his engine. He wanted more.

While serving himself a third plate, he listened to guests laughing and having spirited conversations. It was such an unanticipated experience, enjoying excellent food at the home of a person he'd never met, invited by a mysterious woman who had opened doors to the kind of life he had only dreamed about. How had he gotten so lucky? He had been in Milano less than a month and was meeting Italians who seemed genuinely happy and well mannered. No cursing or angry outbursts from drinking too much vodka. That was what a birthday party in Moscow would have been like.

When his third plate was empty, he carried it to the end of the table, where a caterer took it and immediately disappeared into another room, possibly the kitchen, where he could see other caterers filling boxes with the party's leftovers and utensils.

Vasily walked back to the chair where he had eaten. He looked out a double-paned window at a glimmer of light below. He stood and looked down on an inner courtyard with lounge chairs, umbrellas, and people sitting at tables surrounding a small pool. Another party, maybe. Residents enjoying a Saturday night at these modern apartments, entertaining friends or neighbors, probably as carefree and content as the guests at Giulia's birthday party. How lucky they all were to be living in a society so rich in history, culture, and the good life. Moscow was far away, not just in distance, but in lacking a lifestyle as rich as the one he was experiencing.

He felt a wave of melancholy, knowing that this was a passing opportunity. That feeling was followed by a rare sense of contentment and fulfillment. How long would such good feelings continue? He was familiar with melancholy. He preferred this new feeling of happiness and hoped it would never end. But it would. One day. Soon.

He needed more wine. He returned to refill his empty wineglass. The caterer who had served him was no longer there, but half a dozen half-full bottles remained. He picked one up, poured, and took another sumptuous mouthful of dark red wine, full bodied, with a lingering aftertaste of plums and cherries. He read the label: Amarone della Valpolicella. It, too, was from the Veneto region. The next time he visited a liquor store, he would buy a couple of bottles.

He sipped his wine and saw Betta walking toward him, looking almost as fresh as when he had first seen her that night. "How was the food, Vasily? Did you get your tummy full?" she asked. Her words were a bit slurred, and her eyes slightly glazed.

"Superb! I'm as full as I've ever been in my life. Thank you for inviting me to meet your friends. It's been a pleasant evening."

"It's getting late. The party's breaking up. Walk me home, will you? It's only a couple of blocks. Women don't like to walk alone at night."

"Of course. I'll be happy to."

"Come with me. Let's tell Giulia goodbye. You can wish her happy birthday again."

Giulia was near the entrance to the apartment, shaking hands and kissing the cheeks of departing guests. When they reached her, Vasily followed Betta's example, wishing Giulia happy birthday again and taking the initiative to exchange cheek kisses.

He felt joy just from this touching. The evening had been a pleasure. He had been received well, felt the warmth of Betta's friends, and devoured the delicious Italian dishes and wine.

When they were on the street, the hot, steaming weather had been replaced by cool humidity. Betta took Vasily's arm and inched closer to him, their shoulders almost touching. He felt a closeness to her and was thrilled that she had invited him to walk her home. He wondered what would happen when they arrived. Would she invite him up and allow him to kiss her good night? Or something more?

But it wasn't going to happen. With her hand on his arm, she said, "Don't worry, Vasily. I don't want to sleep with you. Just walk me home."

"Of course. The walk will be pleasant enough," he managed to say, thinking he had made a polite response to her declaration.

"You should know that I don't sleep with any man until I know I can trust him. I need to feel completely comfortable with him. That doesn't happen in a few days, or even a couple of weeks," she said. "Trust is important for me. Do you understand?"

An intimate confession? How bold and definitive. He had come to expect such from Betta. But he had hoped for a different ending to the evening. "Of course I do. I respect your honesty. And thank you for telling me."

She continued, "When I was young and had my heart broken, a friend of my older sister told me, 'Betta, wait before you sleep with a guy. You won't regret it.' She was right. I meet many men—good looking, rich, cultured. But after a few dates, I begin to notice things I don't like. Maybe they're possessive or vain. Occasionally, I sense they're lying. I can't tolerate that, not at all. So, as politely as I can, I send them on their way, knowing that, in a few days I'll meet another gentleman. They're out there, looking for a matchup, just like women."

They walked to the end of the block. She took his arm again to cross at the intersection. They continued in silence, enjoying the fresh, cool air and lack of noisy traffic.

Vasily had never heard a woman speak so candidly about what she was looking for in a man: someone she could trust, believe in, and respect. No man at the party had seemed romantically involved with her, only interested in having a good conversation. Betta had floated around the room like the proverbial social butterfly, talking to everyone, lingering with a few. She had been interested only in good conversation and laughter.

Couples who appeared to be lovers had departed early. Those who had stayed lingered for spirited conversations with close friends. It had been a fascinating night for Vasily. He hoped it wouldn't be the only time he would experience Italians enjoying friends at a celebration.

"My apartment's in the next block, Vasily. I've lived there, let's see, for almost ten years."

"A nice neighborhood. Coffee shops, bakeries, trattorias, and a small park. I see why you like it."

"I do," she said, dropping her hand from his arm. "Vasily… we've known each other for a short time. I thought it was important that I be honest with you so you'd know the kind of woman I am and what I value." She reached up, kissed him on both cheeks, and pressed against him briefly. "Thank you for listening to my little soap opera," she added with a warm smile. "I'm glad we had this talk."

They reached her apartment building, and she pointed up. "This is it, my place. See you Monday for coffee? Same time, same place?"

"I look forward to it."

She pressed a code near the door, and it clicked open. She turned around, smiled, and gave him another finger wave.

And she was gone.

# CHAPTER TWENTY-SIX

The next morning, Simona sat in her office with her door closed, reading a text from Armando. He was trying to soothe her, as she was going to tell Antonella that she was pregnant. *"Be calm. She'll be thrilled at the news and reassure you that you can keep your job,"* he texted.

*Thanks*, she texted back. *I'm going to ask Dario to go with me to see Antonella. Will call later.*

Simona set down her phone, sat back in her chair, and took a deep breath. She had not slept well. She had had a dream that she could feel a butterfly moving in her womb. That feeling would come later. And after nine months, she would hold that butterfly in her arms—and her life would change.

Every waking moment, and whenever she awoke from sleep, Simona could think only about this tiny butterfly. She believed she would be happy being a mother, but she dreaded the change that would come in her professional life. She liked her colleagues and loved her job, with its challenges, excitement, and intrigue. In a matter of months, she'd be staying at home, carrying a butterfly bundle wrapped in a blanket, a bundle that would demand her attention almost every waking minute of her day.

She punched a button on her phone. When Dario answered, she said, "Busy?"

"Hmm, not really. What's up?"

"Can you come to my office for a few minutes? I need to tell you something."

"I was going to, but your door was closed."

"Just come in."

"Be there in a second."

Moments later, Dario rapped once on her door and let himself in. "What's up? Hey, are you okay? You look flushed."

She motioned to a chair in front of her desk. "Shut the door, please."

He pushed the door closed and sat down, studying her face. He recognized her apprehensive expression.

Simona looked at Dario, tapped her fingers on the desk, and took a deep breath. "I'm pregnant," she said, her voice quivering.

"Really? Wow, that's great!" he said, grinning like a child playing with a new toy. "When? You don't look pregnant."

"January."

"Congratulations! But you look worried. What's going on?"

"I have to tell Antonella this morning."

"No need to worry. She'll be happy for you."

Simona frowned. "You think so? I'm not sure. I've been here for only three years."

"Almost four."

She nodded, relieved that she had told her partner. She appreciated their close connection and ability to share occasional personal details of their lives.

One of her vivid memories was when she had confessed to Dario her anger and frustration when the two of them had been on duty on a cold December night more than two years ago, sitting in an unmarked police car to see if a terrorist suspect would leave his apartment. That weekend, she had been invited to Lake Como to attend a holiday celebration with Armando at the home of his friend, American actor George Clooney. Instead, she had spent the evening in the freezing cold on a DIGOS assignment with Dario. He had patiently listened as she had admitted her anger.

When she had bitched about missing the party, Dario had given her soothing counsel and had driven her back to DIGOS later that night as she wept. It had been their most intimate moment, one that they had occasionally referred to during other stressful times. Again, Dario was here for her now as she revealed her anxiety about telling her supervisor that she was pregnant and would be on maternity leave at some point in the coming months.

"Motherhood is not something I'm prepared for, Dario. I'm always excited to come to work every morning. But in a matter of months, I'll feel lost, not coming here every day to see you and everyone else. There's a camaraderie in our office with colleagues we respect and admire. I look forward to that every day."

Dario shrugged and waved his hand. "Don't worry, Simo. We'll still be here—trust me. Italy never lacks for crime. Terrorism is a growth industry; just read the papers. DIGOS is the place to be."

"Exactly. But instead of being in the office, I'll be changing diapers, feeding her—or him—learning how to nurse, having sleepless nights, feeling worried all the time—"

"Hey, stop complaining! You'll be a great mom. Having a baby changes your life."

"That's what I'm afraid of. I don't want to lose what I've been working toward all my professional life. I'm in the perfect place. I don't want anything to change."

"Your position will still be here when you're ready to come back; trust me."

"Are you sure?"

"Absolutely! Antonella will confirm it. She'll want you back. So will I. Say, that makes me wonder who I'll have as a new partner. Probably a new agent. I'll train him until you come back."

"If they let me."

"Nonsense. You're afraid for no good reason. What does Armando say?"

"The same as you. Have you talked to him?" she asked jokingly.

"I don't have to. He's a good man, smart and talented. He's crazy about you. Probably the best man you've ever had."

"Stop it!" She said with a laugh, smiling at Dario. "You're right. He is a good man, the best by far of all the men I've known."

"He'll love being a papa. He's never been married, has he?"

"No."

"You're both ready. Neither of you is getting younger. It's best to have kids when you have the energy and time. Don't wait."

Simona looked at him, reassured that Dario was being positive and encouraging, like Armando. She had wanted to tell Dario first as kind of a rehearsal speech before telling Antonella.

Although her relationship with Dario was sometimes confrontational, they always worked together to accomplish their assignments, and they often received praise from supervisors as well as colleagues. Around the office, they were nicknamed Marshall and Lily, from *How I Met Your Mother*—personality opposites who entertained friends and colleagues with their quirks and frequent squabbles. But in the end, true love triumphed, and life moved on to the next episode.

"Wanna come with me?" she asked, raising her eyebrows.

"What do you mean?"

"Go to Antonella with me."

He blinked. "Why, sure, if you want me to. But this is personal, not professional."

"I'd feel better if you were there. Moral support, kind of."

Dario felt honored by her request. He would go with her, an affirmation of their close relationship and partnership. "I'll go. I'll be happy to be with you. Thanks for including me."

Simona sighed and stood up. "Then let's go, partner, and get this over with." She slapped his back as he opened the door. "Thanks, sport."

He smiled and took her hand. "You'll like it when people start calling you 'Mamma.' It's a privilege."

"Okay, okay. Let's go," she said, gently pushing him as they passed two DIGOS colleagues in the hallway, who noticed they were holding hands. Their colleagues' expressions could only mean, *What is going on with those two? Something's up!*

Simona and Dario didn't acknowledge their stares or snickering. They just kept moving down the hallway. Their colleagues would find out later what was going on.

Simona and Dario dropped their hands when they reached Antonella's open door. Dario knocked, and Amoruso looked up. "Hey, come in. What's up? Something with your Russian?"

"Not really," Simona said. "Mind if I shut the door?"

"Not a problem. Go ahead," Antonella said, a little confused by the request for privacy. Agents walked down the hall all day, and office doors were kept open except in sensitive situations.

Simona and Dario sat down. She glanced at Dario and then took a deep breath, looking at Antonella. "Aaah, *dottoressa,* I have some news....I'm pregnant."

Antonella raised her arms in celebration, a smile lighting up her face. "Hallelujah! That's great news. When are you due?"

"January, the doctor said."

Antonella came around her desk, almost bouncing with joy. She embraced Simona. "Wonderful! This is such great news. I bet *dottor* Lucchini will be delighted as well. Have you told anyone else?"

"Just Dario. It's too early to announce it to anyone except you and *dottor* Lucchini. My gynecologist said the risk of miscarriage is highest in the first trimester. So I'll wait until I'm twelve weeks along before I make it public."

"Of course. Volpara is your partner and buddy. I'm glad he came along with you."

Antonella was still holding her arms. Simona took a deep breath and asked, "Can you tell me what will happen to my career?"

"Not a problem. Come back when you're ready. You have five months of maternity leave. We can work something out. You can drop to half-time, or possibly work from home. Don't worry. Your job is safe."

"Are you sure?"

"Absolutely. I'll want you back. We all will. You and agent Volpara are a great team."

"But what about him?" she asked, looking at Dario.

"Agent Volpara?" Antonella laughed and winked at him. "Don't worry. I'll find plenty for him to do. We have new agents coming in the next few months. He can interview them and find someone he could work with. And he or she might join your partnership before you take maternity leave. The *questore* is promising me two or three women by the end of summer. When you come back next year, you two can decide if you want to have a third person working with you or go back to the way you have it now."

"You make it sound so…easy," Simona said.

"It's routine. Having babies is a part of life. I wish my husband and I had had children, but it didn't work out for us." She managed a smile. "I've made my career my life and have few regrets. I'm involved with another family. You know I brought my sister-in-law and her children to Milano after my brother's funeral. I spend time with them and have helped them over a few rough spots."

"How are they?" Simona asked.

Antonella sat back down. "They're fine. They're living in Monza. I see them once a month. Luisa is doing well in school. She's studying violin and has good friends. Carmela found a good job and is taking night classes to get her accounting degree. Diego, the fifteen-year-old, has started at a hotel management high school and wants to become a chef. He's working hard and is finally becoming a good student. Carmela and I talk often.

She says she uses me as a model for Diego, telling him to stay in school, work part-time, and not hang out with bad characters."

"That's good. Life is easier for them here than in Naples, isn't it?" Simona asked.

"No question. They're happier here by far." Antonella smiled. "Hey, let's share the good news with *dottor* Lucchini. If he's free, we can go to his office right now and tell him."

# CHAPTER TWENTY-SEVEN

Betta didn't show up at the coffee shop Monday or Tuesday. Vasily was unsure if it meant anything. The conversation on the walk back to her apartment Saturday night had been on his mind when he was taking a shower, taking the metro to the coffee shop, waiting for her, and feeling disappointment when she didn't show. Had something happened to her?

Betta intrigued him like no other woman ever had. He had never quite understood female behavior; it had always been a puzzle. When he was growing up, his mother was moody most of the time, rarely talked to him, and flinched whenever someone touched her. Although Vasily had had limited contact with his father, he sensed that that was one of the reasons he had left her. She was an unhappy person.

When Vasily started being interested in girls, he didn't know how to talk to them or ask what they liked to do. It was as if his tongue was frozen. He'd look at them and fake a smile but did not know what to say. Then he would walk away. Other boys, the popular ones, moved effortlessly among girls, chatting freely, making them laugh, and touching them. And Vasily learned that those boys had sex with girls. Not one or two, but any girl they wanted.

But not Vasily. He was sixteen when he had sex for the first time. A rather unattractive girl had teased him and said everyone knew he hadn't had sex yet. She had taunted him and said he wasn't a real man until he lost his virginity. They were behind his apartment in a small alley when she lifted her dress and challenged him.

"You ready for this? Take it if you know what to do."

Wide-eyed, Vasily unzipped his pants and pulled her to him. After a bit of slap and tickle, he had forced himself into her. He soon gasped, had an orgasm, and started to shake. The girl pushed him away, pulled up her underwear, and slapped his face. She scowled and said, "You better learn how to screw, or no girl will ever want you to put your stick in her."

His first sexual experience, over in a minute or two. The girl mocking him haunted Vasily. She had even told her girl-friends about their brief encounter in the alley. When he next saw them, they laughed, pointed at his crotch, made a face, and said something crude.

Vasily knew that this girl had trashed his reputation and that he needed to do something to salvage what he could. That had meant finding a less intimidating girl and propositioning her so he could brag to boys that girls couldn't resist him. It happened a week later, when he met a girl, also not very attractive, and asked bluntly if she wanted to have sex. She nodded. Within minutes, they were standing awkwardly on a staircase in an abandoned apartment building and having at it. Just like before, he unzipped, she lifted her dress, and it was over after a few quick thrusts. Neither one knew what to say afterwards. He zipped up, and she lowered her dress and left him standing in the stairwell, embarrassed and confused. He never saw her again. Was this what sex was about?

Each of Vasily's sexual encounters as a teenager had been like this. After a couple of casual meetings, he would ask a girl to take a walk. When they were alone, he would give them the same blunt proposition. And it was always brief, hurried sex. And then it was over. He had had no relationship with a girl that lasted more than a couple of weeks. He quickly forgot about them, even their names.

His marriage, in his early thirties, had lasted only three years, with many arguments, quarrels, and lingering anger. They had been forced to get married after his girlfriend had discovered that she was pregnant. Their only child, Pyotr, was two when Vasily finally left their home and moved in with an old army friend. In the years to follow, most of his encounters were with women who had sleazy reputations. He found them in almost any bar he frequented.

But Betta was the first woman he couldn't stop thinking about. She lingered in his memory: visions of her laughing, sipping cappuccino, and walking to her apartment after Giulia's birthday party. He replayed in his mind her confession about not sleeping with any man until she was comfortable with him, believed he was honest, and felt respect for him.

After Vasily's daily surveillance of Chiara, while he was having dinner and drinking wine late into the night, Betta was always on his mind. This wasn't what he should be thinking about: a woman he had met in a coffee shop who had been friendly and invited him to meet her friends and socialize with them. He needed to focus on tracking down Volkov, completing his assignment, and returning to Moscow.

But meeting Betta had diverted his attention from his mission. Granted, he had intended for his time in Milano to be more than just completing his assignment. He had also wanted to experience the Italian lifestyle, which he greatly enjoyed. And Betta was the catalyst; she was such a different sort of woman than he was used to. She was quick to engage and express interest in him, but not in a needy way. It wasn't about sex, but more about establishing a relationship based on interests and trust. He didn't want anything to interrupt their evolving friendship.

On Wednesday morning, after a night when Vasily had slept poorly, he arrived at the coffee shop late. Betta walked through the door and came up to him. "Got a place saved for me?" she asked. Her voice was bubbly; she sounded pleased to see him. Direct and friendly. He could feel his pulse throbbing like that of a lovesick teenager.

"I've missed you the last couple of days," he said.

She waved at the barista, who gave her a thumbs up and started to prepare her cappuccino.

Betta laughed. "I've had a few stressful days at work and have had to go in early. I'm on the phone most of the day, talking to doctors and hospitals about treating patients with our drugs. It's serious work. I like it very much, providing medications for patients in need."

The barista delivered her cup, saucer, spoon, and napkin. Betta dropped a five-euro note on the bar, which he picked up.

"Then," she added, "when I get home, I listen to voice messages from my brother in Sicilia, my mother in Roma, and various friends. They want me to advise them on health problems, their children, old lovers, new lovers. It's not like I can help them; I really can't. They have to live their own lives." She paused. "That's what my days have been like. How about yours? Do you have to spend much time on the phone?"

"Well, not really," he answered. "Just a couple of phone calls a day with friends in Moscow." Another lie. He received one or two calls or texts a day, but they were from supervisors. Never his mother or son. His mother had to borrow a phone to call him, which she rarely did. Katya hadn't contacted him in months. Where was she? Did she have a new lover? He checked his phone every morning, hoping someone would call, say that they missed seeing him, and ask how he was.

His mission was secret, so he had to lie to people in Russia and say he was in training. He hated to admit it, but he wanted to hear from Katya and hear her say that she wanted to come back to him. It had been months since she'd moved out. He missed her. Katya was the closest he had come to marrying again.

"Boy, are you lucky," Betta said. "I love my friends and family, of course, but they think I have time to talk to them every day. *Please.* Give me a break. I have a busy life! There aren't enough hours in the day to do all the things I want to do." She laughed again, smiling at the barista, who winked at her.

"Maybe I have too many friends. What do you think, Vasily?"

What could he say? She was far down the road with this monologue, one that he, sadly couldn't relate to. Not only did people not call him—he didn't call them, either. So he simply smiled and shrugged.

She finished her cappuccino and picked up her purse. "Say, by the way, do you want to come to the clinic on Friday? We have a team of dentists and doctors coming to provide medical treatment to refugees and homeless people. So many of them are in bad shape. They have rotting teeth, torn muscles, and even broken bones."

"Friday?" A problem. He was planning to go to Barna on Thursday to see if he could find Volkov's car or his apartment and then stay over until Saturday, when Chiara might come. He could then follow them to Barna and learn where Volkov lived. Vasily had felt frustrated the previous time, when Volkov's car had disappeared near the church, having turned onto one of the nearby streets. Vasily had looked but hadn't been able to spot the car. He was hoping to be more fortunate on his next trip there.

"Yes, I'd like to," he said at last. "What time?"

"Around 11:00 a.m. We already will have been treating people, but things slow down a bit after a couple of hours. I help sign in patients, do some paperwork, and then lead them to the right doctor or dentist."

"I'll be there. Where is it?"

She dug in her purse and found a business card. She dug deeper for a pen, and when she found it, she scribbled on her business card. "Here's the clinic's address and phone number. Ask for me. I'll come out and take you inside."

Vasily took the card and looked at the address and phone number.

"Bye, Vasily. Have a good day. See you tomorrow."

A finger wave, and she was out the door. He stood in puzzlement, holding her card and reaching for his espresso, which was now cold.

Three hours later, Vasily was driving up the hilly road to Barna. He glanced left and right at a few vineyards, pastures of grazing cattle, and fields of hay. This was his second time on the rural road, and he hoped that there would be more time to explore the area. It had an emotional appeal to him. It was close to Lake Como but more secluded. A peaceful rural setting with sparse traffic.

He loved seeing the tall pine forests, lush fields of crops, and farmhouses with fenced gardens. And the birds—so many birds, flying free as the wind from fields to trees, disappearing in the forests. He didn't know the names of most of the birds, but they resembled sparrows and hawks. The birds he did know were seagulls from the nearby lake.

Vasily pulled over to the side of the road and parked. He opened the window and smelled freshly mown hay and a hint of manure. Across a fence, a small herd of brown and white cattle peacefully grazed on tall grass, leaving plops of manure behind.

Vasily felt at peace. He fantasized that he could live there, find solace, and search for meaning to his life. If he was twenty years younger, he'd want to learn how to drive a tractor, raise cattle, harvest corn, and pick apples from an orchard. He would rent a rustic farmhouse, milk cows, and collect eggs from chickens. He'd get a dog with long, shaggy fur, like a sheepdog, and hike with him into the pine forests. He'd lead him to a trail deep into the woods, where they would hear birds sing and see snakes, frogs, and gophers. It had been decades since he had seen a snake or gopher—back when he was fifteen and staying at a friend's dacha. They had stayed there only three days, but every minute of it had involved experiencing nature. How he missed that in the city.

He drove slowly into Barna and turned toward the church but didn't park. The small piazza with the fountain ended at a stone wall between the town and the forest. Vasily turned around and drove down a narrow street, seeing older, well-maintained apartments.

It was a quiet street. Children played with cats and dogs, and parents sat on benches talking. No one noticed him; their attention was focused on their neighbors, pets, and children, not on a stranger driving a rental car in their quaint town.

Vasily parked and walked down another narrow street, searching for Volkov's car and hoping to possibly see him outside his apartment. This was only a reconnaissance mission: find him but not attack. Vasily hadn't packed the toxic vial or pistol. He just wanted to survey the area and become familiar with its streets, shops, parks, and benches. If he was lucky and spotted Volkov and his Italian wife, he wouldn't approach. He would only follow them to learn Volkov's routine—where he shopped, where he stopped for coffee or a meal—and maybe learn where his apartment was and where he parked his car.

As Vasily walked along the narrow streets, he looked up and spotted CCTV cameras. Not every area had them. He needed to identify those close to where he would fulfill his mission. He'd seen CCTV cameras in the piazza, across from the church, on corners around the Carabinieri station, near the two banks, and at the Carrefour Market.

After an hour of walking around Barna, Vasily returned to his car and drove off. No sighting of Volkov or his car. He would return on Friday afternoon after going to Betta's clinic.

Driving down the hilly road out of Barna, he saw the deep blue sky above Lake Como, with a few puffy clouds, white as snow. He drove slowly, enjoying the clouds gliding across the sky, some with flat bottoms due to atmospheric pressure. The clouds looked artistic, like a painting by one of those French impressionists, Manet or Degas. Vasily didn't know much about art.

He parked near a fence where cattle grazed. These were black with spots of white on their heads or flanks. Were they dairy or beef cattle? He didn't know. Again, the scene looked artistic, with the cattle's heads lowered to chomp on grass. He watched them take a few steps to the next patch without ever raising their heads. Vasily felt like he could sit there for hours, watching the clouds passing over and the cattle grazing. The only sounds, other than a slight wind, were those made by flocks of pigeons, seagulls, and crows soaring overhead. They were playing in the sky, frolicking in the clean summer air. "Free as birds" was the saying…so true. He envied the freedom of the birds and the serenity of the cattle grazing with no predators.

As he gazed at a dome of pillowy white clouds over Lake Como, Vasily felt as if he could weep with joy, a feeling that had evaded him for so long. The stillness…the beauty…the peace of this setting. Vasily believed that the Italians who called Barna home were the most fortunate people in the world.

# CHAPTER TWENTY-EIGHT

The clinic was on a dingy, littered street in the Loreto area, with locked roll-up metal doors graffitied with crude political and racial slogans. Homeless people and refugees stood in a long line clear to the end of the block: mothers with children, teenagers of various nationalities, bedraggled men of all ages carrying rolled-up blankets and sleeping bags. These were the forgotten Milanese. They wore old running shoes with torn laces and held plastic bags stuffed with water bottles, boxes of food, and scraps salvaged from garbage bins.

It was not unlike what Vasily had seen in Moscow's blighted neighborhoods, where the homeless slept on benches, their meager possessions stuffed into plastic garbage bags, their dirty hair looking like tangled mops twisted into sticky clumps. Vasily had felt disgusted in Moscow by the sight of humans living like feral animals, arguing, drinking cheap vodka, and tossing bottles into the street after they'd drunk the last drop. How could people let their lives become so horrible—one step from the grave, unwanted by relatives and friends who had given up rescuing them?

Vasily stood in the street, where mangy dogs and stray cats wandered, looking for crumbs from the people waiting to enter the clinic. He remembered that Betta had told him to call and tell her when he was outside.

Before he could do so, however, a familiar face appeared at the open door. "Vasily, come on in. I've been waiting," she said, waving at him and then retreating inside. He stepped through the door and saw volunteers handing out forms for the immigrants and homeless people to fill out with basic information.

Betta came over to him. "Here, please let this gentleman through," she said to the crowd just inside the door. The lobby was crowded with homeless people filling out the forms. Four black teenage boys, skinny as poles, handed their forms to volunteers and then stepped back, staring blankly at Vasily and then looking away. They moved to stand against a blank wall.

"Come in. I want to show you around," Betta said, finishing handing out forms and then taking Vasily's arm. She led him through the crowded lobby, where volunteers questioned the refugees and homeless people, jotting down notes about their health needs, age, height, weight, and medical condition.

"It's crowded today," Betta said. "It's always this way when we have a team of doctors here. We have two shifts: four dentists and doctors from 7:00 a.m. until 2:00 p.m., and then another four from 2:00 p.m. to 8:00 p.m. On normal days, we hand out donated clothing and food from grocery stores and restaurants. We treat patients on Tuesdays and Fridays."

She led Vasily through the lobby into a hallway where immigrants leaned against the wall, wearing torn and soiled shirts and blouses, sandals with no socks, flip-flops, and torn running shoes. They were all waiting to be allowed into the next room, which was crowded with other refugees and homeless people moving around tables stacked with piles of used clothing, shoes, socks, underwear, caps, scarves, and a few backpacks. An assistant supervised the handouts, letting each person choose two clothing items from each pile to stuff into their plastic bag. Then she motioned for them to move toward the back, where there was a door to another room.

Betta led Vasily through the clothing room to a larger room, where the refugees and homeless people slowly walked single file around a table with wooden pallets holding boxes of pasta, cans of sauces, loaves of bread, cans of vegetables and soups, wrapped cheeses, ground beef, and bottles of water.

"Here's where we distribute food. Many have no money. They can't afford to buy even the most basic foods. It is such a pity for people to be homeless, broke, and half-starving. They can take two items from each pallet but only one meat, one package of cheese, one loaf of bread, and four bottles of water."

Betta surveyed the room as Vasily watched with a sense of admiration mixed with sorrow. He had seen so many well-dressed, well-fed, and well-mannered Milanese. These people were the underside of the city: the unfortunate poor, homeless, underfed, and ill.

Vasily heard fragments of Italian, Eastern European languages, Arabic, and African languages he did not know. Everyone was speaking softly, timidly selecting their items as an assistant supervised and courteously asked them to make their choices and leave so the next group could enter.

"Last year, we served 10,000 people with food, medicine, and clothing," Betta said. "This year, we'll serve around 15,000. Our current medical staff is forty physicians and dentists who volunteer once or twice a week. They bring their nurses, physician assistants, and dental hygienists, who you'll see in a minute."

Vasily shook his head. "Amazing. It's hard to imagine—so many desperate people in need."

Betta nodded. "We serve people from Africa, the Middle East, and Asia who hear about us and come for our services. And so many need psychological help after escaping from war or, in the case of many young women, from sex trafficking. We see boys and girls with no parents; we send them to shelters. It breaks your heart, doesn't it?"

Indeed, Vasily had a lump in his throat. He had to swallow before he spoke. "It does....It does."

"Come, let me take you to the medical ward." Betta led him back into a hallway, where they passed a small office with volunteers looking at papers and working at computers. At the end of the hallway, Betta led him into a room with double doors. Vasily noticed that this large room resembled a hospital ward, with air-conditioning, a clean tile floor, and a row of chairs where patients waited.

On one side of the ward sat four occupied dental chairs, where two dentists and their assistants, wearing face masks and gowns, treated patients. In the other two chairs, dental hygienists cleaned and examined teeth and filled out charts. Across from them, two other dentists were treating patients, one holding a high-speed drill in a woman's open mouth, another extracting a tooth from a skinny African boy about twelve years old who gripped the arms of the dental chair. Vasily heard gurgling from the plastic tube in the boy's mouth. A masked assistant wiped the boy's chin as saliva and blood dripped onto his paper apron. The patient moaned, his eyes closed, his arms shaking.

Vasily grimaced. He hated going to dentists—the pain they caused, the dreaded sounds of drilling and scraping, the injection of needles into his mouth. He hadn't been to a dentist in more than a year. He'd have to go when he returned to Moscow.

Betta took his arm and led him to another open room, where teams of medical staff wearing blue gowns, sanitized gloves, and face masks were treating patients on gurneys or on plastic couches. The staff was wrapping arms in bandages, examining eyes and ears, checking pulses, administering blood-pressure tests, and examining scabbed and open wounds. Doctors and nurses spoke in clipped phrases, using medical terms Vasily didn't understand. They were working as fast and efficiently as they could.

Betta leaned toward Vasily and said quietly, "Some of these patients have communicable diseases or fevers. They're tested and given vaccines or medicines. The staff asks them to return. Some do, but others we never see again. No idea where they go. Many have never been to a doctor, even in their home country."

Betta caught the eye of a doctor who looked up. He nodded and spoke to a nurse who was bandaging a middle-aged African woman's arm from shoulder to wrist while the woman whimpered, tears in her eyes. When the nurse finished, the doctor said something to her and then came over, lowering his mask.

"*Ciao,* Betta. Is this the friend you told me about?"

"Yes. Riccardo, meet Vasily, my Russian friend."

Vasily reached out to shake his hand, but the doctor raised his. "Sorry. I'm treating patients and don't want to spread germs."

"Of course. I understand."

"Don't worry. Maybe we'll meet again and can shake hands and talk a bit. Betta says you're an interesting person. I'd like to hear about Russia. I've never been there but would like to go one day."

"Riccardo's just back from Sudan," Betta said. "He volunteers with Doctors Without Borders in Africa, where they treat the poorest of the poor in desperate need of medical care."

"Sudan?" Vasily repeated. "Did you like it there?"

"Oh, my God, the weather is so hot and dry, and everything is dusty and sandy."

"I've been to places like that. I hate deserts."

Betta looked over. "You have? You never told me that before. You said you worked in a bank in St. Petersburg."

He thought quickly. He couldn't fumble and lose credibility with Betta.

"It was a long time ago, when I was in the army. We did training exercises in deserts."

"Where?"

He responded quickly. "Aah, Uzbekistan in Central Asia." Another lie. He'd never been to Uzbekistan. Syria was where he'd been sent on another dangerous mission. But he couldn't say Syria. It would lead to too many questions he couldn't answer honestly.

"Oh, more new information," Betta commented.

"It was blistering hot in the summer. You could barely breathe."

Riccardo said, "Fortunately, we lived in tents that had fans and basic air-conditioning. But on most days, we were traveling to villages far away. It's challenging, dangerous work, but I want to help people who need medical attention in the worst way. Sudan is a part of the world most people don't know or care about."

A nurse called over to Riccardo, and he excused himself, saying, "Sorry, I have to get back to my patients. Nice to meet you, Vasily. I hope to see you again."

"Me, too. You're courageous. I respect the important work you do."

Betta touched his arm. "Vasily, I have to get back to work, too. I'm glad you came. I wanted you to see the clinic and understand why I spend so much time helping people."

"It's impressive, Betta. I admire what you're doing."

"I've invited others to come back later today. Some are contributors who want to see where their money goes. I want them to see how crowded we are here. We treat a tiny fraction of the people who need our services. We're raising money to buy the building next door. It's a vacant shoe store, and we want to knock out the walls and join the two buildings so we have space for more doctors and dentists. We desperately need pediatricians, gynecologists, psychologists, and X-ray technicians."

As they returned to the crowded lobby, Vasily said, "Can I help?"

She looked up at him in surprise. "What do you mean?"

"Can I make a small donation?"

"Why, of course, but that's not why I invited you. I just wanted you to see our clinic."

Vasily reached into his pocket, took out a roll of euros, peeled off five 100-euro notes, and handed them to Betta. "This might help you when you buy the next building."

Betta gasped. "Vasily! I'm thrilled! How generous." She took the bills and reached up and kissed him on both cheeks. "Thank you! Thank you so much! I'll tell my staff you made a generous donation."

Vasily blushed, not sure what to say. He finally said, "I admire what you're doing, Betta. I want to help in the only way I can."

The next morning, Vasily left Milano and drove toward Menaggio. He continued on to Barna, arriving about 1:00 p.m. He parked near the church, speculating that if Volkov was picking up Chiara in Menaggio again, they would return to Barna around 3:30. Vasily didn't want to follow them and risk tipping off Volkov that he was being followed. Instead, he would park on a side street with a view of the hilly approach to Barna. The first time he had followed them, Volkov had arrived at Barna at 3:40 with Chiara in the back seat.

Vasily parked on a side street off of Via Cavour and got out of the car. He surveyed the quiet street, where only a few people were present. He was familiar with the area from his visit two days before, when he had hoped to spot Volkov's car parked on the street.

Vasily walked past apartment buildings with underground garages, which were a necessity, given that cars were crammed into every space on the street and filled small lots that accommodated about ten cars each. No sign of Volkov's black SUV.

At 1:30, Vasily walked past the Carrefour Market and crossed the road coming into Barna. He continued to a small park and sat on a bench shaded by young pine trees. In his pocket, he had a small pair of binoculars and a notebook to make notes of his surveillance. He counted the cars approaching and leaving

Barna, about ten every fifteen minutes, more leaving the town than arriving. A regional bus came up the hilly road, entered Barna, and parked near the Carrefour. Vasily figured it was likely to depart in an hour or so. A sleepy village, even on a weekend.

At 2:15, he spotted Volkov's SUV on Via Cavour from the area Vasily had surveilled. His heart fluttered; he had planned well. He now knew the area where Volkov's apartment was. Vasily took out his cell phone and snapped a photo as Volkov's SUV drove down the hilly road toward Menaggio. Volkov's wife was sitting in the passenger seat.

Volkov was likely driving to pick up Chiara. With his pocket binoculars, Vasily watched Volkov turn at the intersection and drive toward Highway 340 on the way to Menaggio.

Vasily felt relief and a sense of accomplishment. Volkov lived in Barna, but where? As Volkov crossed the road, Vasily watched. He continued walking on the narrow, cobblestone road with two- and three-story apartments and a few houses with gardens and lemon trees in the front yards. He continued two more blocks to where the road slightly curved. He stopped.

A block ahead, he saw the Carabinieri station, with police cars parked at the curb and behind the three-story brown stucco building. On the roof were several antennae, along with CCTV cameras that were pointed at intersections around the station. Near the entrance, uniformed officers stood under trees, smoking, talking, and casually watching as pedestrians passed by, including children walking dogs on leashes.

Vasily didn't want to risk walking behind the station and being recorded by the cameras. He turned left into a neighborhood with apartments on both sides of the street. The street was only a few blocks long and ended at the forest. He followed along, checking out apartments and parking lots. The street curved slightly, circling the piazza beside the church. A block later, he reached a low stone fence that circled the piazza. He turned around and returned on the same street but avoided the area near the Carabinieri station.

Vasily felt hungry and thirsty. He reached Via Cavour and entered a small trattoria with outside tables. He ordered a panino and coffee and took the tray outside to sit under an umbrella. He munched on his panino, sipped his coffee, and watched residents making their way to the Carrefour, picking up children, or out enjoying an afternoon *passeggiata*.

He plotted his next move. If Volkov was picking up Chiara, he likely wouldn't return for an hour or longer. Should he go back to his car and wait to see Volkov's SUV coming up the hilly road? Or would it be better to stay between the trattoria and the Carabinieri station so he could observe where Volkov parked and lived?

Waiting in the street seemed a bit risky. Residents might notice and wonder who the strange man was. He left the trattoria and walked down another side street that extended three short blocks and also ended at the forest. He looked left and right. No parking lots. Just a dirt road with tire tracks along a metal fence. The fence appeared newly installed—no dirt, rust, or signs of wear.

Vasily turned right and walked down the dirt road along the fence. Ahead, he saw a metal gate with an electronic control box attached to a concrete post. When he reached the gate, he studied the control box. He peered over the fence and noticed another control device on the same concrete post but facing the forest. There were two, on both sides of the fence, but without dials or panels for entering codes to open and close the gate.

Vasily realized that opening and closing the gate must be accomplished by pointing a remote device at the shiny metal window on each of the control boxes. Wires from the control boxes connected to the top of the gate.

A security fence. Did this have to do with Volkov? It would explain why Vasily hadn't been able to find his SUV. He looked past the electronic fence and saw what appeared to be the corner of a building down the hill, partially obscured by trees.

Vasily heard feet crunching on pebbles along the dirt road. He looked over and saw a man coming toward him, a cane in one hand and a pouch over his shoulder that looked like a small backpack. When the man saw Vasily, he stopped and looked surprised to see him examining the metal gate and the control boxes. The man was in his sixties, with short gray hair and a neatly trimmed gray beard. He was about six feet tall and dressed in casual clothes and walking shoes.

He greeted Vasily. *"Buongiorno.* Can I help you?" The man looked suspiciously at Vasily.

"Oh, no. I'm just out for a walk."

"Here? No one walks back here."

"I got lost. Sorry."

"Do you live in Barna? I don't recognize you." The man's voice was firm with authority.

Vasily's pulse quickened. He had to get away. "No, I live in Milano. I was just driving around. I saw your village and wanted to explore it."

"Where do you live in Milano? I was a lawyer there before I retired and moved back here with my wife."

"Aah, I live near Via Filzi, near Centrale."

"I know that area. Where's your car?"

Too many questions! "I—I'm parked over there, past the church," Vasily said, pointing behind him and trying not to stammer. "It's a lovely piazza. Very nice."

"Have you been in our church, Santa Maria Maddalena?"

"Not yet."

"Santa Maria is more than four hundred years old. It was begun in the early seventeenth century, when the Catholic Church was exerting its influence by building churches everywhere, even in small towns like Barna, which was nothing more than farms. There were only a few other villages in the area. My grandparents, my parents, my sisters and brothers, and I were all married there. It's where all of our children were baptized. Some still live in Barna and attend Mass every Sunday."

"Wonderful. I'll visit it."

"Would you like me to take you there?" The man's voice had an edge, as if he was still suspicious.

"Oh, no. I know where it is."

"You're not Italian, are you? You have an accent. Where are you from?"

"I'm Polish. From Cracow," he lied.

"Where did you learn to speak Italian?"

Vasily's heart was pounding. He had to get away. This man was interrogating him like a lawyer with a witness in a courtroom. "Aah, I studied foreign languages at university."

"Which university? I've been to Cracow."

Vasily winced. "Ah, the Pedagogical University." One of his students at the GRU was from Cracow and said he had studied there.

"Which department?"

"Aah, po—political science," he stammered, sweat forming on his brow.

"Did you learn other languages?"

"I speak Russian also."

"Where did you learn Russian?" the man persisted.

"Aah...well...I...aah...traveled there...family...aah...you—you know," Vasily stammered, panicking because the man was extracting too much information from him. He wanted to run away, but that would definitely make the man think he was lying and possibly up to something illegal. Which he was.

The man stared at him, not answering. Vasily felt sweat starting to trickle down his face, and his palms were moist. He had to get out of there!

They looked at each other without talking, the man's eyes narrowing slightly, his chest not moving, like he wasn't breathing. The man looked toward the gate and then back at Vasily. "I think you'd better be on your way. This is a private entrance. No one is supposed to be here. The Carabinieri come by sometimes."

"I—I see," Vasily stammered, desperate to leave. "I'll go now." He raised his hand, managed a weak wave, and turned around. *"Ciao. Buongiornata,"* he said. "Nice to meet you."

The man didn't answer. Vasily turned and walked away, trying not to make it seem like he was fleeing. Which he was.

After a few hurried steps, he stumbled on a stone half-buried in the dirt. He reached out and grabbed the fence for support, turning slightly.

The man was still standing there, watching him. He hadn't moved.

# CHAPTER TWENTY-NINE

Lucchini called Antonella into his office and asked her to bring agents De Monti and Volpara.

"Yes, sir, right away," she said, sensing something important, as he had not greeted her with pleasantries like he normally did in the morning. This was a direct order from her boss. She hurried down the hallway, looked into De Monti's and Volpara's open office doors, and said, "Lucchini wants us in his office. Now. Let's go."

They followed her down the hallway, entered Lucchini's office, and stood by chairs. "Sit down, and shut the door behind you," he said.

Dario closed the door and took a chair between Simona and Antonella. They all looked at Lucchini, who said nothing else until they were all seated.

"We had a call from the Carabinieri in Barna. They suspect someone is searching for Volkov in their town." Suddenly, the tension in the room was like a jolt of electricity.

"What did they learn?" Amoruso asked.

"A resident of Barna, a former Milano lawyer, saw a man who identified himself as a Pole from Cracow. He was inspecting the electric gate that leads to the farmhouse where Volkov and his wife live. The lawyer was suspicious and said the man was acting strangely. He spoke Italian, but with an accent. The lawyer asked him a few questions and thought the man was lying or trying to cover something up. Since our informant is a former lawyer, he's likely skilled at questioning suspects or witnesses who aren't telling the truth."

"This could be a break—the first we've had," Amoruso said. "We need to meet with the lawyer and question him. What did he learn, other than that the man said he was Polish and from Cracow?

"Not much, unfortunately. The lawyer was walking to his apartment near the fence and saw the man checking the gate as if he were searching for something. The lawyer said that people in Barna know that a Russian and his wife are living secluded in the forest and that they go through an electronic gate when they leave their home."

"We know that gate," Simona said. "Dario and I went through it when Dmitri drove us back to our car near the trout farm."

Lucchini nodded. "I remember. The retired lawyer said the Carabinieri know Volkov. He paid for the fence and asked permission from the Carabinieri before he had it installed. He's on good terms with them. He pays local taxes and participates on local committees about safety."

"Volkov wants to be seen as a good citizen in Barna, not a hermit in hiding," Amoruso said.

"His daughter said that, too," Simona added. "He's on good terms with the people in Barna."

"Does Volkov know about this new development?" Amoruso asked.

"Yes. The Carabinieri called Volkov, who told them that Volpara and De Monti had been to their home. The Carabinieri commander contacted the *questore*, who briefed me. The *questore* is very concerned that the Polish guy could be a Russian agent sent from Moscow to hunt down Volkov."

"How did the Pole—or Russian, probably—get there?" Dario asked. "He must have a car. The only buses are regional ones to and from Menaggio and Como."

Lucchini shrugged. "More important, if it is a Russian sent after Volkov, how did he find out he lived in Barna? It's very remote."

"Who knows?" said Amoruso. "It didn't take him long to find out. The lawyer didn't get a picture of the Pole or see his car?"

"No," Lucchini said, shaking his head. "The lawyer followed him, but he got away. The lawyer walks with a cane, and the Polish guy probably ran."

"We need to go to Barna to talk to the lawyer and reassure Volkov," Amoruso said. "I'm sure he's worried."

"He must be," Lucchini said. "Volkov's been in Barna only a few months, and already someone is looking for him, most likely a Russian sent from Moscow to kill him."

"You think he's FSB, maybe from the Russian consulate here?" Dario asked.

"Not likely," Lucchini said. "We know all of the FSB agents at the consulate and follow them occasionally to see what they're up to. They do standard intelligence operations and take photos of train networks, airports, anything remotely military. But there's a branch of Russian military intelligence called the GRU. They're the ones who carried out the Litvinenko assassination in London and other places. The Russians wouldn't risk assigning a local FSB agent to search for Volkov. If they were successful in finding and killing him, it would be an international political scandal: Russians sending an assassin from the consulate. Rome might go so far as to shut down the consulate and send everyone back to Russia. No, too risky. They'd want plausible denial, someone sent by the Kremlin."

"That sounds right: a rogue killer with no connections to the consulate or embassy in Rome," Amoruso said.

"I'd bet on it," Lucchini said. "The *questore* informed the Ministry about the suspect and asked if they had intercepted any more intelligence about Moscow sending someone after Volkov. This case has reached the highest level of our national security. We have to prevent assassinations on Italian soil, as the political ramifications would be immense. We've got to protect Volkov and his wife."

They all nodded. "I need to go to Barna with Volpara and De Monti," Amoruso said. "I want to meet Volkov, check out his security setup, and question the lawyer."

Lucchini held up his hand. "Wait a couple of days. I called Volkov, and he said he and his wife are taking a few days of vacation. They're in Varese and going on to Menaggio Thursday to return home."

Simona said, "Yes, Dmitri told us that he and his wife like to take little vacations every week or so. They don't want to be cooped up in their remote farmhouse every day."

"Call Volkov on Wednesday," Lucchini said to Amoruso. "Find out when they'll be home so you can drive up and meet them."

"Let's do it," she said to Volpara and De Monti.

* * * * *

On his drive back from Barna, Vasily cursed to himself about the encounter with the man with the cane. Damn! He had been so careful in his surveillance of Chiara and in finding Volkov, learning where he lived, and not attracting attention. He had followed basic surveillance protocol: Don't stand out from the crowd, wear neutral clothes, wear no hat or cap, don't look people in the eye, don't smoke in public. Melt into the scenery so no one notices you. He had done all that, until the man with the cane had seen him just when he was making a potentially critical discovery: a gate and a road that led into the forest where a corner of a building was visible. And, of all things, he had been discovered by a suspicious former attorney who had questioned him as if he were on a witness stand!

Bad luck, and just when he thought he had made a major discovery. What could he do now? He couldn't return to Barna unless he had a way to evade detection. When and how would he do that?

The drive back to Milano was not as relaxing as other trips. He was familiar with the roads now, where traffic backed up along Lake Como, taking the right exit off the Autostrada toward Centrale, the location of the rental car office.

Vasily contemplated going to the consulate and calling Lebedev in Moscow to tell him of his potential discovery of

Volkov's home—but not a word about the man with the cane. If the Kremlin knew someone had seen Vasily and questioned— no, interrogated—him, he might be sent back to Moscow, and another agent would be sent to finish the job. Vasily didn't want to take that chance. He certainly wasn't eager to return to Moscow.

By the time he reached the suburbs of Milano, Vasily was weighing his options with regard to continuing his surveillance. One idea was to check into a hotel room in a nearby town and take a regional bus to Barna instead of driving his rental car back there again, which might attract suspicion. He *had* to return to Barna to learn more about the fence and the gate, see where the road went, and find out more about the building he had glimpsed.

Had the man with the cane reported him to the police? If so, would they patrol the fence? Could they arrest him for trespassing?

*Damn,* Vasily thought. *Why did this have to happen just when I thought I'd found my target and could plan my next move: swiping the poison in the vial on Volkov's hand or arm or face?* Achieving success now involved a more dangerous venture.

Vasily's sleep on Saturday and Sunday nights was not restful. He kept awakening from bizarre dreams and rubbing his eyes, the nightmares fading from his memory. Normally, he slept well, but not after the man with the cane had questioned him. How had he been so unlucky to be seen at the most critical time of his search? Was this a foreboding, a harbinger that he might not complete his mission? If he was arrested, what would happen to him? Did the Italians torture suspects to extract information, as Moscow did? He didn't want to find out.

When he awoke on Monday morning, he stretched and stared at the ceiling with its concentric stains in the corner.

He rubbed his eyes and looked over at his watch: 7:18 a.m. He picked up his Russian phone and saw a text from his ex-wife:

*Vasily, I have bad news. Your mother died yesterday morning. I was at the hospital. They called me and said I should be there. They couldn't contact you. Where are you? You should have been with your mother during her final days on earth. Why weren't you here? Are you coming for her funeral? You are her only child. You have to come back to St. Petersburg. Pyotr is upset because his grandmother died. He asks where you are. When are you coming to St. Petersburg?*

He read and reread her text, feeling a flood of emotions: sadness, nausea, bitterness. He felt like crying, but he couldn't. He was a man, a strong man. Strong men didn't cry. They showed strength and courage. They didn't break down and weep like women did. No, he wasn't going to cry.

His morning was a blur. He went into the bathroom, turned on the shower, and lingered under the hot needles of water. His mind swirled with the flood of misfortune: his mother dying, the man questioning him at the gate.

He'd been so upset about the man interrogating him that he hadn't waited for Volkov to come back, if, in fact, he had gone to Menaggio to pick up Chiara. It was no wonder that Vasily hadn't been able to find Volkov's car or apartment; he didn't live in Barna but in a forest outside of town.

By the time Vasily got out of the shower, steam was rising from his body. He wrapped a towel around his waist and returned to the bedroom, dripping water onto the floor. He picked up the phone and read the text from his ex-wife again, and then reread it one more time. He set the phone down on the nightstand and hung his head. He shut his eyes, recalling the last time he had seen his mother before he had flown to Milano. Her head was sunk deep into the pillow, her eyes were closed, her face wrinkled. She uttered soft moans but no words. Almost like a corpse that was still breathing.

He glanced at his phone: 8:12. What was he going to do that day? He had planned an early lunch, followed by a stroll around Milano on a hot summer afternoon. But his mood was not going to allow him to enjoy a peaceful day.

His mother had died. He couldn't go to St. Petersburg until he had completed his assignment.

He wanted a drink, something strong. He went to the cabinet and took down the bottle of grappa. He opened it, poured an almost-full glass, and tossed it back. The sting of the strong alcohol scorched his throat. He closed his eyes and gritted his teeth as the grappa flowed down. After a few moments of relief, his belly rebelled at the flood of alcohol on an empty stomach.

He rushed into the bathroom and threw up in the sink. A swoon of dizziness made him grip the sink and hold on so he wouldn't fall.

The grappa had been a mistake. He felt sick, woozy. He returned to the bedroom and lay down on his bed. He looked over at his phone. He couldn't bring himself to read the text again.

He put an arm over his eyes to block the rays of morning sun coming through the curtain. He wanted to escape into sleep, but he couldn't. His mind was racing with the events of the morning and having been discovered by the lawyer. Awake and sick to his stomach, he knew he couldn't stay in bed all day.

He remembered the pistol he had picked up at the consulate. No, he couldn't. Never. *Don't think about that as a solution to end this agony.*

He had to get up and go someplace. But where?

Two hours later, after three cups of cappuccino and a brioche, Vasily found himself at the San Maurizio museum, which he had visited briefly after Betta had recommended it. The first time he had walked around the former church, now a museum, he had stared up at the frescos, impressed by the beauty of Renaissance art. He had spent only half an hour there but had planned to return when he had more time. Today he did. In a damaged frame of mind.

He stepped into the entrance on Corso Magenta and turned left to view chapels set back into the walls, chapels of the Resurrection, St. Stephen, and St. John the Baptist. He turned to observe chapels on his right: St. Catherine, the Deposition, and St. Paul. The somber setting of the chapels soothed his anxiety. He was no longer obsessing about his mother's death and the unfortunate experience in Barna. He felt a sense of calm for the first time since morning.

Staring up at the beautiful frescoes, he recalled childhood memories of statues and icons in Russian Orthodox cathedrals of the Madonna and baby Jesus, the saints, angels, and God in heaven. Byzantine art had made him feel connected to God, back when he was a believer. Later, he lost all interest in religion.

An organ was playing somewhere, possibly behind doors where a musician was rehearsing for a future event. The chords were muted, as if muffled by thick stone walls. Even the faint, almost whispering music gave Vasily a feeling of tranquility, which he desperately needed.

He closed his eyes and remembered back to his childhood when his mother would take him to the Kazan Cathedral or St. Isaac's Cathedral in St. Petersburg during Holy Week. She would clutch his hand, humming as a male chorus behind the iconostasis chanted ancient Gregorian hymns. He couldn't understand the words but felt a spiritual presence for a minute or two, which then dissolved as he looked at the old women wearing long scarves covering their heads and the men bowing and genuflecting repeatedly. Old believers seemed to be in another world, maybe remembering their childhoods and how they had survived wars, famines, and bloody revolutions—and the millions who had not. Religion seemed to mean something to them, but not to him.

Vasily opened his eyes, blinked, and continued to walk around the museum, gazing up at the colored frescoes of saints with halos, angels and cherubs, disciples, the Virgin Mary and baby Jesus, and depictions of the Crucifixion and Resurrection.

He wanted the peaceful feeling to remain. He walked past an altar through a small opening on his left, entering the Hall of the Nuns. He had read in the guidebook that, centuries ago, convent nuns were not allowed in the sanctuary and could only attend Mass behind the altar. They were forced to live in seclusion, devoted to prayer and contemplation.

Vasily circled slowly around the Hall of the Nuns, admiring the chapels and frescoes on the ceiling. The most beautiful one depicted a starry sky with angels, evangelists, and Jesus in the center, looking down, his hand holding up two fingers. Vasily felt overwhelmed by the beauty of the religious themes created by artists long dead, as well as by the way their genius continued to inspire viewers of the majesty of art and religion.

Vasily spent two hours in San Maurizio, his hands often gripped behind his back, his heartbeat slowing. He was able to breathe calmly, immersed in religious beauty. When he exited, he emerged into bright sunlight in the piazza, hoping and even praying he could carry with him the serenity from San Maurizio for the rest of the day. And maybe forever.

He reached up and wiped the tears that were streaming down his cheeks. It was the first time he had cried in many years. He knew he would have to respond to his ex-wife's text later.

His mother was dead. Would he meet her in heaven?

# CHAPTER THIRTY

Simona and Dario came into Amoruso's office later that afternoon. "I talked to Chiara. She heard about the Polish guy," Simona said. "Her father called her after the Carabinieri informed him."

"We received the Identi-Kit the Carabinieri made after talking to the retired lawyer," Amoruso said. "I'll send you the link."

"It will be interesting to see what he looks like," Dario said, "although some are a bit vague—hair color, eyes, mouth. But at least we'll have something to start with."

"And Volkov. Did you talk to him?" Amoruso asked Simona.

"Yes. They're still in Varese, returning tomorrow. He said the Carabinieri would check the gate during the day and be on the lookout for a Polish man or possibly a Russian snooping around. The Carabinieri *caserna* is on the piazza across from the church. Too bad that lawyer didn't get a photo. He didn't have his cell phone with him."

"Who goes around without their cell phone?" Simona said.

"Retired lawyers, I guess," Dario said with a snicker.

"Probably right," said Amoruso. "Clients aren't calling him anymore. In any case, clear your calendars for Friday. I want us to drive up in the morning so I can meet the Volkovs, check their security system, and brief them about any new information we have. Do you want Volkov's daughter to come with us?"

"She can't. She's in Paris this week for work," Simona said. "She won't return until the weekend. The family talked it over. She won't go see her parents in Barna. They might meet in Como or Menaggio."

*  *  *  *  *

All week, Vasily pondered his next move: when to return to Barna and inspect behind the fence. Rather than take a regional bus, he decided he would park, walk along Via Cavour, and turn down the street that led to where the fence started along the granite wall. He'd crawl over the fence and continue into the forest in the direction of the building he had seen.

With luck, the man with the cane wouldn't show up again. And if he did, Vasily would be below his line of sight in the forest on the downward sloping hill.

He would wear sturdy shoes, a dark sweater, and dark pants. In one pants pocket, he would carry the vial of the Novichok. In the other, he would carry his Spetsnaz pistol from the consulate. A back pocket would hold metal clippers, in case he needed to cut through the fence or any other barrier he might encounter. And a knife. He had used a knife in Georgia and Ukraine before and considered it a good luck charm.

His sentimental attachment to knives went back to the time he was growing up in Leningrad. One summer night during the "White Nights," when the sun never sets, Vasily had been walking home from a playground and taking a shortcut through a neighborhood he didn't know well. In the fading light, as the sun approached the horizon, a gang of rough kids had burst out of an alley, chased him, and beat him up. They'd warned him that they'd hurt him even more if they saw him in their neighborhood again.

Vasily had limped home, bruised, with a bloody nose and damaged fingers and wrists. He became determined never to be attacked again. He borrowed his brother's old pocket knife with a dull blade. A week later, he ventured back into the area. When he was confronted by the thugs, he pulled the knife out of his pocket and stabbed one of the boys in his leg, drawing blood. The boy screamed. His friends saw the blood and ran away. Vasily wasn't threatened again. And he didn't go near there anymore.

When he saw one of the boys weeks later walking alone on the street toward him, the boy stopped. Vasily put his hand in his pocket as if he had a knife, which he didn't. He crouched, his hand still in his pocket, staring at the boy, showing his teeth. He made a growling sound deep in his throat. The boy panicked and ran away.

Vasily always carried a knife after that, an army knife. He carried it when he was sent on maneuvers in Belarus. Later on, he bought a red Swiss Army knife in Kiev. He sharpened it and used it to slice bread and cheese when he was traveling on a train. He used the small clippers to trim his fingernails. A knife was a tool, not just a weapon.

The encounter in Leningrad had taught him a lesson: Always be prepared. You never know when you'll need a knife.

At an outdoor market in Moscow, a dealer had displayed a collection of knives, some military and others handmade, as if they had been made in a prison. There were two from the Great War: a German one with a crest of the Kaiser, the other a bayonet from an English Enfield rifle. Both were rusted and probably had been dug out of trenches. Vasily purchased them, along with a Nazi pistol, nicked and battered. The dealer said it had been found in Stalingrad. Vasily had taken the knives home and made a wooden plaque to display them, labeled with the date he had purchased them.

However, after Katya had moved in, he showed her the plaque with the knives, boasting that he was going to collect more and display them in the living room. She had looked at him with a frown on her face and muttered, "Strange. Knives. Ugh."

After Katya had moved into his apartment, she showed him her jewelry case, which contained rings, necklaces, and bracelets, many looking cheap and gaudy. She wore rings on her fingers, a fake pearl necklace around her neck, and plastic-looking jeweled bracelets on her wrists. She had stood in front of the mirror and asked Vasily what he thought of her jewelry, adding, "Aren't they beautiful? I love jewelry! Don't they make me look sexy?"

Annoyed by the pretentious display, Vasily grasped for something complimentary to say, not wanting to upset her so soon after they had started living together. "Why, of course, Katya," he had managed to say. "That pearl necklace almost matches your sweater. You look very attractive."

But Vasily thought jewelry was bourgeois, done to impress. He thought that Katya's collection made her look like a hooker you'd pick up in a bar, one wearing too much lipstick, a wig, a very short skirt, stiletto heels, and lots of gaudy jewelry.

Knives. Jewelry. Everyone had different tastes.

* * * * *

"Sorry, sweetheart. I don't think I can make it to your concert on Friday night," Simona said when she returned home from work.

"Oh, no. I wanted you to come," Armando said, sounding disappointed. "It's at the Verdi concert hall. It's magnificent, with great acoustics. Why can't you make it?"

"We're going to Como on Friday, and I don't know if we'll make it back in time."

"Como, again?"

She nodded, reached down and kissed his forehead, and ran her fingers through his wavy hair. "I told you a little about it. We're involved in a very high-level case. I'm so sorry; I can't say more than that."

"The Russian thing?"

"Yes, that."

"You and Dario mentioned it when we had dinner with him and Cecilia."

"Yeah, it's that. I'm sorry, but duty calls."

"How are you feeling? You looked tired. You could barely make it out the door when you left for work this morning."

"I didn't sleep well last night. My breasts are growing, and they're sore. I worry about the baby, and then I can't go back to sleep because I'm thinking about her. I'm hungry all the time, but the smell of some foods makes me nauseous. Garlic, especially, and onions. Things that have a powerful odor. I miss eating my favorite foods, and I want to make sure our baby is getting enough nutrition to be healthy."

Armando reached out and hugged her. "Just six months to go."

She rustled his wavy hair again and kissed him on the cheek. "Five and a half months."

"Counting the days?"

"Sort of. My parents want us to come to Bergamo this weekend for my mother's birthday. I'm going to say we might have to make it the weekend after next. This Como thing might mean I have to work on the weekend. Sorry about that. My parents really wanted to see you. It's been a while."

"Would they want to come to the concert on Friday? I could get tickets. A birthday present for your mother."

"Hmm, not a bad idea. They could stay over on Friday and go home Saturday for his party. It might work out."

"We need to discuss the wedding, too. I know your mother is anxious about it."

"Yes, she is. She keeps pestering me with calls or texts every day. She's mentioned two dates, September 11 and 18. Would either work for you?"

"Either would be fine. I'm conducting *Così fan tutte* at the Salzburg Festival in August, so September is fine. Either day."

"Good. The next thing we have to decide is whether we want a small wedding in Milano or a bigger one in Bergamo. My father wants to invite all his rich friends; he has so many. But I don't want to stand in front of hundreds of people when we take our vows. And I'll be showing by then; my plump belly will let everyone know what's coming. If it was up to me, we'd just have a small affair here: my parents, a few colleagues from DIGOS, your friends and family, and a couple of my childhood friends from Bergamo."

Armando looked at her. "A wedding is for more than just the bride and groom. It's for the parents and friends as well. My parents will come, as will my brother and sister and a couple of cousins. But your parents will want more."

"They'd rent out San Siro stadium if they could," Simona said, rolling her eyes. "Aaagh! The thought of a big wedding terrifies me!"

Armando stood up, put his arms around her, and patted her back. "Don't stress. We need to include your parents in the planning but maybe set boundaries: the number of guests, the church, and—"

"Papa will want a dinner for his friends after the wedding. What about music?"

"Chamber music would be nice. I can arrange that."

"Good. Music would be important. I want this to be a wedding that people will remember for a long time. But I'm not at the age where I want to impress anyone. I'd like to have it be just you, me, our parents, and a few friends so we can talk and enjoy ourselves. My father will invite people who hardly know me. They're conservative and like to flaunt their wealth. They'll want to show up in expensive dresses and accessories, showing off like it's a public relations event, not a family wedding."

"Don't be concerned about all that. Your father's a decent man, well respected in Bergamo and Milano. We shouldn't disappoint him."

"You're right. Okay. I need to calm down a bit."

"Sit down and relax," Armando suggested, pulling out a chair and taking her arm to guide her over to it.

"Okay, I'll try to calm down. But I wake up in the middle of the night wanting a small wedding, not some big affair that my father will pay for and brag about to his friends—'My daughter, the DIGOS agent who catches terrorists and is marrying a famous conductor.' The media will want to show up and take photos of us."

"I don't mind. Our wedding will interest a lot of people. We should be happy about that."

She sighed.

Armando put a hand on her belly. "It's also for her."

Simona laughed, running her hand through his long hair and reaching over to kiss him. "Her? We don't even know the gender yet. I'll have an ultrasound soon, and then we'll know. But in the meantime, we can start coming up with names for a boy and a girl. Do you have any favorites?"

"Yes, I do."

# CHAPTER THIRTY-ONE

On Friday morning, Vasily woke at 7:11. He yawned, stretched, and opened his eyes. He stared at the concentric circles of brown water stains in the corner of the ceiling. All of his mornings started similarly: staring at the stains, recalling memories of the previous day, thinking about his plans for that day. Thoughts of Betta, Volkov, and Chiara.

He hadn't seen Chiara all week. Or Betta. Volkov was difficult to find, but Vasily would find him. Maybe not that day, but soon. Vasily was in Milano to track him down and fulfill his mission of sprinkling Novichok on him. Most likely, this would occur in Barna. Then Vasily would return to Milano and depart as soon as he could to any destination outside of Italy. Eventually, he would return to Moscow. His days in Milano were limited as he narrowed down his search for Volkov. Hopefully, he would find him within the next few days.

Vasily stretched and reached for his Russian phone. At the top of the screen was a text from Katya, the first contact from her in months:

*Hello, Vasily. I don't know where you are. Maybe you're out of the country.*

*I need to tell you that I'm getting married next month. I hope you don't mind. I met a man who treats me well. I needed a man who loved me and wanted to marry me. He makes me happy. Please don't be sad. You will find a woman to marry, someone who will make you happy. Goodbye.*

He reread the text, stunned by the news and deeply saddened to learn that the woman he hoped might come back to him would never return. She had found someone else. He hadn't. Would he ever?

He struggled out of bed, dizzy, and stumbled toward the bathroom. He tripped over a rug and hit his head on the bathroom door. Then he stubbed a toe getting into the shower, where he lingered under the hot needles of water. When he got out and dried off, his stomach was churning. He felt he could throw up again, like he had when he had gotten the news of his mother's death.

Feeling faint, he sat on the toilet. He felt at a loss like never before. He hadn't regretted it when he had split up with his ex-wife. But she had raised their son, who had become belligerent toward him. His mother had died, and he hadn't been at her bedside. And now Katya had happy news that felt like a knife in his heart. How much more could he take?

As he dressed, he felt weak. Sadness washed over him. Never had he felt so alone. Alone in a city that didn't know him. Traveling with a phony passport and a semiautomatic weapon. And a vial of poison. He loved Milano but knew he would leave soon, never to return once he had completed his assignment. Russian assassins weren't allowed to go back to countries where they had committed crimes.

The worst that could happen would be if he were captured. He would be jailed, tried in a foreign court, likely found guilty, and imprisoned for the rest of his life. His name would be known to the world, stained forever.

He couldn't let that happen. How had his life turned out this way? Could he somehow change his life into one that offered hope of a future without remorse and regret?

\* \* \* \* \*

Early Friday morning, Antonella, Simona, and Dario met with Lucchini in his office. "The *questore* wants to be informed when you arrive in Barna," Lucchini said. "Call me, and I'll conference him in. He's in Rome at the Ministry, which has a high level of concern for Volkov's safety. And tell Volkov we'll provide technical support if he needs it."

"I called him this morning," Amoruso said. "He's looking forward to our coming today. He doesn't seem worried. He said the man who was inspecting the gate might have been nobody in particular, just a coincidence. I told him that I'm suspicious of coincidences. I won't dismiss it unless we can identify the Polish person, or Russian, whoever he is. I suspect he's the assassin Moscow sent."

"We can't take a chance," Lucchini agreed. "The stakes are too high. This is a national security investigation."

Amoruso nodded. "By the way, Volkov's Italian is excellent. He speaks with a Calabrian accent. I told him I was from Napoli.

We have a lot in common. He and his wife were in Napoli when they traveled south."

"He sounds like a decent fellow, not like the Russians I've met," Lucchini said. "They seemed a bit aloof, distant—but that's just my opinion."

"That's been my experience, too," Amoruso agreed, "with the Russians I met at conferences and at the Milano Expo when they had a large delegation in Italy. Volkov is Russian by birth, but his wife has influenced him and shown him how Italians behave. Maybe it's a cultural thing. Who knows?"

Lucchini stood and walked around his desk. "Call when you get to Barna. I'll hold all my calls after that."

"Yes, sir, will do," Amoruso said, standing, followed by Simona and Dario. Lucchini walked them to the door. "At least you'll have a nice day for a drive to Como. I wish I could be with you," he said with a smile and a wave.

"We should be there around noon," Amoruso said, checking her watch. "Traffic along Lake Como is challenging on Fridays, with weekenders clogging the roads around the lake."

"Enjoy what you can. And let Volkov know we'll help in any way we can," Lucchini said as they gathered in the hallway. "And be careful. I want you all to come home safe tonight."

Fifteen minutes later, Dario drove an unmarked Audi police car out of the *Questura* onto Via Fatebenefratelli, turning left toward the Piazza Cavour, a block away, and then heading north through the center city toward the suburbs. Each DIGOS agent had a bottle of water resting in a holder. Amoruso was in the front seat, looking through the morning paper. Simona sat in the middle of the back seat, reading texts on her phone from

Armando and her mother, who wanted to talk about wedding plans and when she would be coming to Bergamo.

\* \* \* \*

Betta spotted Vasily in his usual place at the end of the coffee bar. She did her finger wave with one hand, the other holding the hand of Riccardo, the doctor he had met at the clinic. Riccardo look relaxed and well-tanned. He took off his sunglasses, smiled at Vasily, and walked over to him with Betta.

"*Buongiorno, Vasily. Come stai?*" Betta said. "Nice to see you today. I've missed our morning coffees. I've just been dreadfully busy with work and the clinic." She turned to Riccardo. "You remember Riccardo, the doctor at the clinic I introduced you to?"

Vasily was stunned. Betta and Riccardo were still holding hands, and their arms were almost touching.

"*Ciao,*" Vasily said weakly, his eyes shifting from Betta to Riccardo and back to Betta. He had a sense that he'd been ambushed by two lovers who had likely spent the night together.

Riccardo thrust out his hand. "I can shake your hand now, Vasily, as I couldn't at the clinic." Riccardo's hand had a firm grip. Vasily gave one pump and pulled his own hand back. "Betta says you're from St. Petersburg," Riccardo continued. "That's where the Russian Revolution happened, isn't that right?"

"Yes, in 1917."

Riccardo laughed. "I don't know much about history, but I remember a movie about it, oh, my God, many years ago."

"There have been many movies over the years, Soviet and Western ones," Vasily managed to say. "You probably saw *Doctor Zhivago,* with Omar Sharif."

"You're right! That was it! Lovely movie with a good soundtrack and interesting actors. I think Alec Guinness was in it, too."

Alec Guinness. Who was that?

"Russia in winter looked beautiful," Riccardo continued, "especially that remote village with all the snow and ice."

Vasily managed a weak smile. Talking about an old movie with Betta's lover. She signaled the barista, holding up two fingers, and set her purse on the bar. Vasily felt uncomfortable. He was in a situation he'd never been in before, meeting the lover of a woman he idealized. He wasn't in love with Betta but thought they had a close relationship. Not a sexual one, but he felt they shared an intimacy that he craved from a mature, intelligent woman. No longer.

"What did you think of our clinic?" Betta asked.

"I was impressed by what I saw. The people at your clinic really need medical services. And I respect that you're both volunteering your time."

Riccardo nodded. "My heart breaks when I see unfortunate people whose health is horrible. Many haven't seen a dentist or a doctor in years. In fact, some never have. Imagine how decayed their teeth are. We treat people with broken bones that haven't healed properly. Some have chronic illnesses. We can't help all of them, but at least we provide basic medical treatment to help them survive."

"And thank you, Vasily, for your generous contribution," said Betta.

"Yes, that was very generous. Thank you, Vasily," Riccardo added.

Vasily shrugged. "It was nothing, really."

He didn't know how he should carry on a conversation with Betta and her lover.

The barista brought two cups and saucers, napkins, and spoons and set them in front of Betta and Riccardo, snatching the ten-euro note she had dropped on the bar.

"Do you know how long you'll be in Milano?" Betta asked, her voice casual, as if this was just another morning of sharing coffee together.

"Aaah...maybe another week or so. I don't start my new job until next month."

"Are you looking forward to going back to Russia?" Riccardo asked.

"Of course, but I want to see more in Milano. I went to San Maurizio recently. It's a very impressive museum, with those beautiful frescoes."

"One of my favorite places in Milano," Riccardo agreed. "Betta and I were there before my last trip to Africa."

Another pang of loneliness. Vasily had gone to San Maurizio to find some tranquility after he had learned of his mother's death. Betta and Riccardo had gone there as lovers.

Betta and Riccardo sipped their coffee, smiling at each other as if their morning had begun at Betta's apartment, the one he had walked her to when she admitted she never slept with a man until she knew and trusted him. How long had she known Riccardo?

"Riccardo and I are planning a long weekend in the Dolomites. We're leaving this morning. We'll go hiking and bike riding and enjoy cooler weather than here. You could join us if you'd like."

Vasily waved her suggestion away. "No. Thank you, anyway. I have plans."

"Really? Where are you going?" she asked.

"Probably Lake Como."

"Oh, beautiful! Como's full of tourists in the summer. We usually go there in the spring or fall."

"I like fall better," Riccardo said. "The leaves are changing, evenings are cooler, and the lake looks even bluer than in summer."

What could he say? He suspected that they had been lovers for some time. So why had Betta been so friendly with him? Was she just naturally friendly with men she'd recently met? Possibly so. He was likely just another in a long line of men she'd charmed.

Betta tipped back her head, drained the last drops, and set her cup on the bar. Riccardo followed.

"If you're here next week, we'll meet again. Okay, Vasily?"

Before he could respond, Betta picked up her purse, and she and Riccardo moved toward the door. Betta turned around and gave Vasily her signature finger wave, her other hand clutching Riccardo's.

Vasily stood at the bar, saddened by the shock of seeing the couple in love, oblivious to his emotional dissolution. He had cherished his relationship with Betta.

He left the café feeling bewildered. He walked toward Chiara's apartment but doubted he'd see her. She hadn't appeared all week. But he was too confused and upset to care.

He wandered down the street, overcome with depression and regret. He felt a bitterness rising in his throat. He had to do something to take his mind off of the turmoil of the morning:

Katya's text about her forthcoming marriage, and Betta showing up with Riccardo as her lover.

Vasily stopped on the street, experiencing a swirl of powerful emotions he wasn't sure he could control. He couldn't wander aimlessly for the rest of the day. He made a snap decision to drive to Barna. It would be a pleasant distraction, with scenic views of Lake Como and the hills into town. And it would give him a purpose: to move forward with his mission. He would attempt to explore behind the fence, into the forest and down the hill where he had seen part of a building.

Barna. His memories of the village soothed him—except for the lawyer who had interrogated him. Never again would Vasily let someone surprise him. With luck, he might encounter Volkov and fulfill his mission. He'd stop by his apartment to get his pistol and the vial of Novichok. Maybe the day would end better than it had begun.

\* \* \* \* \*

The drive through the Milano suburbs to the Autostrada took half an hour, congestion beginning as the DIGOS agents reached the ramp. Amoruso flicked the air conditioner on high. The sun blazed down, and the temperature had reached thirty-eight degrees Celsius.

They arrived in Como at 10:15, Dario following the signs for SS 340 to Menaggio and then the exit to Barna.

Amoruso finished reading the paper, dropped it on the floor, and looked out the window at the mountains above Como. She said, "So, Simona, have you made plans for your wedding?"

Simona laughed. "Well, yes and no. Armando and I have had conversations with my parents in Bergamo about it, but nothing is definite yet. We're thinking of a compromise: a wedding in Bergamo next month, and then a reception in Milano for our friends and my colleagues at DIGOS."

"I look forward to it," said Amoruso. "Any date yet?"

"Tentatively, September 18. Armando is in charge of having the invitations printed, hiring a chamber music ensemble, and working on a menu for the dinner. I'll bring invitations to the office as soon as I get them."

"I wouldn't miss it!" Amoruso said. "I'll make sure Carlo is in town that week. His travel usually starts up in early September, but I'll tell him tonight to hold that date."

Dario said, "I'll see Cecilia tonight and tell her the date also. We'll be there."

They drove on in silence for a while, enjoying the beautiful scenery. Then Amoruso said, "I'm going to call Volkov and tell him we're coming into Barna. Lucchini, too. I'll let them both know we're almost there." She picked up her phone as they drove up the road toward the spire of the church.

"This is a nice area," Amoruso said after she checked in with Lucchini. "I like all the animals and farmhouses. And birds! Look at them. We're not far from Menaggio. Tourists don't know what they're missing by not exploring."

She punched Volkov's number on her cell phone. When he answered, she said, *"Buongiorno,* signor Volkov. We're coming into Barna. What do you advise?"

She listened and then looked over at Dario. "The gate. Volpara, you know what he means, right?"

"Yes. It's at the back of Barna, where the forest begins. Along a dirt road, there's a fence that comes to his gate."

"*Signor* Volkov, agent Volpara is driving. He remembers the gate. We're driving a black Audi unmarked police car. See you soon."

Vasily followed a black Audi driving up the hilly road to Barna. It had two antennae on the roof. A man was driving, and a woman with dark hair was sitting in the passenger seat, talking on a cell phone. A woman with reddish-blond curls was sitting in the back seat.

The Audi entered Barna, turned onto Via Cavour, and disappeared. Vasily pulled into the side street where he had parked before, in front of a wooden two-story home with a garden in the yard.

Vasily got out of the car and looked both ways. A regional bus was coming from the piazza on its way out of town. He let it pass and then walked across the road to Via Cavour. He continued past two streets until he reached the third intersection. On the next street were the Carabinieri *caserna* with CCTV cameras and parked cars near the entrance.

He avoided attracting attention, looking down at the sidewalk when he approached other people, not catching their eye. His dark glasses, neutral clothes, and rubber-soled shoes provided a modicum of anonymity. He dreaded the possibility that he might run into the man with the cane again. But there was no sight of him. If Vasily spotted him, he would duck into a retail shop or enter an alley between apartment buildings.

Dmitri Volkov stood a few feet behind the fence and clicked his remote at the electronic lock on the gate. The metal-paneled gate slowly swung toward him. Dario drove through, stopping a few meters past him while Volkov closed the gate. The shade in the forest cooled the air. Streaks of sunlight penetrated the tall trees.

Dmitri walked over and greeted Antonella and Simona, who had stepped out of the police car.

"Welcome to Barna, *dottoressa*," he said, reaching out to shake Amoruso's hand and nodding toward Simona.

Amoruso said, "My colleagues were right. This is quite remote. A village behind us, a shady pine forest, and no people except us. I like this. And where is your home?"

Volkov pointed down the sloping hill. "Just over there about forty meters. When you drive down this path, you'll see the roof and my rooftop garden. How was your drive?"

"Pleasant," Amoruso said. "Heavy traffic along the lake, but once we took the bypass, it thinned out and we could enjoy the pastures and farms. Quite a lovely area. I've never been to Barna before."

"Most Italians haven't, even those who live in Menaggio. I like it that way—peaceful with very little traffic."

"Yes, once you leave the highway, it's mostly cattle farms and farmers working in the fields."

"You're probably a bit hungry from the drive. My wife has prepared a three-course Calabrian lunch for you."

"How nice," Amoruso said, pointing back at the closed gate. "Is that where the lawyer spotted the Polish fellow?"

"Yes. He was examining the electronic device that opens and closes it. The Carabinieri have a remote in case they want to come down. And I have mine," he said, holding it up.

"Do people ever try to enter?" Amoruso asked.

"No, people in Barna aren't snoopy. They leave us alone. I know people on the city council, the Carabinieri commander, and the priest at Santa Maria. They know Valeria and I want to protect our privacy. That's why the lawyer called the Carabinieri. In the summer, there are people who rent apartments or houses nearby for a week or two, mostly from Milano and Como."

"How often do you leave your home?"

He shrugged. "Usually once a day to shop for food or see friends in Barna. We also take little vacations to visit towns in the Lake District. We just came back from Varese, as you know. And on some weekends, we pick up Chiara in Menaggio. But she's in Paris this week. We won't see her until next weekend."

Amoruso said, "It's pleasant here—fresh air, pine aroma, and leaves on the ground. It's been a long time since I walked on leaves in a forest."

"Let's walk a bit," Dmitri said. "I'll show you around the area, and then we'll go into the house."

He led Simona and Antonella down the sloping trail, following the tire tracks on the forest floor. Dario followed in the police car with the window open and his arm resting on the door as he breathed in the pine-scented mountain air. This was certainly a much more pleasant way to reach the Volkovs' home than hiking up the rocky path, ducking under trees, swatting flies and other bugs, and sweating from the physical exertion. Better to arrive in an air-conditioned police car.

Dario parked next to the Volkovs' garage and a caged area where a fluffy orange-and-white cat watched the four of them approaching.

Vasily noticed that there were very few people on Barna's streets on the sticky-hot afternoon. No sign of the man with the cane. Or the Carabinieri. The *caserna* was two blocks ahead, where Vasily could see the CCTV cameras aimed at intersections, the piazza, and the back parking lot.

He turned off Via Cavour and walked toward a granite hillside behind apartment buildings and a few homes. He reached the narrow footpath between the granite and the apartments. The fence ended where it met the granite slab, which towered above the two- and three-story apartment buildings. Vasily looked to his right, where the fence curved out of sight toward the electronic gate. A boy about ten years old with a puppy was walking toward him. Vasily turned away and bent over as if to tie his shoe so the boy wouldn't see his face. He waited until the boy turned onto the street from which Vasily had approached.

When the boy was gone, Vasily looked up and down the footpath. No one visible. He climbed over the fence. When his feet touched the ground, he hurried into the forest, his feet crunching over dried twigs and pine needles. Within seconds, he was out of sight of the path along the fence. He slowed, making his way down the hillside through the pine forest, pushing back vines and thick weeds. To his right, he saw the frame of what looked like a farmhouse, the black Audi he had followed, and a garage with open doors, revealing Volkov's SUV.

Vasily's heart pounded. He had found Volkov's home, in a forest surrounded by tall pine trees with a sloping hill that kept the home virtually hidden from the residents of Barna.

\* \* \* \* \*

"Welcome to our home," Valeria greeted Antonella, Simona, and Dario, who followed Dmitri into the house. "I'm so glad you could come."

"Thank you," Amoruso said, reaching out to shake hands. "You're from Calabria. I'm from Napoli."

"My husband told me. I like people from Mezzogiorno. We have so much in common—good food, big families, a slower pace of life. And no snow, like in Moscow."

They all laughed. Volkov said, "*Amore*, these are our guests. They don't care about what you think of Moscow. We're in Italy."

"I'm sorry. Please forgive me. I'm just so happy to be living in Italy again. And I'm so pleased to finally meet you, *dottoressa* Amoruso."

"Please call me Antonella."

"Then please call us Valeria and Dmitri. Would any of you like something to drink? I have coffee, tea, water, and a little lunch if you'd like. Come into our dining room. Sit down. Relax."

They followed her into the dining room, where the table was set for six, with bottles of carbonated and natural water and a bottle of red wine. Valeria went into the kitchen and returned with a plate of olives, cheeses, prosciutto, and bread. "A little *aperitivo* if you'd like," she said, placing the platter in the middle of the dining table.

"Lovely," Antonella said. "We enjoyed our drive today, even though there was a bit of traffic. Weekenders coming to Como."

They all took forks next to small plates and selected a few things to nibble on. Valeria appeared with a bowl of pasta with *'nduja* and ricotta, and another platter with *melanzane alla parmigiana*.

When they started eating, Dmitri said, "Antonella, what do you think? Do we have anything to worry about regarding the man inspecting our gate?"

"Dmitri, we don't know, but we're concerned that it may be someone from Russia looking for you. That's why we came to see you and inspect the gate and your security system. We want to learn if that person could have seen something he'd want to pursue."

Volkov nodded. "When we finish lunch, I'll show you the security system I have installed."

"Agents Volpara and De Monti told us about it, but I'd like to see it as well. We have resources at DIGOS to supplement any gaps you might have."

They all enjoyed their lunch, during which they talked about the hot summer weather and what it was like living in a forest. The DIGOS agents praised Valeria for her delicious meal. She shared with them her joy of living in Italia again and being close to Chiara, who also liked to visit their new home.

When they finished their lunch, Volkov said, "Bring your water. I'll show you my office, where I have monitors."

"Thanks again for the fabulous lunch, Valeria. It was delicious, I was hungry after our drive from Milano." Antonella said, arising from the table. Simona and Dario stood also. Dmitri led them through the living room into his office. He gestured to wall-mounted computer monitors with split screens showing different locations around the home and on the paths leading to it.

"This screen is from cameras along the trail from the trout farm, the path taken by hikers. I doubt anyone looking for me would approach via the path. This monitor," he said, pointing to the other wall, "shows cameras focused up the hill toward the gate, the fence, and around the perimeter of our home."

Amoruso stepped close to the screen, her eyes moving from one partition to the next. She saw views of the forest, the hill rising toward Barna, and the electronic gate.

She pointed at the tracks coming toward the house. "That path comes from the gate to your home?"

"Yes. And I have speakers in trees to pick up unusual sounds in the forest."

"I think cameras are better," Amoruso said, looking from one screen to the other, right to left, top to bottom. "What's this?" she asked, pointing to the far right of one screen.

"Dmitri, your warning light came on!" Valeria shouted from the kitchen. A red light flashed above his computer, followed by a beep from one of the speakers.

*"Mio Dio!"* Volkov exclaimed. "Someone's coming down the hill! He came over the fence! Who is that?"

# CHAPTER THIRTY-TWO

"De Monti! Volpara! Outside! Dmitri, Valeria, stay inside!" Amoruso took charge. She grabbed De Monti's arm and ran from the office, followed by Volpara. She raised the tail of her blouse, flicked off her holster strap, and pulled out her weapon.

"Volpara, come with me! De Monti, cover our backs, the gate by the trail. Someone might be coming there!"

Amoruso opened the front door a few inches. No one in her line of sight. She pushed it open and stepped onto the porch, her back flat against the house. Volpara followed by her side. She eased sideways to the corner of the house, where she turned and motioned to De Monti. "Go now! I don't see anyone," she whispered. De Monti hurried down the steps and through the yard toward the gate where they had met Volkov.

Amoruso remained stopped at the corner of the house. She held her arm back so Volpara wouldn't come past. "Stay. I'll take a look," she whispered, her voice tense.

Amoruso peeked around the corner, surveying the wooded hill below the fence and gate. Her eye caught sight of a man crouching and dashing from tree to tree about forty meters away, headed toward the house. He was medium-tall and wore dark clothes. He disappeared for a moment and then ran to the next tree. Although she hadn't seen his face clearly, she caught a resemblance to the Identi-Kit drawing. The man appeared again, running toward their parked police car. He was clearly not a hiker or someone lost. He knew where he wanted to go, and soon would be close enough to the house to look in a window. Amoruso didn't think he had seen her.

She turned back around to Volpara. "He's getting closer," she whispered. "I'll run toward our car. You run to the right, toward the trees, and hide behind a big one. When you get there, look back at me. If he sees me, I'll distract him so he won't see you. We'll box him in."

"Right. After you!" Volpara whispered. His voice shook slightly. His heart pounded.

Amoruso looked toward De Monti, who had her weapon at her side and was walking quickly toward the wooden gate and not yet out of range if a pistol was fired at her.

Amoruso took a deep breath, let it out, and nudged Volpara. "Now!" she whispered.

They both dashed from the corner of the house, running in two directions, both looking in the direction of the man, who had stopped behind a pine tree large enough to conceal him.

Vasily saw a flurry of motion. He looked toward the parked Audi and the house. He glimpsed a man and a woman running, crouched over, both with weapons by their sides. The woman ducked behind the Audi, the man behind a tree twenty yards from him.

Vasily was at the apex of a triangle between two people carrying weapons on his left and right. Were they police or security guards protecting Volkov?

Vasily ducked back behind the tree, his heart racing. Just seconds ago, he had been making his way down the hill through the forest, undetected, attempting to discover if this was where Volkov lived.

He now knew he had found Volkov. It was time to complete his mission. Only two security guards were between him and his target. Two against one, but he knew he could handle them. First he would eliminate the security guards, and then he would hunt down Volkov inside the house.

Vasily reached into his pants pocket for his Spetsnaz SR1PM pistol and flicked off the safety. He was an expert marksman. The two guards didn't know that, but he would show them his expertise.

Instead of guards, could they be police? Maybe the Audi was a police car, given the two antennae on the roof. Was it a coincidence that they had arrived in Barna at the same time he had? Or was this another case of his misfortunes that day?

De Monti reached the gate, her eyes searching the woods and the trail below. She glanced up at the security cameras underneath some branches. She opened the gate and walked down the trail a few steps, scanning for any sign of someone approaching. She slowed, worried that she had run quickly for several meters with a fetus in her womb. No more running. She couldn't risk anything happening to her baby.

She pivoted so she could see back toward the house. Amoruso was crouched behind their car, Volpara behind a pine tree. Both had their weapons raised. She wondered if they had seen the man spotted in Volkov's security monitor.

De Monti saw Volkov's front door open, and he stepped out onto the porch. NO! She raised a hand and waved at him to go back inside. He moved toward the corner of the house, pointing in Volpara's direction. Volpara didn't see him.

De Monti kept waving at Volkov to move back into the house. Volkov saw her motion but looked puzzled until he understood what she was signaling. He turned back toward the front door but didn't enter the house.

A fluttering noise above De Monti startled her. She looked up. A flock of birds flew out of the trees, possibly startled by her waving at Volkov. Four or five brown birds with sharp beaks and long tails flapped their wings and screeched as they flew a short distance and settled in the upper branches of a pine tree above the parked police car.

De Monti felt her heart skip a beat, startled by the flock of birds. She swore, disappointed in herself for being distracted by the sudden noise. Her supervisor and partner were in danger. She had to back them up, not be sidetracked by birds. She took a few steps toward the gate and clearly saw Amoruso crouched behind their police car, her weapon by her side. Twenty yards away, Volpara was behind a tree, his pistol raised, looking in the same direction as Amoruso.

De Monti couldn't see the man who had been spotted on Volkov's security camera, but she speculated that he was hidden behind a tree between Amoruso and Volpara. De Monti crept a few feet to her right, just enough to glimpse the man: brown hair, grayish pants, and brown shoes that almost camouflaged him against a large pine tree.

Amoruso looked to her right at Volpara. His held his pistol at waist level against the pine tree. He looked toward Amoruso.

She nodded and clenched her fist, a signal that she was about to engage the man behind the tree. Without exposing her head, she shouted, "Police! Come out! Identify yourself!"

Vasily pressed against the tree, his heart pounding. Police! Not security guards. How had they gotten there just before he arrived?

"Come out! Identify yourself! We're police!" Amoruso shouted, still hidden behind their car.

Vasily realized that a woman behind the Audi was in charge. He glanced in Volpara's direction and saw part of him behind a tree. Only a slim profile of his left side was visible. Upper body, but no head or neck. Vasily glanced up in the tree above where the man was, and he saw the black cone of a camera lens pointing toward him. A security camera! Volkov had set up surveillance at his home. Vasily glanced at a tree next to him and noticed another security camera. He looked behind him and saw a third camera near the electronic gate.

Trapped. Should he run up the hill to the fence where he had crossed over? Risky—they could shoot him. He gripped the pistol in his right hand. His heart pumped adrenalin through his body. His muscles were tensed, and his mind was racing. He wasn't going to identify himself. And certainly he would not surrender. His options were limited: flee or engage in gunfire.

"Police! Come out, hands in the air!" the woman's voice again shouted from behind the parked Audi.

Vasily had never encountered a policewoman on his GRU missions, only men fated to die. He turned when he saw a quick motion to his left. A man dashed from one tree to another only fifteen meters from him. The tree was thinner, a younger pine with branches inches above the man's head and shoulders. The right profile of his body was exposed. Vasily had a target.

Vasily raised his pistol to stabilize it against the tree. He aimed down the barrel at the metal bead to target the man. The SR1PM was excellent at short range; its bullets would pierce a body, shatter bones, and leave a gaping exit wound. Vasily had never seen a victim felled by an SR1PM bullet survive if it entered the neck, chest, or stomach. With so much blood gushing from the wound, the person would be dead within a minute.

The man behind the tree was not fully exposed—only his right shoulder and his arm down to his elbow. It was a small target, but if he hit him, he'd likely fall to the ground, where Vasily could fire again at his body.

Vasily aimed and fired. *Bang!* Birds exploded out of the trees with a chorus of screeching. They flew in all directions.

"Aah!" Volpara screamed. He clutched his upper right arm with his left hand, where a spurt of blood had stained his shirtsleeve. He felt a dull pain, as if he had been hit with a bat, not a bullet. Then hot streaks of pain took over. He winced and reached down to transfer his pistol from his right hand to his left before the pistol could fall on the ground.

*Bang!* A gunshot from the behind the Audi. Another flock of birds erupted from the trees, fleeing from the sound of the gunshot.

A bullet slammed into the side of the tree near Vasily's head, sending pieces of bark and wood pulp into his cheek, nose, mouth, and forehead. Vasily flinched at the stinging. He closed his eyes momentarily, reaching up with his empty hand to wipe bark from his face. He spit, and a sharp piece of bark flew from his mouth.

Too close! She had almost shot him in the head. A couple of inches and he would have been dead.

Vasily heard a sound from the wounded man to his left. Not his main threat anymore. Instead he needed to focus on the woman police officer behind the Audi whose bullet had hit the tree. She was his greater danger. He swiveled slightly to his right, keeping his body from being exposed to her. He had wounded the man on his left. He needed to shoot the woman and at least wound her so she couldn't fire at him again.

But Vasily had to see her first. He took a quick breath, his heart pounding, adrenalin coursing through his body. It was a familiar feeling from when he had been in danger before, and it had helped him perform at the peak of his power.

Vasily peeked around the tree for a split second. He glimpsed the top of the head of a woman with dark hair behind the trunk of the Audi, pointing her weapon at him.

*Bang!*

Vasily jerked his head back just as the bullet impacted the tree, splintering bark, but this time not at his face. Damn, she was an excellent shot! He had to shoot her, but only the top of her head and her weapon were visible. His target was measured in inches, not a full body. He had less than a second to look around the tree, aim, fire, and then duck back behind the tree. Just as he was about to act, two more gunshots came from the direction of the Audi.

*Bang! Bang!* One bullet whizzed past his right ear. The second slammed into the tree near his stomach.

Now! Vasily looked around the tree, aimed, and fired. The woman wasn't behind the trunk anymore.

*Bang!* His bullet shattered the Audi's back window.

He fired again. *Bang!*

His bullet careened off the trunk, making a whizzing ping.

The woman's head reappeared. She aimed and fired.

*Bang!*

A bullet pierced Vasily's wrist, shattering bones. His pistol fell to the ground among dried leaves and twigs.

"AAHH!" Vasily screamed, spinning back behind the tree, blood streaming down his limp hand.

"De Monti! Here!" he heard the woman shout.

Vasily was stunned. The pain in his wrist was excruciating. He gasped, wounded, but couldn't surrender. His mind raced with the danger he was in. He needed to recover to shoot the woman and then escape. Clutching his wounded wrist, he looked at his weapon on the ground. It was a meter from the tree, half covered in leaves. He would have to grab it with his left hand, aim at the woman near the trunk, and fire.

Vasily took a deep breath, trying to ignore the shooting pain in his wounded wrist. He had to act now. He lowered his body and then reached across the leaves to grab his pistol.

*Bang!* This bullet hit above his left elbow, tearing through muscle and shattering bone.

Vasily screamed and toppled to the ground, landing on his right side, where his wrist had been shot. Pain shot through his whole body. He felt like he was going to faint. He tried to raise his wounded left arm to reach for his weapon.

But a man's boot stomped on his left hand. Then a cold metal tube poked the back of his skull. "Don't move!" Vasily heard a man's shrill voice, the man he had wounded.

The boot kicked Vasily's weapon away so he couldn't reach it.

Flaming arrows of pain shot through Vasily's bloodied wrist and upper arm. Within seconds, the pain was unbearable. He moaned and cursed in Russian.

"Volpara's got him! De Monti! Call the Carabinieri!" a woman's voice shouted. "We need an ambulance!"

Vasily writhed on the ground, blood from his wrist and arm moistening the dried leaves and turning them from brown to dark red. He gasped, struggling to breath, feeling faint as the pain overwhelmed him. He moaned, looked up, and saw a woman in black aiming her pistol inches from his forehead. Behind her, another woman ran toward them, her weapon in one hand and a cell phone at her mouth. He could hear her yelling into the phone.

"Volpara, you're bleeding!" the first woman said, glancing toward the man wearing boots and then at Vasily squirming on the bloodstained leaves.

"Only my arm. Surface only. No bones broken," said Volpara.

Vasily opened his eyes and again saw the barrel of a pistol pointed at his forehead. He felt the barrel of a second pistol behind his head.

Vasily heard a siren and closed his eyes. The pain was unbearable.

"Carabinieri here!" a woman's voice shouted.

Vasily fainted.

## CHAPTER THIRTY-THREE

Two black Carabinieri cars drove slowly down the hill from the gate, red lights flashing but no sirens. Behind the cars, two uniformed officers followed.

Amoruso was on her phone to Lucchini, telling him about the shooting and the wounding of Volpara and the man who had shot him.

"Carabinieri just got here," she reported. "An ambulance is coming shortly. I'll call you when we know more about the apparent Russian assassin. We found a vial in his pocket that might be the poison he was going to use on Volkov."

"I'll pass this along to the *questore*," Lucchini said. "He'll inform the Ministry that you may have a suspect."

"I've got a photo I'll send you so you can compare it to the Identi-Kit. It looks close."

"How is Volpara?"

"He's bleeding from his upper arm but says he doesn't think the bullet hit his bone. He's sitting on the ground. De Monti's with him."

"I hope he's okay. Stay in touch."

"Yes, sir." Amoruso put her phone back in her pocket and raised her hand at the approaching Carabinieri. She was standing next to De Monti and Volpara, whose wounded arm hung limply. The suspect seemed to be unconscious, bleeding from two wounds.

The Carabinieri cars stopped side by side. Three officers got out. The driver of one stayed, talking on a cell phone, likely reporting that they had arrived. When he got out and joined the others, he said, "An ambulance will be here soon."

The officers formed a half-circle around Vasily, who lay on his back, his wounded wrist and arm exposed. Blood had soaked his shirt and dripped onto the ground. One of the officers leaned down and put a hand on Vasily's neck to check his pulse. Vasily's eyes half-opened as he tried to focus on the uniformed and non-uniformed police around him.

Amoruso introduced herself to the senior officer. "I'm Antonella Amoruso, deputy with Milano DIGOS. These are my partners, *ispettore* De Monti and *agente* Volpara, who was wounded in the arm."

"So, what happened?" the senior officer asked Amoruso.

"We suspect that this man is a Russian assassin sent to murder the owner of this house," she said, looking toward the Volkovs' home.

One officer looked at Volpara. "How's your wound?"

Volpara looked down at his bloody shirt. "Hurts like hell, but it didn't break my humerus."

"The ambulance will be here soon. They'll treat you."

They all turned at the sound of crunching leaves and twigs, announcing the arrival of an ambulance van, its blue lights flashing as the driver parked between the Carabinieri cars. Three paramedic personnel emerged wearing blue uniforms and carrying medical kits. They joined the half-circle around Vasily on the ground.

"Gunshots?" one asked, bending over to examine Vasily's bloody wrist and arm.

Amoruso nodded toward Volpara. "Yes, but first, take a look at *agente* Volpara's wound."

The paramedic carrying the largest bag came over to Volpara and leaned down to examine his bloody arm. He set down his medical bag, opened it, and pulled out a pair of long scissors. He snipped Volpara's shirt near his neck and cut the sleeve open to the cuff. Using the scissors, he lifted the sleeve to expose Volpara's bloody arm. Volpara winced.

"Sorry. I need to wipe off the blood so I can see the wound," the paramedic said.

Volpara nodded. He winced again when the medic took a white cloth from his bag and carefully wiped around the bloody entrance and exit wounds. "Let's go to the ambulance. You need to sit down while I clean the area and give you an anesthetic."

Volpara stood with the assistance of the paramedic and De Monti. The paramedic took Volpara's uninjured arm, led him to the ambulance, and opened the rear door, motioning for him to sit down.

"So, who is this?" The senior officer pointed at Vasily, whose eyes were half-closed, feet spread apart. Vasily moaned.

Amoruso said, "He looks like the one in the Identi-Kit you made when you questioned the retired lawyer who saw a man acting suspiciously at the gate. We found a metal vial in his pocket, probably a toxic poison he was going to use against Dmitri Volkov, who lives in that house," she said, gesturing behind them.

Standing on the porch, Dmitri and Valeria watched. One of Valeria's hands covered her mouth; the other clutched her husband's hand. Dmitri was visibly shaken, his face pale.

One of the other officers said, "He would have likely driven here in a car, probably a rental. We need to find it. That will give us his identity."

Another officer said, "We'll check the CCTV footage to see what cars drove into Barna since this morning."

"If it's a rental, he probably picked it up in Menaggio or Milano," Amoruso said.

The paramedic driver knelt beside Vasily. He leaned down to look at his wrist, arm, and bloody shirt. "He's lost quite a bit of blood. I can put a tourniquet around his arm, but he needs to get to a hospital for a transfusion."

The senior Carabinieri officer looked at Amoruso. She was in charge. The wounded person on the ground was there because of DIGOS, not the Carabinieri. "*Dottoressa* Amoruso, they should take him to the Menaggio hospital."

Amoruso nodded. "No need to delay. And take *agente* Volpara as well. He needs a doctor to patch up his arm."

"Only room in the ambulance for the victim," the medical van driver said.

"We'll drive *agente* Volpara," the senior Carabinieri officer said. "We'll take him to the hospital, and we'll provide security along the way."

"Fine. I want him to get treated as soon as possible. He's one of our best agents."

Amoruso turned to Volpara, who had just returned from the ambulance, his wound bandaged and his arm in a cotton sling. "Go with one of the Carabinieri cars. They'll provide security and get you to the hospital to get your wound treated. We'll have someone drive you back tonight unless they want to keep you overnight."

"I'm fine either way," Volpara said.

The paramedic driver took out a cell phone and punched a number. "We have two gunshot victims in Barna, a DIGOS *agente* and a suspect in a criminal case. We need to get them to Menaggio right away."

The other two paramedics returned to the back of the ambulance to retrieve a gurney. The Carabinieri officers circled Vasily, looking around at the forest floor. "Any evidence other than the vial and his weapon?" one asked, holding up Vasily's pistol with his pen in the barrel. "Looks Russian; the serial number looks Cyrillic. We can check it out. Nasty weapon. Good at short range."

Dmitri and Valeria left the porch and walked toward the Carabinieri and Amoruso.

Amoruso said, "Have your forensics look for evidence. I went through his pockets while he was unconscious. I think he came down from there," she said, pointing to the path where she had first seen him coming toward the house. "Probably crossed the fence and didn't come down near the gate."

The Carabinieri officers nodded, looking around. "We'll check it out. Anything else in his pockets?"

"About 5,000 euros; two cell phones: a Samsung, possibly Russian, and a cheap Italian TIM phone; and that vial on the ground. Watch out; it could be poisonous."

The senior officer nodded while two of his officers started walking around the scene, examining the ground and the piles of leaves. "We'll have our emergency squad that handles suspicious devices come out. *Brigadiere*, call them."

An officer punched a number on his cell phone and asked for the emergency response team.

The senior officer said to Amoruso, "We've got things under control. Do you want to go to the station and file a report?"

"Not yet," Amoruso said. "First, we're going back into the house to talk to the Volkovs. They're pretty shaken. Could you guard the gate tonight?"

"We'll take care of it. Should we post someone by their house also?"

Dmitri and Valeria shook their heads.

"No, someone at the gate is fine," said Amoruso.

Amoruso and De Monti both turned to the Volkovs, whose arms were linked. Amoruso tilted her head toward their house. "Let's go inside. Let them do a search."

Dmitri nodded. He and Valeria turned around and walked slowly toward their home. They climbed the steps to the porch, and De Monti opened the front door for them.

"Would you like something? Coffee? Tea?" Valeria asked.

Amoruso nodded. "Tea."

"I need something stronger," Dmitri said. He opened a tall, thin bottle, poured some of it into a wineglass, and tipped it back.

"Please sit down," Valeria said. "I'll get some tea." They sat at the dining table, where the dishes and silverware remained from their earlier lunch. Valeria disappeared into the kitchen, and they could hear her getting cups and turning on a burner.

Amoruso, De Monti, and Volkov sat in silence for a few moments. Volkov looked away and then at Amoruso, his voice quivering. "So close....How did he find us? I thought I had a good security system."

"You do," Amoruso affirmed. "But somehow he found out where you lived. He probably followed your daughter when she came here."

Volkov nodded. "Maybe that's where I let my security lapse. I pick Chiara up in Menaggio after she gets off the Como ferry. She wears disguises, but apparently they were not good enough."

"Russian intelligence agents are smart," Amoruso said. "He probably followed her and learned her travel patterns."

Volkov forced a weak smile. "He's likely GRU or FSB. They're trained for surveillance in dangerous situations all over the world."

Valeria returned with a pot of tea and poured it into their cups. Amoruso said, "We need to find out if he was operating alone or had a partner. Or partners. If you'll excuse me, I need to call my boss at the *Questura* again. The *questore* is keeping the Ministry of the Interior informed. The Ministry considers this a national security case. When they have all the information from forensics and from questioning the suspect, they'll likely contact the Russian embassy in Rome."

"What will happen to him? Prison?" asked Valeria.

Amoruso shook her head. "Not up to us. This case will likely go all the way up the chain of command to the prime minister."

CHAPTER THIRTY-FOUR

Four days later, Dmitri and Valeria arrived at Milan's *Questura.* Simona and Dario escorted them from the parking area under the arch on Via Fatebenefratelli. Dario's arm was in a sling.

"Welcome to DIGOS," Simona said. She checked them in at the registration office, handed over *carte d'identita,* and told the guard, "*Dottor* Lucchini is receiving them."

The guard checked the log, scribbled the time and Simona's name, and handed the Volkovs' identification documents back through the window.

"Follow me, please," Simona said. She led them into the building and down a hallway to an elevator. They all got in, and she punched the button to the third floor. The elevator opened onto the vault door with the DIGOS logo. She punched the code to enter and then led the Volkovs down a hallway to Lucchini's office, where he and Amoruso were waiting.

Lucchini invited them into his office and reached out to shake their hands. *"Buongiorno, signor* Volkov. *Signora,* welcome to DIGOS," Lucchini said.

Amoruso said, "Hello. It's nice to see you again—in a safer environment."

"Yes, it is," Dmitri said. "And thank you again."

"Please have a seat," Lucchini said, motioning at the semi-circle of chairs. Simona and Dario sat at the end, Amoruso sat next to Valeria.

Dmitri said, "Thank you for inviting us to DIGOS, *dottor* Lucchini. Such a warm reception. My wife and I are pleased." Valeria nodded.

"Of course. I wanted to meet you," Lucchini said. "I've ordered coffee. We can get to know each other and discuss what happened last week, as well as your future plans."

"I've read about DIGOS investigations into terrorism, criminal syndicates, and crowd control at sports events," said Dmitri. "Very impressive."

Lucchini smiled, appreciating the compliment. "We have an outstanding team of agents," he said, nodding at Simona, Dario, and Amoruso. "DIGOS draws from the ranks of police forces. We select officers who have experience and excellent recommendations."

"We can testify to their professionalism," Dmitri said. "They demonstrated it to us. We wouldn't be here without your colleagues' intervention. It was luck—or fate—that they were at our home when the assassin showed up."

Lucchini smiled. *"Dottoressa* Amoruso says there are no coincidences, but I think this was."

Amoruso said, "I had planned to come after our agents visited you and told us about your security. It was fortunate timing; I'll just leave it that way."

"Do you feel safer now?" Lucchini asked.

"Yes, but I have to admit, I didn't expect we would have someone finding us so soon after we moved into our Barna home."

An aide arrived with a tray of coffee cups, sugar, and cream, and distributed them.

"Forensics said the poison was a form of Novichok, very deadly," said Lucchini.

Dmitri and Valeria looked at each other. She cringed, and he reached over to take her hand. "We're safe, Vale, thanks to DIGOS."

Lucchini glanced at Amoruso, who nodded but didn't look at the couple, who were visibly shaken by the news of the Novichok.

"That's one reason I wanted you to come, *signor* Volkov. We wanted to let you know that our government was disturbed by an armed agent of Russia attempting to commit a crime on our soil. As a result, our Ministry of Interior contacted your embassy in Rome. With the approval of our president and prime minister, they issued a warning to the Russian ambassador that any attempt to harm you would be considered a hostile action. The Russian ambassador would be sent back to Moscow, along with most of his staff. And the consulate in Milano would be closed."

"Thank you for informing us," said Dmitri. "We didn't think what I did in Bern would result in what happened on Friday. When my wife and I were planning on leaving Bern and moving to Italy, I decided I needed a negotiating position."

Lucchini nodded, raising his eyebrows.

Dmitri continued, "I have an attorney in Milano. He will contact the consulate with my offer. I will return half of the money I took from the oligarchs if my wife and I are not threatened. If nothing happens, I will return more in five years."

Lucchini's eyes widened. "That's wise. You were looking ahead."

Dmitri nodded. "What I did was embarrassing to them. I will have my attorney inform them that I was disappointed in Russian political actions in the last few years—assassinations in England and Germany, threats to reporters, the shutdown of independent newspapers and social media. Democracy is crippled in Russia. I don't know what will happen in the future, but I think it will become even more repressive and deal harshly with dissidents."

"Unfortunately, I agree with you," Lucchini said. "When the Cold War ended and Russia began the long process of becoming a democracy, governments in Europe hoped your country would allow political pluralism, tolerate dissent, and grant individual liberties—or at least to start to move in that direction."

Dmitri nodded. "So did I, along with most of my countrymen. Unfortunately, Russia has little experience in representative democracy. The country was ruled by corrupt and incompetent czars and Communists in the twentieth century. I guess we can't expect Russia to develop a stable democracy, with so much tyranny and despotism in its past. I'm sorry, but I don't want to live in a country like that. I want to live in the West, where democracy thrives."

"Me, too," Valeria said. "I'm Italian. We have political and social problems as well, but we have diverse political parties who represent different views and don't put in jail those who disagree."

Lucchini smiled and said, "Italy is not a perfect country… but are there any? We live in a complex world, and there are few problems that have simple solutions. Governments in Europe allow open discussions and disagreements. In the end, voters make decisions, and governments try to follow their guidance. Again, not a perfect solution, but at least people have a right to express their beliefs and not be threatened because of them."

Dmitri nodded. "Russia has a long way to go. I don't think we will see that kind of transformation in our lifetimes."

Lucchini said, "You're still a citizen of Russia and have a Russian passport."

"Yes, but I also received an Italian passport after I married Valeria."

Lucchini nodded. "And that's part of why we wanted you to be safe. All Italians receive protection from our police forces when threatened."

"And what about the man who was wounded? *Dottoressa* Amoruso told me he's in a hospital under police guard. What will happen to him?" Dmitri asked.

"This case is being reviewed by the prime minister's staff. Our government is considering options: putting him on trial for attempted murder, or possibly sending him back to Russia. His injuries will require multiple surgeries, which could be quite expensive. I'm hearing that our government would rather have him receive treatment in Russia and let them absorb the costs, not us."

"I see," Dmitri said. "That does make sense."

"We also know that he received distressing news from Russia just before he traveled to Barna the last time."

"Really? Can you tell us what it was?"

Lucchini shook his head. "Sorry, I can't. Maybe I shouldn't have mentioned it. But it does give us an idea of his emotional state."

Dmitri slowly nodded. "I understand. Even assassins are human."

"He has to face up to what he attempted," Lucchini said. "If he were to go to trial in Italy, it would likely be a long, protracted process that could go on for years with appeals."

Lucchini stopped talking, not wanting to admit that that was his opinion. Let Russia deal with the assassin, rather than having his case tied up in the Italian judicial system for an extended period of time. DIGOS and other law-enforcement agencies had an ample number of cases they were investigating, and they should have their resources focused on those and not have to assign police to provide security to the assassin.

Later that afternoon, Simona and Dario were in her office with the door closed. Betta was sitting in front of Simona's desk. After pleasantries, Simona began to question her.

"*Signora* Cattaneo, we want to ask you what you know about Vasily Egorov. He had an Italian phone that we were able to access. Your phone number was the only one he called, and you called him. Could you tell us about those calls?"

Betta nervously looked at Simona and Dario, clutching her hands in her lap. They were damp with sweat. "I have nothing to hide. I met Vasily a number of weeks ago at a coffee shop on Via Crema, near my apartment."

She looked down and blushed, embarrassed at having to admit a brief friendship with a person who had attempted to commit murder. "It was my fault that we met. I spilled coffee on his shirt. I apologized, and we started talking. He told me he was from St. Petersburg and on vacation before starting a new job."

"Do you remember the date when you first met?" Simona asked, pen poised to make notes.

"Not the precise date, but I think it was mid-June. We met at the coffee shop several mornings before I went to work. He asked me about my job. I told him I was a manager for a pharmaceutical company and that I work with doctors and hospitals, providing various drugs for their patients. I also volunteer at a clinic in Loreto for refugees and homeless people. My position lets me invite doctors to volunteer at the clinic, usually two or three times a month. When Vasily asked me about this, I invited him to an *aperitivo* where volunteers were planning a fundraising event for the clinic."

"After a few morning coffees, you invited him to an *aperitivo*?" Dario asked. Wasn't that a bit forward? You hardly knew him."

Betta looked embarrassed again. "Yes, I suppose you're right. I'm sorry, but that's my personality. I like meeting new people and telling them about my career and especially about the clinic, where we provide critical medical care for those in need."

Dario nodded, recognizing a trait he had seen in a few other people he had met. But he wanted to learn more about the assassin, not confront Betta in a way that might make her hold back important information about him.

"And did he come to the *aperitivo*?" he asked.

Betta nodded vigorously. "Yes, he did. It was at a bar in Quartiere Ticinese. I introduced him to my friends and fellow volunteers. They were kind to him. They asked him about Russia. I think he was surprised at how nice everyone was. I also invited him to our fundraiser at an art gallery, but he said he couldn't attend because he was taking a friend from Russia to see the sights in Milano."

"Did you meet his Russian friend?" Simona asked while she scribbled notes.

"No. He just said he took him to the standard tourist sights—La Scala, Parco Sempione, and the Duomo."

"Did he mention his Russian friend after that?" Simona asked.

"No. Just that one time."

Simona and Dario looked at each other, thinking that maybe the assassin had made up the story and that there wasn't a Russian friend. After all, Vasily had been in Italy to track down Volkov, not to be distracted by social invitations.

"Did you see him after that?" Dario said.

Again, Betta nodded energetically. "Yes, a few more times." She related their morning conversations and that she had invited him to a friend's birthday party and to visit the clinic.

"Did he tell you what his job was?" Dario asked.

"He mentioned one time that he worked at a bank. Nothing more than that."

Simona leaned back in her chair. "What was it about him that interested you?"

Betta pursed her lips, frowning. "That's a good question. He didn't appeal to me as someone I was attracted to, but I was curious about him. I'd never talked to a Russian before. And one more thing: He seemed lonely, in a foreign city with no contacts, just a tourist. He asked me a lot of questions, and I just kept talking," she said, smiling. "I do like to talk a lot. Just ask my friends; they call me a chatterbox."

Simona and Dario smiled.

"I'm interested in people—their lives, hopes, and dreams. I'm just naturally curious. Maybe I probe too much. I think Vasily was flattered that I seemed interested in him."

"Did your relationship ever go beyond these morning coffees and your other meetings?" Simona asked.

"No. Never. One time, I asked him to walk me back to my apartment. That was after my friend's birthday party. I wanted him to understand that I didn't want anything more than a casual friendship with him. I told him that I never got involved with a man unless I knew him well and could trust him." She stopped, weighing how she would bring up Riccardo.

"Perhaps I should mention that I am in a relationship with a doctor who volunteers with Doctors Without Borders. He spent the last couple of months in Sudan and returned to Milano just two weeks ago. I introduced Vasily him to when he came to the clinic, but it was very brief. Riccardo was busy treating patients that day. And then, a few days ago, Riccardo and I met Vasily at the coffee shop. I think he was upset when he realized that Riccardo and I were a couple. Vasily had a hard time talking that morning. Lots of stammering and clearing his throat."

"What day was that?" Dario asked.

"Last Friday. Riccardo and I were going for a long weekend to Alto Adige."

Simona and Dario looked at each other. "Friday morning?" Simona asked.

"Yes."

"Egorov was apprehended in Barna that afternoon, just hours later."

"Oh," Betta commented. "A coincidence?"

Neither Dario nor Simona commented.

Simona reviewed her notes and asked for a few more details. After she had them, she looked up at Dario. "Anything else you want to ask?"

"I think we've learned what we wanted to know. *Signora* Cattaneo met him a few times, and they had some conversations, but he revealed nothing about why he was actually in Milano. He certainly wasn't just a tourist—"

Betta interrupted: "I didn't know a thing about why he was really in Milano."

"We believe you," Simona said, closing her notebook.

Betta cleared her throat. "I have a request."

"What's that?"

"Could I see Vasily?"

Dario responded, "He's in a hospital and has had several surgeries."

"I understand. But if I could see him, I could tell him goodbye. It would close the issue for me."

"But maybe not for him," Simona said.

No one spoke for several moments. Simona looked at Dario and asked, "What do you think?"

"We'd have to talk it over with *dottoressa* Amoruso."

Dario looked over at Betta. "We'll get back to you."

Three kilometers away, Vasily lay on his hospital bed, staring at the ceiling, his thoughts becoming a bit more coherent as the effects of morphine were easing. He leaned over to a tray close to his bed, sipped water through a straw, not touching the lunch brought to him. Next to the water, the remains of a plate of pasta, a vegetable salad, and a piece of bread that a nurse had tried to get him to eat earlier that afternoon. He stared at the leftover meal, not hungry, too nauseous to manage more than the few bites she had fed to him.

His right wrist was in a cast. Metal tubes enclosed his fingers and wrist up and extended up to his elbow. His left arm lay on a pillow, with a cast above his elbow. He stared at his damaged wrist encased in metal casts like it belonged to somebody else. It was numb, with little feeling, dulled by drugs, fortunately.

Vasily's mind was fuzzy, his memories a blur of events with no connection to days or times. He knew he had had surgeries, two or three, with teams of doctors standing over him, injecting him with painkillers. He recalled an anesthetist above his head, counting numbers that didn't go above three. He had awakened later, confused, with racks of plastic bags of fluids of different colors flowing into his left arm. Despite the numbness in his arms, he felt a need to scratch his exposed skin. His lack of motion had apparently done something to his blood circulation. He felt helpless. He let his head sink deeper into the pillow and closed his eyes. He felt drowsy but couldn't sleep.

Over the last couple of days, he had overheard snatches of conversations indicating that he had been brought from a Menaggio hospital to another hospital in Milano. He recalled other bits and pieces about surgeries, as well as medical terms such as "fracture" and "suture." Another surgery was planned for tomorrow. And maybe others after that.

"Your metatarsal bones are damaged, some crushed," a doctor had told him the previous night when he had increased Vasily's morphine drip. "Surgeons will have to repair them, but not all at one time. You'll need multiple surgeries. The doctors will have to see if your injuries are healing."

Morphine was reducing the pain, making Vasily drowsy and unfocused. He was half asleep, half awake. A few hours after his morphine drip, he would start to feel numbing pain in his wrist and arm and then sharp, intense pain, as if a knife was stabbing his bandaged arm and wrist.

That morning, he had heard fragments of a conversation outside his door by police officers armed with automatic weapons. A doctor who had spoken to him when he was in a drug-induced haze had told him the previous night—or was it in the morning—that the Russian consulate had sought permission to visit him in the hospital, but they needed permission from the police before they could get access.

Who would come to see him? Not the consul general. Most likely an FSB or a GRU agent. What would they say? Would he be chastised? Interrogated? Was his hospital room bugged by the police? He didn't want to see anyone from the consulate. He'd had enough disruption and stress. Why add to it by being interrogated? Shortly after the doctor had told him about the potential visit, Vasily had drifted off to sleep as the morphine took effect, numbing his pain and soothing his brain.

He dreaded his future. Would he be tried in an Italian court, found guilty, and sentenced to prison? Or there might be negotiations between Russia and Italy to return him. Both would involve punishment. Prison in Italy or disgrace if he returned home.

He wished that he could see Betta again, although he knew it was not possible. Yes, she had a lover, but she was the only person in Milano who cared about him. Not romantically, but as a person who cared for other people: refugees and homeless in the clinic, a lonely Russian in her country. Did she know what had happened to him in Barna? What would she think of his fate? He would never see Betta again. Why would she want to see him? He was wounded, in the hospital, facing a trial, or prison, or the possibility of being returned to Moscow.

Why would she care? But Betta was the only person he wanted to see.

Had the news been reported in Italian newspapers? It was unlikely that it had appeared in Russian news media. His drug-infused brain quieted, and he drifted off to sleep.

He was awakened by the sound of the door opening. He felt too woozy to look up. He heard voices, a man's and a woman's. Then a soft voice he recognized. *Betta.*

He struggled to open his eyes. Through blurry vision, he saw Betta at the foot of the bed between a man and a woman. The man's right arm was in a sling. Could that be the man he had shot in the forest?

"Hello, V—Vasily," Betta said softly, stammering slightly.

Betta must be an apparition. Was he dreaming, or was she actually in his hospital room?

"I...I wanted to see you," she said nervously. After a quiet moment, she motioned toward Simona and Dario. "These kind officers got permission for me to come and see you. How...are you?"

Vasily opened his mouth but was too dazed to speak. All he could manage was a throaty "Aaahh...whaaaa?"

"I know. You're inj—injured," she stammered. "I hope you get better. I'm sorry this happened... ." She turned to the woman on her right and nodded. He heard her whisper, "I think he's too weak to speak. We can go."

Vasily raised his head from the pillow and opened his mouth, but no words came out at first. Finally, he managed,

"Goodbye…Betta." A wheeze of slurred words. Another wheeze, and then, "Thank you for…," he stammered, but couldn't finish. He didn't know what he was going to say. He lay his head back on his pillow and closed his eyes, which were filled with tears.

When Simona returned home that evening, Armando was packing a bag on their bed, neatly folding clothes.

"*Ciao, cara.* Welcome home. You had a big meeting today?"

She nodded. "More than that. The Russian and his wife. Nice people. They're going to be safe."

"TV and newspapers are filled with the news—pictures and interviews with the Carabinieri and with people from Barna. What a nice town up in the mountains."

"Yes, it is. We were there twice, once before I knew I was pregnant, and again on Friday."

"I know you had to keep this information private. At least now I know why you couldn't tell me before. The media has been sensationalizing it, of course. That's how they sell papers."

"It's hard to keep the media from falling all over themselves to get the story," Simona said. "But they don't have certain sensitive information. We did our job: prevented an assassination by Russia against a Russian with two passports. The Brits weren't able to stop the Litvinenko assassination, but we stopped one here. I don't think there will be a next time."

"Let's hope not."

Simona went into the kitchen, returned with a bottle of green tea, took off her suit coat, and sat on the bed. She took a sip of the tea and ran her hand over the blanket, not looking up at him.

"You're tired," he said. "Do you want to lie down and rest? I can prepare dinner, or we can go out. Let's do that—someplace nice and quiet. I'll make a reservation."

Simona shook her head and leaned back on the pillow. Armando watched her. He could tell that she had something on her mind. When she was contemplating something significant, her behavior changed. She was behaving now as if she were about to make a major statement.

"Dario and I went to the hospital to…to see the assassin."

"Really? Why? He tried to shoot your colleagues!"

Simona shook her head. "There's more I can't tell you. Maybe it will come out in the media. There was an Italian woman who knew him."

"Really? What happened?"

She shook her head again. "Sorry, I can't tell you. It was touching. We took her to the hospital to see him. That's all I can say. Don't ever tell anyone."

"I won't, of course."

She sat up and took a drink of her tea. "*Caro,* I've decided."

"Decided what?"

"The wedding."

"What do you mean?"

"I want it small, simple. Only family and a few friends."

"All right," he said, realizing her decision would be met with disappointment from her parents. She had weighed the ramifications of her decision and might explain. But he wasn't going to probe.

He sat down on the bed and put his hand on her forehead. She reached up and touched his hand. "What happened in Barna—it was over so quickly. We shot the assassin, and

Dario was wounded. If we hadn't been there, who knows what would have happened? The Russian could have broken into the Volkovs' home and murdered them both. A terrible situation, but we stopped it."

Armando nodded and waited for her to continue.

"And so, I've been thinking about those terrible minutes—the gunshots, Dario and the Russian both shot, and me a hundred yards away. Think how close I came to being in danger, possibly shot by the assassin. It made me think about our baby..."

She stopped talking, reached for Armando's hand, and closed her eyes. "Incidents like that make you think about what's most important: safety, good health—and family. Nothing else really matters, does it?"

He nodded. "You're right, *tesoro*."

"So, after what happened, I just feel that a big wedding would be embarrassing. I'd be uncomfortable with hundreds of people there having a good time, pretending it would never end. It seems trivial after what happened in Barna. I was involved in a police action that was over quickly, with two people wounded, one seriously. Not Dario, fortunately."

"How is he, by the way?"

"Fine. His arm is in a sling, and he's taking pain meds. He was with me at the hospital today. Sorry, I can't say more."

"I understand."

"After being involved in a police shooting, it's a little difficult to think about planning a big wedding." She shook her head, still gripping his hand.

Armando nodded. He realized that this was what had occupied her since the previous weekend. She had seemed remote and had not been sleeping well. "I respect your decision."

She put the tea bottle on the nightstand, sat up, and hugged him.

"Let's get married soon. Two, maybe three weeks. Let's just call people and tell them when and where. A small service at a church. A reception at a hotel. That's all." She looked up at him, awaiting his reaction.

He nodded. "Would you want a honeymoon? We haven't talked about that, with everything going on."

Simona pressed her lips together. "Let me think about it. Right now, I just want to call my parents and tell them. And I want a glass of wine tonight." She looked up at him and smiled, the first smile since she'd arrived home.

He grinned. "I can arrange that. Home or dinner out?"

"Here. Just you and me. After a glass of wine, I'll call them."

They sat on the bed in silence, she rubbing the blanket, he holding her hand. Finally, she said. "Honeymoon? Yes. I hadn't been thinking about that. How about Majorca for a weekend?"

"I'll make reservations."

She laughed. "Majorca, a perfect place. That's where this all started," she said, taking his hand and patting it on the little bump on her stomach. "Let's take her back there."

"Excellent choice. She'll like that."

"We'll find out next week if it's a boy or a girl." She laughed, her eyes bright.

"In Majorca, we'll come up with her—or his—name. I have a couple of ideas," Armando said.

"Me, too."

"Let's wait until we get to Majorca."

THE END

# ACKNOWLEDGMENTS

M y journey of researching and writing *The Lonely Assassin* included friends and colleagues in Italy and elsewhere providing valuable information.

I was fortunate to have two Italian researchers helping me. Caterina Cutrupi arranged an appointment with senior DIGOS officers at Milan's Questura, she translated the plot and several questions for them. During our meeting, the DIGOS officers willingly offered ideas and suggestions about the book's plot and investigative procedures.

My other researcher, Elena Ciampella, provided important details on the characters and settings for *The Lonely Assassin*. Elena also served as my researcher and editorial advisor for two earlier books in this series, *Thirteen Days in Milan* and *No One Sleeps*.

In addition, I want to thank friends in Milan for their support: Marco Ottaviano, Bojana Mursic, Eric Sylvers, Aaron Maines, Barbara and Stefano Klaren, Francesco Di Marzio; and Cristina and Roberta Mattioni in Stresa.

Julia Schankin in Bern, Graham Barrow in London, and Bryan Lee, Tom Finnegan, and Lana Bryan in Monterey provided important details in the story.

My editor, Pamela McManus, worked diligently to correct grammatical errors, important timelines, and plot points. I appreciate the time and attention she provided to bring this book to publication.

### THIRTEEN DAYS IN MILAN

Sylvia de Matteo, an American single mother, is taken hostage by terrorists during a political assassination at Stazione Centrale, Milan's train station. She is seized at gunpoint and thrown into the back of a van. Moments later, a Paris-bound train with Sylvia's fiancé and ten-year-old daughter aboard departs Centrale without Sylvia. The terrorists drive Sylvia to a warehouse where she is imprisoned in a cell. When the terrorists discover Sylvia's father is a wealthy Wall Street investment banker, they demand a ransom for her safe release.

### NO ONE SLEEPS

Milan's elite antiterrorism DIGOS police receive a tip that a sleeper cell of Muslim terrorists have received toxic chemicals from Pakistan to make deadly sarin gas.

The terrorist leader has access to Milan's centers of finance, technology, commerce, and entertainment—all high-profile targets with potentially hundreds of casualties in a terrorist attack.

## VESUVIUS NIGHTS

Antonella Amoruso, senior deputy of Milan's antiterrorism police, receives a call to return to her hometown of Naples for the funeral of a family member murdered in a Camorra clan feud.

Amoruso is plunged into the dangerous culture of Camorra, Naple's violent criminal syndicate, which thrives on illegal drugs, prostitution, extortion, and murder. Her goal is to rescue her family from Camorra's deadly grip.

## THE LONELY ASSASSIN

A Russian banker embezzles millions laundering money in Switzerland for Russian oligarchs. He flees with his Italian wife to a remote location on Lake Como near Milan, where their daughter lives.

Putin wants him dead and sends a GRU assassin to Milan to find and poison the banker.

But Milan's antiterrorism police cannot locate the assassin, Vasily Egorov, who is traveling with phony documents, carrying a vial of poison, and speaking Italian. Unexpectedly, Egorov meets an intriguing Italian woman who probes into his emotional life. On a dangerous assignment, Egorov realizes he's an assassin in a deep personal crisis.

# What readers are saying about the Milan Thriller Series

"I'm Italian and I must say that Erickson's view of my country and my fellow citizens is not so stereotypical as it appears in other books about Italy written by a foreign writer. His understanding of our political and cultural situation in *Thirteen Days in Milan* is very deep, his knowledge about food and drinks amazing, and the characters in the story are powerful and realistic."

"The historical introduction to Italian politics in *Thirteen Days in Milan* is very interesting and gives a great foundation for the rest of the book. Once you get to know the characters and the story is headed for a big climax, it's hard to stop reading. It was easy to visualize the scenes because of the attention to detail in descriptions of the environments, sounds, and smells. If you enjoy John le Carré or Raymond Chandler, you might enjoy this book."

\* \* \* \* \*

"*No One Sleeps* is a chilling story that reads like today's headlines. With no leads, DIGOS agents use technology to discover that a cell of Muslim terrorists are using stolen phones to communicate. But the agents don't know that the leader of the terrorists is an Italian with Pakistani heritage who was trained at a Taliban terrorist camp in Afghanistan."

"*No One Sleeps* is a thoroughly researched and soberly told tale of one of today's most pressing issues." KIRKUS REVIEWS

"*No One Sleeps* is both entertaining and all too real. It is obvious that the author did a great deal of research and, although it is fiction, many details are quite accurate, including the training camp in Pakistan. The book is action packed and would make a great movie. It has good plot and character development. I could not put it down."

\* \* \* \* \*

"*Vesuvius Nights* has everything I want in a mystery. A compelling plot, vivid writing, and an Italian setting with vivid details. Erickson's writing style really holds my attention and fully engages me. The pace of the writing mirrors the speed of modern life with the action transpiring over one week. The characters exhibit depth and humanity and become very real. Highly recommended."

"This third book *(Vesuvius Nights)* in Jack Erickson's thriller series moves to Naples with the back story of the leading female detective, exploring the workings of the Camorra, organized crime. Jack's descriptions of Naples and the views of Vesuvius make you feel a part of the vibrant city, and the action will have you transfixed. Can't wait for the next one!"

\* \* \* \* \*

"In *The Lonely Assassin,* Erickson skillfully describes how Putin deals with people who wrong him, even when they leave Russia. I particularly enjoy Erickson's description of the good life in Northern Italy. He also did a very good job of humanizing the 'lonely assassin.' I can't wait for the next book in this series."

*"The Lonely Assassin"* is a cleverly written thriller. The story begins in a bank in Bern, Switzerland. Three Russian government employees are laundering money for Russian oligarch billionaires. One of the three, Dimitri is thought to be off for a few days when another notices that there are some irregular transactions in the accounts Dimitri handles. It quickly becomes apparent that Dimitri has embezzled a substantial amount and that he is not just gone for a few days—he is just gone. The news of this crime reaches all the way up to Vladimir Putin, who dispatches an assassin to eliminate Dimitri and, if necessary, his family.

# THIRTEEN DAYS IN MILAN

As a preview of the Milan Thriller Series, here is an early chapter of *Thirteen Days in Milan*. We meet Sylvia de Matteo's father, Paolo, and her 10-year-old daughter, Angela, shortly before Sylvia is abducted by terrorists at Milan's train station.

## CHAPTER THREE

## DAY ONE

Paolo de Matteo loved his ten-year-old granddaughter, Angela, so much that he bought her pistachio gelato every afternoon.

On their daily walks into Menaggio, Paolo and Angela left the family's hillside villa at noon to have lunch along the shores of Lake Como. They strolled hand in hand down Via Sonenga, a narrow, winding road through a neighborhood of modest homes and apartments. A block from their villa, Angela stopped at a small park where her friends, local boys and girls, played soccer and climbed on the playground equipment.

Angela waved and shouted, *"Ciao a tutti!"*

They waved back. *"Ciao, Angela. Come va?"*

*"Tutto bene. Ciao!"*

Along the route, Angela waved at Italian mothers hanging laundry on ropes strung across patios.

*"Buongiorno, signora!"* she called out.

*"Ciao, Angela. Come stai?"*

*"Bene, grazie. Buona giornata!"*

In the late summer weather, red, pink, and white petunias and geraniums spilled out of flower boxes on balconies and patios. Morning Glory vines spilled over fences, and branches of lemon trees drooped to the ground, heavy with fruit. Ripe tomatoes, green bean vines, plump lemon squash, and purple eggplant hung in metal cages, ready for picking. The air was lush with the fragrance of basil, cilantro, oregano, and rosemary, which would flavor home-cooked meals that evening.

One garden had rows of grapevines with branches poking through the slats of a wooden fence. Angela plucked a few grapes and popped them in her mouth, letting the purple juice dribble down her chin.

"Oooh, these grapes are so juicy, Nonno," she said to her grandfather. "I love them."

Five minutes from the de Matteo villa, Via Sonenga merged into Via Monte Grappa, a steep road that led downhill towards Menaggio.

At the base of Via Monte Grappa, Angela and Paolo crossed the street and walked along stone walls of a medieval castle while enjoying the views of Lake Como's deep blue waters and mountains across the narrow channel.

They walked down a narrow cobblestone staircase between stucco-walled apartments, heading to Via Calvi and their favorite café on Piazza Garibaldi. They sat at an outdoor table under an umbrella and ordered from the waiter, who greeted them like members of his own family. Paolo chose his usual: shrimp salad, fresh Italian bread, and a glass of sauvignon blanc. Angela ordered cheese and prosciutto panini, pomme frites, and a lemon soda.

"Whew, it's hot today, Nonno," Angela said, setting her floppy sun hat and beach bag on an empty chair. Angela wore a different hat every day, all acquired by Paolo, who loved to buy her little gifts. "I can't wait to go swimming. Caterina and Maria are waiting for me at the lido."

"It's your last day in Menaggio, sweetheart," Paolo said. "Are you sorry to see summer end?"

"Oh, yes, Nonno. It's been the best summer ever! I love it here. You and Nonna have been so good to me."

"You have your bathing suit and towel in your bag?"

She slapped her cloth bag. "Right here. Do you have your book?"

Paolo patted his shoulder bag. "I always carry a book. I'm almost finished. I can read and watch you swim."

"Swimming in Lake Como's the best, Nonno. I hate our apartment swimming pool in New York. It's small and yucky with chlorine. All people do is swim laps. And no kids. How boring! Swimming in Como is fun."

"It sure is. I learned to swim at camp in New Jersey," he said, taking off his hat and sunglasses and wiping sweat from his forehead. "We didn't have swimming pools in Brooklyn when

I was a boy. I couldn't swim until I was twelve years old. And look at you, you swim like a fish—and you're only ten years old."

"Eleven in December, Nonno."

Paolo reached over to pat her hand. "I'll never forget December 8. I was with your dad at the hospital, waiting for you to come into the world. I held you when you were only fifteen minutes old. As soon as you saw me, you cried. I thought you didn't like me!"

She frowned, a playful look in her dark eyes. "Nonno, you always say that! Of course I liked you. I just didn't know who you were. I was just a baby!"

When their waiter delivered lunch on large ceramic plates, Angela nibbled her panino and licked warm mozzarella cheese oozing between thin panini slices. "Oooh, I love cheese," she said, closing her eyes. "It's warm and yummy."

Paolo sipped his wine, savoring the soft citrus flavors rolling over his tongue. "I love my wine. It's yummy, too."

"Nonno, you're funny," she giggled. "Wine and cheese are different! Wine is yucky; cheese is lip-smackin' good!"

Paolo chuckled, thrilled by Angela's playfulness. She beamed, delighted that she could make her *nonno* laugh, a jolly "Ho . . . ho . . . ho," a corner of his mouth curling into a Santa Claus grin.

Paolo was a bit like Santa, but more like an Italian version: not a big belly, and taller, with a barrel chest, long legs, and fluffs of curly white hair on his arms and around his neck. His once long, dark hair was stylishly clipped by New York's barbers to accent gray and white streaks that made him look like an aging Italian matinee idol from Federico Fellini's *La Dolce Vita*. Paolo was as generous as Santa, giving Angela gifts, holding her hand on walks, and taking her to Menaggio's lido beach to swim with her Italian girlfriends.

Angela sipped her lemon soda and watched tourists strolling through the piazza wearing colorful short-sleeved shirts, shorts, and sandals, scanning menus posted outside cafés and trattorias. A few yards from their outdoor table, double-decker ferries were crossing Lake Como from Menaggio to Varenna or Bellagio, carving V's in the deep blue waters. Expensive villas behind gated fences were slotted along the steep mountainsides on both sides of Lake Como.

"Boy, the piazza's really crowded today," Angela said, dipping pomme frites into a mound of ketchup and stuffing them into her mouth.

"It's like this every August, the busiest month of the summer," Paolo said, pushing the olives to the side to enjoy at the end of lunch. "Hotels are full, waiting lines for the ferries, and more tour buses show up every day. A month from now, it'll be quiet and sleepy."

"Can we get gelato after swimming?"

"Of course, sweetheart. We can't go home without gelato."

After lunch, Paolo and Angela left Piazza Garibaldi and strolled along the embankment, where waves from ferries slapped against the stone walls. Angela tore crumbs of bread she had saved from lunch and tossed them to ducks bobbing on the waves.

The lake air smelled of the pizza and pasta being served at outdoor cafés, the rosebushes along the shaded promenade, and the diesel fumes from ferries. Paolo and Angela walked past the elegant Hotel Victoria, where uniformed valets were off-loading bulging suitcases from taxis onto carts and wheeling them into the hotel. In front of the Victoria, fronds of towering palm trees were fluttering in the breeze next to flagpoles with American, Italian, British, and Swiss flags.

The route to the lido followed along the embankment past parks, cafés, gardens, and a monument to Menaggio's women silk-weavers from back in the day, when Menaggio had been a village of craftspeople and peasant families.

When Paolo and Angela reached the lido, Angela ran off to the women's locker room to change into her swimsuit. Paolo picked out a lounge chair and umbrella with a view of the beach.

Rows of beach towels were laid out on the lawn. Children and teenagers were sunbathing, laughing, and flirting, suntanned and without a care in the world. Paolo was reading when Angela dashed out of the changing room and dropped her bag next to his chair. *"Ciao, Nonno. Ci vediamo dopo!"* she said, running off with another girl, both speaking in Italian.

Angela's swimsuit accented her long, tanned legs, arms, and bare midriff. She danced across the lawn like a ballerina, her feet barely touching the ground. When the girls reached the beach, their girlfriends jumped up from their towels and hugged them, giggling and energetic as puppies. They sat down on their towels, eyeing young boys diving off a platform and whooping and splashing in the waves.

*Oh, the children,* Paolo thought. *They're so happy and full of joy.* He envied their youth, knowing that in a few years they would know struggles, disappointments, and frustrations. *Enjoy happy times now, children. Life will get complicated soon enough.*

Paolo admired how Angela looked like her mother, Sylvia, when she was her age: stunning good looks, lanky limbs, sensuous dark eyes, and long, silky black hair. Angela would be a beauty—just like Sylvia.

The wine was making Paolo drowsy. He put his book on his chest, took off his sunglasses, and closed his eyes, listening to the children playing, the ferry horns honking, and the waves lapping on the beach.

Paolo loved family vacations on Lake Como, returning to the homeland of his mother and father. After he had made his first million on Wall Street, he had bought his first Menaggio villa, eventually trading up to the present luxurious three-story villa with a wine cellar, enclosed garden, and balcony looking over Menaggio and Lake Como.

After forty years as an investment banker, Paolo was one of the highest-paid executives in his brokerage firm. But he was weary of the grind of long hours, endless meetings, and constant stress. He was ready to retire so he could spend more time in Menaggio and indulge his hobbies of painting watercolors and collecting Italian antiques.

This was a bittersweet day for Paolo. His family would celebrate his sixty-sixth birthday that night. Tomorrow, Sylvia, Angela, and Sylvia's fiancé, Cole, were leaving for Milan and Paris before returning to New York.

Farewells and birthdays were sad occasions for Paolo. Birthdays marked another year passed, and Paolo wasn't sure how many more he would have to enjoy his family. Farewells were sad because loved ones were departing. He and his wife, Harriet, would be alone, a feeling they liked less as they aged and their health deteriorated.

After Sylvia, Angela, and Cole returned to New York, Harriet had a doctor's appointment about her worsening MS. Paolo had another checkup scheduled in connection with the quadruple heart bypass surgery he'd had two years before.

Paolo was also concerned about Sylvia and Cole's pending marriage. They had met at a New Year's party, had become engaged in June, and were getting married in October. *Too much, too fast.*

Sylvia had been divorced for five years. Cole was also divorced, and his preteen son was living in Chicago with his mother. As a conservative Catholic, Paolo was opposed to divorce for all the stresses and complications it caused families—especially children. Like Angela.

As Paolo dozed off, worries about health and family returned like they did every night. Too many situations were out of his control. And Paolo liked control.

\* \* \* \* \*

## Milan Thriller Series
*Thirteen Days in Milan*
*No One Sleeps*
*Vesuvius Nights*
*The Lonely Assassin*

## Novels
*Bloody Mary Confession*
*Rex Royale*
*A Streak Across the Sky*
*Mornings Without Zoe*

## Short Mysteries
*Perfect Crime*
*Missing Persons*
*Teammates*
*The Stalker*
*Weekend Guest*

### True Crime

*Blood and Money in the Hunt Country*

### Noir Series

*Bad News is Back in Town*

### Audio Books

*A Streak Across the Sky*

*Perfect Crime*

*The Stalker*

*Teammates*

### Nonfiction

*Star Spangled Beer:*

*A Guide to America's New Microbreweries and Brewpubs*

*Great Cooking with Beer*

*Brewery Adventures in the Wild West*

*California Brewin'*

*Brewery Adventures in the Big East*

J ack Erickson is the author of international thrillers, mysteries, short mysteries, true crime, and romantic suspense novels. He is a former Air Force intelligence officer, U.S. Senate speechwriter, senior editor for a national trade association, publisher, and freelance writer for the *Washington Post, Washington Star, Washingtonian,* and other newspapers and magazines.

Erickson is the author of five books on the early days of the craft brewing industry, including the award-winning *Star Spangled Beer: A Guide to America's New Microbreweries and Brewpubs* published by RedBrick Press.

Erickson lives in northern California with his wife.

Book Five in the Milan Thriller Series, *Year of the Plague,* will be published in 2023. You'll receive information about the forthcoming book if you sign up for Erickson's newsletter.

www.RedBrickPress.net
www.JackErickson.com

Made in the USA
Columbia, SC
19 December 2022